THE POACHING GANG

A Novel

GEOFFREY EYRE

Mardle Publications

Also written by Geoffrey Eyre

A Plain Village
ISBN 978-0-9554608-1-4

Nutwhistle Farm
ISBN 978-0-9554608-2-1

The Case for Edward de Vere as Shakespeare
ISBN 978-0-9554608-4-5

Curlywigs
ISBN 978-0-9554608-5-2

The Poaching Gang

Published by Mardle Publications

www.mardlepublications.com

mardlebooks@gmail.com

© 2015 Geoffrey Eyre

Typeset by John Owen Smith, Headley Down

ISBN 978-0-9554608-3-8

Printed by CreateSpace

THE
POACHING GANG

1

From happiness to unhappiness only a brief moment of time is needed. University lecturer Dr Ralf Lassiter aged thirty was packed up and ready to leave London to take up a post in California when he received a telephone call to say that his father was ill and likely to die.

The bad news came not from his father Tom Lassiter but from an elderly female relative who lived near him. She urged Ralf to leave London and return immediately to his home village because his father was not only terminally ill but about to move house. 'Do something, Ralf,' she pleaded. 'I wouldn't be calling you if it wasn't urgent. You've got to stop him. He won't listen to me, or to anyone else either.'

'What makes you think he would listen to me?'

'You haven't been home in a long time, Ralf. Your Dad needs you, and he needs you now.'

'Are you sure about him being so ill? He's only sixty. That isn't old these days.'

'Quite sure, and that's why I don't want him to leave his house. You'll think the same when you hear where he's planning to go. You've got to stop him, it will end in disaster otherwise. He hasn't looked after himself since your poor mother died and this is the result. You need to be here, Ralf, sorting it out. How soon can you come?'

Ralf was understandably shaken by this bad news from home, and by a summons that was impossible for any man to ignore. Thinking straight is difficult at such times but a glance at the calendar forced him to concentrate his mind. It was four days until his flight to Los Angeles, four days in which to return home, arrange his father's affairs and then make a last-minute dash to the airport.

He had been camping out in the home of a friend, having

sold his small bachelor apartment. His airline suitcase was already packed so there was no need for delay. After a few farewells and hurried explanations he was soon on his way, calculating that he would arrive home by train and taxi late in the evening. No sooner was he on the train speeding him away from London when he had a new problem to occupy his mind. He felt unwell. He closed his eyes and tried to doze. Instead he began to suffer with a headache which grew steadily worse as the journey progressed.

So it was not a happy homecoming and he was unable to raise much enthusiasm when his birthplace village finally came into view. This was Long Beckles, a picturesque biscuit-tin village featured in all the tourist brochures. He passed the huge ornamental gates leading to the home of the merchant banker and his family who owned most of the village. It was a shooting estate and the wooded plantations where the pheasants lived were closely guarded to deter poachers. There were a great many trees, with notices on them instructing everyone to KEEP OUT. Ralf took it personally. He thought they were trying to tell him something.

His father Tom Lassiter was the long-serving farm manager for the local big estate and lived alone in a stone-built farmhouse close to the church. Ralf paid off the taxi at the end of the drive, hoping to arrive unnoticed. It had been a long warm summer day but the sun was now low in the sky as he stood hesitating outside his old home. Next to the church he could see the gravestones in the churchyard, a painful reminder of his mother's funeral, now five years into the past. A quick glance round at the village was sufficient to reveal that nothing had changed in his absence, he would not have expected otherwise.

At that moment the church clock struck the hour, a sound he had heard many times at close proximity from earliest childhood. It was slow clanking chime with plenty of bell power, even after it had stopped it seemed to go on ringing in his ears. He had left the village for university at the age of eighteen and his return visits had been few and far between.

The elderly relative who had made the fateful telephone call summoning him home was Daisy Lassiter, always referred to by his father as Cousin Daisy. It suddenly occurred to him that she might not have told him the entire truth about his father's condition. Could it already have reached a critical stage? Would his father be upstairs in bed, picking feebly at the blankets and too ill to recognise him? Or in dressing gown and slippers taking his last medication of the day?

The answer was neither. When Ralf finally knocked and entered he found his father seated at the kitchen table cleaning his twelve-bore shotgun. He was squinting down the barrels then polishing them with a soft cloth. He was also smoking a pipe and looking purposeful in a military-style khaki shirt.

They stared at one another with equal amounts of surprise on both sides but it was his father who recovered first. 'Here, come and sit down, Ralf,' he said in alarm. 'You don't look too good, my son.'

'I don't feel too good,' Ralf admitted, accepting his father's invitation to sit down at the table. He was embarrassed to be unwell, and made suitably apologetic gestures.

His father quickly took charge of the situation. 'I thought I heard a car. Where are you parked?'

'I came on the train, Dad. Took a taxi from the station.'

'You should have given me a ring to let me know you were coming. Is something the matter? Is it bad news? What's going on, Ralf? The last time we spoke on the phone you told me you had landed a good job in America and would soon be on your way. Has there been a change of plan?'

'Can we talk about it later? I seem to have come down with something.'

'Are you suffering? Tell me where the trouble is.'

'I've got a vile headache. And I feel sick. How do my eyes look?'

'They're bloodshot.'

'Sorry about this, Dad. Must have eaten something that didn't agree with me.'

His father's speciality during the ups and downs of family

life had been to preserve a rock-like calm at times of stress. He was a hard man to fluster and while he thought it over he refilled his pipe from a tin, sitting quietly on the other side of the kitchen table. Then struck a match, tamping down the glowing bowl with a cindered forefinger.

Having assessed the situation he said, 'Just sit there quietly for a minute or two while I make you a nice strong cup of tea. That cures most ills. I don't think you need the doctor just yet.'

Ralf watched as his father moved slowly around the kitchen. Because he was a countryman who had worked with animals all his life he did everything with a quiet deliberation that both soothed and inspired confidence. Even simple operations such as pouring hot water on a tea bag and stirring in milk and sugar were carried out with solemn thoroughness.

Ralf began to feel a little better, although whether it was his father's calming influence or the heavily sweetened tea he could not be sure. He said, 'Thanks, Dad. You wouldn't have a couple of pain-killers handy, would you?'

His father went to a cupboard and returned with a bottle of aspirins. He shook out two and handed them over. Ralf swallowed them obediently. He knew that anyone would have to be dying before his father considered they needed anything stronger than two aspirins.

He looked round and noted that little had changed, the kitchen being exactly the same as he remembered it. Nor was his father any different. He was tall and strongly built, with the pared-down leanness that can only be acquired from long years of hard work. His big crumpled hands were surprisingly deft and in his weather-beaten face the eyes were as openly honest as ever. He had a steady gaze that stifled the lie or the half-truth long before the words could be spoken.

He said, 'Are you sure you don't want anything to eat? The hens are laying well. How about a nice soft-boiled egg with some bread and butter? You could manage that, couldn't you?'

'Sorry, Dad. I can't face food at the moment.'

'In that case I'll go upstairs and get your room ready. You look as if you could do with a good night's sleep.'

'I surely could. Only don't go just yet. We need to talk.'

'If you're in some sort of trouble I'll do my best to help you. Of course I will. Want to tell me about it?'

'I had a telephone call from Daisy. That's why I'm here. And if what she tells me is true it's you who is in trouble, not me.'

'You know Cousin Daisy. Always first with any bad news that's going.'

'And what is the bad news, Dad?'

'Depends how much she told you. I asked her not to bother you with my trials and tribulations but she was determined to get in touch with you somehow. You're a hard man to get hold of, did you know that?'

'Never mind about me. She said you were ill. Is that true?'

His father was not a man to be hurried and thought out his answer carefully.

'Last winter I struggled a bit with my breathing. Bronchitis. It wouldn't clear up with antibiotics and eventually the doctor sent me along to the hospital to have an X-Ray.'

'Don't like the sound of that, Dad.'

'To be honest, Ralf, it's all happened very quickly, just in the last few days actually. The X-Ray showed a patch on the lung so there isn't much doubt what I've got wrong with me.'

In a trembling voice Ralf repeated, 'A patch on the lung? What does that mean? A growth?'

'I'm afraid so, Ralf.'

'Cancer, Dad? Lung cancer?'

'You're bound to be upset. I was upset too when they told me.'

'Should you be smoking?'

'They say it doesn't make much difference at this stage.'

'Surely you're going to have some treatment? They can't just … '

'Let me die?' His father gave him a sympathetic squeeze

on the arm as though he was the one who needed comforting. 'They don't tell you much even these days but I gather it was too late for me to have the operation. I can't say I'm sorry.'

'This goes from bad to worse.'

'They were very nice to me in the hospital, and they've given me some medication, although I haven't taken any of it up to now. But there's no point in kidding ourselves, Ralf. No one likes saying the word but what I've got wrong with me is cancer, so we may as well start off by being truthful with one another.'

'You take it very calmly, I must say.'

'It's my own fault for smoking all my life. Nothing is going to alter that. You can't blame the doctor either, I should have gone to see him a lot sooner than I did. So there it is, my son. Sorry not to have better news for you when you come home.'

'Couldn't be much worse really, could it?'

'I soldiered on with the farm work as best I could but after I had the X-Ray they made me pack it in. It was a bit of a struggle towards the end but I've never been one for having time off. I enjoyed my work and I'm only sorry I won't be doing it any more.'

Ralf was impressed by the calm way his father had unfolded his story, and by his refusal to feel sorry for himself. His stoical acceptance of this gross misfortune made him feel even more ashamed at losing touch. He said, 'I'm sorry you had to do all this on your own, Dad. Going to the hospital and everything.'

'There's no need for you to feel guilty about it, Ralf. You couldn't have done anything even if you had come home earlier.'

'I could have done something.' Although the telephone call had prepared him for the bad news it still came as a shock to hear it spelled out. 'Tell me,' he said. 'There's no chance of a mistake, is there?'

'What sort of a mistake?'

'Only that you don't look much different to me, Dad. And

I haven't heard you cough once.'

'We've still got the same family doctor. You're welcome to speak to him about it, I wouldn't object to that. In fact it might be a good idea. He could explain it to you better than I can. And tell you what the outlook is.'

'Surely it's not too late for a second opinion? Or for some treatment that would help your condition?'

His father put a consoling hand on his shoulder. 'Sorry if this has come as a shock to you, Ralf. I've had to come to terms with what is happening to me and you'll have to do the same.'

'It's a bit of a sod in other words.'

'Afraid so. I'm not as well as I look and I'm certainly not going to get any better. I've lost some weight lately, and likely to lose more. I don't have any pain to speak of, just discomfort at night when I lie down. Come up and talk to me while I get your bedroom ready.'

Ralf still felt queasy, and longed to lay his head on a cool pillow, but even so the irony of the situation was not lost on him. He had arrived home to help his father only to find that instead his father was helping him. They stood for a moment face to face, both tall men sufficiently alike to be obviously father and son. But there the resemblance ended. Ralf was slim and pale, and his hair was long. His father's hair although grey was razored down short. He was weathered and leathery, with eyes that didn't blink, not a man you argued with or messed around. Ralf knew better than to try.

It was an old house and climbing the narrow staircase was a well-remembered experience, reassuringly familiar. The floor creaked as they reached the landing, a soothing sound long forgotten but instantly recalled. Apart from that, silence. The house was situated in a very quiet part of the country and the only sounds they heard were those made by themselves.

Ralf went to the bathroom while his father made up the bed. Staring into a mirror is often an unsettling experience, forcing unpleasant facts to be confronted head on. So it was for Dr Ralf Lassiter on this fateful occasion, examining his bloodshot eyes in the bathroom mirror while facing up to an uncomfortable moment of truth. He was an only child and so had no brothers or sisters to rally round and share in the help and support. Which meant that if anyone was ever going to do anything for his father it would have to be him. There was no getting away from that sombre fact.

He was desperately tired but felt marginally better after he had washed and undressed before returning to the bedroom. His father turned down the sheet and indicated that he should get straight into bed. He did as he was told, almost expecting to be tucked up and kissed goodnight as though he was a child again.

It was a strange experience, and one not to his advantage. His father had been given an easy opportunity to reassert his parental authority, and had taken it. Tomorrow they would have to talk but Ralf knew in advance that his father was now even less likely to listen to his advice and opinions than he might have been otherwise. Tom Lassiter had been noted all his working life as a hard taskmaster. He expected and received immediate obedience from the estate's many outside workers. Any discussion of the way he wanted things done was of short duration and Ralf knew that if he was set on a course of action no amount of persuasion would change his mind.

Before switching out the light his father sat down on the bedside chair for a few moments. He said, 'Sorry it's come to this, son. I'm sure you didn't want to get mixed up in my affairs at this particular time in your life.'

'Cousin Daisy saw to it that I did.'

'I asked her not to get in touch with you because I didn't think it was fair to worry you with my troubles. Apart from not being sure whether you had left for America or not.'

'I'm glad she told me. You shouldn't have had to go through all this on your own.'

'Life usually has one or two nasty surprises up its sleeve. None of us knows what is coming next. Perhaps it's better that way.'

'I didn't mean to lose touch, Dad.'

'Of course you didn't. And you haven't, have you? You're here now and I'm very pleased to see you.' He tweaked Ralf's big toe through the bedclothes before closing the door behind him. 'I'll tell you what my plans are in the morning.'

Ralf slept for eight hours and awoke refreshed. This long peaceful slumber in his old bed had done the trick and the moment he awoke he knew that he was better. His upset tummy had righted itself, his headache had lifted completely and he was restored to his normal good health.

Already the sun was shining hot and bright so he climbed quickly out of bed and drew the curtains back so that he could take a look through the window. It was a familiar view, one he had looked at virtually every day until the age of eighteen when he left home to go to his hall of residence in exciting central London. On the left he could see the church, and beside it the churchyard where his mother was buried. On his right he could see the rooftops of the village, and it was undeniably a pretty village with thatch and cobbles and tubs of flowers.

Straight ahead was the park, although the big house itself was hidden from view because of the trees. The village and surrounding area was thickly wooded with a great number of trees, now in full summer leaf. From his bedroom window Ralf looked out over a sea of green. The trees were there as habitat for the thousands of pheasants reared on the estate every year, neatly parcelled into woods and plantations. Even those opposed to the countryside pursuit of shooting animals for sport, Ralf firmly among them, would have to concede that it did wonders for the scenery.

So much for the scenery. He had more important matters to worry about and turned his back on the window. He had people to see and much to do in a short space of time so after a quick wash and shave he dressed and hurried downstairs to the kitchen.

'How do you feel this morning?' his father enquired politely.

'Better. Much better.'

'You're still very pale though. I reckon you need a few quiet days to set you up again.'

'Fresh air and healthy country smells. Something tells me I've come to the right place.'

'Yes, you can have them in large quantities here. Fancy anything to eat?'

'How does your garden grow? A lettuce would be nice.'

His father considered this request with his usual deliberation and did not like what he was hearing. 'Don't tell me you've become a vegetarian. You haven't, have you, Ralf?'

Anxious not to start the day on a contentious subject but knowing also that it was unwise to lie to his father he admitted that he had indeed become a vegetarian. But felt entitled to defend his lifestyle. 'Vegetarian food is very nutritious, actually. And while we're on the subject I don't normally take sugar in tea or coffee. If that doesn't put you out too much.'

'No sugar?'

'And just the tiniest quantity of milk. Skimmed milk, preferably.'

'I get it straight from the bulk tank at the farm.' His father took a while to absorb this information but at least it explained something for him. 'Now I know why you're so thin and pale. Nothing will ever convince me that it's healthy to be a vegetarian. But if it's a lettuce you want I've got a whole row of them you can have.'

'Just one will do for now. A freshly cut lettuce straight from the garden. What could be nicer?'

'You can come and choose it. And get started on the fresh air at the same time.'

Having asserted himself he led the way into the back vegetable garden. It was a warm sunny morning and therefore impossible not to feel pleased at being alive. Ralf looked round appreciatively and said, 'The garden looks good, Dad. As always.'

'It's not up to its usual standard. For reasons you will understand.'

This reference to his illness put an end to the conversation, after which it did not take Ralf many minutes to eat his green salad breakfast. As soon as he had finished he said, 'Dad, we need to talk.'

His father's response was to put a match to his pipe, pressing down the glowing tobacco with a blackened finger. 'Let's get it over with. What else did Daisy tell you?'

Ralf pointed to the front hall where there was a stack of cardboard cartons tied up with farm string. 'She said you were moving house. She didn't say where.'

'This house goes with the job, you know that. And I won't be doing the job any more.'

'That doesn't mean you have to leave.'

'That's true, it doesn't. It was my choice to go.'

'A bit drastic though, if you don't mind me saying so. What with being ill and everything.'

'The doctor at the hospital sent a social worker to call on me. A pleasant sort of woman, she spelled out the options. Told me I was entitled to nursing care under the national health service. In view of the fact that I was living on my own in service accommodation with no family support.'

'And what were the options?'

'The general hospital has got a cancer ward where people go to die. I didn't fancy that, not at this stage anyway. If I've got to die I would sooner do it with my boots on and a gun in my hand than in a hospital bed with tubes up my nose.'

Ralf winced. 'Don't say things like that, Dad. Please. Not at a time like this.'

'Cousin Daisy and her husband invited me to move in them. George and Daisy are about the only relations we've got left round here. It was kind of them to offer.'

'Not much of a choice.'

'I don't want you to think that I'm being awkward for the sake of it but I was offered a room in Northbeck and I turned that down too. Do you blame me?'

Ralf flinched on hearing this, Northbeck being the local hospice. He shook his head. 'No, of course I don't blame you. Who in their right mind would want to go there?'

'I'm going to die, nothing will alter that, but I still didn't want to end my days up at Northbeck among all those invalids shuffling about in their walking frames and staring at the walls. Just couldn't face it.'

'A grim decision for anyone to have to take.'

'Not that it's easy to get into Northbeck. The Captain wangled it for me and he wasn't very pleased when I turned it down.'

Ralf could feel his headache coming on again. The Captain referred to was Captain Ives, the Agent who ran the estate, and his father's boss. He said angrily, 'You don't mean that fat oaf Ives is still in charge, do you?'

'He's been very kind to me, Ralf. Please don't make difficulties. He means well, or most of the time he does. He still thinks Northbeck is where I should go and he tried really hard to get me a place.' He pointed through the window. 'You can see it from where I'm sitting.'

Ralf followed his point. Perched on top of a hill at the farthest extremity of the village was a grim stone building, the facing south front painted a clinical white. This was Northbeck. It had once been a sanatorium for tuberculosis patients in the belief that plenty of fresh air and scenery would do them no harm and keep them away from other people. It was now a home for the demented and dying and Ralf could well understand why his father had refused the offer.

'Poor old Dad. I don't suppose you ever thought it would come to this.'

'Things change when you fall ill and can't do your work any more. George and Daisy know I don't want to stay here and when they heard about the hospice they tried again to get me to move in with them.'

'But you still refused? '

'Daisy used to be a nurse years ago, before she married George. I was sorry to disappoint her but the thought of her doling out my medication every hour of the day, standing over me to make sure I took it and telling me what to do all the time put me off the idea.'

'It would put anyone off.'

'Daisy is very house-proud so I wouldn't be allowed to smoke my pipe. George is a chapel man and keeps on about the Lord all the time. I try not to swear when I call to see them but I just seem to do it more, somehow. I like a bet on the horses occasionally, and to watch the horse racing on the television, but they wouldn't allow that, you know they wouldn't. For some reason they don't believe in fires either. I've never known a colder house than theirs. Even the hospice up at Northbeck would be a bit more homelike than that.'

'So where are you going, Dad?'

His father had been putting off this moment, knowing that Ralf's reaction would be unfavourable. He scraped out his pipe and moved his tobacco tin around before replying. 'I'm going up to High Beckles to live. Dick Shillabeer offered me the use of a house and I shall be moving in the day after tomorrow. I should appreciate some help with the rest of the packing, if you can stay a couple more days until I settle in.'

'At least I can understand now why Daisy was so agitated when she rang me. Are you sure you know what you're doing?'

'When Dick heard what I'd got wrong with me he said I was welcome to move in with him. He's a bachelor as you know, and Queenie his housekeeper was willing to look after me. Very kind of them, I thought. It's a big farmhouse so there would have been plenty of room.'

'I take it you refused?'

'Yes. I've lived here on my own ever since Mother died so I'm capable of looking after myself. I told Dick I was grateful for his offer but I didn't want to move in with him. I didn't expect him to offer me the use of a house instead.'

Ralf leaned his head on his hand in a gesture of despair. 'Am I hearing this right? You are planning to go up to High Beckles to live? On your own? And in one of Dick

Shillabeer's tumbledown old cottages?'

'What's your objection?'

'It's so isolated up at High Beckles. You would be cut off from everyone you know.'

'Anyway it isn't one of the farm cottages, it's the stone-built house at the end of the lane that runs up to Beckles Hill. An old retired architect lived there for years and years. Orchard House, it's called. Know the one I mean? '

'Of course. Mother used to send me up there for jars of honey.'

'You're right, the old architect man had a few hives and kept bees for a hobby. Would practically give the honey away to anyone who called. A clever man in his time, by all accounts, and designed some good buildings. He liked being on his own, some people do. No one troubled him up there.'

'I bet they didn't.'

'Dick bought the house when he died, mainly so that he could have some say in who lived there. Put it on the market a couple of times and took it off again. Couldn't get his price and couldn't decide what to do with it. A bit of luck for me, as it turned out.'

'I wouldn't be too sure about that, Dad.'

'The old architect made himself a nice garden. Very nice. It's a bit overgrown after the house lying empty but when Dick showed me round I didn't need asking twice. I can keep my little cat, and my few hens, and have somewhere to park the car and my old van. I might even get one of the hives going again. I've always fancied to keep a few bees.'

Ralf sighed and gave in. He could tell that his father had made up his mind and was not only determined to go but excited at the prospect. In fact looking forward to it with considerable eagerness. Having a last try he said, 'Dad, are you sure about moving house at this point in your life? Have you actually asked Captain Ives if you can stay put here?'

'You can ask him yourself. He sent a message for you to go down to the estate office as soon as you were up and about this morning. He doesn't like the idea of me going to High

Beckles and wants you to persuade me to go into the hospice instead.'

'A message, Dad?'

'You've had three so far. Hope you brought your engagement diary with you.'

'But how …?'

'There's no privacy in this village, or indeed any other village probably. If you thought no one noticed you arriving last night you were wrong. The whole village knows, including Cousin Daisy. She wants to be first on your visiting list.'

'I'll go straight away. If that's all right with you.'

'Perhaps you would kindly bring my washing home. She does it for me now, and there's a load to come back. I'm almost out of underpants and socks, if you wouldn't mind.'

'I'll try and remember.'

'George and Daisy can't help the way they are. Be nice to them, Ralf. I've taught myself to do most things about the house but the bloody washing machine beats me every time and I'm grateful to have it done for me.'

'You said there were three messages. Who was the third one from?'

'Dick Shillabeer. How does he know you're home? The postman told him first thing this morning and he rang just before you came downstairs. It's no good being upset, that's how things get done round here. Anyway Dick knows you're home and he wants you to go up and see him.'

'I'm not sure if I want to see him though. Certainly not today. Tomorrow, perhaps. I'll think it over.'

'Don't try and talk me out of going to High Beckles because I've made up my mind to go. Other people retire and move house. Why should there be all this fuss and controversy when it's my turn?'

'It's not the same though, is it?'

'It is for me. A lot better than disappearing into Northbeck and seeing all my belongings carted off to the tip.'

Ralf was a quick thinker and soon got his head round the

new developments. 'I'm not trying to stop you. I was thinking that Dick Shillabeer must be getting on a bit. Seeing that you're going to be dependent on his good will.'

'Eighty next year, that's how old he is. Lost his licence and had to give up driving but otherwise he's fit and healthy enough. He's likely to outlive me, if that's what is worrying you. Right now I'm more concerned with the packing. There's a load of stuff in the loft to get down, if you wouldn't mind helping me. And I need to clear out the garage and the garden shed. Are you feeling strong?'

This made Ralf smile. 'No, but I'm available. First I'm going to call on George and Daisy and then I'll go and see Captain Ives. I'll help you with the packing as soon as I get back.'

A few minutes later Ralf was knocking on Cousin Daisy's door. Two pairs of estate cottages faced one another across tidy vegetable gardens and hers was the second on the right. Daisy and her husband George were chapel folk, a childless couple who always looked as if they had just come back from a funeral.

'Madness,' Daisy said in exasperation when she answered the door and invited him inside. 'A man in your father's condition going to live in High Beckles. He won't last long up there with those Shillabeer people. You've got to stop him, Ralf. You've got to make him see sense.'

'His mind is made up, I'm afraid.'

'You know how muddy and windy it is up at High Beckles. And what goes on there doesn't bear thinking about. I pity anyone in Dick Shillabeer's clutches. He was never a suitable friend for your father. Are you quite sure you can't stop him?'

'It's all arranged. He's moving in the day after tomorrow.'

'Our offer will always be open. He's more than welcome to come and live here with us for the rest of his days.' She turned to her husband. 'Isn't that so, George?'

'Yes. Tom has got a home here any time he cares to ask for it.'

'The doctor isn't pleased with him either,' Daisy added for

good measure. 'He told your Dad that he shouldn't live on his own any more. Got together with Captain Ives to find him a room in Northbeck, and you know there's always a long waiting list. They never expected him to refuse.'

Husband George was thinking along the same lines. 'We didn't expect it either but if Tom doesn't want to go into Northbeck then the obvious thing for him to do is move in with us. Daisy used to be a nurse when she was younger, a good nurse, and she still knows what to do. She would look after him right to the end. You tell him, Daisy.'

'Right to the end,' she repeated. 'Yes, I would nurse him right to the very end.'

'He doesn't seem too bad just at the moment,' Ralf said hastily, anxious to change the subject. The dismal couple thought and spoke as one, usually about sin and death. 'Dad tells me that you have very kindly been doing his washing for him. If it's ready perhaps I could take it back with me.'

'Doesn't look after himself,' Daisy said reproachfully. She insisted on picking through his father's laundry item by item, showing him the socks she had darned, the cuffs she had turned, the shirts she had mended, the underpants that were worn out and needed replacing. 'Doesn't look after himself,' she repeated. 'And won't spend anything on himself either, even though he needed to look smart for his job. Too late now. Your mother did everything for him, bless her soul, including buying all his clothes, and he's been lost without her.'

'He does the cooking.'

'Unhealthy food though, all done in a frying pan. That isn't proper cooking. And he still smokes his pipe even after what he's got wrong with him. Drinks a lot too, mainly brandy, he says it helps his breathing. It can't be good for him, can it? So you tell him, Ralf. You tell him that he should come here and live with us so we can look after him properly.'

'I'll tell him but I don't think he will change his mind.'

To speed him on his way she pointed upwards. 'I'm sure your dear Mother is looking down on you too, Ralf. She was so proud of you passing all those exams and being so clever. She was clever herself, she could have run the estate office on her own. The Captain depended on her for everything.'

'He did. Yes.'

'I know how close you were to your mother, Ralf, and I'm sure you still miss her. She always knew what to do for the best and I think she will work something out to help you and Tom. I hope so anyway.'

'Trust in the Lord,' George urged him as he left. 'Be patient and do your duty and it will all come right in the end.'

There would have been more well-meant homilies but Ralf knew when enough was enough. He could hear the pious couple still giving him advice as he set off across the park to call at the estate office.

An elderly merchant banker and his family owned the big house. They were direct descendants of the speculators who had struck it rich during the industrial revolution and sought respectability in a country estate. Staying power is much admired in the country and the banker's family had held on tenaciously through good times and bad. They had survived innumerable wars, a sex scandal and a big financial swindle but every time had clawed their way back and were once again doing very nicely.

The merchant banker's main interest in life was game shooting. This interest extended to most members of his family, including the female members. They were all equally keen on shooting and in recent years it had become the main business of the estate, and big business too, with many thousands of pheasants reared every year. It was a posh shoot, with the occasional royal guest or foreign head of state to add an air of respectability to the proceedings.

The Lassiters were an estate family, one of many in the village. George had been a herdsman, Daisy still worked part time in the kitchens of the big house, his father had run the farm and his mother, a clever self-educated woman, had run the office. Ah, his mother. Ralf slowed almost to a stop, unsettled by Daisy's mention of their close relationship.

More than anything else his mother had wanted to go to university and study law. For various family reasons this had not been possible. Although she made up for the disappointment with a well-paid interesting job and a happy marriage she still yearned for the academic way of life. She had used her only child to fulfil these objectives by proxy, as is often the case. Ralf knew himself to be the beneficiary of her thwarted ambitions and acknowledged her skill and determination in steering him through the education system as far as he could go. If the price was being known in the village as a mummy's boy he considered it worth paying. How much farther she could have pushed him no one would ever know because five years ago she had died suddenly after a short illness which everyone, including the doctor, had assured her was not serious.

She had worked for Captain Ives, an amiable old buffer who ran the shoot and made sure things stayed the way the owners liked them. The estate office was situated in the rear courtyard, the coach houses having long ago been converted to other uses, as service flats, garages and offices. There was a four-sided blue and gilt clock over the stables and glimpses of a yew walk leading down to the river. In fact there were pleasant views all round and these included a young woman in skin-tight breeches and a black sweater who was unsaddling a horse. The horse looked glossy and expensive, the woman likewise, and Ralf treated her to an admiring glance.

He was also in luck because exchanging compliments with her in person was Captain Ives, the all-powerful Agent. His smile dimmed a little on seeing Ralf but duty called and he tore himself away. 'Yes, wanted to talk to you, Ralf,' he said genially. 'Heard you were home, no secrets in a village. Step into the office a moment.'

He wore a tweed cap, a chequered shirt buttoned to the wrist, cavalry-twill trousers and gleaming brown brogues that clipped the paving stones with crisp military strides as he led the way. His two black Labrador dogs lolloped at the rear of the procession. Like him they were well bred but carried too much weight.

'Take a pew,' he said, when they reached his office.

This was furnished in the Regency style with striped curtains, a polished wooden floor, two rosewood cabinets and a large ornate mahogany desk. As soon as they were seated he lit a long thin cigar from a silver desk lighter. The portly steward had style, no doubt about that, and Ralf was pleased to see him again, if only because he had been his mother's boss and treated her well. With good reason. As Daisy had said she was indispensable to him and could have run the estate on her own without his help.

The pleasantries did not take long and the Captain soon came to the point. 'This is a bad business, Ralf. About your father's illness, I mean. I take it you are up to speed with all the latest developments?'

'I only came home last night. Daisy telephoned me. But yes, I think so.'

'I couldn't get hold of you myself. Tried leaving messages but they obviously never reached you. Not that I'm apportioning blame, you understand. Just that it's all happened rather quickly.'

'Dad should have gone to see the doctor sooner. He admitted as much to me last night.'

'Got it in one, Ralf. Your Dad is from a different generation, one of the old school of workers. A few more like him and the country wouldn't be in the state it is now. We can't afford to lose him.'

'Kind of you to say so.'

'Too stoical for his own good, I fear. Put up with a lot of discomfort before he was forced to seek medical help. Brought up not to complain. No close family to advise him. Perhaps I could have done more myself. No one comes out of this with much credit.'

'Me least of all, I realise that. Well, I'm here now and I shall certainly do what I can for him. Except that he seems to have made his own arrangements.'

'That is what I wanted to talk to you about. Is it really in his best interests to move house at his time of life? And in his condition?'

'No. I don't think it is.'

'I never expected him to throw in his lot with Dick Shillabeer. Did you?'

'No. But I don't think he will change his mind.'

'We're talking about a sick man here, Ralf. A man with a time limit.'

'How long do you reckon?'

'The medics will never say but I gather the pick-up time was very late, which means the cancer is far advanced. Tom is a strong-minded man in good physical condition so he could prove everyone wrong. But a year wouldn't be far out. Sorry if this has come as a shock to you.'

'A year?'

'I could hardly believe it either but the doctor told me in confidence that he was unlikely to live more than a year. Which is why he and I tried so hard to get your Dad a room at Northbeck. We were surprised and disappointed when he turned it down.'

'Doesn't want to be among sick people. I think that's the reason.'

'It's not bad up there, Ralf. I persuaded the Matron to call on him and explain that he would have his own room and some of his own things so that he could be as independent as possible. Regular meals and constant attention, that's what he would have had at Northbeck. Something he hasn't had much of since your mother died. And of course it's still in the village and not far away if people wanted to visit.'

'Northbeck sounds just the ticket to me. All right. I'll have one last try to persuade him.'

'At the very least he would be receiving some medication to alleviate his condition. Up to now he has been refusing to take anything. Or didn't you know that?'

'He told me.'

The Captain eased his paunch against the desk. 'I'm going

to miss him as much as anyone, looking at it from a selfish point of view. Your Dad was bloody good at his job, but of course you knew that. He coaxed the best out of the men, he looked after a lot of expensive machinery, he got the crops in and out on time, and generally kept the whole thing screwed down tight. It's been a well-run farm, noted for it, and Tom gets the credit. Made life easy for me, I don't mind admitting.'

'Thank you for telling me.'

'Your family has had a long association with the estate, Ralf. I'm sorry that it seems to be coming to an end.' He waved his cigar in the general direction of the outer office. 'Your mother, too. We still miss her, of course we do. Ran the office like clockwork, there wasn't a thing she couldn't handle. How long has it been now? Five years?'

'Yes.'

He heaved himself out of his chair and headed for the door, indicating that the interview was at an end. 'If it goes wrong for you up at High Beckles you always have George and Daisy's tender mercies to fall back on. Give Dick Shillabeer my regards when you see him. I assume you will be seeing him, and fairly soon?'

'Not if I can talk Dad out of going.'

'At least you will be able to visit at the weekends, and in the holidays. Do what you can for him, Ralf. A splendid chap like Tom deserves a bit of help.' He offered his hand. 'Don't be afraid to come to me if you want something done in a hurry. I can fix most things around here.'

Ralf stared into the Captain's round pink face and promised that he would, knowing full well that whatever happened neither he nor his father would dream of ever asking for his help. Ives had been amiable enough and said the right things but Ralf was left with the impression that he had been patted on the head and sent on his way.

In that instant he had a brief insight into why his father wanted to move, and for the first time began to sympathise. He had probably had more than enough of the overbearing

Agent telling him what to do and turning nasty when he didn't get his own way. Being polite and deferential would not have come easily to his father. If he wanted to remove himself to more congenial surroundings while he still had the chance he could not find it in his heart to blame him.

Outside in the bright summer sunshine the sumptuous girl in the skin-tight breeches and black sweater was still playing with her horse. The merchant banker and his family lived in style with French furniture, art treasures and a famous wine cellar. Plus the broad acres of the park, the river, the farms and property, the preserved game, the wealth and the influence. The mailed fist of the landowner throughout the centuries. Feeling like a cottager who had fallen behind with his rent Ralf plodded disconsolately back across the park with his father's bundle of washing.

'No need to ask how you got on,' his father greeted him on his return. 'I can see it written in your face. I hope Ives didn't upset you too much because we've got work to do. Feeling fit, Ralf? Carry those boxes into the hall for me. Time is short.'

Ralf found sleep hard to come by that second night. The room was familiar to him, it wasn't that, but the unaccustomed silence troubled him deeply. The absence of noise made him jumpy, not helped by the occasional animal noise outside his window. He loved London a lot more than he had ever loved the countryside, or the country way of life, and was glad when the sky gradually lightened and it was time to leave his bed.

He drew back the curtains and looked out over the trees. He was facing up to an inevitable course of action that could well ruin his life. Since returning from the estate office he had been unable to shift from his mind the grim prognosis passed on to him by Captain Ives, namely that his father had only a year left to live. There was something in the reconciled way his father was behaving that convinced him he knew it too, and that it was true.

So Ralf had a problem, and a decision to make. Could he turn his back and simply walk out of his father's life again, leaving him to die on his own? What had been only a plane flight and a few hours away now seemed as improbable as a trip to the moon. Yet he flinched from the consequences of unscrambling all his plans and pulling out of his job in California, something that was unlikely to come his way again, and could well torpedo his career. Guilt at the way he had gradually lost touch with his father prompted a second and equally awkward question. Even if he stayed, and his father survived for a year, was that long enough to get to know him and put right all the years of neglect? He doubted it.

Although it was scarcely light his father was already in the kitchen, busy cooking breakfast. He said, 'We didn't eat properly yesterday so we'll start today with a good meal inside us. Hope you brought your appetite downstairs with you.'

Ralf watched as his father turned up the heat under the big black family frying pan. He stood proudly at the stove with the air of a man who had mastered a difficult skill, presiding slice in hand amid swirls of blue smoke. It was the camp-fire school of cookery with lots of sizzling, spluttering and the occasional gush of flame. Anything to hand went into the heavy black pan and came out looking much the same. Tomatoes, eggs, mashed potato, baked beans and fried bread. It was a glorified indoor barbecue.

Ralf was impressed. When he had eaten he said, 'Thanks, Dad. Best meal I've had for a long time. Don't get nice fresh eggs like that in London. Pass on my compliments to the hens next time you feed them.'

His father looked pleased. 'I taught myself to cook when Mother died. Not bad, if I say so myself.' He glanced up at the kitchen clock. 'When you're ready, Ralf. I suggest we start with the shed and the garage before it gets too hot outside.'

Shed and garage were crammed with thirty years of possessions, impossible to sort out in the time available. His father solved the problem by deciding to take the entire contents of both. 'This?' Ralf queried in disbelief, about to throw a box of rusted oddments into the bin. 'Keep stuff like this? It's all junk, Dad. Throw it out.'

His father snatched it back indignantly. 'I need all that to keep my old lawn mower going. Unusual sizes some of those bolts are, you can't buy them any more.'

Ralf knew better than to argue and did as he was told. They had moved back indoors, his father filling the boxes while he tied them up with farm string and wrote sticky labels with a felt-tipped pen. Something occurred to him while doing this and he asked, 'How are you moving, Dad? Are you having a removal lorry tomorrow?'

'Dick is giving me the use of his big cattle truck. Jed is bringing it down with a couple of helpers. I shall be loaded and unloaded in no time.'

'Jed?' Ralf queried. He shook his head in disbelief. 'Jed was still at school the last time I saw him. You mean they let him drive a lorry?'

'He's a strong lad. Dick's right hand man and farm foreman.'

They were discussing the young son of Shillabeer's housekeeper. This helped to loosen Ralf's memory a little but the more he remembered about High Beckles the less he liked the idea of his father going there to live. And as for joining him there for the whole of the terminal year, he knew he would never be able to stick it out, even for a few weeks.

The man who owned and ran High Beckles was his father's shooting friend, Dick Shillabeer. He had combined his farming activities with being a haulier and cattle dealer. Although only small, not much over five feet, he had the reputation of being a hard man to get along with, and a bad man to cross. No one was ever quite sure what went on at High Beckles, his mother used to say darkly that it was better not to enquire. Shillabeer was an elderly lifelong bachelor who valued his privacy above all else. No outsiders ever penetrated his little private fiefdom.

When they stopped for a mid-morning rest his father said,

'You're very quiet, Ralf. Let me ask you a question. Do you believe in fate?'

'I don't know. I should have to think. Probably not.'

'Nor me, but as I've grown older I've come to the conclusion that we don't really have a lot of say in what happens to us. Luck, fate, call it what you will. I get this nasty feeling that everything has been worked out for us in advance.'

'I don't suppose you ever thought you would be going up to High Beckles to live.'

'You're right, I didn't. Mother and me talked a lot about how we would spend our retirement. She was a great one for saving schemes and pension funds. She had it all worked out, how much we would have to pay for a house and how much we needed to live on. She had big ideas and usually got what she wanted. A pity she had to die before she could see it come true.' He lit his pipe and allowed himself a rueful smile. 'I didn't have the heart to find somewhere on my own. Left it too late. Just like a lot of other farm chaps who ended up with nowhere to go.'

'Don't be too hard on yourself, Dad. You didn't know you were going to have something wrong with you. There would have been plenty of time to find yourself a nice retirement house otherwise.'

'I shall be all right at High Beckles, you don't need to worry about me. Dick has always liked you, Ralf. He's asked me ever so many times what you were doing and how you were getting on.'

'I'm sorry you weren't able to tell him.'

'I used to take you up there in my truck sometimes. Even when you were quite small he enjoyed a conversation with you. I can remember you chattering away together long before you started school.'

'You mean he talked and I listened.'

This made his father smile. 'Dick likes the sound of his own voice, that's true.'

'I'm still sorry you weren't able to give him an answer.'

'We didn't really lose touch, did we? We were only a

phone call away. You don't need to blame yourself for anything. If I had given up smoking all those years ago when Mother first asked me to give it up I wouldn't be on the way out now. Not that I intend to die just yet. Not until I've spent some time in the old architect's garden.'

'Don't keep talking of dying, Dad. It upsets me.'

'People always mean well, Ralf, of course they do, I wouldn't pretend otherwise, but a man can only put up with so much sympathy and pity. I've lived a public sort of life, always on view, always on call when anything went wrong on the estate. My life wasn't my own. Any farm manager will tell you the same. Well, now I want to go where I can be left alone and don't have to keep answering questions about my health and how I feel. Can you understand that?'

'I can, Dad. I can.'

He gestured at all the boxes. 'Beats me how much stuff we had crammed into the house. You don't realise it until the time comes to move.'

'You're putting on a brave face. I don't suppose you like this any more than I do.'

His father sighed and rasped his face with his hand, tired and dejected. 'Ralf, you know I'm not a religious man. I've never believed in an afterlife but this last week or two I've started to get worried. Just in case Mother is around somewhere and can see the pickle I've got myself into. I would prefer her not to see the way I ended up when she wasn't around to look after me.'

This bleak admission broke the last of Ralf's resistance. He knew he had no option. He had to stay with his father for as long as it took. Reality in this case meaning a year in High Beckles and he flinched at the thought. His father had talked about fate, and fate exerted no stronger squeeze than progressive illness and certain death. It was a danse macabre that had only just begun.

He stood up. 'If Dick Shillabeer has asked me to see him it would be rude not to go. Is it all right if I borrow your car?' When his father stared at him in surprise he added, 'I'll be back as soon as I can to help with the rest of the packing up. Don't overdo it while I'm gone.'

It was two miles from Long Beckles to High Beckles, and uphill most of the way. At the bottom of the hill was a notice saying No Through Road, there being only the one narrow winding lane which led there and back again. It was a lane much cratered with deep potholes, an effective deterrent. Few visitors troubled the secretive inhabitants of High Beckles who treasured their privacy above all else.

The settlement of High Beckles had grown up around the farm of the same name. It was a straggle of old cottages and a few isolated houses, with here and there a tethered goat or a dozen geese wandering about. Most of it belonged to Dick Shillabeer who made his living from beef cattle and sheep, owning large numbers of both. In addition to the extensive farm buildings he also owned eight hundred acres of the surrounding countryside, including Beckles Hill, a neolithic hill fort dotted over with round barrows where the ancient people were buried.

Shillabeer lived in a rambling old farmhouse with many rooms. Ralf parked his father's car and began walking towards the house, stopping every few yards to look around with interest. As a child he had been a regular visitor to High Beckles, relishing the air of secrecy and seclusion. His father was Shillabeer's shooting companion and so he had been accepted into their small enclosed community, something which is always prized, even in childhood.

It felt strange to be revisiting the farm at the age of thirty. And stranger still to think that he might soon be a resident there himself, if only for the time it took his father to die. Could he bring himself to do it? Could he live with himself afterwards if he didn't do it? He began to experience a deep sense of unease, knowing that he was in the wrong place at the wrong time. It was wretched bad luck to be cornered in this way, having little option except to do the decent thing and support his father through a terminal illness. That it would end unhappily he did not doubt but finally made up his mind to ask Dick Shillabeer for permission to move in with his father, knowing it to be a fateful decision.

Then what? He thought he would prefer not to know what happened after that. Through gaps in the trees he caught glimpses of the Beckles Valley scenery, a broad view, and very pleasant to look at on a warm sunny day. Ralf was not fooled. He knew what it would be like in the winter, and his heart and spirits sank lower still. Even so it was nice to hear a skylark singing, not a sound he remembered hearing very often during his twelve years in London.

Just as there is no sound in the world quite like the mechanism of a shotgun.

Perfected by centuries of gifted craftsmen there is a gentle oiled click as it comes together ready to be fired. It would be no exaggeration to say that Ralf's blood ran cold and he gasped with fright. The sound came from behind him and he whirled round to find himself looking at an elegant single-barrelled lightweight twenty-bore shotgun. It was wielded by a tall young woman, her face half in shadow beneath a straw hat. She had long dark hair curling at the ends and wore a simple slim-fitting white dress with short sleeves, exposing long bare arms. She was pointing her gun downwards and sideways but held it in such a way as to imply that trespassers were not welcome.

If Ralf was startled it was for a very good reason. Why had his father not reminded him that Sonia Shillabeer was part of the deal at High Beckles? And if the young woman with the gun was aware of his reaction she gave no sign, her face expressionless as she waited for him to speak. Nor was she alone. By her side was one of the ugliest creatures Ralf had ever seen. It was a peculiar blue-grey colour, rough-coated and long-legged, with rheumy eyes and a white whiskery snout. Lurchers are the criminal class of the dog world and this was a deerhound lurcher, expertly bred not for looks but for speed, strength and high intelligence. The unlovely animal was tall, its head level with the young woman's waist, and stood protectively close beside her.

'The Witch?' Ralf queried disbelievingly.

This was Dick Shillabeer's dog and he could scarcely believe that she was still alive. She was well over the time limit for a big lurcher, the hair on her face white with age. He remembered her as sour-tempered and smelly, with the teeth and jaws of a shark. She stared back at him unblinkingly, not so much hostile as watchful. She was a silent killer who did not frighten her prey away by barking. 'The Witch?' he asked again, and this time the young woman with the gun nodded.

'I've been away a long time, Sonia,' he apologised. 'Working in London. Got a lot of catching up to do.'

He stopped himself just in time from saying that he had forgotten she might still be living at High Beckles since no woman would take it kindly that her existence had been overlooked. But such was the truth. She was Shillabeer's niece, or more accurately his grand-niece, and had come to live with him while still at school. They had met briefly a few times as teenagers before he went to London, a lapse of twelve years, and he needed a few moments to recover his composure. He assumed she would have married or moved away and finding her still there came as a big surprise. Rapidly he calculated her age and made it twenty-five.

Ralf was badly disconcerted and uncertain how to proceed. By any standards this was a beautiful woman. He tried not to stare but the longer he looked the more certainly he knew that he would fall completely in love with her. His father believed that everything was worked out in advance and now he believed it too.

The simple white dress and the long bronzed arms would have been enough. With the hat, the gun, the dog and the haughty manner he found her irresistible, a presence no man could ignore. The idea of coming to live with her in the same small community filled him with equal amounts of excitement and apprehension. He suddenly found himself more enthused about the idea than he had been a few minutes previously.

They stared at one another for a long time, although neither of them spoke. Even so Ralf sensed that they were communicating. During his twelve years in London he had enjoyed many little affairs of the heart, first as a student and then as an academic and member of the faculty. He liked women and had never experienced any problems with his sex life. He fell in love easily and so far had been able to extricate himself painlessly from each affair in turn before moving on to the next. He had been without a partner for some time, he was overdue for his next romance and fell in love with Sonia on the spot where she stood in her uncle's farmyard.

'We've been expecting you, Ralf,' she said, but said it without a smile. Nor did she relax her grip on the gun, or order the Witch to back off. As a welcoming party it lacked warmth.

'I think the Witch remembers me,' Ralf said nervously. 'Perhaps not,' he added, when the dog responded with a blood-freezing snarl.

'Have you come to see Uncle Dick?'

'Yes.'

'I'll take you in then,' Sonia said, and led the way to the kitchen which was situated in the oldest part of the house. Ralf followed her obediently, with the Witch's whiskery snout warningly up his backside. It was like being marched into a robber stronghold under armed guard.

He would have preferred to walk more slowly and look round as he went but was prodded by the Witch from behind and frowned at by Sonia Shillabeer from the front. 'I'm right behind you,' he assured her as they reached the back entrance to the house. This twisted and turned through a series of brick outbuildings and stone-slabbed yards. Finally there was a large covered area cluttered with old mangles and other domestic equipment no longer used, it being a house where nothing was ever thrown away. There was a stack of logs with an axe embedded in the chopping block, a row of coats hanging on pegs, and pairs of muddy boots waiting to be slipped on. A speckled hen guarding the door to the kitchen turned a beady eye on him, as did a skinny black cat crouched beside an enamel dish of rich farm milk.

The kitchen door was made of oak, and studded with bolts. It had a huge iron latch that clanked and two stone steps downwards, both hollowed with age and constant usage. All houses have a distinctive smell and the moment he entered the kitchen it was instantly familiar, a hospitable waft of tobacco smoke, dogs, mud and roasting meat.

It was a big kitchen with a huge iron stove. Beside the stove was a lurcher sized dog basket and at the end farthest from the door stood a grandfather clock that reached from floor to ceiling. Running the length of the kitchen was a table made of thick oak planks. Ralf remembered Shillabeer telling him as a child that it had been made first and the house built round it, and still believed him. It could have passed muster as a refectory table in an Oxford dining hall. A little more cluttered perhaps but polished by daily use over several centuries. And sitting at the far end of the table was the head man himself, his father's friend and shooting companion, Dick Shillabeer.

'Ralf,' he said, peering at him short-sightedly. 'It's a long time since you've been to see me, Ralf.'

'I need to have a word, Mr Shillabeer. Is it convenient?'

'Join me,' he said courteously, indicating a chair at the table.

He wore a linen jacket with a white shirt and a neatly knotted dark tie. With his wisps of tidily combed silver hair and gentle blue eyes he could have been an elderly country parson enjoying his retirement. An air of quiet respectability pervaded the kitchen.

Ralf said, 'It's about my father. That's why I've come.'

'We've been expecting you.'

'Dad's not as well as he would like to be. Got a bit of a lung condition.'

'So I believe.'

'His house goes with the job. The Captain wanted him to go into the hospice at Northbeck.'

'Even in the bad old days the estate didn't turn a man out of his house the moment he fell ill and couldn't work any

36

more. I've always had a low opinion of Captain Ives and I think even less of him now.'

'I'm not sure that's entirely fair, Mr Shillabeer. I think it was done with the best of intentions.'

'Is it true? About what Tom has got wrong with him?'

'I'm afraid it is. Yes.'

'I'll tell you something, Ralf. They're going to miss him on that estate, not half they won't. Your Dad was the best farm manager they ever had, or likely to have. Kept the costs right down and made a lot of money for them. No salesman ever pulled a fast one on Tom. Knew every trick in the book.'

'Tell me about the house where the old architect used to live.'

'There isn't much to tell. He was a good neighbour and looked after the property so I bought it straight away when he died. It's been empty for over a year. I tried it on the market a couple of times but couldn't get the price I wanted, or find the right people to buy it. I was wondering what to do next when I heard about your Dad being ill and looking for somewhere to live. Couldn't miss it, could I? Company for me and a free house for Tom. No need for him to start paying rent at his time of life.'

'It was a generous offer.'

'Tom has been my pal for a long time, Ralf, you know that. If your mother was still alive it might have worked out differently but with you in London and the Captain turning nasty I reckoned it was up to me to step in and do something. We'll look after your Dad, Ralf. Up here we count him as one of our own.'

'He's looking forward to moving in. All packed and ready.'

Shillabeer leaned closer. His eyes were a faded blue, like little forget-me-nots. 'If what I hear is true he hasn't got all that long. What sort of time period are we talking about, Ralf?'

'A year.'

'Poor Tom. Only a year, you reckon? I knew he was in a

bad way, but not that bad.'

'It's going to change a lot of things. For me, anyway.'

'Did you know Sonia had invited him to move in with us?' He turned from Ralf to his niece who sat at the far end of the long oak table listening to the conversation. 'We would have looked after him, wouldn't we, Sonia?'

'Yes,' she said. 'We would have looked after him.'

Shillabeer nodded agreement. 'We still can. The Orchard House is only five minutes walk from here.'

Sonia spoke again. 'I was sorry to hear about your father having cancer, Ralf. We all were.'

'Thank you, Sonia. It's come as a shock to me, I don't mind admitting.'

Shillabeer turned back to Ralf. 'Did your father tell you that Sonia is the boss now?'

'He didn't mention anything about that. No.'

'She manages the farm. I leave all the decisions to her.'

This gave Ralf his first chance to speak to her directly. 'Quite a responsibility for you, Sonia. Running a farm this size.'

Shillabeer spoke again, replying on her behalf. 'Sonia wanted to change a few things when she took the farm over. Needed to modernise a bit. Very sensible and the right thing to do but she couldn't have done it without Tom's help. He steered her every step of the way. There's not much money in farming right now, Ralf, so we couldn't afford any mistakes. Thanks to your Dad we didn't make any, and we've ended up all right.'

Sonia nodded. 'What Uncle says is true. I couldn't have done it without Tom's help.'

'So we reckoned we owed him,' Shillabeer said. 'And that's not all. I'm officially retired now and stay out of everyone's way but I still want my little shoot keepered properly. Jed is keen but without Tom showing him what to do it would soon have slipped back. We rear quite a few pheasants now and make a good job of it. So you see, Ralf, one way and another we have a lot to be grateful to your Dad for. Letting him live in the house is the least we can do. There's no need for you to feel that he's under any obligation.'

Although Ralf listened he found his gaze straying irresistibly to Sonia Shillabeer. He was unable to conceal his fascination, in fact could hardly take his eyes off her. Although she was sitting down instead of standing up, and did not have the gun in her hand, or the dog standing protectively by her side, he still had a vivid memory of their meeting in the sunlit farmyard. The straw hat she had taken off and placed on the table in front of her. He sensed that she was a woman of few words who spoke only when necessary. She sat silent and expressionless but was listening intently to the discussion about the house.

He flexed his memory and trawled up long-forgotten items of local news told to him by his father in years past. He could vaguely remember Sonia's father being killed in a tree-felling accident, not a nice way to die. Her mother had soon married again and moved far away, leaving Sonia behind to be brought up in the household of her elderly relative at High Beckles.

None of this was lost on Shillabeer who had to place a hand on Ralf's arm to regain his attention. He said, 'Where do you fit into all this, Ralf?'

The crunch question. In a voice that trembled slightly he made the commitment they were expecting to hear from him. He said, 'I had some other plans. They don't seem quite so important now. I should like to stay with Dad, of course I would. For as long as it takes.' He paused, and winced slightly. 'It wouldn't have been a problem in the farm house. Up here it's a bit different. How do you feel about me coming too? I'm willing to pay rent for my share of the house.'

Shillabeer said, 'I don't think that will be necessary. Sonia, it's up to you. Can Ralf move in with his Dad?'

'I'm agreeable if you are.'

'That's settled then.' He turned his attention back to Ralf again. 'I shall look forward to you telling me about London. A very dangerous place from what I hear.'

'In twelve years I never saw anyone carrying a gun.'

Shillabeer paused a moment, sensing criticism, but let it pass. He said, 'Did your Dad tell you I lost my driver's licence? I had a couple of accidents, two years ago now and almost three. Got the blame and that was the result. Disqualified.'

'Inconvenient for you.'

'It certainly was but I decided to do the sensible thing and pack it in. My eyesight isn't what it was and I shall be eighty next year so my driving days are well and truly over.' He seemed lost in thought for a moment and then brightened. 'Perhaps you wouldn't mind giving me a tour round in my old Land Rover occasionally? That would be nice. I hardly ever leave the farm now. We could catch up on the news at the same time.'

Ralf was in no position to refuse a request politely offered but realised that he would be doing it in lieu of rent for his share of the house. He shrugged and said, 'Yes, of course. If that's what you want in return.'

Instead of replying Shillabeer suddenly flew into a rage and started hammering on the table. 'Queenie!' he shouted. 'Why are you never here when you're wanted. Quickly, woman. We've got company for lunch.'

Within seconds his housekeeper appeared from a side door and set Ralf a knife and fork. 'Sorry to hear about your Dad,' she roared at him. She was hopelessly deaf and one of the noisiest people he had ever known. She was a big good-natured woman but kept up a constant commotion, banging pots and pans around, shouting at the kitchen cat to keep out of her way, quarrelling with Shillabeer and hurling coke into the stove. It was instant uproar from the moment she arrived.

'Pour Ralf out a beer,' Shillabeer instructed next, making dumb motions.

'I've made a pie,' she bellowed when she put the glass of beer down in front of him. 'For your Dad. He won't go hungry up here, Ralf, and nor will you. I made the pie bigger when they told me you might be coming as well.'

'Very kind. Thank you.'

'I think Ralf looks hungry now,' Shillabeer told her. 'When you're ready, Queenie. Let's have some food on the table.'

Obediently she produced a joint of cold roast beef from her big walk-in larder and staggered with it to the table on a huge oval plate. It was an enormous joint held together by rib bones two inches thick, almost too heavy to lift and oozing a sticky reddish liquid. Not a sight calculated to quicken the salivary glands of a vegetarian.

Looking more than ever like an elderly non-conformist clergyman Shillabeer drew an old tobacco tin from his pocket. Constant use had given it a lustrous gunmetal finish. Inside on a nest of cotton-wool lay a fragile tangle of glass and wire which he looped over his ears with the slow motion movements of a considerable age.

'You look pale, Ralf,' he said, squinting at him benignly through his tiny spectacles. 'I shall make sure Queenie feeds you up a bit. Try a plateful of this beef.'

Queenie obligingly plied the carving knife and loaded succulent slices of tender underdone roast beef on his plate. Being a vegetarian in cattle farming country was never going to be an option and he abandoned the struggle without putting up a fight. He had not expected his resolve to be tested quite so soon but gave way at once when Sonia Shillabeer moved down the table to sit opposite him. Queenie had also dished out big bowls of oven-ready chips and indicated that as far as she was concerned luncheon was served and everyone could help themselves. Sonia tucked in and Ralf did the same, surprised to find that the cold roast beef went down rather well with a glass of beer and a plateful of chips. Making eye contact with Sonia was less easy but Ralf found it a pleasurable experience to be so close to the long bare arms and the flawless farm-girl complexion. He slowed down, eating the chips one at a time so that he could prolong the moment.

Just as he was finishing his meal the door latch clanked again and in swaggered Queenie's son Jed. He put on a welcoming smile and said cheerfully, 'What are you doing up here, Ralf? On holiday, I suppose.'

'That would be one way of putting it.'

'Some people have all the luck. The guvnor never gives me a holiday.'

'Life is one long holiday for you, Jed,' Shillabeer told him. At which they all laughed, both statements being equally true.

He sat next to his mother and soon caught up, eating at a tremendous rate. He wore jeans and a skimpy yellow tee-shirt, out of which bulged huge muscled arms. His blond hair was long and matted, his clothes filthy dirty. He had an ear ring, a scar on his cheek, and tattoos on his forearms. Although Jed looked more like a fairground prize-fighter than a farm worker Ralf remembered him as amiable and chatty. He had arrived on the farm with his mother as a babe in arms and started full-time work there as soon as he could carry a bucket, shortly after his second birthday.

'Eat up, Ralf,' Jed urged him, as he forked it in himself. He waved his knife in the general direction of the huge joint of beef. 'There's plenty more where that came from.'

Although he did not like to admit it, even to himself, Ralf was finding the slices of roast beef rather tasty. Having already decided to abandon the vegetarian struggle for the duration of his exile in High Beckles he saw no reason not to give way with good grace and cleared his plate with the rest. Aware all the time that Sonia Shillabeer was watching him stealthily from across the table. At thirty and twenty-five respectively they were no longer young, or at least no longer youthful, but their lives had suddenly intersected and they were both acutely aware of the difficulties likely to arise.

Because from now on they would be living close together, would see one another every day, and perhaps several times a day. Sonia was obviously fond of his father so a certain level of family intimacy and contact was therefore guaranteed. She was certain to be affected by the sudden arrival of a man likely to want to be her lover and eyed him warily across the table, trying to work him out. He was not at all like his rugged countryman father but she knew that from their earlier meetings as teenagers. She was looking to see if anything had changed and was able to satisfy herself that nothing had.

Ralf was suddenly conscious of his city dweller's pallor and his soft pink hands, having never done any manual work in his life. On the plus side he knew what women had told him by way of pillow talk. That he had a studious nature and tended to be a little abstracted at times, dreamy in other words, but had a nice shy smile and good manners to make up for these shortcomings. Sonia's eyes kept locking on to his, as they had at their first meeting when separated by the gun and the deerhound lurcher. He sensed that she was a woman very much in control of herself and her surroundings. Unsmiling and intensely serious, she gave no clue to her feelings.

The spell of their private silence was broken by Jed who wanted to make a statement. He stopped eating for a moment and said, 'I was sorry to hear about your Dad being ill, Ralf.'

'Thank you, Jed.'

'He's been good to me, your Dad. Taught me how to aim straight and how to look after guns properly. And how to rear the birds and keep the shoot going. I owe him a lot.'

'Thank you for telling me. It's nice to know he is appreciated.'

'You'll like it up here, Ralf. People leave us alone up here.'

'That I can believe.'

This amused Jed. He speared the last of the fries with his fork and coated them all over in tomato sauce. Then added, 'You being a London man and everything. Won't be quite the same, will it?' And Ralf had to admit that it wouldn't.

At which point another member of this kitchen family decided she was not getting her fair share of attention. And an important member, too. The Witch had been curled up in her large wickerwork basket but announced that she also liked roast beef by coming to the table and digging her long whiskery snout into Shillabeer's arm by way of a reminder.

Ralf thought she was the ugliest creature imaginable, as well as smelly and bad-tempered. Shillabeer slid a hand into his jacket pocket and as though it was a conjuring trick produced a vicious spring-operated switchblade. It was so sharp that he was able to cut off a huge piece of meat with no apparent effort, or no more effort than it took the Witch to swallow it whole.

The kitchen was hot, Ralf had drunk two glasses of beer and could feel a sense of unreality deepening by the minute. As if by an evil spell he had been transported from his busy academic and professional way of life to this beleaguered settlement and put down among these strange people. From London to Los Angeles would have been a long journey, but not nearly so long as the two miles that separated Long Beckles from High Beckles.

How did he find himself at table with the tiny but domineering Dick Shillabeer and his awful dog, his noisy housekeeper and her bruiser of a son? His father was beginning to suspect that such things were ordered by an agency beyond human control, a notion warranting serious consideration. Because by the same process he found himself sitting opposite Sonia Shillabeer, and was unable to stop looking at her, indeed was suffering the sharp pangs of love at first sight. Something the others could not help noticing, or Sonia either, who lowered her head to avoid renewing eye contact with him.

He sensed an air of excitement, guessing that right up until the last minute they could not be sure whether he was coming or not. In a moment of insight Ralf realised that they must have discussed at length what line to take if he turned up at High Beckles wanting to move in with his father, in fact had probably spoken of little else since the local postman brought them news of his arrival. Guessed also that his father had deliberately omitted any mention of Sonia Shillabeer, not wishing to compromise what was likely to be a delicate situation.

With the result that his world had been turned upside down and his settled way of life disrupted with a suddenness he could not have imagined just two days earlier. He knew that he was going to be changed by the experience, it would be unavoidable in these circumstances. Whatever the outcome his life would never be the same again.

Shillabeer raised his voice and hammered on the table. 'Sonia, fetch the keys! Take Ralf across to look at the house. Show him round. Make sure it all works. Let's be nice to our new neighbours.'

2

Standing empty for a year does not do a house much good but after a few weeks of habitation, a bit of cleaning and some running repairs it soon passes muster again. Not so a garden, as Ralf was finding out the hard way. Uncouth nature swiftly reclaims any lost territory but reversing the process requires time and hard labour. Urged to work harder by his father he had toiled for countless complaining hours but made no impression on it at all. It looked exactly the same as when he started.

Not that his father was daunted or put out. On the contrary he was having the time of his life, continually finding items of interest beneath the rampant weeds and the overgrown shrubs. 'The scent!' he enthused, pausing to sniff the air. 'That old architect knew a thing or two about how to plant a garden and lay it out. Someone in his line of business would know where to go for advice, I expect. That's always useful.'

'Does that mean I can stop now?'

'I was telling you about the flowers, Ralf. Mostly old-fashioned varieties, not showy but plenty of scent, that's what he planted. As soon as it gets dark I'll remind you to have a sniff.'

'You're not going to keep me digging until dark, are you?'

His father was not listening. He was gazing round with pride at the tangleweed garden with its overgrown brick paths, unbridled borders and fallen branches as though it was the prize exhibit from the cover of a seed catalogue.

'Keep going, Ralf,' he said encouragingly. 'Time is short to get our vegetable plot started. We need to put those cabbage plants in today. Just another couple of rows, my son. That's a nice bit of ground you've turned over but not nearly enough for all the plants I brought with us.'

'Digging and me don't agree,' Ralf panted. 'Not in this heat, anyway. Couldn't we wait until it rains and the ground is a bit softer?'

'Blisters?' his father enquired genially, working a thumb over his palm. 'All in a good cause. Stick at it. Your skin will soon harden up.'

'No, backache,' he groaned, stamping his prong into the ground and leaving it there. 'I need to have a rest, Dad. Repetitive strain injury. You wouldn't want my union to sue, would you?'

'You can't keep stopping for rests. We're running out of time if you want some cheap veg for next winter.'

'Are you sure we can't buy it all from the supermarket the same as everyone else?'

'Quite sure. I've always grown my own, it's easy when you know how. These Brussels sprout plants are ready to go in as soon as you're rested. Want me to fill the watering can for you?'

'No, I'll do it,' Ralf said with a sigh as he set to work again. 'If this is gardening then I'm glad I don't like it. I never thought I should and now I've tried it I like it even less.'

His father was still not listening, continually finding things to interest him. He said, 'It's clever how the old man laid this garden out. The paths keep leading you back into the middle and round again so that you're never quite sure where you are. Then he planted trees and shrubs to make each part of the garden private. Sheltered, too. That's why the little plants do so well. He was happy up here on his own and I'm beginning to see why.'

Ralf was less enchanted and offered a helpful suggestion. 'Smaller vegetable plot, larger chicken run. Let the hens scratch it over, a very cost-effective way of gardening in my opinion. Or borrow one of Shillabeer's tame old sheep to keep the grass down. Beats digging every time.'

'A change of jobs sometimes helps,' his father offered kindly. 'You use different muscles. I'll give you a hand to saw up that old fallen apple tree if you like. Burns nicely on a fire, apple wood. You'll think the same next winter.'

'Do you want the long answer or the short answer?'

His father chuckled and put a match to his pipe. 'Back to work, my son. There's a lot to do yet and summer won't last for ever.'

'You mean people do this for pleasure?' Ralf grumbled, spitting on his blisters. 'They actually enjoy it?'

'I'll tell you what we'll do,' his father said. 'I'll finish off the digging while you hook down some of this long grass.'

'Must I?'

'Let me sharpen it for you,' he replied imperturbably, a man not easily discouraged. He produced a small piece of carborundum from his trouser pocket and used it to sharpen the grass hook.

'Not too sharp,' Ralf pleaded, watching his father testing it with his thumb. 'That looks a dangerous weapon to me.'

'Not everyone can use a hook, that's true.' His father looked pleased with himself, the common reaction of those who possess a skill watching someone who doesn't. 'You'll enjoy the feel of it when you can swing a hook properly,' he assured Ralf, giving a few lazy swishes by way of demonstration and laying bare a square yard of brambles and thick grass. 'It's only a knack. Now you do it.'

Ralf tried but however hard he hacked and swiped at the weeds and tall grasses they remained as upright as ever. The only difference being that his wrist ached instead of his back and his blisters formed in a different place. It also meant that he was scratched by thorns, stung by nettles and bitten by vicious insects. 'Not as easy as it looks,' he conceded, wiping the sweat from his eyes. 'I think I preferred the digging.'

'Now what's the matter?'

'I've cut myself.'

'Badly?'

'If the blood comes out, that's bad. Blood is supposed to stay inside. I need a tetanus injection right away. Can you run me down to the surgery?'

'Don't keep stopping, Ralf, or we shall never get these jobs done. Try again. Me, I'm going to have nice cold beer from the fridge. I'll bring one for you too, you look as if you need it.'

When he returned with the cans of beer they sat down together on a wooden seat under a plum tree. The seat was beside a wide brick path bordered by a profusion of cottage flowers giving off a gentle scent in the hot summer air. One of the hives was still occupied and the bees were hard at work on the flowers. The sound they made was pleasantly drowsy but the bees put them to shame by continuing to toil in the bright sunlight while the two gardeners took their ease in the shade beneath the plum tree.

'Know what, Ralf?' his father said, putting a companionable arm along the back of the seat. 'I should have moved on years ago. People get in a rut and don't realise it until it's too late. I stayed on that farm too long.'

'Yes, I think you probably did.'

'Mother would have loved it up here. I'm sorry she isn't able to share it with me.'

'So long as you're pleased. That makes it worthwhile.'

His father took a sip of beer and leaned back against the seat. 'I know it's a funny thing for a man in my position to say but I feel as if I'm on holiday.'

'I don't suppose you've had too many holidays, Dad.'

'It was one of those things Mother and I were always planning for when we retired. This isn't what either of us had in mind but I intend to enjoy it just the same.'

Ralf was inclined to agree. 'There's something about High Beckles, isn't there? Because it's so cut off, I suppose. It's like going back a century or two.'

'Either way it's a thousand times better than going to the geriatric home. Or moving in with George and Daisy.'

'Can't disagree with that, Dad.'

His father turned to him with troubled eyes. 'It's grand to have you with me, Ralf, but I still think you shouldn't have come. A man's career is the most important thing in his life and I don't want to be responsible for buggering up yours.

education.'

'It was an easy decision to make. I don't regret it, if that's what is worrying you.'

'Even so.' He gave Ralf's arm a quick squeeze. 'I was wrong to think I could live here on my own. I realise that now. If you hadn't turned up to help me I would never have survived the first week.' He paused, finding the words difficult. 'It means a lot to me, Ralf, you being here. I know you made a big sacrifice to make it happen but I hope you can stick it out a bit longer.'

'Dad, I told you, I'm staying.' He patted his father's hand. 'No need to upset yourself and talk about sacrifices. You sit here and take the air while I do some more digging.'

'Don't go for a minute. There's something I've been meaning to tell you.'

'Something personal?'

'It's about Sonia. Did you know that Dick had signed the farm over to her?'

'He told me she was running it. He didn't tell me she owned it as well.'

'She does, but there's a catch.'

'Isn't there always?'

'It was a deed of trust and the seven years aren't up until next year. On Dick's eightieth birthday to be exact, which comes on the first of May.'

'Not all that long to wait then. What's the problem?'

'If Dick dies before his birthday she has to pay a lot of tax. Things aren't very special in the farming world right now, Ralf. In fact times are as hard as I've ever known them. Sonia might have to sell off part of the farm. None of us want that to happen.'

'Dick seems healthy enough, even if he is nearly eighty. He should last round until next May. Only another ten months. Easy.'

'Listen carefully, Ralf. Sonia and me have been pretty close these last few years. She lost her father a long time ago and I never had a daughter, so we made do with one another, in a manner of speaking.'

'She's very fond of you. I realise that.'

'Farming is a man's world, always has been, and always will be. Before very long she won't have either old Shill or me to protect her and she'll have to manage on her own. That's what she's working towards. Won't let anything distract her. Wants to be ready when the time comes.'

'I can understand that.'

'Ever since Dick signed the farm over to her she's thought of nothing else. There aren't many women farmers around and she doesn't want to fail. She wants to see out her days here just like all the other Shillabeers who had the farm before her.'

'You still haven't got round to telling me what the problem is. Come to the point, Dad.'

'It's her uncle, you didn't really need to ask, did you? The closer he gets to his birthday the more nervous she becomes. Me too. We wouldn't want anything to happen to him now, not having got as near as this.'

'He smokes cigarettes and drinks gin all day. I don't suppose that helps.'

'Never seems to do him any harm, though. You're the brainy member of the family. What's the explanation?'

'Must be a protective gene.'

'A pity I never had one. But it isn't just his health that Sonia is concerned about. He takes risks.'

'What sort of risks?'

'It was a relief to her when he lost his driver's licence and had to come off the road. He drove that huge cattle truck all over the place until a couple of years ago. He was starting to get a bit reckless and drove too fast. That's what worried her.'

'You mean for an old guy he makes a lot of trouble for everyone? What else does he get up to?'

'Losing his licence made a big difference to him. He was used to getting around the country, going to sales and markets and having a good time. Being stuck on the farm all day didn't suit him so he was soon up to mischief.'

'I don't think I want to know but you had better tell me anyway.'

'He started going out at night with his gun, to shoot pheasants mainly. Boredom, I suppose. Calls it his hobby. Dangerous for a man of his age in the dark, wouldn't you say? That's what Sonia thinks, and I agree with her.'

'But she can't stop him?'

'No, short of locking him up. To make matters worse he takes Jed with him, practically every night last winter. Sonia needs Jed to help her work the farm, in fact she is absolutely dependent on him. He's a strong lad but even he can't stay out all night shooting pheasants and still work hard all day as well.'

'Sonia has a problem. I can see that. Why can't her uncle see it too?'

'I know Dick is my pal, and I never find fault with him, but he likes to have his own way. Always has, all his life, always done just as he pleases, and up here he still rules the roost. He's fond of Sonia, of course he is, she's family, and he thinks the world of her. But ask him to give up something he likes doing and it's a different story.'

'Why are you telling me all this? It doesn't have anything to do with me, does it? Or does it?'

'Well yes, it does, now that you've started driving him out and about in his Land Rover every day. Sonia is hoping that a sensible chap like you might be a restraining influence on him. She's relying on you, Ralf. More than you think. She's hoping that you can keep him out of trouble for a few more months.'

Ralf could feel his headache coming on again. 'Hold on a minute, Dad. Driving him round in his Land Rover is one thing. Keeping him out of jail is not part of the agreement.'

'Putting it bluntly she needs him kept alive until the first day of May next year. She would never admit that was the main reason, even to herself, because she's very fond of old Shill and doesn't want him to come to harm. Me neither, of course I don't, but I want to live round long enough to see her clinch the inheritance. So you would be doing it for me as well as Sonia.'

'You've got me worried now. What have I let myself in for?'

'Sonia and her uncle aren't getting on too well just at the moment. Neither of them likes backing down and they can both be a bit high-handed when it comes to telling other people what to do. It's over Jed, as I've just explained to you. Sonia wants him full time on the farm, not going out at night to poach pheasants. Me, I take her side but Dick shows no signs of giving way.'

'Sounds to me like a family argument. Common sense tells me not to get involved.'

'You like Sonia, don't you?'

'What's that got to do with it?'

'She likes you.'

'How do you know?'

'It's the way people look at one another. Or don't look at one another. She thinks you're very polite and nice, I can pass that little bit of information on to you. That is if you're interested in hearing it.'

'We don't have much to say to one another. She's always busy and I'm supposed to be looking after you.'

'She was nineteen when Dick signed the farm over to her and she's dedicated her life to it ever since. It's a big farm, and a lot of work and responsibility. Did you know she has never had a boyfriend? Not even as a teenager.'

'Now that is interesting.'

'It's also true. There's never been a man in her life. Like I said, she won't allow herself to be distracted. Doesn't see it as a sacrifice.'

Ralf was not really surprised, he had guessed as much from other hints that had been dropped, and it fitted in with what he had seen for himself. His father closed his eyes and proceeded to doze, finally falling asleep. Ralf remained sitting alongside him, his hands clasped between his knees, pondering on what he had just learned about the brooding heiress of High Beckles. A young woman who led a strange existence, separated from the world, and apparently celibate from choice.

Jed referred to her as the boss lady and she certainly expected to have her own way, not just on the farm but over everything else that happened in the isolated outpost of High Beckles. Ralf frowned and sighed, doubting his ability to cope with such a strongly motivated woman. According to Jed she hunted deer, apparently as a form of relaxation, teaming up with her uncle's dog. If Jed was to be believed she could run almost as fast as the Witch. The deer lived on the thickly wooded slopes of Beckles Hill but made a break for open country when pursued. The Witch pulled them down for Sonia to finish off with a knife, more than that he did not want to know.

Ralf sighed again and shook his head in mild disbelief at what his father had been telling him. A huntress and a virgin, whatever next? Beckles Hill was a mysterious dark place, with several Bronze Age burial mounds at the top and the remains of a yew grove on the lower slopes. The hill had been in the ownership of the Shillabeer family for many generations. It was in the middle of their farm with no footpaths or rights of way over it, allowing them to maintain its privacy.

Ralf was intrigued in spite of himself because it did not need much imagination to see Sonia as an enchantress descended from hunting ancestors buried on the hill. That he was strongly attracted to her he could not deny but twelve years fending for himself in London had taught him some hard lessons, the first of which was that temptation was always better avoided than resisted. He decided for his own sake as well as his father's to keep his feelings under control. Complications and heartbreak he could well do without at this difficult period in his life. Much as he was fascinated by Sonia Shillabeer he steeled himself not to fall under her spell.

At which point his father woke up from his doze and said,

'You had a good education, Ralf, the best the country could provide. I know you're putting up with a lot of aggravation for my sake so I hope it won't be too hard for you living here.'

'Dad, why do I have this nasty feeling that my education is only just beginning?'

This made him smile. 'It's a funny thing, Ralf, but Dick has always liked you, and he doesn't like many people. Hardly anyone in fact.'

'People who take risks usually have a death wish. Is that what Sonia is afraid of? That he intends do himself in before the seven years are up?'

'You didn't know what you were letting yourself in for, did you, coming up here to live? Do what you can to help her, Ralf. You would be doing it for me as well.' Unable to prevent some emotion affecting his voice he added, 'I really love this garden. I'm happy here and I don't want to have to move house again.'

3

Dick Shillabeer was so eager to set off for his drive every day that he was sitting in the passenger seat of the Land Rover waiting for Ralf to arrive, his arm around the Witch. He was as fond of her as if she was a child, and she certainly behaved like one, peering eagerly from side to side as if they were on a school outing.

Their pleasure in touring the countryside was hard to resist and Ralf had no wish to spoil the party. Shillabeer was at his most benign and apple-cheeked, beaming at Ralf through his innocent blue eyes as though he was an elderly clergyman setting off on a round of parish visits. He was always smartly dressed, usually in a favourite navy blue suit, worn with a cloth cap. The suit had a waistcoat and when he was in a good mood, which was most of the time, he hooked his thumbs in the pockets and hummed a jaunty tune. A white shirt clean on every day, and a carefully knotted tie, made it a natty outfit. He was dapper in appearance, nimble on his feet, and mentally alert at all times, never missing a trick. For a man in his eightieth year he had a teenager's zest for life and mischief, and Ralf was beginning to understand what his father had been trying to tell him.

Between the Shillabeer farmhouse and the old architect's house now occupied by Ralf and his father lay a wide stretch of grass known as Beckles Green, all that remained of an area of common ground from previous centuries. Surrounding the green were two pairs of farm cottages and some other small properties, all of them now owned by the farm. The occupants supplied the extra labour required on the farm throughout the working year. Dick Shillabeer may have been small but he was master of all he surveyed. The cottagers were all under obligation to him in some way. The men worked off arrears of rent by digging his garden while their womenfolk cleaned his house and polished his furniture. Everyone who lived in High Beckles took care to keep things the way he liked them.

And also the way Sonia liked them. She intended to carry on in the same way, exerting her authority and guarding her territory closely. She agreed for her uncle's daily Land Rover tour to start with a patrol of the perimeter fences, to check that none of their animals had escaped in the night, and that all their water troughs were in working order. The sheep took little notice of their daily visits but the beef animals were more friendly and ambled towards them.

'Start counting,' Shillabeer commanded, an instruction Ralf ignored, knowing that he loved them all dearly and would have known in an instant if one was missing. 'Rustlers,' he explained. 'Can't trust anyone these days.'

'Is that so?' Ralf replied, a general-purpose answer he found useful. It indicated that he had been listening but showed just the right amount of polite disbelief.

'A lot of rogues about in the countryside these days, Ralf. It's a sign of the times. There's money in meat and one of these beefers would be a nice little earner for someone if they could get close enough with a truck.'

The Land Rover rocked as the hefty curly-coated white-faced animals rubbed against it, and licked and pulled at his sleeve through the window. 'It would be a clever rustler who pitted his wits against yours, Mr Shillabeer,' Ralf told him, at which he looked pleased.

'Where shall we go today? How about taking a trip to Huckle?'

'Whatever you say. Just point me in the right direction.'

'Only a sleepy little village but there was a new farmer moved in last year. Let's see what sort of a hash he's making of it. Go the back way.'

This was the most frequently repeated of his instructions and tested Ralf's knowledge of the district to its limit. Shillabeer liked to keep an eye on his neighbours and made full use of the many ancient tracks and green lanes that hid him from the road. Not that Ralf minded. It was good fun driving the Land Rover Defender which would go almost anywhere. They careered through woods, splashed along the beds of streams, bumped over ploughed fields and climbed the steepest hillsides with no effort at all.

Shillabeer always had plenty to say and now that he had a captive audience whiled away the time by thinking aloud while Ralf drove. Long rambling monologues that seemed to suit the lazy summer days and the aimless driving around the countryside. Ralf only listened with one ear but even so Shillabeer's main interest in life soon became apparent. He was not unduly surprised because his father had already alerted him to this interest, which in Ralf's opinion amounted to an obsession – pheasants.

How to rear and shoot them was a subject that interested him above all else and he returned to it again and again. Until by the time the summer had turned to autumn their drives began to take on a different purpose. Instead of meandering around the neighbouring villages he began to devote his drive time almost exclusively to the shooting coverts of the estate.

'Overstocked,' he whispered one hot sunny afternoon in August when they were parked in a gateway as close as they could get to some release pens and a feeding station. 'Thousands and thousands of pheasants they rear every year and don't know how to look after properly.'

'Captain Ives loves each one personally. And hates poachers.'

'Quite true, Ralf. He does.'

'And the same goes for the gamekeepers and practically everyone else on the estate. They aren't going to make it easy for you.'

'I know a lot about pheasants. Your Dad does too, but not as much as me. How about you, Ralf? Have you made a study of the pheasant and its ways?'

'I like to see them on a menu. Adds a touch of class. That's a good start, isn't it?'

'The Captain made a big mistake last year. Sacked his head

gamekeeper and replaced him with a college boy. Can you imagine that, Ralf? A gamekeeper who handles a computer better than he handles a gun.'

'It's all about profit margins these days, Mr Shillabeer. Accountants rule the world, in case you didn't know.'

'Accountants don't catch many poachers though, which is what interests me. We shall be doing them a kindness by shooting a few of their spare birds. We're going to have some fun this winter, you and me.'

'Don't count on it.'

'Ralf, you owe it to your father to get even with Captain Ives and this is the way to do it. By cleaning him out of pheasants. His job will be on the line then so we'll see how he likes being on the receiving end for a change.'

'You've got hundreds of pheasants of your own. Thousands, probably. And I bet you couldn't give them away.'

'You're wrong there, Ralf. There's money in pheasants if you know where to get it, and I'm going to show you how. A young man like you ought to be taking this more seriously. I'm putting you in the way of making a few sovs so the least you can do is show a bit of interest.'

The Witch had been listening intently to this conversation, turning her head from one to the other as they spoke. She could detect a note of irritation in her master's voice and pressed her whiskery white snout to Ralf's ear as a warning against making too many smart answers. He did his best not to flinch from her poisonous breath. She made it plain that she did not trust him and watched him suspiciously with sideways glances of her clouded eyes. Shillabeer knew when it paid to be silver-tongued but his doggy minder had no intention of softening up. If Ralf did not swing the wheel fast enough after receiving the order to change direction she treated him to one of her blood-chilling snarls.

'The Witch wants her pie!' was one of his regular battle cries. As a treat he would buy her a steak and kidney pie with gravy from a roadside restaurant. Whether she did or not she began to quiver in anticipation when she heard the words.

Ralf was forced to the conclusion that she could understand much of Dick Shillabeer's conversation, whether directed at her or not, and he never failed to be impressed. 'Switch off and talk to me,' was another of his favourite commands, but then did all the talking himself. This suited Ralf very well as he did not need to listen. Shillabeer preferred to muse aloud without having his train of thought interrupted and invariably returned to the subject which absorbed his interest to the exclusion of all others – shooting pheasants. Preferably those belonging to someone else.

He lit a cigarette and nudged Ralf's elbow to be sure of his full attention. 'I expect you would like to start practising. Remind me when we get back. I've got exactly the right gun to lend you.'

Speaking slowly and with emphasis Ralf made a careful reply. 'Mr Shillabeer, I hope you won't mind too much but the truth is that I am not in favour of killing harmless woodland creatures, for whatever reason, and certainly not as a hobby. Also I am strongly opposed, on principle, to all forms of hunting and blood sports. That includes shooting pheasants, whether illegally at night or with beaters during the day. I hope that is clear so that I don't have to keep repeating myself.'

'Ah, but this is a special poacher's gun, Ralf, a four-ten. It folds up, the neatest thing you ever saw. On a windy night you can just charm the birds down from the trees with it.'

'You didn't listen to a word I said.'

'Jed and me have got it rigged up with a gunlight and a silencer. It's a handy piece of kit, if I say so myself.'

'But would be wasted on me. I haven't fired a gun since I was eighteen, which was the last time Dad took me out shooting. My views have changed since then and are unlikely to change back again. Sorry.'

'Yes, you need to be able to shoot straight to use a four-ten properly. Fancy a walk round with it tomorrow? I don't like pigeons any more than your Dad does. Or crows, or squirrels, or foxes and a lot of other pests we could do with less of. You can do us both a bit of good by sorting a few out.'

Ralf tried hard to be patient, and mostly succeeded. Although counting down to his eightieth birthday Shillabeer made no concessions to age whatsoever, in fact did not seem aware of being old. He was a seventy-nine year old juvenile delinquent, his delight in misbehaviour undimmed by the passing years. Ralf could well understand how he exasperated his handsome niece as she tried to run the business.

Every so often he made a strenuous effort to take up the slack in Shillabeer's conversation, trying to haul in the ravel of useless information that had made a long dry summer pass more pleasantly than it might have done otherwise. But failed. Trying not to sound unduly disapproving he said, 'The estate has those pheasants guarded day and night. No poacher would stand a chance.'

'That's where you're wrong, Ralf. This is a once-in-a-lifetime opportunity and I don't intend to miss it. Don't worry about getting caught, I'll show you how it's done.'

Remembering what his father had told him when they had their conversation on the seat under the plum tree Ralf was suitably apprehensive. Shillabeer was softening him up as a replacement for Jed on his night-time pheasant shooting activities and he wanted to make it clear right from the start that he had no intention of becoming involved. He said, 'I hope you're not including me in these plans. You're going to be disappointed if so.'

'Of course I am. I'm properly retired now and can put my mind to it. You're here to help me and the Witch can still do the business when a pheasant hits the deck. So we're going to make ourselves some money and have fun at the same time.'

'Your idea of fun isn't quite the same as mine. And there is no money to be made from shooting pheasants. Even I know that.'

'Ralf, not many weeks from now, as soon as we get the first frosts, you and me are going to help ourselves to so many of the Captain's pheasants that the shooting syndicate will complain about their poor sport. So would you complain if you knew how much it was costing them. His lord and master in the big house won't like that so we'll see how he likes having a boot up his asshole for a change. The fat bastard.'

'I don't dislike him that much. Really.'

'But Ralf, I'm putting you in the way of making some money.' Shillabeer sighed in despair. 'Young people today! Never mind, head down to those buildings of mine at Claypits Farm. We've got a little consignment for my nephew Oliver. Your old school pal.'

'What makes you think that Oliver Biggs was ever a friend of mine?'

'Young Biggsy's wife has just had another nipper, number five by my reckoning. He needs all the readies he can get. I thought you would be pleased to help him.'

By long tradition the butcher's shop in their nearby market town did not open on Monday afternoons. Biggs & Son Family Butchers closed at midday and their shop window was filled with clean white trays decorated with sprigs of plastic parsley.

This was relevant because every Monday afternoon Shillabeer would enquire courteously, 'Where shall we go for our little drive today, Ralf? How about a trip down to those buildings of mine at Claypits Farm?'

Ralf was not supposed to comment on this arrangement and always pretended not to look when Jed threw some gruesome packages through the rear door of the Land Rover. Packages that landed with a thud and were heavy enough to lower the rear axle. Followed by a message, delivered to Ralf through the driver's window. 'Just a couple of heifer calves. Tell Oliver they were the best I could do this week.'

'I shall be sure and remember.'

'If he says anything tell him I've got a really big heavy old sheep looked out for next week. That should keep him quiet.'

'I would prefer not to know. If you don't mind.'

Jed lowered his voice to a whisper. 'The boss lady is really happy now that you're keeping the guvnor amused and out of her way. Things have really improved since you came up here

62

to live, Ralf. It's great to have you.'

There could be no sensible reply so Ralf spun the wheel and set off on a cross-country route to Claypits Farm which was about halfway between High Beckles and their nearby market town. Only the buildings and a few paddocks remained of this small farm, the land having been absorbed long ago into larger neighbouring farms. Shillabeer used this cluster of dilapidated old barns to store hay and straw, and also as a secluded place in which to meet his nephew, Oliver Biggs the butcher.

Ralf was not very happy about this arrangement and sneaked a look over his shoulder to see large plastic sacks oozing blood. They contained large chunks of raw animal butchered into crude joints and not for the first time in Shillabeer's company he mused wistfully on the past pleasures of a wholesome vegetarian diet.

Meanwhile he had to eat to stay alive and in High Beckles that meant meat, lots of it, mostly home killed. His father shot partridges and rabbits, the Witch caught hares and deer, and where the rest came from he preferred not to know. His father could not conceal his relief, fearing for his son's health if he had continued living on grated carrot sandwiches and watercress soup. Parents are allowed to make personal remarks and Ralf did not take offence.

It was necessary to stop and open a couple of gates on the way to Claypits Farm, after which he was able to plunge the Land Rover down off the hill and bump along a rutted track between thick hedges so that they arrived at the isolated farm buildings unseen. After only short acquaintance as the robber chief's driver it had become second nature to go the long way round and the back way in.

Ralf and Oliver Biggs the butcher were the same age and had been exact contemporaries at the school in their local market town. This was one of the old grammar schools, now independent and with a sixth form college. Together with its chapel and some almshouses it was situated in the older and more photogenic part of the town, much visited by summer tourists. Meeting up with old school friends can be an agreeable experience and Ralf was warmly welcomed by the butcher every Monday. He was always there first, sitting behind the wheel of a large van out of sight from the road, and any customers of Biggs & Son Family Butchers who might be passing.

'Hotter than ever,' he greeted them cordially, mopping his face with his sleeve as he climbed out of the van. 'You're late. I was falling asleep.'

'We're here now,' Shillabeer said soothingly. 'And I expect Ralf will give you a hand if you ask him nicely.'

Ralf sensibly stayed put and allowed the & Son to do the portering. Oliver Biggs looked every inch a butcher being stout and strong, with a big red good-natured face. He wore a grubby white coat liberally daubed with bloodstained finger marks and when the meat had been transferred and was safely out of sight he drew Ralf aside for a chat.

'Never have time normally,' he apologised. 'We've been shorthanded in the shop ever since my Dad died so I have to do most of the work myself.'

'No need to be embarrassed, Oliver. What would you like to talk to me about?'

'It's about this little arrangement Uncle Dick and me have with the meat. Just a quiet word.'

'You're having it now.'

'You see, Ralf, it's well, what you might call 'unofficial'. This little dodge with the meat.'

'But which an unkind judge might describe as 'illegal'?'

'You could put it like that. A small family business like mine can't compete against the supermarkets. Uncle Dick and me have got together to cut out the middle man. Does that make me a criminal?'

'It's what it makes me I'm worried about.'

'Just a little bit of spare cash that the usurers and money-changers and tax-gatherers can't lay their hands on. Have you any idea what it's like being a butcher these days?'

'Difficult, I should imagine.'

'Bloody well is. And much the same for farmers. These are hard times for us country chaps, Ralf. Not like you city slickers on big salaries.'

'Oh, my aching sides.'

'It's no laughing matter, mate. We had a problem after Uncle lost his licence but you've turned up to do the necessary this year. We like to keep it in the family so to speak, and you're one of us after all, which means we don't have to trust outsiders. We go back a long way, Ralf, so please don't say anything to anyone about the meat.'

'Who did you have in mind? I don't meet so many people these days.'

The butcher laid a big hand on his shoulder to indicate that he had no wish to hurt his feelings. 'I know you wouldn't turn us in on purpose, Ralf, but you tend to be a bit, well you know, not quite up with the game sometimes. You might mention it to someone without thinking. In which case we all end up in front of the magistrates pleading for leniency.'

'I'm not that dreamy and out of touch. I don't want a prison record either. I shall say I was only obeying orders.'

'Good man,' his old school-fellow said, giving his shoulder a squeeze. 'We must meet up together one evening. We've got a lot to talk about.'

'I should like that, Oliver. Whenever you can arrange it.'

'A steak, a bottle of wine, and a pretty waitress in a black frock. I'll treat you to all three, in whichever order you prefer.'

'I'll let you know on the night.'

Oliver Biggs smiled at this and their business having been concluded Ralf accompanied him to the door of his van. Before they went their different ways he lowered his voice and said, 'Sorry to hear about your Dad being ill. Sonia told me the bad news about Tom after he had been to the hospital. Came as a shock to all of us.'

'He's managing all right at the moment. The fine weather helps.'

'My old man died from cancer two years ago, so you have

my sympathy. Colon cancer in his case. It was not a nice way to die. Perhaps your Dad will have better luck.'

'I'll do what I can for him. He doesn't want to be treated as if he was an invalid.'

'Your father and my father were shooting mates, that counts for something, doesn't it? They had some good times together up at High Beckles, helping Uncle Dick to keep his rabbits under control.'

'A shame that their good times had to come to an end.'

'We really do go back a long way, Ralf. My Dad and your Dad went to school together as well, just like we did. One of my grannies was a Shillabeer so we're all in it together whether you like it or not.' The butcher beckoned Ralf to move a little closer. 'How are things looking up between you and Sonia? Any developments yet?'

'I don't know what you mean, Oliver.'

'Bloody sure you do. Sonia is special. Not many women as good-looking as her in a route march, as my old Dad used to say, although what he meant by it I was never quite sure.'

'I'm not sure either.'

You fancy her, don't you? What would an old married man like me give for the chance!'

'She works too hard. I never catch up with her.'

'That's a feeble excuse.' The butcher folded his arms and paused a moment to collect his thoughts. 'I know we shouldn't be talking about Sonia like this but she's a cousin and I'm fond of her, of course I am. The point is, Ralf, that none of us want to see a good woman going to waste and right now it looks as if she could end up an old maid like Aunt Edie Shillabeer. You remember Aunt Edie, don't you? My granny's sister. Never did get married and lived on into her nineties.'

'Yes, I remember her well. Used to look after the geese on Beckles Green. Bent over a stick. I was more frightened of her than I was of the geese.'

'We wouldn't like to see Sonia go the same way. There's a farmer sniffing round but he's only after her land. You would suit her much better, Ralf. That's what we all think.'

'We?'

'Me, Jed, his mother, your Dad. Uncle, too. He likes you for some reason. Although right now I think he's getting impatient.'

Shillabeer wanted to count up a few more pheasants and was indeed becoming increasingly restless. 'Time to go,' he called from his passenger window. 'When you're ready, Ralf.' On hearing his displeasure the Witch obliged with a blood-curdling growl.

Oliver Biggs took the hint and they parted. He drove off back to his shop while Ralf resumed his travels in the Land Rover. Obeying instructions to avoid roads he meandered over hill and dale, following a zig-zag route along green lanes and field-edge tracks. Shillabeer always had a destination in mind but liked to keep him guessing, saying suddenly, 'Take a right,' or 'Go left here,' instructions accompanied by a snarl from the Witch to make sure he obeyed at once.

Ralf did as he was told until eventually he was ordered to stop in a secluded gateway. They were visiting the Larch Plantation and as always they had gone the long way round and the back way in, arriving unobserved. The sun streamed through the branches making a view good enough for a calendar, except that the scenery was not what they had come to admire.

'Best birds on the estate,' Shillabeer whispered confid-entially, nudging Ralf's arm to be sure of his full attention. 'Look at those little beauties hiding in the bracken over there. See what I mean?'

'They look just like any other pheasants to me,' Ralf replied truthfully.

'Every year the Captain saves these for the special Boxing Day shoot. Pampered birds, Ralf. They're as fat and tame as your Dad's old hens.'

'You mean even I couldn't miss?'

'Nor me either. Which means that Captain Ives and his boss and their rich pals are going to find the larder bare.

Because we shall have had the lot.'

'Who are we talking about now?'

'You, me and the Witch. We're going to make a great team.'

'I agreed to be your driver, not your accomplice. Think again.'

'Can you see them all in there,' he exulted, once again worrying Ralf's elbow. He pointed. 'Look, Ralf. Hundreds of the little buggers just waiting for us to come and get them. I can hardly wait.'

Ralf did not respond because he was lost in thought and had mastered the art of detaching his mind while Shillabeer enthused about the estate pheasants, occasionally murmuring a vague reply to keep him happy. He was thinking about Sonia, and what Oliver Biggs had told him. And was slowly coming to realise that he was not only being set up as Shillabeer's idiot apprentice for the poaching season but also as Sonia's future husband.

When Shillabeer nudged him a third time he said, 'Dad loved the Boxing Day shoot. Sometimes he followed behind to pick up the fallers and other years he was in charge of the beaters. I'm sorry he won't be doing it ever again.'

'Me too, Ralf. Me too.'

'Well, do you want to stay here? I fancy a change of scenery.'

'Why not? There's a nice little estate between Long Beckles and Huckle with more birds than they know what to do with. Shall we take a look? We might be able to do some business with them later on.'

'Steal some of their pheasants, I think you mean.'

'They won't miss a few, or even a few hundred. Take a left here and go down that track. A good short cut that is, make a note of it.'

Ralf promised he would but guessed that it would be swiftly erased from his memory. He had plenty to think about these days, and much to occupy his time. What with one thing and another he was on the go from morning till night. His father left most of the work in the garden to him, and increasingly the shopping and housework as well. America he put firmly from his mind. If it didn't hurt then it wasn't a sacrifice and he was determined to have no regrets, whatever the cost.

Most of all he was disturbed by the handsome presence of Sonia Shillabeer. Every village had its beauty, soon seduced and married off. Sonia was something else and they all knew it, and were acutely aware of having such a proud and beautiful woman hidden away in their isolated farm settlement. Ralf kept asking himself if he would have been as smitten by her if he had met her in different surroundings, at a drinks party in London for example, with other attractive women on view He came to the conclusion that he would. Sonia was tall and possessed of darkly beautiful good looks but it was not these features alone that had ensnared him. Nor was it her farm-girl complexion, her athletic fitness and her glowing good health that he found so irresistible. It was her unshakeable strength of purpose that set her apart. She was completely self-absorbed, always focused on the job in hand. Which in her case meant securing her inheritance, and to this end she allowed herself no distractions.

It was impossible not to be constantly aware of her in such a small community and he knew that their lives were starting to converge. They were the object of much curiosity, speculation even, because the others openly hoped that a romance would start between them. He pretended indifference but it was a pretence he did not feel. When he pulled back his bedroom curtains in the morning his first thought was to peer from side to side in case he could see her somewhere on the farm, or passing by in the lane. When he visited the farmhouse and clanked open the iron latch on the kitchen door he experienced a stab of disappointment if she was not there. He had really got it bad and was utterly miserable if a complete day passed without seeing her.

Meanwhile he did his best to humour Sonia's elderly scallywag of an uncle, as well as trying to keep him out of trouble, an impossible task. 'You're very quiet, Ralf,' he said suspiciously, aware that he was deep in thought.

'How would you prefer me?'

'An answer for everything. Never mind those pheasants, we can count them up another day. Head for that big eating place on the main road. The Witch wants her pie!'

4

The world was full of matchmakers and the good folk of High Beckles were no exception. Sonia was twenty-five, unmarried, and likely to remain unmarried. For the reasons Ralf's father had explained to him.

Although she was a competent businesswoman well able to look after herself, and set to inherit a farm that was big enough to guarantee her independence for life, Sonia was a captive in her surroundings. High Beckles was so isolated that she was likely to become as unworldly as the other members of the Shillabeer family who had held the farm before her. And like them she was bound by a strict old-fashioned morality. Although Ralf had spent the last twelve years of his life in London he retained much of his folk memory and needed little reminding of how things had always been done in the farming community.

Nothing had changed, or was likely to change, certainly not in this part of the countryside. Money, land and property needed to be kept within the family for as long as possible, the only acceptable alternative being a secure lifelong marriage, preferably with a relative. If his father was to be believed Sonia had no intention of compromising her inheritance with either a lover or a husband and had chosen celibacy and the single life instead. This was made easier because she seldom left the farm and so was unlikely to meet anyone who might want to fall in love with her, still less meet someone she might fancy herself.

A situation that had changed with his arrival in High Beckles. For the first time, and perhaps for the only time, Sonia now had a prospective suitor whose presence she could not ignore. Her uncle was in favour, Tom Lassiter even more so, as were Oliver Biggs the butcher, Queenie the house-

71

keeper and her son Jed. They all wanted Ralf and Sonia to fall in love and get married. He was not an outsider, he was the son of Shillabeer's best friend, a man who was also a father-figure in Sonia's life. They reckoned she would never have a better chance.

There was another reason, and Oliver Biggs had spelled it out. They did not want Sonia to end up like Shillabeer's Aunt Edith.

Oliver had asked him if he remembered Aunt Edie, and he did. She had been one of the more vivid memories of childhood. Miss Shillabeer, as she was always known, spent the last years of her long life on the green at High Beckles tending her flock of geese. Her favourite form of greeting was to brandish her stick as a warning, just in case you might be up to something. The hissing geese were scarcely less intimidating.

Stooped and grim, with a formidable presence, she had survived to a great age not by being soft and cuddly but by being gnarled and cantankerous. She was a fierce old party determined to guard the family interests, and did, right up until the day she died.

At the far end of the kitchen at High Beckles was a low doorway, slightly misshapen and with a wobbly brass handle. It opened into a small communal sitting room where Jed and his mother snoozed at intervals during the day. Ralf once had to wait while the robber chief spoke on the telephone, and stepped into this quiet side room to drink the mug of coffee Queenie had brewed up for him with rich farm milk. She was obeying Shillabeer's orders that he had to be given food at every opportunity. This was to build up his strength. Shillabeer was determined to recruit him as his poaching partner instead of Jed, and was having him fattened for the winter.

While sipping his scalding hot coffee Ralf looked around him with interest. The room contained a glass-fronted mahogany cabinet in which stood some family photographs, most of them old. He was immediately drawn to one of a strikingly beautiful woman in her twenties. It was a portrait photograph, disconcertingly lifelike. The expression on the young woman's face was vigorous and intense. Her eyes seemed to follow him, as is often the case with full-face photographs. Written on the bottom was her name, Edith Shillabeer.

And having seen it he could better understand why the others were so concerned, because it could have been a photograph of Sonia, they were so alike. He found himself surprisingly disturbed. Not just by the resemblance but because it was hard to accept that the scary old battle-axe who tended the geese on Beckles Green had once been the ravishingly beautiful young woman in the photograph. Jed was too young to have any memory of Aunt Edith but Queenie and his father could remember her, and of course Shillabeer himself. They would all have seen the photograph many times and could not have missed the close resemblance with Sonia at the same age. Hence their wish to avoid a similar outcome.

A new inhabitant was rare at High Beckles so he was now better able to understand the effect that his arrival had on this small enclosed community. They were getting ready to welcome his father, Tom Lassiter, when the postman brought them some even more exciting news. Tom's son Ralf, who had vanished from sight at the age of eighteen, was returning from London to stay with his father for the duration of his illness. They did not need to be told that the presence of a young man joining the family would make a difference to their lives, and to Sonia's in particular.

It explained why she had been waiting, gun in hand, for him to present himself. She wanted to take a good look at him first, before he made it to the house and kitchen to meet the others. Standing protectively beside her the Witch also gave him the once-over. A reception committee of two, guardians of their territory, unsmiling and watchful, and both reaching the same conclusion. They found him wanting. He lacked the nerve and balls needed to make the grade in their hillside frontier outpost.

Unfortunately for him he had been much changed by twelve years of university life and was now strongly opposed to all forms of hunting for sport. At first he had not believed that the boss lady, as Jed called her, hunted deer on foot with the Witch but then found that she did so regularly. His father hinted that Sonia had a wild streak, inherited from another side of the family, and he could well believe it. Either way he knew that a love affair was not in either of their interests, viewed sensibly. But when was love ever rational and sensible? Ralf knew that his principles would not hold out very long if he could get close enough for a kiss.

Alas for the matchmakers there was a storm cloud brewing. An impending quarrel rather than a tender romance.

His father had explained the situation to him. It was a battle between Sonia and her uncle over which of them had first claim on Jed's services. He found himself uncomfortably squeezed between two strong-willed people who both expected to have their own way. But on one thing Sonia and her uncle were in full agreement. The problem would be solved at a stroke if he agreed to replace Jed on the nightly poaching expeditions in the coming winter. Neither of them could understand why he kept refusing.

Few days passed without meeting Sonia, either in the kitchen or around the farm. They were aware of the interest in them and for this reason found conversation difficult. She spoke more freely when they met away from the farm and one day in September he met her head-on in the narrow lane that joined High Beckles to Long Beckles. He was driving his father's car and on his way to the town, while Sonia was on her way back.

She had a Land Rover of her own, newer and smarter than her uncle's battered version, and as they approached she flashed her lights and pointed to a gateway, indicating that she wished to speak to him. There being no other traffic to worry about they stepped from their respective vehicles and leaned over the gate. The open spread of autumn countryside in front of them would have inspired an artist but Sonia was not interested in scenery and came straight to the point.

She said, 'I need Jed to run the farm properly.'

Ralf replied patiently, 'I know. Dad explained it to me. I understand the problem.'

'Uncle Dick is too old to go out at night on his own.'

'Try and persuade him to stay in then. Everyone else watches television, why not him?'

'I can't. He won't.'

'If he won't listen to you he certainly won't listen to me. I don't have any influence over him, Sonia. None at all.'

'I feel a lot happier when I know he is with you, Ralf.'

'I can't help you. Really.'

'He takes risks. Unnecessary risks for a man of his age. The winter is going to be a difficult time for all of us.'

'It isn't really my problem though, is it?'

'I need him to survive the winter.'

'Dad explained that to me as well. About his eightieth birthday next May.'

'It means a lot to me. Which is why I want you to help Uncle with the pheasants.'

'I can't do that, Sonia.'

'Oh. Why not?'

'You know perfectly well why not. Helping him with the pheasants means poaching from the estate. Poaching is against the law. I could not possibly be involved.'

'If you don't go with him Uncle will insist on taking Jed instead. And I need Jed on the farm.'

'You must stand firm. Tell Jed not to go with him.'

'He would threaten to go by himself, which would be even more dangerous.'

'I find it hard to understand, Sonia, I really do. Your uncle has got plenty of pheasants of his own. Why does he need to shoot other people's as well? To steal them, in plain language.'

'It's his hobby.'

'Sonia, that is not what is meant by having a hobby.'

'Well, it's what he does in the winter since he lost his driver's licence. Are you sure you couldn't go with him this year?'

'It wasn't part of the agreement.'

'If you don't go it means I shall have to take it in turns with Jed.'

Ralf felt like scratching his head in the forlorn hope of finding a compromise that would satisfy everyone. Nothing occurred to him and he knew that nothing ever would because it was a problem with no solution and no easy exit route for either of them. Sonia was too proud to plead, all she could do was keep explaining the problem to him. All he could do in return was to continue to refuse as politely and firmly as possible.

He was unhappy about it and tried to soften his refusal by spreading his hands and putting on an apologetic smile. 'I just can't do it, Sonia. I have my career to consider. The answer is 'no'. It will always be 'no'. I don't like to keep refusing when you ask me to do something for you but I can't do what you want. Don't ask me again. Please.'

This was not what Sonia wanted to hear and for a moment she allowed her displeasure to show. Ralf guessed that she had been to the town on business because she was not wearing her farm clothes. It was a bright but cold day and she wore a navy blue overcoat with a double row of gold buttons. The overcoat swelled in and out very nicely to follow her shape but when the gold buttons began to heave and her eyes to smoulder Ralf knew they were on a collision course.

Of the two bossy Shillabeers she was exerting more leverage than her uncle but there could be no doubt of the price they both wanted in return for living in the Orchard House and enjoying the architect's garden. Making a big effort to sound more conciliatory she said, 'Uncle Dick enjoys your company, Ralf. He looks forward to his drive with you every day.'

'Good listeners are always popular.'

She thought this was funny, and smiled. 'It's made a big

difference already. I just wanted to thank you for helping to look after him.'

'He is under the impression that he is looking after me.'

She smiled again, then changed the subject, lowering her voice. 'It's terrible about your father being ill. Really awful. Poor Tom.'

'Thank you for being so nice to him.'

'He's helped me in all sorts of ways. I'm very fond of him.'

'He's fond of you, too.'

'It was good of you to give up your job to come home and look after him.'

'He loves living in the house, Sonia. And the garden. I've never seen him so happy.'

'We like having him up here with us. You too.'

'It's been a lovely summer. Couldn't have worked out better.'

Their conversation had come to its natural end but neither of them made the first parting move. There was no need for haste. At High Beckles time was always in plentiful supply so they continued leaning side by side over a wooden farm gate taking in the view. Having the attention of a beautiful woman was testing Ralf's resolve to the limit. None of the reasons for keeping his distance seemed quite so compelling when she was standing close enough for him to admire her unblemished outdoor-girl complexion.

He said, 'Does it seem strange to you, meeting again after such a long time? It does to me.'

'It wasn't something I expected to happen.'

'Must be ten years, the last time we spoke together. Just before my second year at university. I still remember it.'

'Uncle and Tom were out on the hill shooting rabbits. You talked to me about London.'

'What did you talk to me about?'

'The Witch was younger then. Uncle had been teaching her to do a lot of clever things. I told you some of them but I don't think you believed me.'

'I certainly couldn't believe it when I saw her still alive. Do you know how old she is?'

'Not exactly. She's getting on a bit but just as clever.'

'You were still at school.'

'I had one more year to go. I left when I was sixteen.'

'You were very pretty. If I had known then what I know now I wouldn't have gone away.'

'You said that with a smile, Ralf. I don't think you meant it seriously.'

'Oh but I did. I would have wanted to be your boyfriend. Most certainly I would. First in the queue.'

'You were more interested in London. I expect you still are.'

'Not necessarily. I'm going to be here for quite a while.'

'You didn't ask me when you had the chance. I don't think you're asking me now.'

Ralf sighed. 'It's difficult. You know they all want us to fall in love and get married, don't you?'

'Your father certainly does. He keeps dropping hints and asking me how we're getting on.' She thought about it a little longer and then conceded the point. 'The others do as well. They watch us all the time.'

'We don't give them anything to watch though.'

'You're right. We don't.'

'It wouldn't work out, would it? For all sorts of reasons.'

'Probably not.'

Ralf sighed again. 'I know we have to be sensible but I'm in love with you, Sonia.'

'That's a silly thing to say.'

'Not from where I'm standing it isn't.'

'It needs a lot of thinking about.' She thought he was going to try to kiss her and moved back towards her Land Rover. 'You shouldn't have said that, Ralf.'

'I meant it.'

'I must get back to the farm. Work to do.'

'Stay and talk to me a moment. Don't run away.'

'I heard what you said. I'm flattered, of course I am, but I still think you shouldn't have said it. Not the way things are.'

She slid behind the wheel but he kept hold of the door. 'You're quite a woman, Sonia. You can't blame me for falling in love with you.'

'It's too soon. I'm not ready.'

'I'm not going anywhere. I'll wait.'

'I don't want you to say it again. It would be better if we didn't meet.'

'It won't change anything. Not as far as I'm concerned.'

'Ralf, you're very nice, and I'm not saying 'no' I'm saying not yet. Not for a long time yet. Ask me again after Uncle's birthday and if you haven't changed your mind by then I'll start going out with you.'

He wailed in despair. 'No man could wait that long. Be a bit nicer to me, Sonia.'

'I am being nice to you.' She smiled but gestured him to shut the door. 'I really do have work to do.'

'You need to relax more. I could show you how, if you would let me.'

This forced another smile but no concession. 'You can be very persuasive, Ralf. Ask me again later.'

'Don't go. We need to talk.'

'No. I have to go. Think over what I said about helping Uncle.'

'You mean that if I really loved you I would do what you wanted?' He winced slightly. 'That's a lot to ask, Sonia. If I was caught poaching at night it would mean the end of my career. That's a hard bargain you're making.'

She started the engine but did not drive off. No woman could remain unmoved after a declaration of love, even one that was followed by two unhappy faces rather than a joyous embrace. Sonia looked disturbed and troubled while Ralf was angry with himself for acting on impulse and bungling his chances. Not that it mattered because he knew instinctively that whatever happened theirs was always going to be a fraught relationship and a doomed romance.

His father had explained it clearly enough. A pre-marital

love affair was not on offer, and never would be. In Sonia's case only marriage would be considered, and then after a lengthy formal courtship overseen by their elders. Whatever her true feelings towards him she was reluctant to commit herself because she knew there was a time limit to his stay. When his father died he would be free to go, and would have to go, since he needed to earn a living and could not pursue his career from High Beckles. Doomed romance was right. They had no future together. He knew it, Sonia knew it better still.

He shut the door and stepped aside as she drove away uphill to the farmhouse at High Beckles. Left alone in the middle of a narrow lane Ralf stayed where he was, watching until her Land Rover disappeared from view. He was deeply dejected and knew that he had only himself to blame. He had started a love affair where there would be no sex, and most likely no kisses or cuddles either. Not the smartest act in his life for a man who was supposed to be clever.

Time was different in the country. What seemed an interminable wait to him was far less so in a farming calendar geared to the interval of the seed and the harvest, or the gestation length of a cow. Sonia might well consider it a short wait until next May but to a man who found his enforced celibacy uncomfortable it seemed an eternity. Even when the Land Rover had long gone from sight he remained indecisively with his hands in his pockets, unable to motivate himself to continue his journey to the town. All he could think about was the snugly fitting navy blue overcoat and the double row of gold buttons heaving gently in displeasure.

No need to ask whether he loved Sonia or not. For the first time in his life he was suffering the anguish of unrequited love, and it was a most wretched feeling.

5

Ralf decided that he did not much care for the month of October. The leaves were falling, the temperature likewise, and the mornings were cold and dark. The general air of holiday and optimism that had surrounded the move to High Beckles finally came to an end. Sonia avoided him, which made him even more miserable. They met in the kitchen but only when Queenie was there, or on the farm with Jed and her uncle, never alone.

His father always looked forward to the shooting season so he was much happier. He got up at first light to walk the stubble and hedgerows, a cartridge belt round his waist and gun at the ready. He had used a gun all his life and didn't feel dressed without one, always returning with something eatable. One day it would be a hare, the next a high-flying duck that had strayed off course, or a brace of partridges, more often than not an old cock pheasant too bold for its own good. He shot so many rabbits that their kitchen needed a game larder. He had promised Ralf that they wouldn't go hungry, and they didn't. He knew several ways of cooking rabbits, all of them delicious, including baking them in a pie to eat hot and finish off cold for supper. Stewed with herbs or roasted in the oven with a couple of game birds, better still. The weather may have been bad but the living was easy.

As the evenings became ever shorter they pulled the curtains and stacked the fire. This was an open fire in a wide stone hearth, and because it was so comfortable and pleasant they both stayed up late, seldom going to bed before mid-night. With no women to boss them around or tell them to be a bit tidier it soon became a rough-and-ready bachelor existence, much to their liking.

His father spent a lot of time in the kitchen, either cooking or preparing food, while Ralf spent time in a small side room which he had converted into a study. 'Your office', as his father referred to it. He had used some of the family furniture to provide himself with a desk and a bookcase, and soon made it comfortable with a few ornaments, a couple of prints on the walls, and a reading lamp. He had plenty of household chores and gardening jobs to occupy him during the day but in the evenings he made it plain that he wanted, and needed, time to himself. He kept the door open so that his father did not feel excluded and then opened up his laptop computer. This reconnected him to his former way of life and kept him in touch with the outside world.

When it was time to rejoin his father in the sitting room they sat in armchairs facing one another, rather than side by side, in order to make conversation easier. And after some initial awkwardness through being apart for so long they soon found plenty to talk about. On hearing strange voices large friendly insects appeared to investigate who was doing the talking. Giant spiders circled the walls, curious to see who was providing the new-found warmth. The roof timbers creaked appreciatively, the tiles settled themselves more comfortably, and there were inexplicable gurgling noises from the plumbing. All evidence that the house had become a home again.

Once a week his father cleared the kitchen table and spread out his gun cleaning kit. Ralf doubted if his guns needed cleaning but he could see that taking them apart and putting them together again was pleasurable to his father. He had an aerosol can of oil, a rod and brushes, plus a selection of soft cloths for polishing the barrels and stocks. It was a form of occupational therapy, combined with pride of possession.

'Your cabbages are growing fast,' he told Ralf as he squinted through the barrels of his favourite twelve-bore shotgun, a quarter-choke boxlock ejector with double triggers. 'That rain we had came at just the right time. There's some old plastic netting in the garage. It might pay you to hang it over some sticks to keep the pigeons out. The little sods are starting to get a bit hungrier now.'

'I'll do it first thing tomorrow.'

'Artful birds, Ralf. I've waged war on them all my life, and lost. Lead shot is the best medicine but a few nets make them think twice. They soon get the message and move on somewhere else.'

'I don't intend to let the pigeons have them, Dad. After all those blisters? Not likely! I've just changed my mind about field sports. Leave the gun handy and I'll do the job myself.'

His father smiled and handed over his empty glass. 'Fill this up for me, there's a good chap. My breathing isn't quite so good tonight.'

Ralf did as he was asked, as he had done many times since they moved to High Beckles. First he spooned plenty of sugar into the glass and then poured in enough brandy to cover the sugar. They had brought the big black family kettle with them and it steamed gently on the stove day and night. He filled the glass with hot water, gave it a stir and handed it back to his father.

It was late in the evening when Ralf finally came to believe in his father's illness. As fatigue began to overtake him late in the day his appearance began to change. Ralf could see it in the texture of his skin, and the hunched way he sat in his armchair. His eyes were dark, and his breathing increasingly harsh and irregular. Even so he continued to refuse all offers of medication. He had long ago announced his intention of dying with his boots on, and saw no reason to change his mind.

When the television failed to hold his attention he switched it off and enquired where Ralf had been on his travels with Shillabeer. On being told he would reminisce about the local farms, speaking slowly in his quiet gravelly voice. Ralf let him talk, knowing that he had no real interests other than farming and shooting. What went on in the outside world concerned him as little as it did the other inhabitants of High Beckles. Ralf could not help wondering how long he would have to live there before the same thing happened to him.

Their country market town was some five miles distant and he drove in two or three times a week. Sometimes with his father but mostly on his own, his father increasingly reluctant to be long away from the carefree garden with its bees and weeds and half-tame birds. Ralf seldom failed to visit a stationer and bookshop in College Street where he bought a newspaper and tried to stay in touch with the wider world as it functioned daily away from the much smaller claustrophobic world of High Beckles.

College Street was named after the college where he and Oliver Biggs, and both their fathers before them, had received their education. Oliver was never a star pupil but made up for it by heft in the rugby scrum, a game he played with vigour. It was originally a grammar school founded four hundred years into the past, and had gone through many changes. Together with its chapel and the almshouses opposite it formed the old part of the town. The College had been Ralf's direct route to university and the good education he received there had prepared him well for the academic way of life, for which he would always be grateful.

Back in High Beckles he had more immediate matters to attend to, namely the overgrown garden of the Orchard House. A spell of warm weather fired his father up for one last big onslaught. 'May and October,' he informed Ralf as he urged him on. 'The two big gardening months. Put your effort into those two months and the rest of the year will take care of itself.'

'Is that so? I'll try and remember.'

'You're coming along nicely. Look at the expert way you handle that spade! Told you I would make a gardener of you, didn't I?'

'You did, Dad. You did.'

'And here's another little job you can do for me. This big clump of Michaelmas Daisies needs dividing. Dig them up for me and pull out the weeds.'

Obediently Ralf eased a garden fork all round and began to prise them from the ground. He said, 'We had these at home.

Mother was very fond of them.'

'She was that. I always planted them where she could see them from the kitchen window. Nice of you to remember such things.'

What they saw next was less pleasing. As Ralf began to lift the clump of woody stems from the ground he found there was a root of convolvulus embedded in the middle, and almost impossible to separate. He waited for instructions.

'Disgusting stuff,' his father said, eyeing it in distaste. 'Dig a bit deeper, Ralf. Don't let it break off or it will only grow again.'

Convolvulus is the pretty bindweed that flowers all summer and autumn with delicate pink and white trumpets. The flowers are pretty but the roots are ugly and twisted, long cancerous tendrils that cling tenaciously to the soil. If broken off they just grow again with renewed vigour. When Ralf finally managed to ease them apart he threw them quickly into the wheelbarrow and covered them over, not wishing to be reminded of his father's illness.

If his father noticed he gave no sign but in October the days are short and as the evening approached he decided they had worked long enough. He pointed to the sun which was a spectacular red disc vanishing fast behind the dark outline of Beckles Hill. He said, 'That's the fellow to watch, Ralf.'

'The sun, do you mean?'

'One more circle round him isn't too much to ask, is it?'

'If I could arrange it for you, I would.'

'A year seems a long time to a man in my condition. I always kept the Michaelmas Daisies going in the garden at home because Mother was so fond of them. I should like to see these bloom once more.'

'You may yet.'

'Over five years she's been gone now. It's passed very quickly. For me, anyway.'

'For me too, Dad. They were busy years at the university. It's a competitive line of business, believe it or not. Passed in a flash.'

'She was a clever woman, your mother. When she was young she set her heart on going to university but her parents were against the idea and she never went. Which was lucky for me personally because she came to work in the estate office instead and we soon got ourselves married. It was a good move for you too because she was determined that you should have your chance to do what she couldn't.'

'I owe her a lot. I know it even more now. I shall never forget what she did for me.'

His father scraped the mud from his boots and nodded agreement. 'She always put her mind to things, that's true. And could find a way out of most family problems. Not that I think even Mother could rescue me from the fix I'm in now.'

'Maybe we should ask George and Daisy for advice.' Ralf pointed upwards. 'They have friends in high places.'

This made his father chuckle with amusement. 'You said it, Ralf. Perhaps it works on the same principle as direct line insurance? Cutting out the middle man. Or middle woman in our case, seeing that we've got a lady vicar.'

'It could be that George and Daisy and all the other chapel folk know something good that we don't.'

'Maybe they do. Me, I prefer to wait and take my chance. I'm in no hurry to find out whether it's all true or not.'

Ralf winced slightly, as he always did when his father's condition was referred to, however obliquely. He said, 'I know I grumbled a bit at first. About helping you in the garden. I was pleased to do it really.'

'I know you were. And we'll have the benefit of it when the cold weather comes. That big old apple tree you sawed up for logs will burn nicely on the fire. We'll save them for Christmas.'

'I was thinking more of all the things we planted.'

'I can hardly wait for the spring to come round. When all the bulbs have come up, and with the border weeded from end to end, it's going to look a picture.'

'We've got the winter to get through first. That isn't going to be easy.'

'We'll manage. I never had the time or the inclination to do much with the garden at home, except to keep it tidy and grow a few veg. This is different. This is the sort of garden I've always dreamed about.'

'Enjoy it while you can.'

'I intend to.' His father touched him briefly on the arm. 'Ralf, I know you don't like it mentioned about what I've got wrong with me but if I breathed my last in this garden I should die happy. I would like you to remember that.'

'I hear what you say. If it's what you want I'll bear it in mind. That's a promise.'

His father seemed pleased and pointed to the sunset again before going indoors. 'Not often you can see the sun and the moon in the sky together. One coming up and the other going down. I reckon that means a sharp frost in the morning and a nice day again tomorrow.'

'The moon looks big. And close. Wouldn't want it to get too close and drop in.'

'It's what they call a hunter's moon, Ralf. Bright enough to read a newspaper by later on. Did you know the old retired architect who lived here had a telescope?'

'I seem to remember Mother mentioning it, yes.'

'He was an interesting man, not that I could ever spare much time to talk to him, but he told me that he bought the telescope because it was so dark up here at night. Got a good view of the moon and stars, he told me. Nice for retired people to have a hobby, don't you think?'

He went indoors before he could hear Ralf's answer, which would have been ambivalent on the subject of suitable hobbies for elderly men. Left on his own to clear up and put the tools away he paused for a moment to study the evening sky. Mention of the hunter's moon made him very thoughtful.

It made him thoughtful because Beckles Hill was where Sonia Shillabeer hunted deer with the Witch. The red sun was slowly disappearing from sight behind the hill, which was a mysterious place, circled near the top with a neolithic ditch and some Bronze Age burial mounds. The lower slopes were thickly wooded with yew trees and juniper bushes, the home of many wild creatures, including some plump roe deer.

Sonia was supple and athletic, and took her pleasures seriously. Her uncle boasted that he had taught her how to catch the deer, and how to butcher them up when caught. Oliver Biggs had a game licence so the dark venison meat sold in his shop soon found its way into the kitchens and then on to the dinner tables of the large houses in and around the town.

Although the light was fading fast Ralf went on looking up at the hill which was obviously a special place for Sonia and her delinquent uncle. It occurred to him as a strong possibility that as well as owning it and keeping it private the Shillabeers were direct descendants of the ancient folk who had made their home on the hill. Not an unreasonable idea even if it required them and their forebears to have been in continuous occupation of the area over two millennia. If so he wondered if they had some pagan wedding ceremony handed down through the generations. Perhaps a fire at midnight among the round barrows where their ancestors were buried, incantations to the moon, dog and all, with the contract sealed by the mingling of blood.

Now that was an attractive idea, well worth further thought. A wedding fire on the hill, then making love to Sonia under the stars, what could be more fitting for a wild and beautiful huntress? And when the night ended they could watch the sun come up, just as the ancient people buried there must have watched anxiously every day for the return of the light. Dreaming and reality were awkward bedfellows but just occasionally, given the right set of circumstances, they sometimes overlapped and came together. Could it happen that way for him? He stood for so long fantasising about making love to Sonia that his father opened the back door and called out to ask him if he was all right.

He signalled back with a thumbs-up and with his train of thought interrupted busied himself putting the gardening tools away and tidying their implement shed. By the time he had finished the sun had slid gently out of sight behind Beckles Hill, leaving only a red glow behind.

'You look cheerful,' his father said suspiciously when he kicked off his boots and joined him in the kitchen. 'Want to tell me what put the smile on your face?'

'Just an idea I had,' Ralf replied.

'Never apologise for an idea, son. Ideas are important. Ideas are what make things happen.'

'I wasn't apologising.'

His father reconsidered. 'Ideas mostly cause a lot of trouble in the world. Which is why people with ideas aren't popular.'

'I would like to make this one happen.'

This made his father even more curious. 'Well? Aren't you going to share it with me? Your big idea.'

'Sorry, Dad. It's personal.'

'In that case excuse me for asking.'

'But it's something you would approve of, I can tell you that much. I'll let you know when the time comes.' Adding superstitiously, 'If the time comes. You said it yourself, Dad. Whatever will be, will be.'

6

Ralf was in a bad mood because Shillabeer had altered his job description. Instead of being driven round in the Land Rover for his treat every day he insisted on being accompanied for a walk instead.

Ralf would have refused except that his father, as well as Sonia, pleaded with him not to let Shillabeer leave the farm on his own. They both feared that he would be getting up to something and urged Ralf not to let him out of his sight. This was an unwelcome development and Ralf began to grumble as their daily mileage increased steadily. 'Walking doesn't agree with me. It wasn't part of the deal.'

'Necessary though,' Shillabeer told him earnestly. 'I'm breaking you in gently, Ralf. I'm showing you how to do it properly. We can't afford any mistakes when we go after those pheasants. Walking is all part of the drill.'

Shillabeer's obsession with poaching pheasants from his neighbours was starting to irritate Ralf. While the sun shone he had listened indulgently with one elbow on the window of the Land Rover, his mind elsewhere, more often than not daydreaming about making love to Sonia. But now the wind blew cold and Shillabeer's ambitious plans for the fast approaching winter did not seem nearly so amusing.

For a small man not much over five feet tall Shillabeer covered the ground quickly and Ralf had a job to keep up with him. His grotesque dog limped alongside. Age for age she was even older than he was, and almost as big. She came up to his waistcoat pockets, her rough deerhound coat as stiff as wire wool. She still peered at Ralf from the corners of her rheumy eyes, not sure whether he could be completely trusted or not, but coming to the conclusion that he was at least harmless.

'Carry the gun for me,' Shillabeer pleaded. He liked to strut and swagger with a gun over his shoulder but was never able to carry it very far and soon had to concede age. 'Be a pal, Ralf. I'm finding it a bit heavy.'

'Why bring it then? I agreed to be your chauffeur, not your caddy.'

'Because we're practising. I told you, we've got to do things properly. You know I leave nothing to chance. Thoroughness, Ralf. That way we stay out of jail.'

'So long as we don't trespass on estate property. Is it a stiffer penalty for the one caught carrying the gun?'

'You worry too much. This is just part of the routine. It becomes second nature when you've done it enough times.'

'Hand it over then. But spare me the lecture.'

'Be careful with it, Ralf. This is my old Remington, my favourite gun. The best shooter I've ever had. Look after it for me.'

It was a .22 rifle and Ralf found it heavy and awkward to carry. Shillabeer's favourite gun was a sixteen shot automatic fitted with a telescopic sight and a silencer. Even Ralf had to admit that it looked the business. But still had his doubts. 'You must show me your firearms certificate when we get back. No doubt you have a firearms certificate?'

'This is my rabbit gun, Ralf. Thousands of rabbits I've shot with this gun.'

'Is that so?'

'Mainly at night from the Land Rover. Jed has got a hand lamp and shines it through his side window. He's a good lamp man, holds it rock steady and the bunnies don't move. Using a silencer means they don't get frightened off either. They never hear the shot that kills them.'

'Or a sheep that might be standing in the way.'

'Sheep's eyes show up green at night. Don't worry, we know what we're shooting at. Foxes eyes show up orange, they're easy to kill at night. Why don't you give it a try. You sound interested.'

'I'm not. Sorry.'

'With the scope I go for a head shot every time and hardly ever miss. Nothing to it if you can shoot straight.'

'You make it sound easy. I'm sure it isn't.'

'Mostly the rabbits run towards the banks and the hedges and then sit there sideways on, so even if I miss the bullets don't go very far. I only use low power ammo anyway. Hollow-nose bullets don't do much damage.'

'I'll take your word for it.'

'Jed has rigged up a spotlight on the Land Rover, he's good at things like that. We've got a big collection of lamps, remind me to show you when we get back. Some are the plug-in type and work off the engine, very good they are. And some are battery operated and fit on the rifle. Just the job for going after the pheasants at night when they're up in the trees.'

'It doesn't sound very sporting though, if you will excuse me for saying so.'

'Sometimes we stand on the back of the pick-up truck and lean on the cab roof to shoot. We've had some good fun over the years, your Dad and me.'

'Yes, I know he enjoyed his rabbiting. But as I keep telling you my views are not the same as his. I am strongly opposed to cruel and unnatural sports. Please believe that I mean what I say.'

'Yes, we've had some great nights out on the hill. Me and your Dad in one truck, Jed and Biggsy in another. I'm only sorry your Dad isn't up to it any more.'

'Not half as sorry as I am.'

'Fancy a go at some rabbits tonight? You could take his place. Give Oliver a ring and fix it up. Let's get it started again.'

'You never listen to a word I say.'

'You don't damage the eats with a head shot. It's the same with pheasants. No one wants to chew on lead shot and bone splinters. Look after your customers, Ralf, that way you stay in business. It's all about marketing a good product these days. That's what young Biggs and me provide.'

'Biggs is involved in your poaching activities? I might have known.'

'He's a licensed game dealer. He will sell all the pheasants we bring him and still want more. We're cutting you in, Ralf. You should be pleased. We wouldn't do it for anyone else.'

'You've been very kind to Dad and me, Mr Shillabeer, and I appreciate it. But I don't feel under any obligation to break the law just to show my gratitude. Please don't ask me again.'

'Biggsy is one of the family and we look on you in the same way. That's why we want you to come in with us.'

'The answer is still 'no'. How many more times must I tell you? Anyway it's time to go back now. Walking and me don't agree. I would prefer tarmac and four wheels from now on. And if it's all the same to you I should like to know where you're going when you take me on the scenic route. All these mystery tours are bad for my nerves.'

Shillabeer pretended that his feelings were hurt. 'Of course I'll tell you where we're heading, Ralf. Every time. You're my partner now. We're heading for Doggrells Copse, a favourite place of mine.'

'Not mine though,' Ralf said, as he fell in behind. There was sunshine but no bird music in Doggrells Copse. Everything in it that moved had been shot long ago by the estate gamekeepers to preserve the pheasants. Even so he had to admit that the broad views over open hillside were worth a casual glance or two. The stubble fields were still golden and the late October sunshine was pleasantly warm. The fresh air was nice too, the only thing that spoiled it was having to supply the sprightly local godfather with his captive audience.

Not only spry and garrulous but vain as well, never less than smartly dressed, more often than not in his favourite navy blue suit, white shirt and neatly knotted tie. He had a selection of headwear, including a straw hat for the summer, and a cap with a long peak given to him by a machinery rep that he wore around the farm. For his trips out he mostly wore a cloth cap. And wore it with style, marching along with his thumbs hooked into his waistcoat pockets, the Witch trotting dutifully at his heels.

This left Ralf to plod behind with the gun, not a role that filled him with pride. In the hierarchy at High Beckles he knew that he ranked among the cottagers as just another supplier of cheap labour for the boss lady and her devious uncle.

'See that?' Shillabeer whispered indignantly as soon as they arrived and found a gate to lean on. He drew Ralf's attention to a pheasant that was making its way stealthily along a ditch, hoping not to be noticed. 'The hen birds stray off all the time but those two lazy keepers do nothing about it. Captain Ives should be ashamed.'

'You're complaining? They aren't straying off, they are all packing their bags and flying up to your place to live.'

'Independent creatures, pheasants. They go where they are appreciated.'

'You mean they go where they are fed best. Would they choose High Beckles if you weren't so generous with food to entice them?'

'How much do a few raisins cost? A handful of corn? A peanut or two? Can I help it if they prefer my place? If you were a pheasant would you want to stay in those dark gloomy old woods down in Long Beckles? It isn't just the food. I know how pheasants prefer to live and I've got it all planted and set out just how they like it. I make them feel safe and snug. I make them feel wanted.'

'They might feel differently when you have your shoot. Dad is looking forward to it already.'

'Lovely creatures,' he said wistfully. 'I've always liked pheasants and tried to understand them. Keep still a moment. Here comes an old cock bird. He'd make a tasty supper with a couple of rashers wrapped round his backside.'

They watched as the cock pheasant picked its way cautiously through a clump of bracken, its metallic green neck ringed with white, its head flashed with red. It came bobbing out into the sunshine with one beady eye fixed warily on them while the other searched for an escape route. Prudently it opted not to fly and edged away until it was safe.

'What a lovely sunny spot for the hens to bring their chicks,' Shillabeer enthused, and Ralf realised that he really did love them, even if it was only to slaughter them in large numbers every winter. 'They don't like their chicks being wet,' he explained. 'After it's rained they search for a nice sunny place to get them dried off. Ralf, hundreds and hundreds of birds I've shot in this copse over the years. And hope to again very shortly.'

'Hundreds?'

'A lot anyway,' Shillabeer conceded as they resumed their walk. 'Jed opens the sack for me and they fall off the trees straight in.'

'We're agreed then. Jed gets the job.'

'Yes, he's a strong lad and he knows the drill. I've known him walk for miles carrying a hundredweight of pheasants. You'll be able to do the same with a bit of practice. It's a matter of wearing the right gear and distributing the weight equally over the body. Leaving your hands free for picking up and using the lamp.'

'Something tells me I am not getting through to you, Mr Shillabeer. What use would I be as your getaway man? Be sensible.'

'I'm trying to explain my problem to you. Rabbits or pheasants, Jed is the best helper I've ever had but I don't want to upset Sonia, you know I don't. She needs Jed to help run the farm properly. It's a big farm with a thousand head of livestock. I promised her I wouldn't take him out any more.'

'Even Jed is entitled to his beauty sleep.'

'Don't make jokes about it, Ralf. This is serious. You'll come in with us instead, won't you?'

'Us?'

'The Witch and me. We need a big strong helper to carry the birds home.'

'I am not going to. Do not include me in your plans. How many more times must I tell you before you believe me?'

Shillabeer sighed with vexation and indicated that they

95

were returning to the farm. 'When I was a young man I could carry my own pheasants but now I need a helper.'

'Don't expect sympathy from me. If you choose to spend your old age wandering about at night making a nuisance of yourself with a gun, that's up to you. Me, I prefer a blameless night's sleep. It's called a clear conscience. I've got one and I intend to keep it that way.'

'Let me explain again why we need to practise the walking. Remember my words, Ralf, because no one else will ever spell it out to you quite so clearly. People who use a vehicle to go poaching at night soon get caught. Vehicles make a lot of noise and need lights. Big mistake. Whether they are after deer, or pheasants, or salmon, or trout, the gamekeepers or the water bailiffs nab them pretty soon. Which is why you and me will be doing it on foot.'

'We won't. I keep telling you.'

'The countryside looks different at night. Did you know that?'

'Given long enough to think about it I could have worked it out for myself. If that answers your question.'

'A mist can throw you right off course, even somewhere you know well. So can the moon if it's bright enough. Ralf, by the end of the winter you will be able to walk round these woods blindfold. Know where we are now?'

'Apart from trespassing on the estate, no.'

'It's a small place that keeps horses, Brunswick Stud they call it. They lost a lot of tack some years ago and ever since they've kept the yard lights on all night. A real glare, you can see it a mile off. If I lose my bearings I look for the light at Brunswick and soon get a fix and know which way to go. You will be able to do the same.'

Ralf was interested in spite of himself. Although it was not a very edifying hobby Shillabeer's commitment was absolute. It occupied his mind completely and he talked of little else. Ralf may have been interested but he was unconvinced.

He said, 'You talk as though gamekeepers didn't exist. They are on duty day and night to prevent anyone stealing their pheasants. My Dad thinks they do a good job, and I believe him. What is more they have the law on their side. Poachers wouldn't stand a chance.'

'Nothing will go wrong if you learn the drill, and that's what I'm teaching you. The keepers aren't looking for trouble. They might shout and holler but they won't risk a fight. You may not believe it but they will be more frightened of you than you are of them.'

'You're right. I don't believe it.'

'The Witch won't let anyone get close without warning us. If they do we separate. Got it? We run off in different directions and the Witch will make her own way home. I'll give you a demonstration if you like. How about tonight?'

'I'm a paid up law and order man, Mr Shillabeer. Sorry.'

'You're not listening. No gamekeeper will chase a poacher very far. The important thing is not to panic.'

'Are you serious? Anyone in their right mind would panic if they were chased by a gamekeeper in the middle of the night. Gamekeepers carry guns, don't they? And always glad of an excuse to use them, I have no doubt.'

'It's dead easy to escape in the dark. You're a local man. You won't get lost.'

'I won't be putting it to the test, that's why.'

'They've got to catch you red-handed with the birds on you to charge you. Dump the birds and they can't touch you.'

'I wouldn't be too sure about that. I should consult my legal adviser if I were you.'

'Generally it pays to keep still and listen. If you racket about they can hear you because they know the paths and the gateways and where to stand. Just keep moving quietly away is the best advice I can give you. Say nothing and melt into the darkness.'

'Sounds simple. I bet it isn't.'

'If you're cornered stand still and keep your mouth shut. Last year Jed was caught out on a small private shoot not far from Claypits. It's run by two brothers by the name of Hounsome, real hard nuts they are, nasty bits of work, particularly the younger one who had Jed cornered. But Jed kept his nerve and never made a sound, just stood perfectly still until I could creep up behind and hit young Hounsome over the head with my gun. He had a pick-axe handle he was going to hit Jed with so I reckon it was fair do's. There's far too much violence these days. I blame it on the government.'

'You shouldn't have told me that story, Mr Shillabeer. It's put me off even more.'

'Ralf, we're surrounded by shooting estates of one sort or another, some big, some bigger still. Between them they rear thousands of pheasants every year and don't know how to look after them properly. Why let the foxes have them? Which is what will happen otherwise.'

'If I come back reincarnated in another form I just hope it isn't as a pheasant. I think my life expectancy would be very short.'

'I've started practising. By the time we're ready for the big haul in December my aim will be smack on target. The Witch looks forward to it every year the same as I do.'

Even Ralf was forced to revise his low opinion of Shillabeer's dog when he saw her in action. Until now he had only seen her curled up in her verminous basket beside the Aga, or sitting between them on the bench seat of the Land Rover, or scratching herself with boredom in a roadside eating place while her master talked. And talked, and talked.

Moving freely on the hill she was a different creature and never missed a trick. With hedgerows to patrol, up one side and down the other, she exerted a natural authority over lesser creatures. If a hare started she overtook it in a blistering turn of speed and crunched it in seconds. Shillabeer had taught her to jump while running and she sailed effortlessly over any gate or fence in her way. Or from the ground could soar six feet to pull an escaping pheasant from the air.

Ralf was impressed. She was a murderous lurcher bitch, trotting lightly in delinquent stealth as she checked the route, apparently well aware of the difference between right and wrong. And seemed to share the common view that wrong was more fun, provided of course that you didn't get caught.

From their walks Ralf soon discovered that she knew exactly where the boundary of the farm began and ended, and that she had only one purpose to her life, namely to protect her master and his interests. She had ears finely tuned for the slam of a car door or the tread of a hostile foot, ranging backwards, forwards and sideways, constantly checking for danger from any quarter.

Shillabeer trusted her implicitly and would change course the moment she recommended evasive action. Although he boasted endlessly of his cleverness, claiming never to get lost even on the darkest night, or to let the gamekeepers feel his collar, Ralf knew who was really responsible and should take the credit.

He was as fond of the Witch as if she was a child. Ralf was beginning to understand why.

7

It rained, and in muddy High Beckles it was no light sprink-
ling or mild growing rain, no passing gentle shower. It was
relentless driving rain that tested Ralf's resolve to breaking
point.

The cold wet weather was not doing his father any favours
either. He was breathless after the slightest exertion and no
longer able to go out with his gun every morning. His
condition was noticeably beginning to deteriorate, even if
slowly. He was not one to give way without a fight and
insisted on doing his share of the household work.

'Laundry day tomorrow, Ralf,' he reminded him after their
meal one evening. 'Now's your chance if you want anything
washed. I'm just getting a load ready for you to take down to
Cousin Daisy.'

'Perhaps George will say a prayer for us.'

This made his father turn reproachful eyes on him. 'We're
short of relations, in case you hadn't noticed. Even George
and Daisy are better than no relations at all. Be nice to them,
Ralf. You never know when we might be glad of their help.'

'It's only the weather getting me down.'

'You've been very quiet this last couple of days. It can't be
much fun for you here in rain like this.'

'It's the same for both of us. No doubt we shall survive.'

'I hope it isn't wet like this for Dick's shoot next week.'

It was Ralf's turn for the reproving stare. He said, 'Dad,
are you sure it's a good idea for you to go on the shoot?
Whether it rains or not I don't think you should go.'

'I've been helping Jed to get ready. Don't worry about me,
Ralf. I shall be all right. I'm looking forward to it, of course I
am. Aren't you?'

'It's taking a big risk with your health. It's not just the

shoot, it's all the boozing afterwards. Too much exertion. Too much excitement. Too much whisky. Don't risk it, Dad.'

His father gave him a consoling pat on the shoulder as he poured himself a tumbler of brandy and hot water. 'If you can't stick it out here any longer you had better say so. I'm nicely settled in now and there isn't much more you can do for me, one way or the other. I shan't think any the less of you if you want to take yourself back to London. Or go to America, just as you've always wanted. Don't let me stop you.'

'It's too late for that. You know it is.'

'I don't see why. No point in us both suffering.'

'Dad, say no more. I made you a commitment so I shall be staying. It's just the rain getting me down.'

His father did not seem convinced but did not pursue the matter and went to the kitchen to begin preparing a meal for the next day. Ralf went to his study, opened his laptop and settled down to some work in progress. He was sorry that he had allowed his dejection to show, and sorrier still an hour later when his father was sick over the kitchen floor, uttering a loud cry of dismay as he did so.

When he had recovered he mumbled an apology. 'Sorry, Ralf. Couldn't help myself.'

'Poor old Dad. Sit down while I clear it up.'

'What a state to be in. Might as well be dead.'

'Anyone can be sick. Sit still while I deal with it.'

His father watched, deeply shaken and depressed at this involuntary proof of his slowly worsening condition. Willpower alone was not enough. It may have been slow but it was inexorable, the malignant cells remorselessly seeking new lodgements. When Ralf had finished cleaning up the mess his father said, 'Promise me you won't send for the doctor. They would only cart me off to bloody Northbeck. I would sooner die, and that's the truth.'

'I've promised you, haven't I? No doctors and no Northbeck. Here we are and here we stay, whatever happens. Both of us. Satisfied?'

He nodded but remained cast down. Ralf coaxed him to

have an early night and he gave way without a fight, allowing himself to be steered up to bed. He would soon need to have this downstairs but was reluctant to concede invalid status, the result being that he spent most nights slumbering uneasily in his armchair by the fire.

Next morning Ralf was woken by an explosion.

The noise was so loud that he woke in a fright, not knowing what had caused it. He had been in a deep sleep and it took a while for his drowsing brain to work out that what he had heard was a gunshot. A gunshot from his father's bedroom next door. With his ears ringing, sobbing with fright, and now flung into a terrible awareness, he stumbled into the next room expecting to find his father on the floor with his brains blown out. Instead of which he was fully dressed, wearing a hat, smoking his pipe and looking pleased with himself, standing by an open window with his twelve-bore shotgun.

'I got him, Ralf,' he said exultantly. 'The pigeon that's been eating your cabbages. Right up the backside! The feathers are still coming down and that's about all there is left of him.'

'You did what?'

His father was startled by the violence of his reaction. 'Steady on, Ralf. What are you glaring at me like that for?'

Ralf ran forward and snatched the gun from his father's hands. 'Are you crazy? I was asleep, I could have died of shock. What do you think you're doing, shooting a gun off indoors?'

They stared at one another in horror, appalled at this sudden quarrel. His father muttered apologetically, 'Sorry, Ralf. I wasn't thinking straight.'

'Let the pigeons have the wretched cabbages if they want them.'

His father put a consoling arm round his shoulders. 'It's cold. You had better get dressed. I'll go down and make us a pot of tea. That steadies the nerves.'

When Ralf joined him in the kitchen he was grateful for the

scalding-hot heavily-sweetened tea but refused the offer of a dash of brandy. He said, 'I'm sorry too, Dad. I spooked when I heard the shot. Guess my nerves aren't up to all this gunfire.'

'I should have known better. I realise now what you must have been thinking when you rushed in.'

'It wouldn't have been a nice way to go.'

'If there was a nice way to go I would have taken it, and so would a lot of other people in my position, I expect. No one wants to suffer, or be a nuisance to the people looking after them.'

'Don't talk like that, Dad.'

'I saw a man with his head blown apart once. A shooting accident on the estate. It never appealed to me afterwards as a way of committing suicide.'

'I'm glad to hear it. People keep telling me what a dangerous place London is but I never saw anyone carrying a shotgun the whole time I lived there. Up here they not only carry them they shoot them off as well. And talk of little else.'

His father pulled back his sleeves to begin cooking their breakfast. 'This particular pigeon was an artful little sod. He didn't fly in, he landed behind the hedge and walked the rest of the way. And then started eating those lovely cabbages you planted.'

'I wouldn't have begrudged him one. Not if he was hungry.'

'This morning I was waiting for him by the back door. I had the gun loaded but I couldn't get an angle on him. So I crept upstairs and leaned out of my bedroom window. Ralf, that was one very surprised pigeon.'

'He wasn't the only one who was surprised.'

'I would have put him in a pie except that I blew the little bugger to pieces.' He sighed and rolled his sleeves down again. 'You don't look as if you've got an appetite.'

'Sorry, Dad. Not hungry.'

His father came and sat with him at the kitchen table. 'It's starting to get to you, isn't it? Living in this godforsaken place. I'm surprised you've stuck it this long.'

'I can stick it a while longer yet.'

'I've been selfish, I realise that, wanting to have you with me. No one wants to live alone, or die alone, I guess that's what it amounts to. But I've said it before and I'll say it again, I don't hold you to your promise. If you really can't stand it any longer pack your suitcase and go. I got you into this mess and I can get you out of it. I'll drive you to the station and you can carry on with your own life instead of sitting around here waiting for me to die.'

'I've asked you before not to say things like that. This is now my life too, Dad. And it's never going to be the same again, is it? For either of us, whatever happens.'

His father rasped his chin, sighed, and put a match to his pipe. Then asked a question to which there could be no rational answer. 'Tell me something, Ralf. You're an educated man. How do two sensible chaps like us come to find ourselves in this predicament? Can you offer any explanation?'

'Perhaps we should consult George and Daisy. Make use of their high level connections.'

'Not such a bad idea. Someone somewhere has got it all planned out for us in advance. Fate, destiny, call it what you like, it comes to the same thing. Some people believe in it. How about you?'

'Shall we say that I'm less inclined to disbelieve it than I once was.'

'I take it that means 'yes'. Knowing that you're going to die sets you thinking about these things. Perhaps it is fate after all, and we don't have much say in what happens to us.'

'I go along with that,' Ralf agreed, and he meant it.

There had been a relentless inevitability in the sequence of events that started the moment he put the phone to his ear and found Cousin Daisy, the great communicator, ready with her tale of woe. With plenty more still to come as their printout continued to unfold. The patterned hieroglyphs had been arranged like notes of music to which they executed a slow danse macabre.

8

The Monday meeting at Claypits Farm with Oliver Biggs the butcher still went ahead, which meant a drive in the Land Rover rather than a country walk. Ralf looked over his shoulder and saw that the weekly cargo consisted of dark meat that oozed blood.

'What is it this week?' he asked Shillabeer, who sat on the front bench seat with his dreadful dog between them.

'The Witch had a bit of luck on the hill.' He gave her a pat and she blinked modestly. 'The old girl can pull a deer down in two minutes flat, and that's from a standing start. Impressed? Not bad for her age, is it?'

'I don't think either of you will go to heaven, Mr Shillabeer.'

He lit a cigarette and looked pleased, taking it as a compliment. 'The cleverest dog I've ever had. Learns things quicker than most people.'

'You both seem to share the same bad habits though.'

'Not me, Sonia. It's her hobby. Why don't you go with her and see how it's done?'

'Catching deer doesn't appeal to me. Not even as a hobby.'

'Sonia and the Witch make a great team. Are you sure you wouldn't like to be included next time?'

'Quite sure. But thank you for the offer.'

'You remember Sonia's father don't you? Saul Shillabeer, my brother's boy.'

'Vaguely. What about him?'

'He was a handful, I don't mind telling you. Wild as a hawk he was. Could catch any living creature you care to mention. Loved the hill and was up there most nights with his dog. That would be the Witch's mother.'

'What happened to him?'

'Fell out of a tree he was lopping, broke his neck and died young. My brother Lemuel died the same way, only he fell off a horse when he was drunk.'

'Gravity. It kills a lot of people.'

'You're right, Ralf. It does.'

'Shall we go? Mustn't always keep Oliver waiting.'

'Did you know that Sonia butchers them up as well? She's a clever girl, whether it's a gun or a knife in her hand. Got a good eye, essential for the meat trade. Never wastes a morsel.' He sighed proudly. 'I taught her myself, everything she knows.'

'A posh Swiss finishing school could have done no more.'

'No need to be sarcastic, there's money in it. I told you, my nephew Oliver is a licensed game dealer and a lot of his customers in the big houses appreciate a joint of venison if it's well hung.'

'I don't think Oliver will go to heaven either.'

'Lots of uses for venison, even the pubs like it if it's cheap. People never notice what they're eating after a drink or two. Adds a bit of flavour to a pie, goes a treat in sausages, and stretches out the mince. Oh yes, a little deer meat goes a long way in a butcher's shop.'

'It goes a long way anywhere. Most people don't like it.'

'They might not like a lot of things but they eat them just the same. Better not to know sometimes. Go the back way, Ralf. I saw a woodie down by Stunch Thicket last week. Nice eating, a woodcock. Keep your eyes open.'

Ralf preferred to look where he was going and ignored this advice, just as he ignored most of the other advice Shillabeer gave him. Off-road driving was good fun. The crumpled Defender would go almost anywhere and after delivering the weekly consignment to Oliver Biggs, and passing the time of day with him, Shillabeer ordered a tour round. Although this was only to note where the pheasants were hiding Ralf enjoyed it, plummeting down steep hillsides and slithering along muddy tracks.

He was always rather downcast after meeting the hard-working and good-natured butcher. At school Oliver had suffered from endless crops of boils on his face and neck, although this did not stop him being attractive to girls. To earn his pocket money he had worked in his father's butcher's shop from the age of eight onwards, fitting in school where he could. His academic achievements were modest but from his father he learned the art of flattery to make the lady customers feel good about themselves, while charming the money from their purses. The shop was run as live theatre with lots of sawing, hacking, chopping and knife sharpening as a backdrop to the sales banter. It had always worked, and still did.

During their tour round in the Land Rover afterwards they saw almost as many wild or semi-wild pheasants making out on their own as there were sociable colonies enjoying the hospitality of the estate. Shillabeer had a territorial memory and marked down these wily rooster pheasants one by one to come back for later. He may have been nudging eighty but a tail feather glimpsed at fifty yards was all he needed to book a cartridge and someone's tasty supper.

'The Witch wants her pie!' he said suddenly, at which she quivered in anticipation. 'Head for that big roadside pub we go to. I'm hungry and they serve up some good grub.'

Ralf was hungry too and scoffed his fair share from a big plateful of beef curry. All the hill walking he had done lately, combined with the digging and sawing, had done wonders for his appetite as well as his muscles. Nor was he such a dainty eater as when he arrived. His days of goat's cheese and broccoli soup were over for the time being. Now he was more concerned with the size of the helpings.

Shillabeer also liked to eat well and soon cleared his plate. He was just as rosy-cheeked and dapper as ever, all blue-eyed innocence as he beckoned Ralf to lean forward. They were in a quiet alcove diner and could speak without being overheard.

He said, 'Am I right in thinking that you don't have a gun of your own any more, Ralf?'

'You are. I don't.'

'In that case I can do you a good turn. I've just acquired a gun that would suit you nicely. I took it off a farmer last week in exchange for a debt.'

'Mr Shillabeer, please listen to what I keep telling you. I do not need a gun. I do not want a gun. I have no intention of buying one or using one. I do not approve of shooting wild animals for fun.'

'You didn't say that when your father taught you to shoot all those years ago. What happened to the gun he bought you?'

'My views changed when I went to university so I gave the gun back to him. I don't think he has it any more.'

'You need another one in that case. The gun I'm talking about would be just right for you. It's important for a gun to feel comfortable. You can't hit the high birds with a gun the wrong length that doesn't balance properly.'

'There's a catch. There always is when you want to sell me something.'

'You're six-foot plus, about the same size as the farmer I took it off. Thirty-two inch barrels. Good pointability but a bit long for most people these days.'

'How much was the debt? Sounds as if the farmer got the best of it.'

'It's an over-and-under. Ever used one? A lot of people get a better aim on the second barrel with an O U.'

'If you can shoot straight it makes no difference.'

'It's a heavy gun, hardly any recoil. A bit on the slow side for reloading but that's no reason not to give it a try out. Tomorrow morning suit you?'

'My Dad wouldn't have it in the house. Try selling it to someone else.'

He sighed with disappointment. 'In a leather case. Beautiful. You should see the engraving.'

'Right now I'm more interested in one of Grandma's Home Made Apple Pies. I don't suppose they really are home made but they're very nice all the same.'

'Order one for me, too. And get a bar of chocolate for the

Witch. She likes plain chocolate best. Better for her teeth.'

It was a sticky pie and suspended their conversation for a few minutes. To give it his full attention Shillabeer looped on his glasses, a tangle of gold wire and tiny lenses kept on cotton wool in an old tobacco tin. With his tidily combed wisps of silver hair, a clean shirt and a tie, he was the picture of pensioner respectability.

Except that he still had only one thing on his mind, and only one topic of conversation. His offer of the gun having been rejected he started to sulk and be difficult. But refused to give up. Leaning forward and speaking with great seriousness he said, 'We're one short on the team, Ralf. We need a big strong helper to carry the birds for us. When you came home to look after your father I knew my prayers had been answered.'

'They haven't. I keep telling you.'

'Mostly they drop straight down for me to pick up but if I lose one the Witch can always find it for me. Wonderful eyesight. She loves it more than anything, and so do I, but we need someone to carry the birds.'

'Someone like Jed, do you mean?'

'Don't spoil it for us. It was a good summer for rearing the pheasants which means there are thousands down there in Long Beckles just waiting for us to come and get them.'

'I fear they will wait a long time in that case.'

'Listen carefully. Sonia runs the farm entirely on her own now so I've got a clear winter ahead. All my life I've dreamed of having one really big season before I'm forced to pack it in. I'm almost eighty for Christ's sake, and the Witch won't see another winter after this one. We need you, Ralf, and we need you now.'

'Mr Shillabeer, will you please stop talking to me about poaching. Which is a criminal activity, in case you weren't sure. I am a responsible citizen, a professional man, an academic. I've written a book and almost finished another one. I teach people, I am respected as well as respectable. Does that explain why I have no intention of being implicated in your poaching plans?'

'Keep your voice down,' Shillabeer hissed, looking round in alarm. 'Not so loud, Ralf. Do you want the whole bloody world to know?'

Ralf also leaned forward until their faces were almost touching across the restaurant table, then spelled it out even more clearly. 'No one gets away with poaching round here, not for long anyway. The gamekeepers and the landowners and the police have got it well under control. Read the local newspaper. Two young men came up in front of the magistrates last week and had to pay a hefty fine as well as having their guns and their vehicle confiscated. Not to mention being named and shamed.'

'Amateurs, Ralf. Just ploughboys out for a bit of mischief. Of course they got nicked, and a good thing too.'

Ralf propped his head on his hand in despair. 'I never get through to you, do I? I know the estate only has two gamekeepers but it's all hi-tec surveillance equipment these days. Night-scope binoculars, radio alarms, trip switches, ground sensors, infra-red beams, image intensifiers, satellite cameras. Poachers would stand no chance.'

'You don't want to believe everything our local postman tells you. That's the sort of horse shit he comes out with every year.'

'Actually it was my father who told me, and I believe him. So if you want my advice you'll start looking for a more appropriate hobby to while away your old age.'

'I'll look after you, Ralf, you know I will. Why are you being so nasty about it?' He lit a cigarette and squinted at him bitterly through the smoke. 'Let's have some more coffee. We've got to talk this through, once and for all.'

'How long have you being doing it?'

'What harm can an old man like me do to a great estate like that?'

'Quite a lot, if what you tell me is true. How long did you say?'

'I've dabbled at it all my life, off and on, but I've never

had the time to devote myself to it properly. While I had my driver's licence I was too busy making money but now I'm properly retired and can put my mind to it full time. This is the year I've always dreamed about. We're mates, aren't we? You'll come in with me, won't you?'

'Which of us will serve the six months in jail? It doesn't sound much like fun to me.'

'Fun?' he said indignantly. 'This is business, Ralf. I do it for money. Biggsy can't sell them fast enough.'

Ralf groaned and lowered his head to the table. 'Never in a million years did I think that my path would cross with wretched Biggs again. Unbelievable!'

'What are you carrying on like that for? Oliver can shift all the birds we bring him. Oven ready or table ready he sells them through the trade, including some big London hotels, if that interests you at all. Cruise liners, the best restaurants, all the other butcher's shops for miles around, deli counters, posh supermarkets, he can keep them in his big freezer and sell them all the year round. Never heard of the export trade? All over the world my pheasants go.'

'I think you mean the estate's pheasants.'

'Eating habits have changed. People want low-cholesterol meat and they're willing to pay extra to get it. Meat doesn't come much more natural than venison and pheasants. Biggsy and me have made plenty of money from game these last few years. I catch it and he sells it.'

'You didn't answer my question about the six months in jail. I don't fancy sharing a prison cell with Oliver Biggs.'

'We could make a start tonight. We're wasting valuable shooting time, don't you realise that? How about the Riverside Plantation? It's close to home, dry underfoot, not many brambles and nice bare branches. So as to break you in gently and show you how we go about it.'

'You need someone with stronger nerves. The answer is 'no'. The answer will always be 'no'. How many more times?'

Shillabeer finally gave up, shaking his head sorrowfully.

He seemed lost in thought, slowly unlooping his fragile glasses and stowing them away carefully in their tobacco tin. He heaved a deep sigh. 'One night last year Sonia and me shot a sackful, and we hardly moved. It was a windy night and the birds were down low, they were lined up for us like pot-shots at the fair. That was in the Riverside Plantation. Jed carried the birds home for us.'

Ralf refused the bait. Shillabeer kept trying to tempt him by offering a night out with Sonia, not a very edifying attempt at bribery and one he was determined to resist. He and Sonia did not agree on much but they both disliked being the object of other people's curiosity.

A little way past the Orchard House was a wide entrance into a field of stubble turnips where she parked sometimes when she was out and about on the farm. If he saw her go past in her Land Rover, and was free to leave his father, he would slip out of the house and hurry along the lane to join her. He climbed into the passenger seat and they talked, even if edgily and at arm's length.

She asked after his father and in return he asked her to tell him about the farm. He knew enough to carry on a conversation, indeed was well aware of the difficulties facing a livestock farmer during the winter months, and was sympathetic. He avoided all contentious subjects, such as telling her that he loved her. Although they both knew it was unlikely to lead anywhere Sonia allowed herself to be courted, enjoying the attention and the flattery. If it was true that she had never had a boyfriend then being wooed was a new experience and she was making sure it went slowly one step at a time.

They understood one another perfectly because they knew what was at stake. They were both constrained within a time frame, running concurrently side by side. He was pledged for the duration of his father's illness, Sonia's life was on hold until her uncle's birthday. Neither of them wished to compromise this arrangement, knowing only too well the risks of getting it wrong. Sonia was the first to put the difficulties into words.

'If it wasn't for your father being ill you would never have come up here to live. And when he dies you will want to leave. That's true, isn't it?'

'Dad talks a lot about dying. It upsets me.'

'You didn't answer my question.'

'That's because I don't know the answer. Would you marry me if I stayed?'

'You would have to ask me again nearer the time. A lot nearer.'

'Are you sure you won't let me take you out? You always refuse when I ask you.'

'I've asked you to wait, that's all.'

'Waiting isn't easy, Sonia. It's going to be a long miserable winter if you won't even let me kiss you.'

'It's the same for me. I'm not complaining.'

'That's just teasing me. Turning it into a challenge. Well, one of these days I'm going to surprise you.' He made a sudden movement towards her. 'Today, perhaps.'

She knew he was not serious and indicated that she had to get back to work, reaching for the ignition. He stayed put for a moment, mainly as a small gesture of defiance, irritated that she always seemed more in control of the situation than he was. Being bossed around and treated as the subordinate partner in their relationship, if such it could be called, did not please him. He was older and sexually experienced but had made little progress and it was starting to annoy him. He sulked and said, 'You think I'm not serious, don't you? You think I'm going to take off in a puff of smoke the moment my father dies.'

'I'm not sure. I don't think you are either.'

'One day we'll find out.'

'Yes. We will.'

But she did not predict which way it would go and he could not work it out either, in spite of thinking about it constantly. Was he in love with Sonia enough to want to marry her? Well, was he? And when the time came would he be willing to find himself a local teaching job if that was the price he had to pay? Or was he just lonely and miserable and would have fallen for any unattached good-looking woman who happened to be living next door?

He was still slowly and painfully working out his answer to this question. It was beginning to occupy his thoughts day and night. The problems seemed insuperable, and yet he knew that he was properly in love for the first time in his life. There is one sure-fire test for love which is to consider the prospect of losing out to another. When he applied this test Ralf was in no doubt of his feelings. The thought of another man taking her away from him was unbearable. Even the alternative of her remaining single and ending up like scary old Aunt Edie with her flock of geese brought him little consolation.

'Well?' Shillabeer enquired, prompting him after his long silence.

'Well what?'

'Don't you think it's time to give it a try? I'll get Queenie to fix you up an extra big feed. Come over about nine o'clock. We'll have some grub, and then sort out a few of the Captain's birds afterwards.'

But Ralf had something just as pressing on his mind. He said, 'I'm worried about Dad, Mr Shillabeer. Very worried.'

'Why? Has something happened to him?'

'He's set his heart on coming to your shoot tomorrow.'

'I know. There's nothing stopping him, is there?'

'I'm not sure he's up to it. I fear the worst. I think it could finish him off.'

9

The big event of the year at High Beckles was the annual shoot, Shillabeer's turn to play the host and entertain his shooting friends.

Ralf's father was up early and dressed ready to go. He had thought of little else for weeks and in the final days had spent many hours at the farm helping Jed with the preparations. Ralf had enough sense not to keep protesting. If it was to be his father's last day on earth, and he knew it, this would be the way he chose to spend it, a shooting party with friends being his idea of heaven.

Even so Ralf had one last try. He had hardly slept all night, kept miserably awake by a window-rattling east wind and a grim sense of inevitability. Whether or not Shillabeer's irresponsible behaviour came at the prompting of a death wish did not concern him greatly. That his father's behaviour was equally irresponsible gave him a restless and deeply unhappy night, overshadowed with the foreboding of death. Unable either to sleep or to force himself fully awake he endured nightmarish images of his father falling on his gun and shooting himself, carried home muddied and bloodied in the farm truck, driven by a weeping Sonia.

He felt the certainty of impending disaster just as strongly the following morning when they set off for the farm. He said, 'Dad, I'm sure there's a way out of this. You could shoot on the first drive and then sit up in the truck with Sonia. No one would mind that and you would still enjoy yourself.'

'Stop fussing, Ralf. I shall be all right. And if I'm not all right I shall only have myself to blame.'

'It's a bit soon to be apportioning blame. You've got a lot to lose if it goes wrong.'

'You worry too much.'

'With good reason. I've got a lot to lose as well.'

'I intend to enjoy myself and my advice to you is to do the same. Come on, it's time to go.'

When the shooting party assembled in the muddy farmyard at High Beckles they were a real desperate crew in Ralf's opinion, his father included. They looked as if they were on their way to start a war. Prominent among them was Oliver Biggs, hugely stout and jovial in a cap and a green quilted shooting jacket. There were two burly farmers, the local cattle-feed salesman, and the landlord of the public house providing the food after the shoot.

It was going to be a challenging day for the local wild life. Anything eatable that showed itself was likely to get shot.

Ralf had seen many shooting parties in his youth, it was part of growing up on the estate. Captain Ives organised them with military precision, the beaters were silent and disciplined, nothing ever went wrong. On the other hand no one seemed to be enjoying it much, perhaps it was too expensive to be fun as well. Whatever the reason they made it seem a grim way of amusing themselves.

Shillabeer's gun-toting pals were a much more cheerful gang, and better shots as well. They were a crack private militia which meant business, judging from the boxes of spare cartridges they had brought with them. They were cheerful because even at ten o'clock in the morning a lot of whisky was being drunk. Flasks were produced from side pockets, tobacco smoke billowed on the wind, and there were manly guffaws at everything that was said. Even the dogs were enjoying it no end and waited for the order to move off with lolling tongues and stupid grins.

'Shooting your own just isn't the same,' Shillabeer admitted with a sigh, drawing Ralf's attention to a stray pheasant wandering injudiciously in nearby stubble. 'Not nearly so much fun.'

'It's the same for the pheasants.'

'A short life but a happy one. Is everyone ready? Give Jed the nod and we'll make a start.'

Jed waited beside a tractor-and-trailer loaded with bales of straw on which sat a party of beaters with sticks. It was a big day for him, too. After much preparation and careful organising it was now his responsibility to put the birds up for the guns. To send a succession of high-curling pheasants over the middle of the line was not easy, in fact very difficult, but the shoot was soon under way and past the point of no return. There was nothing Ralf could do to influence the outcome and although he still feared for this massive strain on his father's health he did not want to spoil the party, and tried not to let his feelings show. His father viewed life and death with a calm fatalism. He had little option in his present circumstances except to do the same.

Shillabeer was aware of his anxiety and hastened to re-assure him. 'You can stop worrying. I've fixed it so that Tom does hardly any walking. He'll have the best peg on every drive. Don't spoil it for him, he's having a wonderful day out.'

'Me too,' Ralf said, trying hard to sound as if he was telling the truth. 'Thank you for inviting us. Let's hope the rain holds off.'

Jed and his beaters had gone into a copse on the far side of High Beckles and were slowly working the pheasants out towards the edge. When these found themselves in the open some tried to find cover but most opted to escape by flight. The pheasant can fly strongly, but only for short distances, and soon has to land again. Most of them were too well fed for their own good and made easy targets.

Shillabeer had the shooters perfectly spaced out in the field sloping downhill from the copse, so that the driven birds had just sufficient time to gain height as they flew over the guns. The first ones to chance it were the only ones to survive. They burst out of the undergrowth and launched themselves into sudden blundering flight, they were past the guns and planing away to safety before anyone had got the range. But soon the pheasants began to rain down, landing with a thud and an explosion of feathers.

It was a desperate business and Tom Lassiter was hitting his fair share, including a spectacular right-and-left to bring down two birds flying high and fast in different directions. It was a bitterly cold day with a sunless dark grey sky and a thin wind, not the ideal conditions for a sick man to be exerting himself. Any lingering hopes Ralf may have had for a leisurely day's shooting in mild drizzly weather faded fast as the cold wind blew and the slaughter intensified.

Drink and determination generated a fierce air of competition. They shot at everything and seldom missed, mainly pheasants and partridges but as they moved from a kale field into the open they blasted away at rabbits and fast jinking pigeons with equal success. Also, to his dismay, a hare. Why Ralf should have felt differently about a hare he was not sure but he did, and hoped it would escape.

No such luck, these men were all deadly with a gun in their hands. The hare survived a long time, twisting and turning, first running crouched in a furrow, finally sprinting flat out for a gateway in the corner. There was a shout of, 'Yours, Tom,' and his father made no mistake, waiting with his gun raised until it presented itself sideways on and then fired.

The hare was going so fast that it went bowling over in a back somersault, then lay stretched across the cold earth. A brutal end. Ralf fetched it and carried it to the farm truck where Sonia took it from him. He found it long and heavy, more like a dead dog, a good enough reason why field sports no longer had any appeal for him.

After which he cheered up slightly, for the very good reason that he had been assigned by Shillabeer as Sonia's assistant to pick up the fallers. She was following close behind with a liver-and-white spaniel belonging to her cousin Oliver Biggs, and as usual bending her mind to the job and refusing to be distracted. She had followed each drive closely and memorised all the pricked birds which had flown on before finally coming down into waterlogged ditches or impenetrable thickets of briar and bracken.

Ralf was a man in love and the opportunity to spend time

with Sonia softened the edges of a sombre day in his exile at High Beckles. He said, 'You're looking good, Sonia. As always.' She did not reply, but looked pleased at the compliment.

She was wearing a waxed jacket with a fedora hat and a woollen scarf. 'Quickly, Ralf,' she said, nudging him as he stood surveying the corpse-strewn battlefield. 'Mark that bird over there. You're not concentrating.'

'Sorry, Sonia. Thinking about something else.'

'There's another one under that tree. Try not to slow down, they're moving off again.'

Obediently he fetched the dead pheasants she had pointed out to him and watched as she deftly looped them together with a piece of string cut to length, and then hung them by their necks on a rail in the back of the farm truck. They were a brace, a cock and a hen, now dangling side by side feet downwards in a posthumous marriage.

When he still seemed distracted Sonia was concerned enough to ask him what was the matter. He pointed to his father. 'This isn't doing him any good. He shouldn't be doing this, he really shouldn't.'

Sonia moved closer and touched his arm for a moment. 'I know. I know. But he was looking forward to it so much. I'm glad you didn't try to stop him.'

Ralf shrugged and made a gesture of helplessness. 'It's bad luck about the weather. A mild day and he might have got away with it. This cold wind is the worst thing out for his breathing.'

'Poor Tom, it would have broken his heart to leave him at home. You couldn't have done that to your poor father.'

'He isn't as well as he looks. I've got a bad feeling, Sonia. This could end in disaster.'

She touched his arm again. 'Uncle will look after him. He's having a lovely time and hitting some good birds. Let's not spoil it for him before we have to.'

Ralf enjoyed this brief snatch of conversation with Sonia in a sympathetic mood. They could not speak again for some time but when they next had a moment to themselves her subject matter was less to his liking. With a frown she said, 'Uncle is getting very upset because you won't help him with his pheasants. He takes it out on me, and he takes it out on Jed. He's been giving both of us a hard time lately.'

'Sonia, you know I can't go poaching with him. I wish you wouldn't ask me.'

'All you have to do is carry a few birds. Why are you making such a big deal of it?'

'It would certainly be a big deal for me if I was caught. As in professional ruin. You can't get a much bigger deal than that in my line of business.'

'Oh, you needn't worry about that. Uncle Dick won't get caught.'

'It isn't him I'm worried about. It's me getting caught and prosecuted that puts me off the idea.'

'Someone has got to go with him to look after him. I need Jed on the farm and if you don't go it means that I shall have to go.'

'Sonia, you know how fond I am of you but I just can't do it. Even for you I can't do it. And right now I'm more concerned about Dad's health. I fear the worst.'

Not for the first time Ralf thought that for an old man looking at his eightieth birthday Dick Shillabeer was making a lot of trouble for everyone else at High Beckles. It had escalated into a battle of principle. He insisted on having his own way, Sonia was standing firm. Neither would back down but both agreed on the solution to their otherwise intractable problem. Which was for him to volunteer as Shillabeer's night-time legman and freight carrier, the role Jed was so anxious to give up.

Eventually the sound of gunshots died away as the slaughter drew to a close. They had run out of whisky Oliver Biggs informed him, so they all drove down to Long Beckles where a hot buffet lunch had been arranged in a public house. There was no afternoon session as with a posh shoot. The fun was over and the serious part of the proceedings was about to begin, the eating and drinking.

There was a log fire in a low-ceilinged room and with so many big men in a small space it soon became over-poweringly hot and noisy. Ralf kept an eye on his father and did not like what he saw. He was laughing at the banter as the shooters ribbed one another about easy birds missed, and also keeping up with the tots of whisky being drunk. Not quite what the hospital had in mind for his treatment. He refused to come when Ralf tried to ease him towards the door so he did not insist. These were his father's lifelong friends and neighbours and he did not want to leave a party that was nowhere near ready to break up.

Ralf turned his attention to Sonia Shillabeer instead. She had removed her hat, coat and scarf and was looking good in jeans with a pink top. In a roomful of men she could not help being the centre of attention, with more than one pair of eyes following her every movement. Oliver Biggs had been chewing on a drumstick and guzzling a pint of beer but took time out to stare openly in admiration. Ralf was slow off the mark and experienced twinges of apprehension as the younger of the two farmers was first to her side with a drink.

The burly young farmer soon had Sonia cornered, his broad back an impassable barrier. Ralf could not even get near her to speak. He watched them with disquiet, and with good reason. The farmer was leaning close to whisper in Sonia's ear, and generally behaving in a roguish manner. He had her to himself and was making the most of his opportunity.

He felt a nudge and found Oliver Biggs by his side. The butcher said, 'Good grub, Ralf. Eat up.'

'I'm not hungry.'

'Uncle Shill always spreads a good table. I like my food. Always have. What other pleasure can a married man expect to get three times a day?'

'I'm not married. You tell me.'

'In the bedroom these days I go for quality rather than quantity. My three times a night days are over. If you follow what I mean. Long over.'

'We're soon past our best. That's true.'

The good-natured butcher had finished his drumstick and was now munching a pork pie. He said, 'Your Dad is enjoying himself, Ralf. It will have done him good to have a day out.'

'You think so?'

'Did you see the way he knocked that hare over? Must have been all of forty yards.'

'It was a good long shot. Certainly.'

The butcher was aware from these brief replies that he did not have Ralf's full attention, and soon worked out why. Ralf was looking over his shoulder to the far end of the bar where Sonia was still head to head with the whispering farmer.

Even as they watched the farmer placed his hand on Sonia's waist and kept it there. If Ralf had any remaining doubts over his true feelings towards Sonia Shillabeer he now found out what they were. Because the sick feeling of disappointment and jealousy was almost more than he could bear. He ground his teeth in fury as the farmer's hand began to spread, grip and explore.

His tortured expression was not lost on Oliver Biggs who came closer and drew him aside. 'Well, there he is. That's our Freddie Foxwell for you, never slow off the mark where the ladies are concerned. You remember him at the College, don't you?'

'Yes. I remember him all right.'

'Captain of rugby, and all that.'

'You don't have to remind me.'

'A good shot with a gun, though. Very good. You can't take that away from him.'

'I saw.'

'Good farmer, too. His old man croaked it a couple of years ago. No brothers or sisters to pay out so he copped the lot. Big herd of pedigree cows, lots of milk quota, four hundred lovely acres and a modern farmhouse to live in. Lucky chap, wouldn't you say?'

'He looks pleased with himself. Is that what you meant?'

'He chose a good bed to get born in, that's always a smart

thing to do. How you start off in life is important.'

'Don't look at me.'

'A successful man, our Freddie. Did you see his new Mercedes in the car park?'

Ralf said suspiciously, 'Where is this leading, Oliver? What's it got to do with me?'

'Freddie has asked Sonia to marry him. Thought you might just like to know that.'

10

Considering the amount of hard liquor that had been drunk the shooting party dispersed safely after much handshaking and hearty farewells. As soon as they were back indoors Ralf helped his father to remove his outdoor clothes and take off his boots. Then persuaded him to sit quietly in his armchair until he had recovered.

At first he was not too bad and Ralf began to hope that his fears would not be realised, and a disaster averted. It wasn't to be. The cumulative effects of the exertion, the boozing and excitement eventually took their toll. His father's eyes were dark, and glittered with exhaustion. By eight o'clock in the evening he was in serious difficulties with his breathing and no longer able to conceal it from Ralf.

'I know, I know,' he grunted. 'No need to tell me. I should have stayed at home.'

'I didn't say so.'

'That was a good day out. A bloody good day out. I don't care if it does kill me.'

The likelihood of this increased steadily as his face became mottled and congested. He sat with his hands gripping the arms of his chair, his shoulders hunched and his face now an alarming mulberry colour. He was weak and becoming increasingly distressed.

Ralf knew that he had to act soon or not at all. He said, 'You need to see a doctor, Dad.'

'No, no,' he gasped, making agitated gestures. 'You promised, Ralf.'

'I can't let you get much worse before I do something.'

'I shall be all right by the morning. Fix me a drink with plenty of brandy. That will ease my chest.'

It did but not for long and soon he was scarcely able to

breathe. Ralf knew that he ought to assert himself on his father's behalf but could not bring himself to do it and held on, hoping his spasm would ease. Once again he said, 'You're in a bad way, Dad. I ought to ring the hospital.'

His father, unable to speak, just shook his head and wheezed, 'No. No. No.'

A bleak moment, interrupted by a knock on the back door. It was Jed. He had come with a message. 'The guvnor sent me over. He was a bit worried about Tom. How is he?'

'Come in and see for yourself.'

'Bloody hell,' Jed said in alarm. 'You don't look too good, Tom. I must go back and tell the guvnor right away.'

Not long afterwards Sonia's Land Rover drew up outside. Ralf opened the door and she came in followed by Jed, and then by Shillabeer who grimaced and spread his hands in remorse. 'It was my fault. I should have persuaded Tom to sit up with Sonia and go round in the truck. It was too cold out there for him today.'

Ralf said, 'Dad doesn't want to go to the hospital.'

Sonia knelt down and unbuttoned his shirt to allow him to breathe more easily. The veins on his neck and chest were vividly defined and his lungs made an awful sound. 'Ralf's right,' he gasped. 'I don't want to go. Don't make me.'

Sonia said, 'We've got to take you, Tom. You know we have.'

Shillabeer came and stood behind his niece. 'You're going to die otherwise, Tom. Which is it to be?'

He hesitated a long time and they were all afraid he was going to opt for dying where he sat. At the last minute he gasped out, 'All right then. But you'll have to be quick. I can feel myself going.' He stared round with barely suppressed terror, believing himself about to die.

Sonia took charge. She said, 'We haven't got long, Ralf. I'll ring the hospital to let them know we are on our way. Can you pack a suitcase with some of Tom's things?'

Still blaming himself Shillabeer asked, 'What would you like me to do, Sonia?'

'Help Jed take Tom out to the Land Rover and both of you sit with him in the back. Can you find a rug or something to keep him warm?'

Although he had not mentioned it to his father Ralf knew that an emergency like this was certain to happen sooner or later and had taken the precaution of preparing a hospital suitcase in advance. It did not take him long to fetch it, calling from halfway down the stairs, 'We're ready, Sonia.'

'Let's get going then. Tom's not going to make it otherwise.'

The prodigiously strong Jed had already carried Tom Lassiter out of the house and helped him into the back of Sonia's Land Rover. Ralf sat in the front passenger seat feeling somewhat subdued, aware that Sonia had swiftly rescued a losing situation. She drove smoothly downhill to Long Beckles and from there to their nearby town and the general hospital's emergency unit.

Shillabeer was apologetic and contrite but it was a case of being wise after the event. He kept saying, 'It was too cold. He shouldn't have come with us on the shoot. I realise that now. Poor Tom. Poor Tom.' Speaking as though it was already too late.

Sonia would have none of this defeatist talk, confident that she had acted in time. She said over her shoulder, 'Keep him warm, Jed. Tom's going to be all right, I keep telling you. Hold on to him, we're nearly there.'

She was right because Tom Lassiter did not die. She had delivered him in the nick of time and the hospital's emergency services pulled him back from the brink. It was touch and go for several days, after which the medical authorities acted swiftly to determine his treatment and best long-term care.

With the unwelcome result that a week later he was put in an ambulance and transferred to the hospice at Northbeck.

11

So in spite of all his efforts to stay out he had ended up there just the same. It was the final irony in a brave fight to escape the invalid life he dreaded, however benign the regime, or well-intentioned the carers.

When Ralf made his first visit to Northbeck he was surprised at how quickly his father had rallied. The enforced rest in the general hospital had done him good. He was not only recovered but determined to leave.

He greeted Ralf with the words, 'Get me out of this place. I'm fine now, and I want to go home.'

'The doctor says you've got to stay.'

'Sod the doctor. It's a free country, is the car outside? If so I'll leave now, this minute. Bring my clothes.'

'They've ganged up on us, Dad. The Matron is under orders not to let you go.'

'They can't stop me. Speak to the doctor yourself. Tell them I'm better and that I'm going home.'

'I have spoken to him. He's determined that you're going to stay and have some treatment. Not chemotherapy or anything nasty like that but it will make you a lot more comfortable he told me. Anyway, I've promised.'

His father was adamant that he did not want to stay. 'It wasn't your promise to make. They can't force me to stay. You can't force me either. I can ring for a taxi and leave here any time I like. And I want to leave now.'

'Dad, yesterday you were in an intensive care unit. Be sensible.'

When he realised that Ralf was not going to change his mind he gave way and sat down dejectedly on a chair. He said, 'You were right and I was wrong. I know you didn't want me to go on the shoot.'

'I didn't try and stop you.'

'I know you didn't, but perhaps you should have.' He folded his arms in despair. 'If I had listened to you and stayed at home I would still be there now.'

'You said it yourself. It's all worked out for us in advance. It had to happen.'

'Going to make a big difference though. You off now?'

'I'll be back tomorrow. Cheer up, Dad. You're in the warm and dry. Look on the bright side.'

'Sonia came to see me in the hospital. She saved my life, I reckon. That's how I look at it.'

'Can't argue with that, Dad. She did.'

'Remember to thank her for me, won't you?'

'I already have.'

'Ralf, I know you won't like me talking about it but a man in my position doesn't have much left to look forward to. If I thought that you and Sonia might make a go of it together I should die a lot happier than I am right now.'

'Tell me about Freddie Foxwell.'

'Ah, yes. You've got some competition there, Ralf.'

'Serious competition? Oliver says he has asked her to marry him.'

'It's a business proposition really but Sonia is a businesswoman and she's considering it, I can tell you that much. He's asked her before, lots of times, every time they meet, I expect. Their two farms run together would make a big spread. Economies of scale. Any accountant will tell you the same.'

'How seriously is she considering it?'

'She certainly won't make a move until her uncle's birthday next year. The first of May isn't long to wait. Then she can decide what she wants to do with the rest of her life. And who she wants to spend it with. If anyone.'

'Thank you for telling me.'

'Don't be too downhearted. Sonia likes being the boss lady and if she married young Foxwell it would be like handing the farm over on a plate to someone else. She isn't going to do that. There are other reasons, too.'

'Tell me what they are.'

'Some other time. Keep your nerve, Ralf. In this life if you want something you've got to make a bid for it, all the more so where women are concerned. Particularly one as good-looking as Sonia. Because if you don't, sure as hell someone else will.'

'I'll give it some serious thought.'

'Do that. I'm tired now. Come and see me again tomorrow.'

Ralf did not sleep very well that night. He had forgotten about Freddie Foxwell since their schooldays at the College but after meeting him again at the shoot he recognised him as a formidable rival. He was troubled by the memory of Freddie's large hand spreading further and further round Sonia's waist and down over her shapely haunches. Since the moment he came to High Beckles and met Sonia again his peace of mind had deserted him. Falling in love is always an unsettling experience but unrequited love is more painful still. For the first time in his life he was suffering the torment of jealousy. Until a few months ago he had been firmly in control of every aspect of his life, secure in his career trajectory, happy with his diet, untroubled by thoughts of love or pangs of conscience. He could not believe that it had all unravelled so quickly.

When he visited Northbeck the next day his father asked yet again to be taken back to the Orchard House and would not be put off with soothing promises. 'Why not?' he asked angrily. 'They can't keep me here if I don't want to stay here. You can fix it for me, can't you?'

'Dad, you're going to have to stay here for a while.'

'How long does that mean?'

'Most of the winter. Until the end of February anyway. After that I'll bring you home, I promise. But not until the warmer weather.'

'That's months! I can't stick it that long.'

'At least you've got your own little room. The matron told

me they would let you be as independent as possible. You will soon get used to the food, and the staff couldn't be nicer. What more do you want?'

'It's invalid food and I don't want to get used it.' He reached out suddenly and gripped Ralf's hand. 'I asked Sonia about the house. Whether you could stay on there.'

'What did she say?'

'She said you could stay for as long as it took. So that you could come and see me every day.'

'That was good of her,'

Still holding on to Ralf's hand he said, 'You'll keep the house on for me, won't you? So that I can go back there in the spring.'

Ralf was shaken by the anguish in his father's voice and acted swiftly to put his mind at rest. 'Better than going down to live with George and Daisy. Of course I'll stay.'

His father still kept hold of his hand, gripping it tightly, and went on staring into his face with pleading eyes. 'Ralf, I don't care what you have to do so long as I've got the house and the garden to look forward to next spring.'

'I've promised. No need to upset yourself.'

In tears his father said, 'You know how much I love that garden. Please, my son. Please don't give up the house. I would do anything rather than die in this miserable bloody place.'

12

So Ralf had a problem.

His father was pleading for the chance of one last summer in the garden of the Orchard House. He had fixed his mind on a point in the future when he would exchange the winter hospice for summer sunshine among the heavily scented flowers, the friendly bees and the half-tame birds who shared the seat under the plum tree with him.

He could think of nothing else, indeed wanted to think of nothing else. If it was to sustain him during a bleak internment at Northbeck then it had to be a realisable dream. A dream which only Ralf could make come true. He could do so by staying put instead of returning to London and rescuing his career. It was a price he was by no means sure he was either able or willing to pay. Which was a long winter at High Beckles being harried by the lunatic Dick Shillabeer.

There was an alternative but it was even less appealing. Their local postman was always busy at times of dislocation, in this case relaying messages from Cousin Daisy, another social worker manqué. She urged Ralf to scrape the mud from his boots and return immediately to the gracious and civilised surroundings of Long Beckles, and her spare bedroom. He declined but took the precaution of asking the postman to transmit his refusal as politely and diplomatically as possible. Just in case.

He laid low while he thought it over, ignoring still more messages from the postman that Shillabeer wanted to see him. Then one evening he gave way and trudged the short distance to High Beckles farmhouse where he presented himself in the kitchen. Not because he wanted to see the robber chief, nor yet hoping for a glimpse of his niece, the sulking heiress. Sonia could see coming ever closer the night when she would

131

have to accompany her uncle on his poaching expeditions. Jed was equally apprehensive, since he would have to take it in turns with Sonia if Ralf still refused to help them out.

No. Ralf was visiting the kitchen for a more practical reason. He was driven there by hunger, being too demoralised to shop and cook for himself. Just at that moment the person he most wanted to see in all the world was Queenie the housekeeper, and his luck was in.

'Sorry to hear about your Dad,' she said, and she said it as if she meant it. Then went through her noisy ritual of hurling coke into the stove, shouting at the skinny black cat that lived in the kitchen, and banging pots and pans around. 'You haven't been eating properly, Ralf,' she scolded him. 'I can tell. Men never cook when they're on their own.'

'Dad did most of the cooking. I shall have to learn.'

'Why don't you eat with us now he's up at Northbeck? No one ever goes hungry here.'

'Thanks, Queenie, I will. If you're sure it's no trouble.' He pointed to the other side of the long kitchen table. 'Perhaps I could have some of what Jed is having.'

'Of course you can, Ralf. Sit down while I get it ready.'

Jed was about to start his evening meal and indicated with his knife that Ralf should sit opposite him. But tonight there were no smiles. Shillabeer's top hand had a heartfelt grievance and lost no time telling Ralf what it was.

'The guvnor's not happy. Says you still won't carry his birds for him. Is that right?'

'My agreement was to take him for a drive every day. Not to be his partner in crime.'

Jed waved this aside. He had his own plate on which all his meals were served. It was an oval willow-pattern serving dish big enough for a regimental dinner. His mother had loaded it with mounds of potato mashed with butter, huge chunks of tender fillet steak and a big tin of baked beans, all swimming in thick rich gravy. After shovelling in a few mouthfuls to get started he explained why Ralf had no need to worry.

'It's only a crime if you get caught, and the guvnor is far

too smart to get caught. You'll be all right, of course you will.'

'I certainly will because I won't be doing it. When will you all believe me?'

Jed frowned. 'He only takes it out on us. Best do what he wants, Ralf. That way we all get some peace and quiet.'

'I've been telling him 'no' ever since I came up here to live. If he hasn't got the message by now he never will. I can't think why he wants to do it, anyway.'

'It's his hobby.'

Ralf turned his eyes upwards in despair. 'Jed, stealing game birds from an estate is not a hobby. Try telling that to the magistrates and watch them fall about laughing.'

'If it keeps him out of mischief what does it matter? I think it's nice for retired people to have an interest. Something to occupy their mind. Anyway, you're supposed to be looking after him, not me. I work for Sonia now.'

'Let me spell it out to you, Jed. Trespass with a firearm is against the law. Poaching at night is against the law. Using a hunting dog to take game is against the law, lamping is against the law, practically everything your guvnor wants me to do is against the law. He should find something else to occupy his mind. Preferably something a little less illegal.'

'I've never seen him so disappointed. He was looking forward to a good season with the gun and now you've spoiled it for him.'

'You won't get any sympathy from me, Jed. A man of his age should spend his evenings sipping a hot milky drink in front of the television before going early to bed. Not wandering off into the night with a gun and a dog to go poaching.'

Ralf stopped talking when Queenie put down an equally mouth-watering meal in front of him. She was a rough and ready chuck-wagon cook only one notch up from his father but she seemed to have access to an abundant supply of prime-cut meat. There was always a huge joint roasting in the oven, or juicy steaks sizzling in the pan, so what her meals lacked in elegance and sophistication they made up for in quantity.

Queenie knew that young men had hearty appetites and liked their plates piled high. Ralf had spent a lot of time in the open air since his arrival in High Beckles and was no longer quite so pale. He had also done a considerable amount of hard physical work with the result that he had bulked up with a lot more muscle-weight than when he arrived. Good wholesome hunger was the result.

Jed had finished eating but continued to sit scowling and picking his teeth. Ralf could sympathise. Jed's face had lit up in smiles when he arrived unexpectedly with his father because he thought his days of providing the head poacher's cheap labour were over. Finding it not to be so was a bitter disappointment. He could see himself working round the clock, driven on by each of the equally high-handed Shilla-beers, both accustomed to having their own way and too proud to back down.

Jed said sourly, 'The agreement was that you kept the guvnor amused and out of our way.'

'Your guvnor has gone funny in the head.'

'What difference does that make? The boss lady isn't very happy either. You're not in her good books any more, Ralf.' He pushed back his chair and headed for the door in a temper. His long matted hair was encrusted with what looked like blood, and probably was blood, as were his arms. His muscles bulged ominously as he had the last word, and it sounded like a threat. 'I hope you know what you're doing, upsetting us all like this.'

He left, slamming the door behind him, allowing Ralf to finish his meal without further interruption. Queenie had taken off her apron and disappeared into the sitting room at the far end of the kitchen, the room that contained the photograph of Edith Shillabeer. Aunt Edie, as his father referred to her, the scary old goose woman of Beckles Green.

Ralf was left alone with the Witch. She slumbered peacefully in her smelly basket beside the Aga, occasionally whimpering in a dream sequence, limbs twitching as she chased deer and rabbits on Beckles Hill. Apart from the Witch snuffling in her basket the only sound came from the long-case clock in the other corner of the kitchen, nearest to the interior.

Most of the contents of the house were old. The grand-father clock reached from floor to ceiling and sliced away the centuries with a slow steady tick. It was a house that sought no contact with the outside world. It existed comfortably in its own time zone where old and new overlapped, and both seemed much the same.

He thought back to London and the flight from Heathrow that would have taken him to Los Angeles. Ralf closed his eyes in despair, thinking over the sequence of events that had exchanged his dream of America for a seat at Shillabeer's kitchen table and Queenie's Wild-West cookery. Could he have done anything that would have produced a different outcome? Or did his father have a point, namely that it was all worked out in advance, and no amount of squirming on the hook would have made the slightest difference? And if so what could he expect to happen next?

He did not have long to wait because the iron latch clanked and Shillabeer appeared in person. He came and sat in his seigneurial place at the head of the long oak table. He was a great one for observing the niceties of polite behaviour and removed his cap, placing it on the table in front of him. 'You eaten?' he enquired.

'Queenie has very kindly fed me. Yes.'

'Time for work then.' He leaned forward and gazed up at Ralf with his innocent blue eyes. 'Well, how about it? You haven't got anything better to do or you would be doing it. So what say we make a start on these birds tonight?'

'We seem to have had this conversation before. Many times.'

'You're upsetting Oliver as well. He keeps on to me about it all the time, which I don't like. He says I promised him a load of birds and now he wants to know where they are. You wouldn't want him to sue us for breach of promise, would you?'

'Us?'

'Yes, us. He's got his customers to consider. That's most of the other butchers for miles around and most of the hotels. About once a fortnight Jed runs a load up to London for him. We're letting a lot of good people down, Ralf.'

'Maybe so but don't worry about the breach of contract. I will give you my opinion free of charge. Hasn't got a case.'

Shillabeer did not care for this reply much. He fetched his gin bottle from the cupboard and when Ralf refused poured himself a glassful and lit a cigarette. 'They're getting away out there!' he grieved. 'The Captain has had one big shoot already, with some good drives. Birds we could have had, Ralf.'

'Could we talk about something else, please? Anything except pheasants and poaching. Is that too much to ask?'

Shillabeer squinted at him morosely through the cigarette smoke but refused to give up. 'Perhaps I should have explained it to you differently. We would be partners, Ralf. Fifty fifty. After I've paid the women for pulling the feathers off I'll give you half what I get from Biggsy. Do we have a deal?'

On hearing the displeasure in his voice the Witch uncoiled herself from her basket beside the stove and treated Ralf to one of her blood-freezing snarls. He was intimidated but resolute. 'No, we do not have a deal. Believe it.'

'Wait!' Shillabeer commanded.

He stood up and began the struggle of removing his bankroll from his trouser pocket. Ralf had seen his cattle-dealer hoard before, it was big enough to sink him like a stone if he ever fell into the river that ran so prettily past Beckles Mill. And where Ralf would gladly have dunked him at that moment.

Parting him from money was like drawing teeth. He winced and swore as he unrolled his wad of high value notes, then heaved an even more desperate sigh as he a weeded a few off and threw them on the table. 'Have it your own way then. No one has ever screwed me down as hard as this before. You want me to show you the money? Here's a couple of hundred quid in advance. Let's get going.'

Ralf was spared a final showdown when the iron latch clanked again. This time it was Sonia Shillabeer who entered the kitchen from the outside door. His heart started beating a little faster as it always did when the deer huntress of High Beckles put in an appearance. Nor did she disappoint him on this occasion.

She was dressed in black. Black needle-cord trousers that fitted very snugly indeed, and a black polo-neck sweater. As always she was neatly coiffed and groomed, her hair tied back with a dark green ribbon, a severe style that Ralf particularly liked. And as always she was unsmiling, intensely serious, brisk and business-like, allowing nothing and no one to distract her from her purpose.

In one hand she held a gun. In the other she carried what looked at first sight like a selection of horse harness. She walked towards Ralf, uttering at the same time the command, 'Stand up!'

Then put her arms around him.

13

But not for an embrace. It was to buckle a leather belt round his waist. A poaching belt with loops. Although the contact was only brief her hair brushed his face, and their breath mingled.

He realised at once that this was his own individual moment of truth, and had about five seconds to make up his mind. If he gave way now he was done for. This was the instant when he needed to make his firm stand and refuse once and for all. He should have unbuckled the poaching belt and thrown it to the ground immediately.

But he didn't. The touch of her hand and the mingling of breath and perfume knee-capped his indignation and sandbagged his resistance in one fell swoop. He had been outmanoeuvred by a resourceful and determined woman and had little option except to capitulate with as much grace as he could muster, which wasn't much.

Sonia also knew that the moment for refusing had come and gone. She instructed him even more confidently, 'Keep still!' Ralf obeyed as in a dream, only to have a leather harness strapped over his back and shoulders. The next command was, 'Turn round!' Again he obeyed automatically as she tightened a buckle and pronounced him ready.

'There!' she said. 'All done.'

She hefted the gun sling over her shoulder then put her arm through his. Followed by an announcement. 'Ralf is taking me out for the evening. We shall be late back. Don't wait up'

On the other side of the kitchen three equally surprised people lined up side by side. Shillabeer had been quickly joined by his housekeeper Queenie, and then by her son Jed. First to react was Jed, who could hardly believe his luck. He grinned from ear to ear to see Ralf kitted out in the carrying gear he normally wore himself. He grinned because he was thus assured of a good night's sleep, and confidently expected it to be followed by many more.

'Well done, mate,' he said. 'Hope the weather keeps fine for you.'

In spite of his age Shillabeer's brain worked quickly enough. He did not need to have it explained to him that Sonia had achieved in two minutes what he had failed to do after months of wheedling, coaxing and bullying. He too hastened to help matters along.

He said, 'The Witch will look after you, Ralf. Remember all the things I told you and nothing will go wrong.'

Nor was the Witch slow on the uptake. On seeing Sonia with the gun she left her basket by the stove and advanced to run a critical eye over the new recruit. She was not quite so hostile or distrustful of him as she had been at first but seemed less sure about having him on the night-shift team, and reserved judgement. Ralf was equally sceptical. The Witch was long overdue for her old age pension and he did not fancy trusting his precious liberty to such an ancient and decrepit creature.

Sonia did not intend to give him time to change his mind and led him by the hand through the kitchen door and along the stone-paved passageway into the covered part of the courtyard. The others followed and they all hesitated for a moment as they exchanged the warmth of the kitchen for the chill night air.

On one side cosy security. On the other the wild wood. Even with Sonia's arm round his waist Ralf's nerve began to fail. 'Loops,' she said, drawing them to his attention. She gave a tug on his belt. 'Just push the pheasants in by the head and pull the strings tight, okay? It's very quick.' Next she indicated some metal V-prongs studded back and front on his leather harness. She explained that pheasants could be quickly slotted by the head for carrying purposes and she promised not to overload him on his first trip. Last of all she patted his pockets to see if he was carrying a torch.

'Sonia's got the lamp,' Shillabeer explained, and to prove it she pulled it over her forehead on an elasticated band. 'We've got quite a few different lamps we use. We'll soon have you trained up.'

More instructions followed. Sonia said, 'Never shine a lamp sideways in the open, Ralf. Straight up into the trees, yes. Straight down on to the ground, yes. Sideways, no. Got it?'

'Whatever you say.'

'You don't talk either. Remember that, Ralf, it's important. The Witch doesn't bark and you don't speak unless spoken to. Least of all call out names. Understand?'

Shillabeer nodded sagely. 'That's good advice, Ralf.' He peered out and gave them his expert opinion. 'Not too dark. Not too cold. Just right.'

Still looking as surprised as Ralf felt he waved them goodbye. Queenie and Jed lined up beside him and watched as Sonia and Ralf disappeared into the night, the Witch trotting behind them with her tail curled down between her back legs.

From her uncle's arsenal of weapons Sonia had chosen a powerful air rifle fitted with a battery operated snap-on spot-beam gunlight. She handed it to Ralf and he carried it without protest in spite of the weight, and it was very heavy. He was fearful but also excited, wondering if there was after all a slight chance that the evening might end favourably for him by way of reward. It was the bit that came first that was worrying him right now. He could only hope it would not be too high a price to pay.

Sonia was wearing hiking boots and covered the ground quickly. She led him back past Orchard House, along the lane where they sat and talked in her Land Rover, and from there across the side of Beckles Hill until they reached a stony track. This was one of Shillabeer's favourite routes. Several smaller tracks branched off it on both sides, giving access to almost anywhere they wanted.

Although Sonia let go of his arm she stayed close and occasionally gave him a pat on the behind by way of encouragement. The clouds were high and there was enough moonlight for him to see her marching alongside. With the exertion of a climb along the side of the hill he could not only hear her breathing but also from time to time smell her breath in the clear night air. That part was nice but every step took them nearer to the estate enclosures and his level of fear began to rise.

The Witch had been following closely behind but suddenly surged past them in a run, and was lost to sight in an instant. Ralf remembered from his long walks with Shillabeer in the autumn that she knew to an inch where the boundary of his land began and ended. The moment they crossed into enemy territory she took off on a reconnaissance mission.

'We're heading for the Larch Plantation,' Sonia whispered as they came to a gate and altered course. 'Can you see all right, Ralf? Your eyes will get used to it after a few nights.'

Ralf was worried. He knew that his safety depended on the dog. She had gone ahead to check it out, but where? How could he be sure that she had gone to the right place? He decided to ask and whispered back, 'How does the Witch know we're going to the Larch Plantation? Did you give her directions in advance. If so, when? And how?'

'Not so loud,' Sonia cautioned him. 'What did I tell you before we left? Voices carry a long way in the open.'

'That doesn't answer my question,' he complained, although not surprised. The boss lady was more concerned with giving orders than answering questions. It occurred to him as a possibility that she was as keen on poaching as her uncle. As a family the Shillabeers had a reputation for unconventional behaviour and it was asking a lot to suppose that Sonia would be any different. If her father Saul Shillabeer could be described 'as wild as a hawk' it was hard to imagine that she saw any future for herself as a docile wife and mother. It was probably already too late. Having had her own way for so long she was most likely untameable. Ah, well.

So he sighed and once more did her bidding, which was to follow her down a steep incline and along a rutted track until they reached another gate. On it was nailed a wooden signboard with the words KEEP OUT in large letters. Here they waited. Several minutes passed but Ralf guessed why and this time did not enquire.

Just when he had given up hope that the dog would ever find them again he heard noisy breathing coming their way. Wheezing and panting the Witch returned from her scouting expedition which Ralf guessed had taken her right round the Larch Plantation and back through the middle to make sure it was safe for her mistress to enter.

Like a grey shadow she glided to her side. Ralf watched with astonishment as Sonia dropped on one knee and put an arm round her shoulders until their faces were almost touching. It seemed this was to receive her report because after some silent communing Sonia seemed satisfied that it was safe to proceed.

'She says it's all clear ahead,' Sonia whispered for his benefit. 'This is it, Ralf. The Larch Plantation. Stay close to me. And remember to keep quiet.'

Ralf knew that pheasants live on the borders of woods and field edges, where they feel safe during the day, but are vulnerable after dark. To avoid predators such as foxes they roost in trees, taking up their favoured positions while it is still light and staying there until shortly after dawn, being reluctant to fly in the dark.

Although some go quite a way into the woods, most pheasants stay close to the edge, so that they can fly out easily in the morning. Shillabeer had explained to him that his preferred method was to search along the borders from the inside. In this way the expert poacher could work without haste, and with minimum risk of detection.

It was different inside the plantation. It was darker, warmer, softer underfoot, and the larch had a turpentine evergreen smell. Within seconds of entering Ralf began to panic, having lost all sense of direction. Low branches scratched his face, ivy and brambles tangled round his feet and did their best to trip him up. Sonia must have sensed this and made soothing noises until he calmed down, holding his hand to guide him forward.

Soon she stopped and looked upwards. The night was cold and dry with very little wind so the birds were riding high. Vaguely Ralf glimpsed first one huddled shape, then another, dark black against ordinary black. 'We go for a head shot every time,' Sonia explained as she angled her lamp for a better look. 'Head and neck, Ralf, that's the target. You don't damage the eats with a head shot.'

'So your uncle keeps telling me. Okay. Now let's see you do it.'

Shooting with a small bore rifle is difficult at the best of times and he stayed absolutely still as she lined up the shot. It was a gas-powered semi-automatic and the battery operated spot-beam gun-light did the rest. The pheasant it picked out obligingly leaned forward. The pencil beam moved along its stretched-out neck and came to a stop on its head. As soon as the bird was hit it flapped its wings violently for a few seconds before tumbling down through the branches, landing in the undergrowth not far away.

'Yours,' Sonia instructed him but then quickly fetched it herself and handed it to him. The soft warm floppy corpse lay awkwardly in his hands as he fumbled to secure its neck into one of the loops on his belt. 'Like this,' Sonia whispered, guiding his fingers. 'Okay? Here's another one we can have. Try and keep up.'

Another jolt from the rifle and again Sonia retrieved the bird, this time slotting it into a hook on his back-harness for speed. After two more she touched his arm to indicate that they were moving deeper into the plantation. Ralf was happier near the edge and could only hope that she knew what she was doing and could get him out again. After missing a few times the next bird she hit flew a few yards before tumbling to the ground out of reach. Without being asked the Witch went in search and returned with it to Ralf's side for him to take from her mouth.

'Give her a pat,' Sonia whispered. Ralf obeyed, gingerly

digging his fingers into the wire wool of her coat, the first exchange of affection between them.

If he thought the worst was over he was sadly mistaken. Sonia was enjoying her night out with the gun and in no hurry to leave. Even though he was badly frightened it was not lost on him that he was spending time with the woman he loved, and that she was lithe as well as graceful, which excited him at the same time. She moved easily and seemed to know exactly what she was doing, which could not be said of him. The main problem being that his centre of gravity was affected by the swinging bodies of the pheasants. If he fell he doubted if he could have struggled back to his feet because of the awkwardness of the weight.

By this time his nerves were at twanging point. He was exhausted, frightened, angry, disorientated and profoundly unhappy. Only the presence of Shillabeer's bossy niece redeemed a nightmare experience.

'What was that?' he asked her. 'What did you say?'

'Feathers,' she repeated. 'You're not concentrating, Ralf.'

'What do you mean, feathers?'

'Can't you hear? The Witch has got some feathers stuck up her nose. Pull them off for her.'

'And lose my hand? Not likely.'

'Don't be such a baby. She won't hurt you.'

Fearfully Ralf stretched out his hand but the aged creature seemed to know what was being said and stopped snuffling while he wiped her nose. Then it was his turn to surprise Sonia.

He said, 'You're not really going to marry Freddie Foxwell, are you?'

She had the gun to her shoulder and was about to pull the trigger when he asked her the question. Slowly she lowered her gun and said, 'This is hardly the time to ask me questions like that.'

'It's as good as any other.'

'I knew you weren't concentrating. Keep still. I can see another.'

'Forget about these wretched birds for a minute. Stay still for once so that we can have a sensible conversation.'

'Not now, Ralf. And please keep your voice down. Behave yourself.'

She was more distracted than she sounded because her next bird was only winged and steepled up into the air before crashing back with considerable noise. A runner.

The Witch plunged after it, making even more noise. She pulled it down from some low branches but pheasants are heavy birds and she lost it again in some brambles. In Ralf's panic-stricken ears the uproar sounded like the clash of armies and he was still shaking when the Witch finally did the business and the bird was secured to his belt.

'That's enough,' Sonia decided. She called up the dog and the Witch led them straight to the fence. Much to Ralf's relief they emerged into the open and began the long walk back to the farm.

Soon they reached the safety of Beckles Hill. This was Shillabeer land so the Witch considered her night's work done and dropped back to troop alongside the new recruit. She looked as clonked as he felt, understandably so considering all the extra miles she had run. With her tail curled round in a treble clef between her back legs the evil-tempered old bitch limped by Ralf's side giving him grizzled blinks of approval. As far as she was concerned he had passed his first test.

As High Beckles loomed into view so the sky lightened and some stars appeared, followed by a lemon-slice of watery moon. Ralf was learning that the sky is not uniformly dark throughout the night, it brightens at intervals depending on the cloud cover just as it does during the day. Nor is it as dark in the open as it is near trees, or in a valley. What a lot he had learned it one night. And was likely to learn a lot more fairly soon.

In front Sonia led the way, purposeful as ever with the gun over her shoulder. When they reached the farm she waited for him to catch up, then guided him into the kitchen courtyard where she opened the door of a spacious brick-built outhouse.

His legs were on the point of collapse as he stumbled and almost fell, finally staggering to a halt as soon as he entered the building.

Sonia switched on a light, making him blink after the hours outside in the dark. Then came to help him as he began to unbuckle himself and let fall his load. She busied herself sorting through the pheasants she had shot, smoothing and straightening them with her hands so that they set in shape. Then looped string round their necks and hung them up one by one from a row of nails in the ceiling rafters.

He sensed that her mood had changed. His question about marrying her farming neighbour had spoiled her fun night out. When they set off she was in exuberant high spirits, having acted boldly and decisively, and was one up on her uncle who had tried and failed to recruit him into their gang. Now she was subdued and wary, uncertain how to proceed.

Once was not enough. She still had to persuade him to do it on a regular basis and she guessed, correctly, that having had a taste of her uncle's hobby he would refuse even more firmly than before. Ralf watched, completely exhausted, leaning against a dusty table to ease his aching legs and back. When he had recovered his breath enough to speak he said, 'I never met anyone like you in London. Or anywhere else for that matter. How do you do it, Sonia? Keep your nerve, I mean. I didn't enjoy it but I can't help admiring you.'

'Thank you for helping me. Not too difficult, was it?'

'I couldn't go through that again. Even for you.'

This was the answer she had feared. Once again she had to ask for his help but without seeming to plead. Trying to speak calmly she said, 'Nothing is going to stop Uncle Dick going after those birds. You know that, don't you?'

'Of course. It's his hobby.'

'I wanted to show you what it's like. What he wants you to do.'

'You showed me. I can't do it.'

'You could if you wanted to. Ralf, I need you to make sure he survives the winter. I'm frightened of him falling or hurting himself. He's an old man, even if he doesn't act like one. He needs someone to go with him and look after him. It's only for a few weeks. You could do that for me, couldn't you?'

'Try and persuade him to have a more suitable hobby. It's the only sensible solution. That way we all get some sleep and stay out of jail.'

'It's too late for that.'

'It certainly is if you're going to marry Freddie Foxwell.'

'Having two men ask me is very flattering. At least Freddie means it. I don't think you were serious, Ralf.'

'I was, Sonia. I still am.'

'You can ask me again next summer then.'

'Provided you don't marry Freddie in the meantime.'

'You needn't worry. I'm not planning to marry anyone.'

'I couldn't bear the thought of you marrying someone else. I'm still in love with you, Sonia. I want you to love me.'

She had been facing him but turned away on hearing this and lowered her head, visibly upset. 'I didn't want this to happen. There are lots of reasons, you know very well there are.'

'Not very good reasons though. If you don't mind me saying so.'

Ralf was thinking quickly, not wishing to lose the moment. He had given his father a solemn promise that he could return to the Orchard House and was therefore committed to seeing out the winter at High Beckles. He did not want to be continually harassed by Shillabeer, and he did not want to lose Sonia to the farmer. She had repeatedly asked him to do something for her, something important to help secure her inheritance, and this was the moment for him to back up words with deeds. Instinct told him he was in a now-or-never situation and in a rush of blood to the head he gave way to the impulse of the moment.

He kissed her.

She had been half expecting it but did not pull away, with the result that it was a nice warm kiss of several seconds duration. Everything seemed to go quiet afterwards, so quiet that they were aware of the night wind outside, and the sound of their own agitated breathing.

In a shaky voice Sonia said, 'You shouldn't have done that, Ralf.'

'I should have done it before. I wanted to.'

'I know you did.'

Still keeping his arms round her to prolong the moment he said, 'I'll do a trade with you, Sonia. One kiss like that for every night I go out with Uncle Dick.'

'To carry his birds, do you mean?'

'You've been pleading with me to do it for long enough. Well? Do we have a deal?'

'I'm not sure I understand you.'

'I think you do. One kiss a night. Starting tomorrow. You could manage that, couldn't you?'

She made to pull away but he kept his arms round her. He could almost hear her working it out in her mind and calculating the risk. She seemed to be coming to the conclusion that his resolve would not last long and that the number of kisses could be very few. For a moment he thought she was going to refuse to have anything to do with such a dubious arrangement but after thinking it over for quite a long time she said, 'Did you say you would start tomorrow?'

'See what being in love does for you? I must be the biggest fool ever, even to think about it. But yes, I'm on if you are.'

Sonia hesitated, and it was plain that she was not wildly enthusiastic at the idea. After another long pause she said, 'Just a kiss? I would not allow anything else.'

'Sonia, believe me, a kiss will do nicely.'

To prove his point he kissed her again by way of ratifying their agreement. Not a very romantic setting surrounded by a row of stiffening dead pheasants in a dimly lit outhouse, both wearing winter clothes.

But a kiss is a kiss, the most intimate of all human contact, and his instinct as a man who had made love to quite a few women in his time was that he would soon soften her up and earn some compound interest. Just the thought of it made him excited and aroused and he began to pull her into an even closer embrace.

Only to find that she was holding the gun between them. In a low voice she said, 'Tomorrow night, then. We'll be expecting you.'

14

The next night they set out all four in a procession. Having no suitable clothes of his own Ralf had borrowed some of his father's creosote-coloured outdoor gear, including a thorn-proof jacket and a pair of heavy cleated boots. To keep his ears warm he wore a knitted woolly hat that he seemed to remember had belonged to his mother. He was aware that his appearance was not heroic.

'We're giving The Holt a try tonight,' Shillabeer informed him as they mustered in the covered walkway that led away from the kitchen door. 'Nice bare branches in the Holt, they'll be lined up for me like ornaments on a mantelpiece.'

He was wearing a long green shooting waistcoat to go with his jaunty cloth cap, and underneath it a clean shirt and a tie. A tie! Ralf sobbed hysterically for a moment before he recovered himself and pretended to cough. Why had no one bothered to tell him that you dressed smartly to go poaching with the Shillabeers? Because Sonia was also at her best in another classy outfit of tiny boots, snugly fitting trousers and a ribbed jumper. Her hair was neatly tied back, her complexion flawless, and round her throat she had a green silk scarf knotted in a stock.

A touch of glamour and a bit of style that made Ralf more in love with her than ever. This dash of flamboyance and family pride bound Sonia to her uncle more surely than a deed of trust. The Witch had it, too. For a brief moment he stood facing all three, aware that they were looking back at him and asking themselves the same questions. Would he ever make the grade? Would he be able to strut and swagger as they did? And more importantly, would his nerve hold when it was put to the test?

They weren't sure, Sonia least of all. He was troubled by

150

her steady assessing gaze. She was a woman with a purpose, which was to defend her territory and protect her interests at all times. Her uncle was nearly eighty so the time could not be long delayed when she would have to cope alone in the tough trade of livestock farming. He guessed that her life for many years past had been a preparation for that moment, and she did not intend to fail when it came.

So could there ever be a place for him in her life? He was beginning to doubt it, much as he loved her, and whatever his father said to encourage him. The differences between them, and the situations in which they found themselves were too great, offering little hope of a workable arrangement. Although he would bravely pretend otherwise he knew instinctively that theirs was a doomed romance, destined to end unhappily.

They set off at a fair pace, Shillabeer walking proudly beside his niece, who carried the gun. Behind them the Witch trotted lightly in delinquent stealth, and bringing up the rear came Dr Ralf Lassiter, once a scholar, an author and a rising academic but now a poacher's leg-man ordered about by everyone. When they reached the small wood known as The Holt he was already tired out, and grateful for a rest while the Witch loped off for her recce.

Although Shillabeer boasted endlessly of his cleverness Ralf was under no illusion as to which was the key member of the troupe on whom their safety depended. Once again after a long wait he watched in polite disbelief and astonishment as the dog returned, wheezing and panting, to give her report. Sonia and her uncle knelt on either side, all three in silent communion but apparently able to understand one another.

'She says it's all clear,' Sonia informed him in a whisper. 'Stay close to me, Ralf. We're going behind the trees now.'

Secretly Ralf was impressed but had not changed his mind. He said, 'If the dog dies on us I'm packing it in immediately. Immediately, do you hear?'

'She'll see the winter out,' Shillabeer assured him sooth-ingly. 'Let's get on with it, shall we? Standing here yarning won't fill Oliver's big freezer up.'

It was another nightmare experience for Ralf as they slipped inside a dark wood in pursuit of illegal game. Sonia handed the gun to her uncle, then shone her lamp into the branches of the trees. The light picked out the pheasants one by one and the deadly head shot followed the beam. Shillabeer took his time, holding his aim with unflinching nerve until he was sure of a hit. Ralf recognised him as a creature of the night. Silent, cunning, and deadly.

Sonia picked up the pheasants and loaded Ralf fore and aft. He guessed they were following a well-practised routine, the only difference being that he was providing their cheap labour instead of Jed. They did not appear in the least nervous and worked methodically without haste. When a bird fell out of reach the Witch searched and retrieved, returning with it in her mouth.

'I trained her from a puppy,' Shillabeer sighed proudly. 'Beautiful!'

It was another strange experience for Ralf who could only hope they knew what they were doing and were as good as their word when it came to keeping him out of jail. He was desperately frightened but determined not to show it, pretending a confidence he did not feel. Soon it was Sonia's turn with the gun and the weight of dead pheasants began to mount, heavy enough to make him protest indignantly.

'All right, we're done,' she said, giving way. She called up the dog who led them out of the wood and back into the open. High Beckles was uphill from any direction and once again Ralf faced a weary trudge with his load of birds. They swung awkwardly and affected his balance. His back was almost breaking and his legs wobbled with fatigue as they approached the farm, and safety.

Once again the decrepit lurcher bitch fell back to pace companionably beside him, both equally zonked after their efforts. Shillabeer refused to disclose her true age, which made Ralf even more apprehensive. His life, his liberty, his whole future was now dependent on this ancient bronchitic creature. By way of fellow feeling he gave her a pat, silently praying that she would survive long enough to keep him from the disgrace of a prison cell.

In front it was a different story. The two Shillabeers strode tirelessly ahead, Sonia sturdy and purposeful with the gun over her shoulder, her uncle strutting proudly beside her. They were hunters, Ralf realised. Natural born hunters, driven by a compulsion he would never understand.

But he was a quick learner and when they reached the farm he staggered round to the brick outhouse where they dealt with the pheasants. Shillabeer and the Witch soon took themselves off, leaving Ralf alone with Sonia. She busied herself smoothing down feathers to keep the birds in shape, then hanging them from a row of nails in the rafters to prevent rats getting at their night's haul.

He was exhausted and leaned back against a wall, watching her at work. He could feel the tension beginning to prickle. The single electric light bulb was so dim that her face was half in shadow as she avoided looking at him. He was the first to speak.

'When does the shooting season end? Remind me.'

'Uncle has usually had enough by the end of January. Sometimes he goes on a little longer. But even he has to stop eventually.'

Ralf gulped, and tried not to look too stricken at this news. 'You said it would be only for a few weeks. Tell me you're joking! I couldn't possibly last that long. Even for you, Sonia.'

She treated him to an encouraging smile. 'It wasn't too bad tonight, was it?'

'Yes.'

'You're coming along nicely. There's nothing to it, really.'

'Why does no one ever tell me the truth? I'm not tough like my father. I'm a Mummy's boy, I was brought up soft. I can't do this, Sonia. However hard I try, I'm not going to be much help to you or your uncle. Sorry.'

This amused her. 'Oh, don't apologise, Ralf. We'll soon

make a man of you.'

Her smile fired him up. It was a challenge he could not refuse. She would soon find out whether he was a man or not. None of his sex partners had complained so far and he was going to make doubly sure that she was not the exception. He moved towards her. The time had come to claim the first of his kisses.

She saw him coming, and registered the change in his expression. He advanced very slowly as though trying to gain the confidence of a shy animal that would prefer to flee but is persuaded to stand still. Her face was tense, her eyes wary, her body stiffening slightly as though to resist.

He said, 'It doesn't hurt, Sonia.'

'Who said it did?'

'Some people even like it.'

'I didn't say I didn't like it.'

'Well then.' He slid an arm round her shoulders and began to pull her into position. Because he not only wanted a kiss, he wanted the maximum body contact permissible within the terms of their agreement. One kiss but a nice warm cuddle first, and a slow disengagement afterwards.

He whispered, 'You smell nice, Sonia. Lovely.' Then kissed her softly on the lips.

It was over all too quickly but a kiss is always a kiss, delightfully and deliciously erotic. Breath mingles, eyes half-close, bodies touch, lips are warm and soft. A kiss is the most intimate form of sexual contact, personal and profound. What starts with a kiss can lead almost anywhere.

Not that a brick outhouse with its butcher's shop row of dead pheasants dangling from strings was a good place to start. Nor in winter clothing, although snug and cuddly as they moved apart. With her eyes still cast down Sonia opened the door and switched off the light.

She said, 'Tomorrow night it will be just you and Uncle.'

'And the Witch too, I hope?'

He sounded so alarmed that she hastened to reassure him. 'Yes, the Witch too. Uncle wouldn't leave her behind.'

'That's a relief. I feel a lot safer with her around.'

Sonia smiled at this, then gave him his instructions. 'At the far end of the covered yard there is a small side door into the house. It's painted green. Do you know where I mean?'

'Yes.'

'I'll meet you there, just inside. I'll leave the door unlocked.'

'What time?'

'Does nine o'clock suit you?'

He replied, 'I'll be waiting, Sonia. Believe me, I'll be waiting.'

Then plodded back to his lonely, if cosy, bachelor bed.

15

Ralf slept when he could but always found time during the day to visit with his father in the hospice at Northbeck. Then in the evenings he put on his night-time gear and walked the short distance across Beckles Green to Shillabeer's ancient farmhouse.

This he did with eagerness and keen anticipation. Firstly to claim his nine o'clock kiss from Sonia, and secondly to sit down at the long oak planks of the kitchen table and tuck into the meal Queenie had cooked for him.

She still maintained that he needed feeding up and served him Jed-sized portions of everything. Wondering what delicious food she would have prepared gave him something to look forward to every day, and she never failed him. He feasted on roast meat, lots of it, including game and poultry. Not his preferred diet in recent memory but he was no longer a university lecturer, a pale and dreamy academic. He had become a hunter, and hunters were always hungry.

Queenie was equal to the challenge. She was a dab hand with the skillet and after a plate of her juicy steak and chips he could just about face another night in the woods with the robber chief and his felonious dog. If he looked in during the day she insisted on ladling him out a bowl of her delicious soup. This simmered on the stove in a huge black cauldron. It was meaty and highly seasoned, second cousin to a stew, and went down very well with a few hunks of bread and butter. Shillabeer often joined him, laying aside his cap in a show of good manners as they spooned up bowls of soup side by side.

Queenie also made a succulent date pudding with custard, which was his favourite, while Jed preferred her bread pudding, a substantial dish heavy enough to sink a ferry. Jed's duties included milking two house-cows, bringing back a huge pitcher of milk twice a day. A creamy rice pudding was usually the result, not Ralf's fare in more refined and sophisticated circles, but warmly appreciated now.

The iron latch on the bolt-studded kitchen door opened with a clank, a sound now embedded in his memory for ever. Shillabeer was always there waiting for him, passing the time by slumbering peacefully in his chair. He liked to doze with a gun across his lap and his leather boots toasting against the stove. By his side sat the Witch, gazing adoringly into his face.

He yawned and stretched when he heard Ralf arrive. 'You're on time, Partner. I like a man who's keen on business.'

'If you say so, Mr Shillabeer.'

'You're doing fine, Ralf. Sonia tells me she has come to an arrangement with you. Is that right?'

'Yes.'

'Good. She didn't tell me what sort of arrangement but if you're getting something out of it that's fine by me. Sonia handles all my finances now. A clever girl with money, Ralf.'

'Women usually are. My mother was the same.'

'Bang on the table, there's a good chap. Queenie can fix me some grub, too. Swallow of gin?'

Ralf declined but was always careful to be nice to Queenie to ensure that the generous helpings kept arriving on his plate. 'Been to see your Dad up at Northbeck?' she yelled at him.

'Every day,' he yelled back. 'Never miss.'

'Does he like it any better yet?'

'No. Still wants to come home.'

'Give him all the best from me.'

'I will.'

Queenie was part of the team too, an important part. In the brick outhouse she spent her mornings helping to pluck the pheasants he had carried back to the farm, allowing for a few days hanging on the nail first. It was a big job. Another woman from one of the cottages on Beckles Green came in and helped her, and even Shillabeer lent a hand when the haul had been good and they had a load of birds to process.

Queenie was in charge. She set a high standard, frowning at torn skin or a tiny feather not removed. She removed the insides, a smelly job, then trussed the birds ready for sale. Finally she dusted them with flour and laid each one carefully on a tray for delivery to Biggs & Son Family Butchers. Mostly the pheasants were larded with a rasher of bacon and decorated with a tail feather ready for distribution to retail outlets. Others were selected to be taken indoors and roasted in the oven. These Oliver Biggs delivered in the evenings to hotels and restaurants over a wide area.

Any unsold birds went into his big freezer to dispose of later through the cold-chain network. New outlets were opening up all the time, he informed them. Cooking programmes on the telly and recipe pages in magazines had created a demand. Nicely packaged game was all the go. However many they shot he still wanted more. Which meant more for Ralf to carry and he was in no hurry to leave the beautifully warm kitchen a moment sooner than necessary, particularly if there was a joint due out of the oven. As there was tonight.

First came a waft of heat as though from a furnace when Queenie opened the oven door, then staggered to the table with a great slab of meat almost too heavy for her to lift. Ralf was puzzled for a moment, but not for long, correctly identifying it as a whole haunch of venison. He knew better than to ask but guessed that Sonia and the Witch had teamed up yet again to provide the weekly meat order.

Shillabeer always treated meals with a great show of ceremony, laying aside his cap, drawing up his chair then looping on his fragile tiny spectacles in order to carve. To do so he put a hand into his top waistcoat pocket and produced his vicious spring-operated switchblade, all in one movement like a conjuring trick. It was razor sharp and he used it to carve off a big plateful for Ralf and an equally generous portion for the Witch. He then cut one wafer-thin slice for himself, which he ate slowly and solemnly. With his tidily combed wisps of silvery hair he looked more than ever like an elderly retired clergyman. It would not have surprised Ralf to see him put his hands together to say grace.

'Well?' he enquired politely when he considered that the time had come to set off in search of more product. 'Are you feeling strong, Ralf?'

'No. But I'll manage.'

'Better see what we can do then. Off we go!'

He liked to strut in front with his thumbs hooked into his waistcoat pockets. The Witch trotted faithfully at his heels while Ralf tramped some way behind, carrying the gun and still wondering how he came to be included in this strange procession. Shillabeer never told him where they were going, not that he wanted to know particularly, but his doggy minder seemed to know without being told.

Two tiny criminal brains that chimed as one. The moment they crossed the boundary of his land in any direction she surged away eagerly into the darkness to check the route, and never got it wrong.

How did they communicate? Ralf never found out but it was plain that they could and did understand one another, and that Sonia could understand her too. When the Witch returned panting and wheezing Shillabeer would drop on one knee, put an arm round her shoulder and receive her report, their heads together in a voiceless exchange of information. Usually she gave the all-clear but every so often he would say, 'Sorry, Ralf. We shall have to go the long way round. She says it's not safe this way.'

The long way round to Park Wood, to Doggrells Copse and Godwins Farm, to the Riverside Plantation and Skinners Clump, a recital of English place names. To Swanmead, Shearcroft, The Norrice, The Holt, Fettlers, Steeplecourt, Stunch Thicket, Grimes Wood, Bellwether Hollow, Dauncey's Bottom, Edney's Piece and Packhorse Meadow.

All these and more Ralf came to know during that long winter, and learned to distinguish them in the dark. He grew used to seeing the lights of villages and farmhouses disappear behind clumps of trees and then reappear from a different angle. He learned to identify the silhouettes of the big houses in the district, and the bulk of the church on its mound, and to orientate himself by the sound of its inharmonious clock clanking out the hours on a windy night.

'Biggsy wants more!' was Shillabeer's battle cry. 'Did you hear that, Ralf? Just had a special order from one of the big posh Mayfair hotels. A banquet. Visiting royalty, an extra hundred birds needed asap. No sleep for us this week.'

He wasn't joking either and Ralf no longer had the spirit to complain. He lived in a state of permanent exhaustion after the incessant walking, most of it carrying heavy weights over hilly ground. Compounded by a permanent state of apprehension, fearful that the Witch would slip up and allow him to be caught with his haul of pheasants. He tried not to think of the steps into the dock, the meticulousness of the judge explaining why a custodial sentence was appropriate in his case. Followed by the steps down into the cells, the handcuffs, the prison van, the sound of prison gates shutting behind him.

'Why do you keep on about gamekeepers?' Shillabeer demanded irritably. 'You've got more important things to worry about than the two idle bastards working for Captain Ives. They aren't out looking for you, they're cuddled up to their womenfolk, fast asleep in bed.'

'Where we should be if we had any sense.'

'Not while there's money to be earned. Hand me the gun, Partner. Here's a couple more we can have.'

And so for weeks on end Dick Shillabeer indulged his hobby at the expense of his neighbours. He was scrupulously fair to the extent that he would take game from any source, not just from the estate. By never flashing a light that could be seen, by going everywhere on foot however long the slog, by never treading the same ground twice, by using a well-trained hunting dog, and by working at different times of the day and night, he had plundered a surprisingly large number of expensively reared game birds.

So far with no opposition.

16

Every day without fail Ralf went to see his father in North-beck. Every day without fail he dozed off in the visitor chair.

'It's the heat,' his father growled. 'I keep asking them to turn it down but they won't. Or can't, perhaps. It's like an oven in this place, no wonder they all look so unhealthy. What's the weather like today?'

'Started off with a frost. Turned to rain. Not too bad.'

'Can't tell one day from another in here. Fresh air is what I miss more than anything.' He beckoned Ralf to come closer. 'Have you brought that bottle of brandy you promised me? I've got a good hiding place looked out.'

'It's too risky while you're on medication.'

'Thought you wouldn't. I put the pills down the lavatory when they're not looking so there's nothing to stop you bringing me the brandy next time you come. Did I tell you they took all my tobacco away?'

'Perhaps it was time for you to give up smoking.'

'I wouldn't miss it so much if I could have a glass of brandy occasionally.' He waggled his feet. 'See those? Carpet slippers! Look what they're doing to me, Ralf.'

'You had to come to it some time.'

'Comes hard, though.' He gestured round at his room, which seemed very comfortable and nice to Ralf. 'Library books. Jigsaw puzzles. Hot milk to drink at bedtime. The Matron reckons they're going to soften me up. What do you think?'

'I think they're going to have a job, Dad.'

He chuckled, but not for long. 'The vicar came to see me this morning. I suppose they added me to her list. Nice enough woman, been in the village a few years now. Told me the Lord loved me. A great comfort that was.'

'George and Daisy aren't the only neighbours with high-level connections then?'

His father chuckled again. 'Yes, it goes with the job, doesn't it? We're all cowards, that's what it amounts to. Everyone wants to die peacefully in their beds, no one wants to suffer. So we're all polite to the vicar hoping she can arrange it for us.'

'Perhaps she can. Don't risk it, Dad.'

He chuckled for the third time. After years of pipe smoking his vocal chords were permanently kippered and his voice was slow and gravelly. He said, 'They brought her in a cup of tea and she told me that went with the job, too. Every house she visits she gets offered tea to drink. Must have wonderful bladder control.'

'You're very chirpy today, Dad. It can't be all bad in here.'

'Better than discussing me and my ailments. Perhaps it's the right time for a little chat about you. And your future.'

'Go ahead. You've got plenty of time to talk and I've got plenty of time to listen. What's on your mind?'

'I reckon you've done your bit. There's no need for you to keep coming to see me in this dismal place. If you want to pack your suitcase and go back to London, that's all right with me.'

'And miss Queenie's cooking? Not likely.'

'That first week when they sent me here I said a lot of things I didn't really mean, and I won't hold you to them. I've got used to this place now and I reckon I can stick it out for as long as it takes. So if you want to jack it in and go back to London, go. Tomorrow, if you like.'

'It's washing day tomorrow. I couldn't deprive poor Daisy of the pleasure of boiling up my underpants.'

'She's been very kind to us in her way, and George too, of course. We used to be quite a big family at one time but everyone seems to have died off or moved away. When you were christened we had a full house afterwards. Now it's just you and them. That won't fill the church for my funeral, will it?'

162

There could be no reply to this bitter remark so Ralf took refuge in silence. He could not help being deeply affected by the sight of his stoical old father slumped dejectedly in a hospital chair, reconciled to his fate but dying a very slow unwilling death. No one likes to see a proud man brought low and Ralf decided in advance that he would erase these painful memories and remember his father as he was in his prime.

A man much deferred to in the village by reason of his top job in charge of the estate's farming activities. A supremely self-reliant man who never had to scratch his head or consult with the office first. Tom Lassiter had the reputation of being a problem solver, confident in his ability to get it right every time. Telling other people what to do, and making sure they did it, seemed to come naturally to him. He was a man's man, good at his job, straight in all his dealings, and held in great respect by just about everyone who knew him.

For relaxation on his day off he went rabbiting on Beckles Hill with his pal Dick Shillabeer, two free spirits who loved the dark mysterious yew-clad hill and the wild creatures they shared it with. Ralf could now better understand his despair at having his tobacco pouch removed, wearing carpet slippers on his feet and given a warm milky drink at bedtime. A hospice was no place for such a man and Ralf sorrowed on his behalf.

When it was time to go he said, 'I shall have to leave you to it, Dad. See you tomorrow.'

'I hope so, Ralf. I certainly hope so. I don't want to breathe my last in this miserable hole.'

'You won't. I've promised you.'

'February. That's what you promised. I'm holding you to it.'

'It will soon come round. Be patient.'

'It can't come soon enough for me.' At the door he put his hand briefly on Ralf's arm. 'I didn't mean it about you going back to London.'

'I know you didn't. And I'm not going.'

'If I didn't have your visit to look forward to every day I should either top myself or give up and die.'

'No need to do either. I look forward to it as much as you do. A nice sit down in the warm, a little chat, a cup of tea. Beats working every time.'

'Almost word for word what the lady vicar said to me.'

'There you are then, Dad. It's called a bedside manner. Perhaps I should consider holy orders myself if all else fails. There are worse ways of earning a living.'

So they parted with a smile but when Ralf looked into his father's wounded eyes they seemed to stare at him from deep within, as through some dark transparency. And was in no doubt that he spoke the truth about preferring to die rather than eke out his remaining days in the hospice.

The memory of this conversation carried over to the next day, mainly because his father had joked grimly about filling the church for his funeral. It reminded Ralf that it was time he paid another visit to his mother's grave in the churchyard at Long Beckles.

At midday there was no one else around to distract his thoughts as he made his way to the grave and stood at the foot so that he could read the inscription on the headstone. Funerals are desolate affairs at the best of times and this one had been unbelievably wretched, a day of driving rain in the middle of winter. Even the sheep couldn't stand it and moved down off the hill to huddle on the other side of the churchyard railings as the committal took place, his father gripping his arm as they watched the coffin being lowered.

'What will do you do now?' Ralf had asked him afterwards. A pointless question since his father had little choice except to carry on.

'Make the best of it, I suppose. Don't have much option, do I?'

He didn't, a stark truth, but standing beside the grave, now almost six years later, Ralf could better understand the loss for his father. His wife dead at a comparatively early age, his son already living and working in London and unlikely to return. An end to his family life.

Ralf had been close to his mother and acknowledged

ruefully to himself that he could do with her advice again now. From her desk in the estate office she had learned how things got done in the world. She saw at first-hand how the merchant banker and his kind ordered their affairs, and copied them. How to make use of contacts, how to get the better of obstructive officials, how to research opportunities, how to apply for grants and loans, how to invest money, and how to look after it once invested.

From close involvement with the estate she also knew that farming was lifelong hard labour, as well as financially precarious, with no upturn likely in the foreseeable future. She was determined that no son of hers would have anything to do with farming in any shape or form, and did her best to prevent him from taking an interest in country matters.

His father had accepted this decision, taken early on in his childhood, and if he was disappointed he was too loyal to his wife to say so. And although Ralf had spent a lot of time in his mother's company he had also enjoyed some quality time with his father, who had taught him to fish in the river, and more relevant to his present situation, how to shoot properly. For his sixteenth birthday his father had proudly given him a new shotgun and encouraged him to use it as often as possible. Which he did, until university education changed his views on field sports.

It is never easy to judge one's parents, still less to think of them as lovers, although that is what they undoubtedly were for the whole of their married life together. Ralf felt his eyes drawn to the empty space below his mother's name on the headstone. It was left blank for his father's to be added later, and the idea of seeing it there fairly soon was hard to take.

He looked closer and was sobered to see how quickly the stone had weathered in those few years. The incised lettering with his mother's name and the dates of her birth and death were already less sharp, they were filled in with little scabs of lichen, impossible to remove by picking at them with his fingernails.

Time passes, even for the dead.

17

When Oliver Biggs still demanded more Shillabeer aug-
mented the haul by shooting during the day as well, starting at
home in High Beckles. The farm included several long thick
hedgerows, plus a wood covering thirty acres.

'Shooting your own just isn't the same,' he said
sorrowfully. 'Not nearly so much fun, and not so profitable
either, considering what it costs to feed the little buggers.'

'But the same for the pheasants, if you will excuse me for
pointing that out.'

'We need your help, Ralf. I can hit them sitting still but I
can't hit them on the wing any more. Have a look in my gun
room and take whatever you think will suit you best. The
Witch will put the birds up for you. She enjoys that.'

Having given way over the poaching Ralf had enough
sense to realise that it would be futile and self-indulgent to
make a fuss by refusing to do as he was asked. He knew that
Sonia would be watching, and that his father would hear how
he had performed, so he put his mind to doing it as efficiently
as possible.

Lessons learned in childhood last for ever and his father
had taught him to shoot at an early age. He was able to swivel
off the front foot in the classic manner, following the flight of
each bird from the back end so that it careered into the flurry
of lead shot. Birds don't fly backwards, his father told him, so
put the shot where they are going, not where they have just
come from. The mantra he was made to repeat had stayed
with him ever since. *'Bum, belly, beak, BANG'!*

They were mostly wild birds the Witch flushed out for
him. They swerved in all directions, usually straight back the
way they had come. Driven birds fly straight for home but
these rocketed out like a lot of fireworks, here there and

everywhere. He found it a testing exercise.

However many he shot, and he shot plenty, Shillabeer still repeated his battle-cry, 'Biggsy wants more!'

So in the afternoons they drove out in the Land Rover and took it in turns to shoot from the windows. Shillabeer used his trusty Remington while Ralf made do with a five-shot bolt-action rifle using rimfire cartridges for minimum damage at short range. It was fitted with scope sights and a silencer, ideal for birds hiding themselves in open ground or tangles of grass, with just sufficient height from the Land Rover to pick them off. The birds sat tight until the last second when they mostly opted to run and dodge about rather than fly.

Shillabeer had acquired an affinity with pheasants and knew where they hid up, during the day as well as by night. There were plenty of unguarded nature reserves run by well-intentioned but naive environmentalists, and these they cleaned out first. There were also lots of little privately owned spinneys and roadside clumps of bush and bramble, even isolated small trees beside streams scarcely more than a trickle he knew to be the secluded haunt of a few stray birds, and they suffered the same fate.

Ralf realised that their aimless drives in the summer had not been quite so random after all. While he had been admiring the view, munching on junk food and imagining himself making love to Sonia, his partner in crime had been carrying out a pheasant census. He remembered them all, and was coming back for them one by one.

He was rapacious and remorseless, keeping Ralf at it virtually round the clock. He seldom slept himself and did not expect Ralf to want any rest either, or to occupy his mind with anything else. The geographical area they covered was extensive, and the terrain diverse.

Ralf had to admire his agility for a man who would be eighty next birthday. He slithered down railway banks while trains roared by underneath, scoured motorway verges in the early mornings as soon as it was light, invaded Ministry of Defence establishments at weekends, worked his way methodically through beauty spots and lover's lanes, and waded the length of every stream and ditch. Anywhere a pheasant bobbed up and showed its head he was squinting at it down a barrel.

Nothing was sacred to Shillabeer who picked off an old hen bird perched trustingly on a headstone in the town cemetery. They might have thought they were safe in forest and footpath but ended up in Queenie's oven just the same. The muffled crack of the rifle being fired was reduced to a fizzing sound by the silencer. The Witch retrieved, even at her age able to leap a gate with a heavy pheasant in her mouth, then bound over the tailboard of the Land Rover as they zoomed off, leaving not a trace behind.

'Pheasant chicks hatch first so they need a good start with the insects,' he informed Ralf. 'Crane flies are their favourite, they love them more than anything. Beetles, too. *Look after the pheasants and the partridges will look after themselves.* That's an old saying.'

'I've never heard it. I think you made it up.'

'There's so much to learn. It's taken me a lifetime and there's still a lot I don't know, particularly on the veterinary side. Pheasants have quite a lot of diseases and ailments and things that can go wrong with them. You would be surprised. I'll tell you about them one day. Remind me.'

'I shouldn't imagine that lead shot does them much good either.'

He chose not to hear this and carried on with his lecture. 'They like to snuggle up in the ivy on an old tree but not all pheasants jug upstairs, it's important to remember that. A rhododendron bush in a quiet drive suits them very well, or a good thick clump of bracken, or a nice bit of swampy ground. The more water to slosh about in the happier they are. If Captain Ives knew that he would know why so many of his birds stray off the estate.'

'I was under the impression that you offered them illegal payments to put themselves on the transfer list. Football managers have to resign if they're caught doing it.'

Shillabeer ignored this and continued with his lecture. 'It's an art, keeping game. The biggest killer is the weather so they need a lot of looking after all through their lives. Rearing the little birds, controlling the predators, planting crops to give them cover at just the right time, cutting out the rides so that they aren't in a draught, it all needs careful thought. Your Dad got me to use maize strips with a bit of millet mixed in, just the job they are. Work a treat.'

'I shall remember to tell him.'

'I never stint on my pheasants, Ralf. Only the best top quality food will do, and hand feeding them when necessary. It's all down to preparation and that includes organising the shoots properly. He's been a big disappointment to me, Captain Ives, because he never gets any of it right.'

'Dad doesn't bear him a grudge, Mr Shillabeer. Neither do I.'

He sighed, and lit a cigarette. 'I think we've swept up most of the loose birds, don't you? Good. That leaves us free to concentrate on him. The foxes are a bit hungrier now but they won't have nearly as many as you and me, Partner. I know we've had a lot already but we are going to have a lot, lot more. We're going to clean him out, that's what we're going to do.'

'So long as you don't become too over-confident. I've got more to lose than you have. I should be obliged if you would bear that in mind.'

'You're a big help to me, Ralf, and I'll look after you. You know I will.'

'I ought to feel comforted. Somehow I don't.'

Shillabeer squinted at him sideways, and the Witch turned her head to do the same. He said, 'As a matter of fact I thought you were beginning to enjoy yourself at last. You've been a different man lately. Something is agreeing with you, and I can only suppose it must be Queenie's cooking.'

Well, he was wrong about that but at least it was proof that so far no one had discovered the secret of his evening meeting with Sonia in the secluded doorway. They were careful not to be seen and had managed to keep the arrangement a private affair. Neither the matchmakers nor the intrusive local postman were on to them, and Ralf fancied that Sonia rather enjoyed the conspiracy. Since it suited them to embrace in a darkened doorway away from prying eyes they saw no reason to do otherwise.

The only thing to spoil it for him was the suspicion that Sonia was also seeing Freddie Foxwell, the enterprising young farmer whose land marched with hers. Ralf had never suffered from jealousy before and raised the subject of his rival during an afternoon visit to Northbeck. His father assured him that he was worrying himself needlessly.

'There's nothing in it, Ralf. I've told you before.'

'Are you sure?'

'Quite sure. Sonia and Freddie both belong to the same buying group. It's a basic sort of co-operative. They get their cattle feed a bit cheaper, that's the attraction. Fertiliser, too. A big item these days.'

'They see one another. Oliver tells me every time they meet.'

His father explained it to him patiently. 'They see one another at meetings, that's all. Every so often one of the suppliers will treat them to a sit-down meal at the Bear Hotel. Very sociable. Oliver is just making mischief. Don't read too much into it.'

'I should like to believe you.'

'Don't give yourself such a hard time. Young Foxwell is a bad man for women, Sonia knows that. He's usually got more than one on the go. Sluts mainly, or married women who ought to know better.'

'That puts her off?'

'He's a big spender, that puts her off even more. So long as he's spending his own money, fine. Would she give him the chance of spending hers? Ralf, you know the Shillabeers better than that. Take it from me, he isn't in the frame.'

'Thank you for telling me.'

After a short silence, while Ralf brooded on this information, his father asked him a question. It was the same question that Oliver Biggs had asked him in the autumn.

'You remember Aunt Edie, don't you? Dick's aunt. She's been dead a few years now.'

'Of course I remember her. I was more scared of her than I was of the geese.'

'You're right, that's how she ended her days, surrounded by geese on Beckles Green. Made money out of it too, lets not forget that. But never married. Never met the right man, I suppose. None of us would like to see Sonia go the same way.'

'Me neither.'

'Old Shill thinks the world of her, you know he does. He would love to see her happily married before he dies. He's got you picked, Ralf.'

'Sonia understands the difficulties even if you don't. My line of work doesn't fit in with hers, and there's no getting round that. No easy way, at least. My career isn't on track any more so I shall be looking for a lecturing job. There are plenty of universities to pick from but none of them close to High Beckles.'

'You never let on how you feel about Sonia but I know she thinks a lot of you. And of course I'm very fond of her myself. Because I never had a daughter of my own, I suppose. Time is running out for me faster than it is for old Shill, even if he is nearly eighty.'

'You don't need to keep reminding me.'

'Don't be upset, Ralf. I can't help how I feel and I should die a lot happier if I thought there was a chance that you and Sonia might get together. When she started to grow up, and everyone round here could see that she was going to be something special, it was the first thought in my mind. That she would be a marvellous wife for you. Because you had left home and gone off to make your way in the world I thought there was no hope, so it was just a dream. Then when you came back to live with us again … ' He pointed upwards. 'It seemed to me that someone up there wanted to make it happen. I often wonder if Mother is still keeping an eye on us.'

'I've come round to your way of thinking, Dad. It's called Fate. All planned out for us in advance. If it's going to happen, nothing we can do will prevent it from happening. Or not happening, as the case may be.'

'Exactly. That's why I'm sure it will be you or no one for Sonia Shillabeer.'

Ralf could only hope that he spoke the truth. Because he now had something to look forward to from the moment he woke up in his own bed every morning. The hope that one day he would wake up in Sonia's, with the heiress snug and warm beside him.

18

The weather suddenly turned much worse for the poaching gang.

One night they walked home during a thunderstorm, vivid sheets of lightning and nightmare claps of thunder. Anyone who met them would have fled in terror at seeing Shillabeer with his gun and strange dog, accompanied by an apparition hung all over with dead pheasants. As they walked they were illuminated every few seconds by shimmering pale blue strands of lightning, followed by cracks of thunder that rocked the ground. Ralf found it a frightening experience.

Another time it snowed, thick wet blobs swirling down from an angry black sky. This was on the outward journey. They were plastered from head to foot within minutes but Shillabeer refused to turn back and insisted on staying out until he had shot his quota.

The snow only lasted a few days, and was replaced with heavy rain. Ralf regretted complaining about the snow because the drenching rain was infinitely worse. It was blown in his face by a howling gale, as well as being pitch dark and achingly cold. He had put up with a lot but on this particular evening he suddenly felt himself at breaking point when he clanked open the latch and reported for duty.

He was exasperated beyond endurance at the sight of Shillabeer snoozing peacefully with his hands clasped over his gun, and the Witch's grey snout in his lap. There was something unfair that he should be so well-adjusted and healthy while everyone else suffered, and Ralf allowed his feelings to get the better of him.

'You never hear me swear,' Shillabeer said virtuously as he woke up and turned to face Ralf's angry glare from the table where he sat nursing a hot drink. He gave the Witch's ugly head a scratch and she closed her eyes with pleasure. 'Is something troubling you, Ralf?'

'Only madmen would go out on a night like this.'

'What?' he cried, looking shocked. 'Best weather going for our trade, this is. I hope you're feeling strong because I'm certainly feeling lucky.'

He was right, and that night bagged a record haul, almost more than Ralf could stagger home with through the mud. But at least it kept his old College friend the & Son happy. The ready roasted birds were a big success this year Oliver informed him when he delivered them along with the other free-enterprise meat at their Monday rendezvous. Queenie was kept busy at the stove and Ralf lost track of time as he was working virtually non-stop to keep up.

But the peak had passed. By now the ground had been well shot over by the estate syndicate with some successful drives. Bad weather and predators accounted for a lot more. As it grew near Christmas the supply of pheasants began to dwindle, until one night they faced the prospect of returning to the farm empty-handed. To improve their chances Shilla-beer revisited some of the places where they had enjoyed success earlier in the winter, and delayed their departure from the farm until well after midnight. With an even worse result, their first nil haul.

Instead of breezing along in front he trooped disconsolately beside Ralf and was so cast down that the Witch whimpered in sympathy. 'It's not your fault,' he said, comforting his awful dog. 'Be nice to her, Ralf. She thinks I'm blaming her.'

Ralf declined the invitation although he was surprised to find the wheezy old bitch sensitive as well as cunning. She was the ugliest creature imaginable. Distrustful, ill-propor-tioned, foul smelling, bad tempered and unlovable. Her rough winter coat was a dingy grey colour, white with age on her muzzle. Her back and flanks were stitched over with barbed-wire scars, inflicted in younger and more impetuous days by running headlong into fences at forty miles an hour in pursuit of hares and deer.

Shillabeer paused in a gateway and considered. 'We're not far from Chantry Copse. A lot of holly trees and blackthorn down there. They could have gone in for shelter. Shall we take a look?'

'Changes of plan never work. That's what you've always told me.'

'It's a windy night and pheasants don't like a draught. They'll be tucked up in those holly bushes, I'm sure of it. It's not a change of plan, Partner, just a change of direction. How about it? Any other objections?'

'We should be on the wrong side of the river if anything went wrong.'

'You're right,' he conceded, altering course again. 'Take the gun and we'll head for home. Queenie can cook us an early breakfast.'

They had walked about a mile and were not far from Shillabeer's boundary when the Witch rejoined them, sliding noiselessly along the moon shadow of a hedge. She had ranged ahead as usual and even Ralf could sense that she had bad news to tell.

'There's someone heading our way,' Shillabeer whispered, kneeling to receive her report.

For a long time they could hear nothing. Perhaps it was only his imagination or the thudding of his heart but Ralf soon began to hear the steady approach of footsteps, and the dislodgement of stones. They were caught in the open with nowhere to hide. It was seven o'clock in the morning with hazy moonlight and high, fast-moving clouds.

'What shall we do?' he whispered.

'Keep still and listen.'

Which they did, all three crouched down out of sight. After a few minutes the Witch started to get agitated. 'What does she say now?' he asked hoarsely.

'She says run for it. Let's shift ourselves, Ralf.'

He ran, Ralf and the dog followed. They scrambled through some fences, jumped a ditch and finally knelt in a muddy gateway. 'You ran the wrong way,' Ralf whispered, his voice anguished. 'High Beckles is the other way.'

'We don't want to lead them straight back to the farm, do we?' He took a tight grip on Ralf's arm, afraid that he might panic and go bolting off. 'Take it easy, Partner,' he said soothingly. 'We'll get out of this all right.'

'She doesn't think so,' he replied, pointing to the dog. He watched Shillabeer and the Witch communing head to head, riffling through the possibilities until they got a result.

'Two of them,' he explained. 'And coming from different directions. That's what confused her at first.'

'You're right, I can hear voices. I think they're talking to one another on mobile phones. Coming closer, too. What shall we do? I don't want to get caught.'

'I don't think they know where we are. Not exactly. Keep still and listen.'

Ralf's bladder drummed with fright and he might well have lost his nerve and gone running off in a panic, except that Shillabeer put a firm hand on his shoulder and held him down. The footsteps came nearer until they could see the outline of a man. He was approaching cautiously, and was soon close enough for them to hear him breathing.

His image seemed to be reflected by the mist and magnified by the moonlight, it made him look about eight feet tall. He was a bulky figure dressed in combat gear, and carrying a gun. He came to a stop about twenty feet away, and they could then hear the second man closing on them from behind. Even if the two men could not see them they knew they were there. Ralf had never been so frightened in all his life.

Shillabeer felt around on the ground, searching for a suitable stone. Having found one he pushed it into Ralf's hand, indicating by dumb show that he should lob it in the opposite direction. He did so, hurling it high in the air to land with a clatter some way off. It had the immediate effect of making the first man curse in surprise, and the second to call out and ask what was the matter.

They then had a stupendous piece of luck.

A charcoal cloud the size of Africa suddenly obscured the moon. For a moment it was as black as the bottom of a coal mine. Ralf did not need Shillabeer to hiss at him to run for it. All three of them fled in an instant and did not stop running until they were safely back on High Beckles territory.

Breakfast was in progress when they arrived at the farmhouse, entering by the kitchen door. Sonia and Jed were both sitting at the long oak table, Jed tucking into a big plateful of fried food. Shillabeer removed his cap and sat down in his place at the head of the table, thanking Queenie politely for the little pot of tea she placed in front of him.

Another day another dollar for the good folk of High Beckles, except that Ralf had not recovered from his fright and was in a terrible state of nerves. Queenie was the first to notice and honked with alarm.

'Has there been trouble?' she bawled at them. 'Has Ralf had an accident? He's all of a shake.'

'No, no, nothing like that,' Shillabeer assured her as he spooned marmalade on to the dainty triangles of toast she placed in front of him. 'We ran into a couple of men with shooters. Coming home the back way from Chantry Copse.'

Sonia and Jed both looked up with interest. 'Not gamekeepers, then?' Sonia said. 'Farmers, perhaps?'

'Weren't dressed right for farmers, Sonia.'

'A couple of poachers by the sound of it,' Jed offered as his contribution. 'Couldn't have been after our birds, could they?'

'Poachers?' Shillabeer mused as he looped on his fragile spectacles. 'Yes, it could have been a couple of locals trying their luck. A long time since we've had trouble with poachers. There's no discipline in the schools these days. I blame the government.'

Ralf began to sob in despair but cheered up slightly when Queenie banged a huge plate of delicious fried food down in front of him. 'And a nice hot cup of tea with plenty of sugar in it,' she trumpeted, noisy as ever. 'How do you feel now, Ralf? Getting over it a bit?'

He wasn't, but the sight of Shillabeer's wisps of silvery hair and faded pale blue eyes had a reassuring effect. Sipping his tea and eating his toast and marmalade he presided at the head of the table with an air of genteel respectability. Ralf's pounding heart gradually returned to normal but even so he sensed disquiet around the table. They were afraid he would lose his nerve and refuse to go out again, leaving them with the same old problem. One by one they hastened to jolly him along. First to calm him down, and then to stiffen him up.

'Yes, Ralf kept his nerve,' Shillabeer informed them. 'He made the grade all right. Stood his ground and frightened the poachers off. For a minute or two I thought he was going to let them have a barrel to teach them a lesson. Just to help them on their way.'

'The right man for the job,' Jed said staunchly, trying hard to look impressed. He had the most to lose if Ralf bottled out so he was fulsome in his praise. 'Well done, mate. Nice one.'

'Nerves of steel,' Shillabeer said for good measure to rally the faint-hearted. 'Never flinched.' He pointed to his misshapen dog, now curled up asleep in her wickerwork basket by the stove. 'Even the Witch was proud of him.'

'Our hero,' Sonia said.

She thought it was funny and her face broke into a smile, not something that happened very often. This prompted Ralf to square his shoulders and live up to his reputation. He smiled back, got on with his breakfast and tried to look a little more heroic than he felt. Secure in the knowledge that at nine o'clock in the evening he would be meeting Sonia in their secret doorway and claiming the next of his kisses. He could hardly wait.

He was easily distracted but the boss lady's mind was never far from the job. She finished eating then suddenly pushed her plate away and put her arms on the table. Her uncle paid attention. 'Yes, Sonia. What is it?'

'I'll tell you what I think. I think what you saw was the Turkey Patrol.'

'She's right,' Shillabeer said immediately. 'All the poultry keepers get together on one of these Farmwatch schemes. I should have thought of that myself as it's so close to Christmas.'

'Inconvenient for you,' Sonia said sympathetically.

'Certainly is,' he replied. He sounded aggrieved. 'We can do without a lot of trigger-happy chicken farmers wandering around with shotguns. What can we do about it, Sonia?'

'Put Jed out for a night or two. He won't mind, will you, Jed?'

'Yes, I bloody well will,' he said indignantly. But was outvoted.

A decoy,' Shillabeer explained for Ralf's benefit. 'Whichever way we go Jed will go the other. Flash lights around. Let off a few bangs. He'll lead them a pretty dance, I can tell you.'

'Take that old twelve-bore in the corner cabinet,' Sonia instructed him 'It goes off like a cannon. That should keep everyone amused.'

Ralf leaned his head on the table in a brief gesture of helplessness and despair. They were mad, all of them, stark staring mad.

'Thank you, Queenie,' Shillabeer said courteously as she filled his cup. He drank tea only once a day, at breakfast, and had a little tea set of his own. A small pot, a china cup and saucer, and a napkin in a silver ring. He sipped appreciatively every morning as though in a deanery.

And that night took Ralf out with him again for no better reason than he loved to be on the hill at night with a gun under his arm and a dog by his side. Whatever drove him on, or what he was trying to prove, and to whom, Ralf was no nearer finding out and doubted if he ever would.

He thought again of the Bronze Age burial mounds dotted along the top of Beckles Hill. He was convinced that Shillabeer and Sonia were direct descendants of these ancient people through continuous occupation of the site. It was their territory and they were determined to hold on to it, come what may. They had survived down countless centuries by tenacity, fortitude, adaptability and cunning, above all by their inherited skill in hunting.

Everyone else perished but Shillabeer was immortal. With his hunting dog and a fire he could survive until the end of time.

19

If Sonia had expected Ralf to crumple after a few nights out with her uncle he had the satisfaction of proving her wrong.

His resolve was lasting longer than either of them had believed possible. The weeks passed and he was still able to keep going, if only just. He was at the limit of his endurance, often so exhausted that he was more asleep than awake as he traipsed home behind Shillabeer and the Witch. Alas for keeping in touch with the outside world, he had not looked at his laptop since the night Sonia had seduced him into the poaching gang, His brain was unable to concentrate on anything else because he was so tired.

What sustained him? His nine o'clock kiss, of course.

He had something to prove and something to gain. When it was time to set off he drew some deep breaths to fire himself up for the task. This was what Sonia had asked him to do, and he was doing it, even though he was suffering physically and mentally as a result. He knew it was his best and only chance to impress her that he meant what he said, and was serious in his wish to marry her.

So every evening at nine o'clock he spoke words of love to the heiress of High Beckles before he kissed her. It was not ideal, but better than nothing, decidedly better than nothing. A regular meeting, a guaranteed embrace, and a chance to plead his case with loving words and a shared moment of intimacy.

He had entered into the strangest period of his life, one he knew that he would never forget, whatever the outcome. For the sake of this one kiss he wandered the night as Shillabeer's idiot apprentice, while at the same time being pathetically dependent for his liberty on the wits of a degenerate dog. Not quite the career trajectory his mother had in mind for him at the age of thirty.

In the mornings he slept. In the afternoons he visited with his father at Northbeck. Then as soon as it began to get dark his thoughts turned to his nine o'clock assignation with Sonia. As the hour approached he could think of little else until it was time to make the short journey across Beckles Green to the farmhouse of High Beckles. Which he did with the mixture of excitement and apprehension common to all lovers, never knowing quite what to expect.

It was an ancient house with a small hidden doorway and it was there that Sonia waited for her kiss. She was always there first in the half-darkened stone-flagged passageway that led to the covered courtyard, and from there to the kitchen door. They were not aware of being watched but to make sure Sonia allowed him to step inside her door into a part of the house that was little used.

Once inside he breathed the special smell of the house, the smell of all old houses perhaps, of earth and stone and time-trapped dust. They met and embraced in a dimly lit tiny hallway at the end of a narrow passage, a secluded and intimate rendezvous for a clandestine affair.

In theory the kiss was to thank him for his previous night's escorting duties but in practise it was just sufficient to stiffen him up for yet another gruelling expedition with the natty robber baron and poacher-in-chief, master of all he surveyed and quite a bit else besides. Ralf's remit was to ensure his survival night by night, and it didn't get any easier because Shillabeer was now casting the net ever wider in raids on the pheasant populations of neighbouring villages.

At first they had referred to this, exchanging thanks with great formality. Sonia would say, 'Thank you for going out with Uncle again last night. I'm sorry the weather was so awful. It never stopped raining and you must have walked miles.'

He would respond by thanking her for the embrace. 'Worth it for a kiss though. That was lovely, Sonia. Thank you.'

It wasn't much, but it was enough. This backstairs meeting kept their romance alive and moved their courtship forward.

Although a kiss is considered to be a sociable and seemly way of greeting it is also an intimate body contact, and Ralf's kisses were as passionate as he could make them, and his embrace slow and lingering.

To delay the kiss as long as possible while still holding his arms around her he held back in the last second before their lips met and engaged her in conversation. Usually by whispering, 'I'm in love with you, Sonia.' To which she always made the same reply, 'That's nice.' But with downcast eyes, and then only after a long pause.

This pause began to nag away at Ralf's self-confidence. It was not exactly an enthusiastic response to his whispered endearments and declarations of undying love. And he knew why. It was because she was still not taking his offer of marriage seriously. She believed him incapable of resisting the lure of London and other faraway places and did not want to commit herself to a relationship that was likely to end the moment his father died.

Although his father's illness was never mentioned it was pivotal to their love affair, such as it was. Had his father not fallen ill he would never have returned to High Beckles in the first place. Similarly, because his father's illness was known to be a terminal one, it meant there was a time limit to his stay. A countdown they expected to come to an end during the following summer.

After which he would be free to return to London and this was the unspoken question at the end of every kiss. Would he still feel the same about her, and whisper words of love and proposals of marriage, when there was nothing else to keep him in muddy High Beckles? Well, would he?

Obviously Sonia did not think so. Whether this was the only reason he could not be sure, but it was certainly the main reason, and his inability to convince her that he meant what he said was starting to get to him. He thought he had been clever in thinking of the nightly kiss but as with all dubious ploys for getting a woman into bed, love has the last laugh. Grimly he soldiered on as Shillabeer's bird-carrier night after night in order to claim his reward, but as the number of kisses mounted up he found that it was him, and not Sonia, who was being hurt the most.

Not that Sonia was untouched by the experience. His words of love and impassioned kisses were having a cumulative effect, as they would on any woman. But she was disturbed by it as well, troubled by the intensity of his feeling for her. He could tell that she was scared as well as excited, scared of her own feelings perhaps, the reason she did not warmly share his kisses and turn them into lover's kisses. She held back because she did not trust him to be around for long, once he was free to leave, and did not want to be hurt any more than necessary.

How could he convince her of his love and faithfulness? Answer, he couldn't. And as a consequence he began to suffer the agonies and ecstasies of an unrequited love affair that haunted his thoughts day and night. Combined with anxiety over his father's failing health, and exasperation with Shillabeer's so-called hobby, he was soon on the verge of collapse and a nervous breakdown. Growing concern for the effect on his career and the fear of being caught had turned the whole experience into an ongoing nightmare, made ten times worse by his doomed love for Sonia Shillabeer.

He quarrelled with Oliver Biggs, accusing him of being responsible for the plight he was in. 'I blame you, Oliver. This is all your fault,' he told him angrily when they met for the latest delivery. When the butcher seemed hurt and surprised he went even further. 'I mean it, Biggs. You're the only one who gets anything out of all this poaching. You drive the old man on and that causes me a lot of inconvenience. You put him up to it in the first place and you'll end by killing him. If you can't make a living with your shop then change your occupation. Are you hearing what I'm saying?'

He felt slightly better after this outburst but it affected his behaviour with Sonia and only made matters worse. During the day he endured a desolate feeling of separation and tried everything he knew to prolong the few minutes he spent with her in their secluded hallway. Followed by an interminable twenty-four hour wait until the next time. Afterwards he thought back over every word she said to wring the last drop of meaning from them.

Worse, much worse, he suffered the misery of jealousy every time he thought about his rival, the dashing Freddie Foxwell, former rugby captain at the College, a crack shot and successful farmer. Oliver Biggs said that Freddie was only interested in Sonia's money and property but he knew better. He knew from the way his old school chum had kneaded her jeans with his big farmer hands that he was just as interested in her body.

Even when exhausted after his night's labours he could not sleep through jealousy, and the fear of losing Sonia to the neighbour whose joined-on land combined with hers would make them married owners of twelve hundred acres. An infinitely better match for her than a bumbling unwaged college lecturer whose bright future was already far behind him. He found to his dismay that he was no different from any other lovesick halfwit who cannot prevent himself uttering words of banal stupidity that only make a hopeless situation worse. The best education the nation could provide had not delivered common sense along with its other benefits.

So one night, instead of a pleasurable embrace, he gripped Sonia jealously by the arms. 'Oliver said you had lunch with Freddie Foxwell yesterday.'

'Ralf, that is my business. Nothing to do with you.'

'You don't let him kiss you, do you? Do you?'

He sounded so anguished that Sonia took pity on him. 'No, Ralf. I don't.'

'But he tried? He's a bad man for women, everyone knows that. Please don't let him kiss you. There's no telling where he might have been.'

'That isn't a very nice thing to say about Freddie. After all, you were at the College together.'

'If he asks you again you can tell him you're going to marry me. That should shut him up.'

'You're hurting my arms.'

'Tell me! Tell me! I've got a right to know. I thought I had heard the last of poxy Foxwell. I never want to hear you mention his name again.'

So began their first quarrel. Sonia did her best to calm him down. She refused to speak until he had relaxed his grip and then said, 'Ralf, you know very well that I am not going to make any plans for the future until after Uncle's birthday. And probably not even then.'

He was distraught. 'I won't have changed my mind. I'm in love with you, Sonia. I want you to love me.'

'It's too soon. I keep telling you.'

'You think I'm going to back out when the time comes. That's what you think, isn't it?'

'No one would blame you. It's easy to make promises.'

'What more must I do to convince you?'

'I didn't ask you to fall in love with me.'

'You mean you don't want to make a commitment. You don't want to get hurt. Well, I've got news for you. It's not something you can avoid, Sonia. Everyone gets hurt where love is concerned.'

She began to cry. She had almost cried on other occasions but managed not to, and now could not prevent herself. Between sobs she said, 'I was happy before you came up here to live. I wish you had never come.'

He was desolated to see her cry, and hear such words spoken. He knew that she was confused, angry and unhappy, and that he was responsible. He felt like crying himself and could not have been more miserable at the wretched way he had ruined his great romance. He was immediately contrite and tried to coax her into an embrace, telling her he was sorry. She dried her eyes but refused to let him touch her. She said, 'Ralf, it's time to stop this. I don't want you to kiss me any more.'

This had the effect of calming him down completely. He realised that he had been getting more and more hysterical and suddenly came to his senses. By now he understood Sonia well enough to know that having said it she would never change her mind.

Anxious not make the situation worse he offered a quick apology. 'I should never have talked you into it. Sorry, Sonia. It was my fault. I realise that now.'

They stared at one another without speaking, uncertain how to part. It suddenly seemed very cold in the dimly lit hallway. Ralf was shaken to realise how badly he had mishandled the whole affair from start to finish. Because of his higher education and his twelve years in a nice part of London he had believed himself superior to the homespun farming folk of High Beckles. Even if he had taken care not to show it he had felt it, and his behaviour had been inexcusable. He had been smugly over-confident and conceited, quite sure that his big city expertise in making love to women would make it equally easy for him to seduce Sonia as he pleased.

First the pride and then the fall because in spite of her sheltered life and limited experience she had behaved much better than he had. Now that it had come to an end he was deeply ashamed of the way he had coerced her into such a demeaning arrangement. Far from being clever he had humiliated a proud woman and she was unlikely to forgive him in a hurry. If ever. In which case he would have only himself to blame.

'What will you do now?' he asked her.

She shrugged and forced a smile. 'Someone has to go with Uncle. I shall take it in turns with Jed.'

'That won't be easy.'

'He can't go on for ever. Thank you for what you did, Ralf. It was a big help. I'm sure we can manage on our own from now on.'

Ralf needed to think quickly. Was the situation retrievable? He thought it might be. So he said quickly, 'No need to do that, Sonia.'

'Oh? Why?'

'I made a commitment to you, and I shall honour it. Of course I will.'

'You will?'

'The end of January, I think you said. I can handle that.'

'You don't have to.'

'I know I don't have to but it would make me feel better. I shall stick to your Uncle Dick like glue until he decides to pack it in. I can't promise to keep him in one piece until his birthday but I shall do my best. Leave it to me, Sonia. I'll look after him for you.'

Without giving her a chance to refuse his offer he turned and walked quickly away. As he had done every night since their arrangement began, the only difference this time was that tonight there had been no kiss. Instead of shutting the door behind him Sonia followed him out into the covered walkway. She stood with her hands in the pockets of her coat watching him make his way towards the kitchen entrance.

He sensed her continuing presence and looked back. They stared at one another from a distance. She was standing alone where he had left her, on the cold stone-floored dimly-lit passageway. At that moment they seemed a long way apart.

20

The break with Sonia came just before Christmas so any hopes of a festive cuddle had to be forgotten. Ralf remained subdued for a long time after the quarrel, knowing that he had only himself to blame. It had been a chastening and dispiriting experience.

To honour his promise to Sonia he soldiered on as Shillabeer's second-string minder. The Witch had spent the whole of her life keeping him out of trouble, he settled for being her assistant. He no longer bothered trying to stay in touch with the outside world and concentrated on survival instead. Never had High Beckles seemed so cut off from mainstream civilisation as it did during that long winter. News of conflict, disasters, sporting triumphs and celebrity scandals never reached them, and would not have interested them if they had.

On a livestock farm one day is much the same as another so Christmas came and went with little change in the routine. Sonia he saw only at a distance. She had her own part of the house upstairs and stayed there rather than come down to the kitchen. Sometimes he saw her Land Rover parked in a gateway as she sat looking out over a ploughed field. Farming was a lonely occupation. What she was thinking about he could only guess.

Unfortunately for him the shooting season continued without a single break. Shillabeer pursued his craft relentlessly while everyone else made merry, not wishing to miss a moment. He rubbed his hands at the thought of Christmas Eve and Christmas Day, two days ripe for plunder as the entire workforce of the area stayed indoors for the annual booze-up, an orgy of over-eating and self-indulgence.

Not that Queenie stinted on the eats and even though

utterly miserable and lovesick Ralf scoffed his share of the Christmas goodies. Shillabeer offered him a cigar and Jed got drunk, the twin highpoints of their yuletide revels. He made his daily visit to Northbeck, spending as much time with his father as possible. It was the first Christmas they had shared together for many years, and was also likely to be their last, not something either of them wished to mention. Whatever lay ahead they preferred not to know.

'All worked out for us in advance,' was his father's opinion, frequently repeated. 'Pointless to worry about any of it, Ralf. What is to be, will be.'

In this way the holiday season came and went, it disappeared swiftly into the past, leaving not a trace behind. The weather in January was atrocious, testing Ralf's resolve to the limit. With every night that passed he reminded himself that the shooting season must surely be coming to an end, which meant his ordeal did not have much longer to run. Or so he hoped.

He should not have allowed himself even to think such things because their worst night of the winter was about to happen.

The night in question began like any other. Queenie took it as a personal compliment that he was visibly putting on weight, most of it solid muscle because of all the hill walking and carrying. She claimed the credit for her cooking and Ralf sat down at the long oak table to give his full attention to a plate of beef casserole with dumplings. This was followed by baked apples and custard, a huge slice of cherry slab-cake, and a mug of heavily sweetened coffee boiled up with milk from the two house cows.

Shillabeer dozed with a gun across his lap, opening his eyes every so often to nod indulgently while Ralf stoked up at the refectory table. The grandfather clock in the corner had a melodious but jangled chime, as though played on a harpsichord. When it struck ten the head poacher began to yawn and stretch and rub his eyes. This was the signal for the Witch to uncoil herself from her malodorous basket beside the stove

190

and report for duty. He scratched her head affectionately and she sighed with pleasure.

'Oliver and his wife have got another nipper on the way,' he informed Ralf. 'Number Six by my reckoning. I think he intends to go on until he's got himself a football team.'

Ralf had made it up with his College friend after quarrelling with him and was suitably impressed on hearing the news. 'I must buy him a drink next time I see him. And ask him what his secret is. Plenty of people would like to know.'

'He keeps on to me that we can't keep him supplied with enough pheasants. Quite a little industry he's got there. He puts a plastic wrapper and a fancy label on them now and sells them to the supermarkets. Fresh, frozen or ready roasted he still says he can sell everything we bring him and wants more. With a wife and all those kids to support I expect he needs the money.'

Ralf was not surprised to learn of the hard-up butcher's good stock-getting record. While still at school he concluded that only regular, frequent and strenuous sexual intercourse would cleanse his blood of the impurities which caused his endless crops of boils. A fortunate man to have an ambition so easily realised. Not that he was entirely sympathetic, and said so to the head poacher. 'Selling pheasants is a lot easier than carrying them home. I reckon Biggs owes me. What do you think?'

'I think it's time for work. Are you ready?'

'Have I ever not been ready?'

'Let's shift ourselves then. They're getting away out there.'

But Ralf was in no hurry to leave the warmth of the kitchen and insisted on finishing his scalding hot mug of coffee before slowly dressing himself and buckling on his carrier harness. Since his quarrel with Sonia he had no kiss to look forward to, his father was stepping up his campaign to return home, the weather was atrocious and there was no end in sight to the poaching season. With little to smile about he forced himself to appear cheerful and willing.

'Got the necessary?' Shillabeer enquired politely, handing him the gun. 'Don't let me run out of ammo, Ralf.'

He patted his pockets. 'Unless you're planning a war we're well supplied.'

'Good. Where shall we go tonight? How about Bellwether Hollow?'

'Are you serious? That's miles away.'

'The last time I paid my respects to that nice little copse at Bellwether they were lined up for me side by side like a chicken roost. It won't take us long once we get there. A lot of big fat tame old birds sit the winter out very quietly down at Bellwether. I intend to give them a big surprise.'

'I still think it's too far.'

'We've got all night. What time is it now?'

'Half past ten.'

'What's the weather like?'

'Raining. Need you ask?'

'Shall we go? Standing here arguing won't make either of us rich.'

'You're the one doing the talking. Let's get on with it.'

They set off in their usual procession, Shillabeer swanking in front, the Witch trotting daintily in the middle, and Ralf the walking game larder bringing up the rear. It started to go wrong almost immediately. The heavy showers of rain had alternated with a drying wind, the end product being mud as thick and sticky as glue. It clung to their boots and made walking slow and tiring. The last lap of a long and arduous journey was across a ploughed field, and it was so slippery that they both fell.

'At least we've arrived,' Shillabeer whispered. 'What's the time now?'

'After midnight. I told you it was too far in this weather.'

'That's bad,' he agreed. 'Considering that we've got to walk all the way back again. The Witch isn't happy about it either.'

'That's because the poor creature can't see where she's going. You'll have to buy her a pair of spectacles to go with her white stick and her bus pass.'

'I can't see where I'm going either,' Shillabeer admitted. Since leaving the farm it had become progressively darker and they could hardly see one another a foot apart.

'Why take risks? The only sensible thing to do is to go back home. And even that won't be easy.'

'Can't see a fucking thing,' he agreed, still trying to make up his mind. In the end he opted to shoot, as Ralf knew he would. 'We've hacked it all this way. Might as well have something to show for it. I feel lucky tonight.'

'You say that every night.'

'We'll go once round the outside and then pack it in. Can't risk getting into the trees, we should never find our way out again. Ready with the lamp?'

Slowly they worked their way down one side of a long narrow copse. Ralf shone his lamp into the trees but could not find a single pheasant. The Witch continued to grizzle and whine and refused to leave Shillabeer's side, which made him irritable. Instead of ranging ahead she made it clear that she was lost, and Ralf knew that if she was lost they were all lost. He was not pleased, and said so. 'Let me know next time you feel lucky. I'll stay at home instead.'

'No need to be sarcastic. If you're so smart perhaps you would kindly lead the way back to the farm.'

'If the dog doesn't know, how do you expect me to know?'

'Uphill,' Shillabeer decided. 'That's usually right.' He handed Ralf the gun to indicate that the expedition was over. 'Let's hope to Christ that it doesn't start raining again.'

It didn't, but they made even slower progress than on the outward journey. The first field they came to was maize stubble and they had no choice except to plod laboriously across. The earth was soft, they sank in with every step, by the time they reached the far side they had slowed to a wretched floundering crawl. The nail-paring of a moon had long disappeared, it was impenetrably dark and achingly cold with a freshening wind. To add to their misery it began to rain again.

'That was all we needed,' Shillabeer wailed, taking it personally. 'And not one miserable bloody pheasant to show for it.'

They came to a gateway and flopped down for a rest, all three equally dead beat. Shillabeer lit a cigarette and tried to console his wretched dog, who seemed to be blaming herself for the predicament they were in. They stayed a long time gathering strength, also hoping that the sky would lighten. It did briefly, just enough to give them a fix.

'Got it,' Shillabeer said. 'I don't know how but we've ended up not far from Claypits. See those farm buildings over there, where the light is showing? I reckon that's Skinners Farm. They milk three times a day at funny hours, I think I can hear the machine running in the milking parlour. Just finishing up the third milking by the look of it. Or starting the first one perhaps. But at least we know where we are.'

Ralf groaned. 'If that really is Skinners Farm then we're farther away than ever. We must have been walking in the wrong direction.'

'No point in sitting around. We've got to hoof it back again. Ready?'

They trudged off, walking three abreast this time so as not to get separated, but were soon confronted with another choice. They arrived at a T-junction and needed to select right or left. They agreed on left but half a mile later the road forked again and they had to choose a second time.

'I don't know,' Shillabeer admitted. 'I'm not sure that was Skinners Farm after all. I just don't know where we are.'

'We can't go on walking in circles. There must be a building around here somewhere. We shall have to shelter up for the night.'

'Get going then. Let's hope we can find a place.'

It was too dark to see much but after they had plodded a slow mile the road widened, and they could see the outline of houses. This revived them and they walked a little faster. All might still have ended well but just at that moment the heavens opened and the rain came down with enough force to make them stagger.

Ralf had seldom experienced rain like it, there was absolutely no escape. It teemed down hard enough to make them gasp with shock. Even the angry gushing sound was frightening, like a mountain torrent sweeping aside everything in its path. They could scarcely see, their eyes and faces deluged with water, their clothes clinging to their bodies as if they had fallen into the river.

They stumbled on, heads down against the driving rain which swept over their feet in clay-coloured foam. They had forgotten about their trusty minder but ever dutiful she had gone on ahead as usual then suddenly reappeared through the downpour and advised a change of direction, growling an urgent warning.

Hardly able to believe what they were seeing they froze in their tracks as a party of men in gleaming oilskins loomed out of the rain in front of them. They were carrying powerful hand lamps which were soon aimed straight at them. Who the men were Ralf never found out because he turned and fled in an instant.

Shillabeer cursed and would have stood his ground but the Witch fled too so he swore viciously and legged it after them, having little option. Immediately they started running there were shouts and calls for them to stop, and the sound of running footsteps in pursuit.

They came to a big house with an open drive and charged up it panting for breath. They ran right past the house and into the garden where they blundered through some flower beds, overturned a seat but made it safely to the far end where they clambered over a fence and escaped their pursuers. Once more they found themselves in a darkened field and kept going until they reached the other side where they collapsed to their knees in exhaustion.

'The sods,' Shillabeer wept. 'Any ideas? They looked like soldiers out on night exercises.'

'The postman told me that one of the villages is flooded. Council men were out late last night putting down sandbags.

Could have been them.'

'You shouldn't have gone bolting off like that. I hope you've still got my gun.'

'It's here.'

'If we knew where we were we could hide it and come back for it later. Tell me the time.'

'Two o'clock, straight up.'

'There must be some shelter around here somewhere. Lead the way, Ralf. Even a pig sty would be better than nothing.'

They did eventually find shelter of a sort, a double tier of giant round bales of straw stacked up in the corner of a field. With the gun and a few kicks Ralf dug out a big enough space at the bottom for them to crawl in between two of the bales and escape from the rain.

Shillabeer had enough spite left to curse but the Witch was completely exhausted. She wriggled in beside them and slept as though dead.

21

Thus they saw out the night, and a long dark cold wet night it was too. Ralf found that the Witch gave out a pleasing warmth, and her smell was bearable, given their situation as bedfellows in adversity. Shillabeer soon fell asleep and eventually Ralf went under himself, in spite of being wet, cold and miserably unhappy.

He was woken towards dawn by a familiar sound, or at least one he had heard all too often in London and elsewhere, but seldom in the beleaguered outpost of High Beckles. A giant airliner crossed the sky slowly, lights flashing, pacing itself for a long journey. He could picture the scene on board as the passengers settled down to enjoy the flight.

Where were they going? It was a huge plane, and from the sound of it, heavy with fuel. In ten hours it could be landing on a strip of blinding runway in a land of perpetual warmth. A land where the sea was blue, and where bronzed bare-legged women strolled languidly along the beach. Ralf stirred uneasily, trying to free his mind from these unsettling thoughts. Having been celibate for many months, and committed to more of the same in the months ahead, he preferred not to agitate himself unduly and switched his mind to less distracting matters. Dick Shillabeer, for example.

The sound of the airliner died away but it had been a reminder of the outside world that never seemed to intrude on Shillabeer and his robber kingdom. Even a war made little impact since they never read a newspaper and were too busy most of the time to watch television. The inhabitants of High Beckles were marooned in their own ageless community where time was suspended and a century here or there made little difference in the scheme of things. The space age had come and gone without them noticing, the microchip had made no impact on their lives, the Internet still less, but the print slots of a deer's hoof seen near the farm would occupy their thoughts and conversation for several days.

Shillabeer still slept and Ralf could only hope that his immune system would see him safely through, inching him another notch towards his eightieth birthday. The first of May seemed an eternity away at that moment, and his survival by no means certain, given his irresponsible behaviour. Why did he make life so difficult for everyone? There had to be a reason and Ralf gave it some serious thought.

Partly mischief and partly vanity, was his conclusion. Shillabeer knew that he was putting his loyal entourage to a great deal of inconvenience but still insisted on being allowed to indulge his disruptive hobby. All done with silvery charm but fuelled by an anarchic sense of mischief. He was vain, a show-off, always needing to prove his cleverness. He had perfected a method of stealing game birds from his neighbours, mostly from the estate. The birds were well guarded so it took nerve as well as consummate skill to get away with it, and he was hooked on the excitement of the chase.

Shillabeer knew that it exasperated his niece, and strained the patience of Jed and his mother, who had long ago ceased to find his exploits amusing. Ralf now realised why he had been made so welcome. Shillabeer was pleased to recruit someone more easily impressed, someone who could fully appreciate what a clever and unusual old man he was. On that point Ralf had to concede. Whatever his faults, and they were many and varied, Sonia's delinquent uncle was quite a guy.

When at long last the sky lightened they crawled out of their cave of sodden straw and trekked once more uphill in an attempt to orientate themselves. It was no longer raining but the air was damp with low cloud and mist, and their clothes were wretchedly cold and wet.

'What time is it?' Shillabeer enquired.

'Just after six.'

'Still not working?' he asked next, referring to Ralf's

mobile phone.

'I'm afraid it isn't.'

'Modern technology. Always lets you down when you need it most.'

Ralf was too dejected to answer back. He had been trying ever since he woke up but either the battery was flat or the signal was too weak and he could not get it to work. He blamed himself because it was an old phone in need of replacement. He had been negligent in not doing so and had only himself to blame. Just at that moment he would have liked to pound it into little pieces between two heavy stones.

'Well?' Shillabeer prompted him. 'You're the one with the eyesight. Worked out where we are yet?'

Ralf pulled him round to follow a point. 'Down there, can you see? That's Huckle church.'

Shillabeer flinched on hearing this. 'Are you sure?' When Ralf nodded he groaned aloud. 'That's five miles from home.'

'More like six.'

'How did we get this far off course? I can't make it back, Ralf.'

'Sure you can. Three miles an hour. We shall be indoors eating breakfast by eight o'clock. We shall only catch pneumonia if we stay here talking.'

'Try your phone again.'

Ralf obeyed, cursing as he did so, but it was hopeless. It would not work and he closed his eyes in despair. Shillabeer tried hard to conceal his disappointment but took Ralf's arm and they moved off slowly, the lurcher bitch trailing miserably behind them. They made steady progress but after about ten minutes it suddenly started to rain again. Rain so heavy and prolonged that they had no choice except to seek shelter.

'Up there,' Ralf said, pointing to a clump of stunted trees. It was a good decision because the clump contained a yew tree which provided almost complete protection against the rain. Better still there was a fallen branch on which they could sit down and recover their breath after scurrying uphill as fast as their legs would carry them.

'I've had it,' Shillabeer admitted. 'Sorry, Partner. Can't walk another step.'

Wearily Ralf tried his mobile phone once more, shaking his head in despair. 'We should never have gone out last night. This is all your fault.'

'Is it my fault your phone won't work?'

'No,' Ralf conceded, watching the rain sweep in sheets across a sodden hillside. 'It's my fault for listening to you.'

'Quarrelling won't get us anywhere.'

'You're the expert. What do we do now?'

'We send the dog for Sonia.'

'How?'

'Best way out of this little difficulty. It's not too bad here. We can sit it out until Sonia arrives. Better than walking six miles in the rain.'

On hearing this Ralf had another try with his phone before bowing his head in utter despair. 'I don't believe this is happening to me.'

Shillabeer hastened to mollify him. 'Don't be cross, Ralf. You're right, we should have turned back last night. I should have listened to you.'

'You didn't. You never do.'

'It won't take long if I send the Witch. Bear up.'

'What do you mean, send the Witch? How can she tell Sonia where we are?'

'Couldn't be easier. We're on the old rabbit warren above Marchants Farm in Huckle. Sonia knows where it is. She bought some calves off them a couple of years ago.'

'Maybe she does know where it is but how can the Witch tell her this is where we are? Come to that how can you be sure the Witch even knows where we are? One rabbit warren is probably much the same as another if you're a dog.'

'The Witch wouldn't get it wrong. Knows the district too well for that.'

'I've got a better idea. You stay here and look after the dog while I leg it back to High Beckles and come back for you in the Land Rover. An hour and a half, less probably. How about that?'

'The dog will be a lot quicker. Leave this to me, Ralf. Sonia will be picking us up in an hour so that's what I'm going to do.'

Ralf was sceptical to say the least as he watched the Witch receive her instructions and then set off after a touching farewell embrace. She had been standing disconsolately beside him, her tail curled so far round in dejection as to be out of sight. Eager to redeem her reputation she turned her silvery snout downhill and limped off into the mist and gloom of a foul January morning. She was soon lost to sight and Ralf was left alone with the downcast robber chief.

They waited, and they waited. After an hour Ralf said, 'You should have written a message in blood and tied it round her neck.'

'She'll do the business all right. Be a bit nicer to her, Partner. She knows you're one of the family now.'

'I'll give her until eight o'clock and then I start walking.'

'No need to do that. Ralf, I've got a treat in store for you. As soon as we're finished with the pheasants I'll ask Sonia to take you out with the Witch to show you how we catch deer. How about it? One day soon?'

'It's got to be better than this.'

'Hares and deer, that's what the old girl does for a living. Helping me with the pheasants gives her something to occupy her mind during the winter.'

'It's time she drew her pension. You'll finish her off with all this running about.'

'It would break her heart if I left her at home one night. I shall never have the patience to train another dog to do all the things she can do. Don't spoil it for us, Ralf.'

'Oliver Biggs is putting me to an awful lot of inconvenience. He must be getting more out of it than he lets on. I ought to check the prices he charges his customers. His mark-up must be considerable. He wouldn't be so keen on it otherwise.'

'I don't begrudge him his profit. Life is hard for the independent butcher.'

'It can't be that hard if he can afford to make his wife pregnant every year. You keep saying he wants more. I think he's had more than enough of my time already.'

'I think I would sooner have the time than the money. Biggs is short of one and I'm fast running out of the other. Don't grow old, Ralf. It's no joke, I can assure you.'

'I'll try and think of an alternative. For your information another hour has passed. Would you like me to go in search of your dog? She must be well and truly lost by now.'

Shillabeer was too miserable even to reply. He put his hand in his pocket for a cigarette but produced only a sodden squelch of cardboard which he threw down irritably. He started to droop. 'I shall have to wait for Sonia now that I've sent the Witch. But you can go, Ralf. No point in us both dying of pneumonia. Leave me the gun and the belt. That will put you in the clear.'

Ralf tried hard not to keep looking at his watch but the minutes crawled past and they were still sitting it out under the yew tree. 'No doubt the Witch is curled up fast asleep in her basket by now. Nice and warm beside the stove.' He sighed in despair. 'How did I ever let myself be talked into this?'

'Be fair, Ralf. You didn't know anything about pheasants, did you? Admit it. You've learned a lot from me, one way and another.'

'Mostly another. Come on, it isn't raining quite so hard now. Can you make it down as far as the church? You can sit in the porch while I fetch help. A taxi will be quickest.'

Ralf had suddenly realised that the masterful Shillabeer was waiting to be told what to do. Obediently he stood up and took Ralf's arm. He swayed and looked shaky for a moment, then stepped out into the rain and they started walking together down to the church which was about half a mile away.

They had not gone many yards when they both heard it.

The sound of a four-track vehicle heading in their direction.

Hardly daring to believe that it was coming to their rescue they stopped to look and soon afterwards saw a pair of powerful headlights shafting through the rain and low cloud. They heard the toot of a horn, in this case the musical sound made by Sonia's shiny new Land Rover climbing effortlessly towards them. A few seconds later she had drawn up alongside. The Witch was sitting in the passenger seat, peering anxiously through the windshield to see if her master was intact and well.

'Nice work, Sonia,' Shillabeer said with heartfelt sincerity, greeting her with a kiss as she stepped out to join them. 'Not a minute too soon.'

'I was out with the sheep. I came as quickly as I could.'

'Of course you did. And bloody glad we are to see you, too. Aren't we, Ralf?'

'We surely are.'

'Queenie packed a box. It's in the back.'

Ralf lifted it down for her and Sonia produced a thermos flask containing a litre of heavily-sweetened scalding-hot coffee, pouring it into two big mugs. Ralf had not realised how cold he was until he felt that coffee going down inside him. He held on to his mug with both hands until he stopped shivering. 'You've just saved my life,' he told Sonia. And he meant it.

'Biscuits,' she said next, handing them round. 'Here you are, Ralf. And you, Uncle. You'll be okay now. I'll tell Queenie to run you a hot bath as soon as we get home.'

'Whatever you say, Sonia.'

Ralf was glad to be rescued but flinched from her displeasure. If he was supposed to be nurse-maiding her uncle then he had not done a very good job and was guilty of dereliction of duty. He needn't have worried because she was too busy taking charge and asserting herself to scold as well. It was girl power in action, driving cross-country to the aid of two hungry, dirty, bedraggled and exhausted men. He thought she was entitled to look just a little pleased with herself as she doled out the rescue biscuits.

'What went wrong?' she asked her uncle.

'Don't be cross, Sonia. Things didn't go according to plan.'

'We got lost,' Ralf admitted. 'It was a very dark night.'

'Lost? Where did you get lost?'

Ralf was about to reply irritably that if he knew that they wouldn't have been lost but thought better of it when he got a whiff of the boss lady's lemony perfume as she came close and refilled his mug with coffee. He had enough sense to realise that she was not blaming him. She seemed relieved to find that her uncle was alive and apparently none the worse for his ordeal. And might yet make it round to his eightieth birthday party.

Shillabeer was embarrassed at needing to be rescued, but recovering fast. 'Got anything else in that box, Sonia?' he enquired, putting an arm round her waist.

He brightened visibly when she handed over a packet of his favourite cigarettes and a bottle of gin sent by the faithful Queenie. 'This will keep the cold out,' he rejoiced. He opened the door and climbed into the back seat, being promptly joined by the Witch who came and snuggled up beside him. 'You can finish off the coffee, Ralf,' he told him. 'You've earned it.' He lit a ciggie, put his arm round the Witch, took a long swallow from the gin bottle and then held it up in salute. 'Beautiful! Beautiful!'

He slammed the door and this left Ralf alone on a desolate hillside with Sonia Shillabeer. It was a month since their quarrel in the stone passageway, and the first time they had spoken face to face. There was a brief moment of awkwardness, the memory of their nine o'clock kisses not something either of them was likely to have forgotten. Ralf certainly hadn't, each one was still individually fresh in his memory, and he suspected, and hoped, in Sonia's memory also.

He said, 'Thanks, Sonia. For galloping to the rescue. You saved the day.'

'You look as if you have both had a rough night.'

'It was very dark. We didn't have a clue where we were. And the bloody mobile wouldn't work. Not one of our finest hours.'

'I don't suppose it was your fault. I've never known Uncle be lost before.' She permitted herself a rueful smile. 'Old age must be catching up with him at last.'

Ralf pointed to her Land Rover where they could see him sitting in the back, drinking gin with his arm clasped round the dog. He did not look like a man at instant risk of death from hypothermia but Ralf was genuinely concerned, having now become quite fond of him. He swallowed the last of the coffee, then shook the drops from his mug. 'We had a lot of rain in the night. He needs some dry clothes as soon as possible.'

The cold misty morning suited Sonia's complexion, she was a good advertisement for the benefits of a cool climate on the female skin. He thought she looked lovelier than ever. Nor was she moving away, and seemed to be offering a reconciliation.

She said, 'I must get him back to the farm. You too, Ralf. Or neither of you will make it round to next summer.'

'It seems a long way off on a day like this.'

At the last moment, with her hand on the driver's door, Sonia asked curiously, 'Why do you get on so well with my uncle, Ralf? There has to be a reason.'

'It's easy. We dislike the same people.'

She considered this for some time before saying, 'That sounds stupid enough to be true.'

'It is true.'

'He likes you. You like him too, don't you?'

'Yes.'

'Jump in then. Let's get going.'

They spoke very little during the journey, but it was not a strained silence. Ralf was happy again, hardly daring to hope that by keeping his half of the bargain Sonia had forgiven him and was ready to make it up. He turned round to exchange rueful smiles with Shillabeer who still sat with the gin bottle in one hand and his other arm round the dog. He was not surprised to see that the Witch was also more than a little pleased with herself. He thought she was entitled to look smug, having played a big part in their rescue.

The longer he had to think about it the more Ralf was impressed. He knew the Witch was intelligent but guiding Sonia back over several miles of open country from the passenger seat of a Land Rover required cleverness of a much higher order. He had been trying to work out how it could have been done, so far without success, and admitted as much.

He said, 'Sonia, you must tell me how the Witch did it. How she explained to you that we needed help. And then directed you back to us. I should really like to know that.'

'It's a family secret.'

'Of course. I should have known better than to ask.'

'It's a good thing she could or you would still be walking.'

He was intrigued, and persisted. 'At night then, tell me this. When she goes off on her own to check ahead, how does she know in advance where we're going? How do you direct her? How does she communicate with you when she comes back? Please tell me.'

To which she replied, 'One day. One day I'll tell you, Ralf. One day I'll tell you lots of things.' And with that he had to be satisfied.

22

Two days later Ralf was in a good mood because he had been given the night off. Shillabeer had left with Jed on a long journey in the big cattle truck and would not be back until the next day. Nights off were few and far between so he had kept a long-standing promise to have dinner at the Bear Hotel with his old College friend Oliver Biggs.

First he made the daily visit to Northbeck to see his father. Although his father had never been reconciled to living there and still wanted to return home, Ralf had to concede that the hospice was doing its work well. All institutions however benevolent have their methods of dealing with the awkward squad and absorbing them into the system. His father had soon been persuaded to stop smoking and no longer smelled of tobacco and the farmyard. His greasy old hat had disappeared, along with his working clothes. The cardigan and slippers which had looked so out of place at first now fitted him comfortably.

Nor could Ralf imagine him taking his guns to pieces and cleaning them any more. It had taken a while for him to be softened up but it had happened. Now when he visited, for the first time in his life, he knew himself to be bigger and stronger than his father. A discovery that gave him no pleasure.

So they had both changed. And both noticed the changes, not difficult in his case because he had suddenly grown tired of his long hair. On a trip to the town he had visited the barber's shop and had it removed and clipped down short instead. His father's bristly grey stubble on the other hand had been allowed to grow out, and his hair was now neatly parted and fluffily clean. It was a reversal of fortunes as far as their hair was concerned, and for both of them it altered their appearance considerably as a result.

'You're looking very smart and up together, my son,' his father said admiringly. 'Going somewhere? Got a date, perhaps?'

'I have. But not with Sonia, if that's what you're thinking.'

'Not another woman, you don't mean?'

'Don't look so alarmed. No, I'm meeting Oliver Biggs for a meal tonight. At the Bear Hotel. I treated myself to a new shirt.'

'Very smart it is, too. Give Oliver all the best from me.'

'I will.'

'I hope you have a nice time and enjoy yourself. You deserve an evening out. The food is good at the Bear. Your mother and me used to eat there quite a bit after you left home. To save her having to cook all the time.'

'I'm pleased that you were able to have quality time together. I know you both had demanding jobs. Nice for you.'

'Never went there much afterwards. Not after she died. Didn't fancy sitting at a table eating on my own.'

'Dad, you're making me feel guilty again. I'm sorry I was never part of your life after I left home. Or mother's life. I must have seemed very ungrateful after all you had both done for me.'

'Not entirely. We should have liked a bit more contact, of course we would, but the whole point of being parents is to get your children safely out into the world and making a go of it on their own. You seemed to be doing all right so we were happy for you.' He gave a wry smile. 'Mother always said that we should hear from you soon enough if you weren't all right. That's true of all children away from home, isn't it? However old they are.'

'Yes. I guess most people head for home when they're in trouble.'

'You're an understanding sort of person, Ralf. Sometimes I think you're like me and other times I think you're more like your mother. Funny old game, genetics. Even doing it with sheep and cattle isn't as easy as it looks. People who try for improvements usually end up with worse animals than they started with.'

'You said it yourself, Dad. Fate deals the hand for us. We just jump through the hoops.'

He grunted and nodded agreement, then got slowly to his feet. 'Off you go and enjoy yourself. Don't hang around in this dreary bloody place any longer than you need to.'

'It can't be too bad. Where else would you find a wine and spirit merchant who delivered to your door?'

'God bless you, my boy. Hand it over.'

'It must be a good hiding place you've found,' Ralf told him as he passed across the flat half-bottle of brandy and took the empty one in exchange. 'That's it, Dad. Now you're stocked up again I'll be on my way.'

'Notice how much lighter the evenings are now?'

'I haven't forgotten my promise.'

'As soon as the weather warmed up, you said. It can't come too soon for me. Most of the bulbs in the flower beds should be showing through by now. I don't want to miss anything. You know how much that garden means to me.'

'I do, Dad. I do. Not long now. Be patient for another week or two.'

Ralf knew that his father retained a strong visual memory of the garden at Orchard House and remembered where everything was planted. He wanted to hear the bees around the hive, see the plum tree in blossom, and walk up and down the long brick path beside the border. Ralf was committed to making it a reality for him.

The brandy might not be what the doctor ordered but the conspiracy against authority had kept his independence alive. He had tried hard not to become institutionalised and was determined to return to the Orchard House as soon as he could persuade Ralf to arrange it with the doctor.

Ralf was sympathetic. He could not see much evidence of the peace and tranquillity that was supposed to reconcile the inmates to their fate. They all looked pretty glum about it to him, none more so that his father who hadn't wanted to be there in the first place.

He had other reasons to be cheerful. The shooting season was coming to an end and in spite of the odds stacked against him he had not only survived the ordeal but come out ahead. Constant exercise combined with Queenie's cooking had done wonders for his health. Lack of sleep was no longer a problem, his muscles had developed to cope with the work, and best of all he began to experience a sense of physical wellbeing. He felt good, and people were starting to tell him that he looked good, so at least he had something to show for his lost year.

On his way back to the main road he stopped the car. There was a gap in the scenery which allowed him a distant glimpse of the High Beckles farmhouse. He sat looking at it for several minutes, turning over some thoughts in his mind.

It was a pleasingly large and rambling house, with many rooms. The oldest part was built of stone, and was certainly of medieval construction. The next oldest section was built of small narrow bricks from the late Tudor period. Succeeding generations of Shillabeers had built bits on in a higgledy-piggledy fashion, in all directions, rather like joining up words at Scrabble. The result was a lovely old house and he could understand why they were so proud of it and never wanted to leave.

There were twenty rooms at least, and that was not counting all the built-in cupboards and wardrobes, the big walk-in larder, the many brick outhouses, and the covered courtyard. Inside, rooms opened up unexpectedly out of one another. There were short flights of steps to level up the floors, and little corner landings. There was a cellar below and an attic above, it was a miracle that the house had survived virtually intact into modern times.

Some of the solid doors in the oldest part of the house were beautifully made and swung on big brass hinges, with handles worn smooth with age. There was a wide wooden staircase, the banister handrail polished by daily use over several centuries. In the central entrance hall, which was paved with smooth stone slabs, stood an iron-bound wooden chest with the date 1685 and the initials SS carved on the lid. The chest had belonged to a Silas Shillabeer and Ralf could understand why Sonia with the same initials worked every waking minute to secure her inheritance.

Ralf allowed his imagination to run on a little. He was thinking what an enchanting house it would be for children to grow up in. A house where the future present merged with the ongoing past. This was because nothing was ever thrown away. Every room was stuffed with belongings from members of the family who had died long ago, and who therefore in some way still lived on through their possessions. He had not been all over the house but had seen enough to know that every drawer and cupboard contained bundles of letters, diaries, recipe books and similar articles that would be of great interest to a historian. More poignantly perhaps he had seen a baby's crib, a rocking horse and other toys and trinkets that had not been played with for many years.

It had been a house without children for as long as anyone could remember. What had happened to those huge Victorian families for whom the house had been enlarged? How would it respond to a new family of children running round exploring its hidden treasures and secret places? Children with him as their father and Sonia as their mother? He thought it would be pleased.

There is dreaming, and there is reality. Sometimes the two overlap making it difficult to be quite sure which is which. Sometimes dreams can be turned into reality and to this end Ralf applied his mind. His father inclined to the view that everything was predestined and would happen anyway. He was less sure, although willing to be convinced. A little luck, a helping hand, a lot of perseverance and some judiciously applied pressure to the backside of circumstance, and who knows?

It might then happen the way he wanted it to happen.

23

'It's tax deductible,' Oliver Biggs assured him as he studied the menu in the Bear Hotel. This had a stuffed black bear in the entrance hall and was the town's best known hotel. 'Entertaining business associates. That's a legitimate expense, isn't it?'

'Absolutely. Don't stint on me, Oliver.'

The butcher proudly eased his paunch under the table. 'We come here for the Chamber of Trade, always eat too much. And drink too much on Lodge nights. My wife keeps on to me about it but I like my food. Always have. You won't catch me going on a diet.'

'There is nothing wrong with food and sex, Oliver. In moderation, of course.'

'Who said anything about moderation?'

'Who said anything about sex? Let's not lower the tone of the conversation.'

They had already enjoyed drinks at the bar before taking their seats in the restaurant, with the result that Oliver Biggs was even more jovial and red in the face than ever. He laughed at everything that was said and beckoned Ralf to lean forward. 'I expect you're wondering why I wanted to sit on this side of the table.'

'Tell me then. Why did you want to sit on that side of the table?'

'So that I've got my back to the bar. So that I can't see the barmaid.'

'Is there something wrong with her?'

There was a bar at the end of the restaurant and two young people serving drinks, one male and one female. They were both dressed in regulation black and white, and looked crisply smart. One was a youth, slim and spiky-haired, the other a young woman who carried a bit more weight. Much of it straining open the buttons of her blouse.

'Never seen breasts like it on a young girl,' the butcher complained. 'They shouldn't allow it, I've a good mind to complain to the management. I try and look the other way when I'm buying drinks. It's a wonder I haven't gone cross-eyed.'

'Everyone else looks at them. Why not you?'

'Because they upset me too much, that's why. I didn't want to be put off my food while I was eating.'

'What you need is a hobby. Look what it's done for Dick Shillabeer.'

'I know what I need mate, and my wife won't let me. She goes right off sex when she's pregnant. I'm not going to be able to last out.'

'Lusting after barmaids is nothing to be ashamed of. No need to feel embarrassed. It's part of the British way of life.'

'It's easy for you to say that, Ralf, not being married. Honestly, it makes me go all weak and funny inside to think of the endless hours of happy sex fun you could have with a girl like that.'

'Fantasy. Easily the best sex you can have.'

He heaved an ulcerous sigh. 'You're right there, mate. We get a lot of women in the shop and I've fantasised about having sex with just about all of them at one time or another. It's good fun being a butcher if you like women. It's a wonder I haven't amputated half my fingers, the state they get me in. They like to watch you handling their meat. The more you slap it around the better they're pleased. You should hear some of the things they've said to me. Respectable women, too. You would have been shocked, my boy, deeply shocked. But not half as shocked as their husbands would have been if they could have heard them.'

'Say no more. I'm easily shocked myself.'

'I suppose you knew we were expecting again?'

'Shill told me.'

'We've got four already. Or is it five? My wife would

213

know.'

'Yes, I expect she would. Women tend to remember things like that.'

'How am I ever going to support all those kids, Ralf?'

'With difficulty, I should imagine.'

'You're a big help.' He sighed once more. 'My wife is keen enough on having sex when she's not pregnant, but because of that she soon gets pregnant again, the silly cow. Do you think a marriage guidance counsellor would help?'

'No.'

'You're probably right. Oh well, I shall just have to console myself with this steak. While you sit there and feast your eyes on the barmaid's tits.'

As they ate Ralf looked around with interest. Even if it was long past its red-plush heyday the Bear Hotel still prospered in a thriving market town where there was plenty of disposable income. It was a good feeling to have his knees under a restaurant table again. It was another little reminder of the real world that existed outside High Beckles. How long would he have to live there before he lost touch himself? It was a seductive place and he warned himself not to let it happen.

'How's Tom getting on up at Northbeck?' the butcher asked him. Ralf was not surprised to find that his big red friendly face still bore the scars of the endless crops of boils he had suffered in an over-ripe puberty. His skin was a pitted moonscape of acneous craters.

'Doesn't like it,' Ralf replied, in answer to his question. 'Wants to come out.'

'Not very likely, is it?'

'The doctor is agreeable, actually. There isn't any more they can do for him and provided I'm willing to look after him they are going to let him leave as soon as it's a bit warmer. I've promised to make it happen. Not long to wait now.'

'My Dad died two years ago. Had colon cancer, poor old bugger.'

'Not a nice thing to have wrong with you.'

'It certainly wasn't. He wanted to die at home which meant I had to hire nurses to look after him. It cost me plenty but I didn't begrudge it to him.'

'It's a grisly business, dying. Wherever you choose to do it.'

'You can say that again. My old man lingered and it wasn't very pleasant. He had several strokes and then pneumonia, the medicine men should have had the decency to ease him out while he still had some dignity left. But they didn't, they even brought students along for a free look because according to their text books he should have died the first time. I threw them out but they only sent more.'

'Oliver, I'm glad you told me that. I'll make sure it doesn't happen to my Dad.'

'I admire you for standing by him, and looking after him. You gave up a lot to do it, we all realise that.' He poured some more wine into Ralf's glass. 'I did the same for mine. Went to see him every day, just like you do up at Northbeck. The doctors let him suffer in my opinion, and I hated them for that. I cried like a baby when he died. Not that I would tell anyone else. A father is special, isn't he? Got to be.'

'Every time.'

'Anyone who tells you that death is easy is a liar. You'll find out.' They had finished their steaks and turned their attention to the sweet trolley. 'Enough of this serious talk.' He pointed to a multi-layered trifle swimming in an acid-green liquid. 'That trifle looks just the ticket to me. You've got a good digestion, haven't you? I'll ask for two big portions.'

Ralf thought it looked absolutely awful but spooned it up without making a fuss. The butcher was good company and it was nice to have a friend in difficult times. He said, 'Thanks for the meal, Oliver. Very generous.'

'You've been a big help with our little deliveries. I owed you.'

'It's called diversifying. You're doing the right thing.'

'I shall remember that if we have a run-in with the law. I

shall tell them I was only diversifying.'

'Never forget the two magic words, Oliver. The first is 'natural' and the second is 'organic.' Keep repeating them and they can't touch you.'

'Sonia and me have had some serious discussions lately. On much the same lines.'

'Tell me. I should be interested to hear.'

'We've been thinking of a joint venture. A game department. Deer, hares and rabbits, pheasants, partridges, snipe, woodcock, even grouse. Reared in a natural environment, no antibiotics or anything like that, and fed only on natural foods. Sonia would do the rearing and looking after them and I would do the packaging and selling. Could be a nice little earner. What do you think?'

'It could be an idea whose time has come.'

'I've got to do something soon, us old-fashioned butchers are on the way out, fast. But I enjoy being in business and a game farm would be right up my street. Pretty much what we're doing already, if you think about it. Only we need to do it properly. Sonia knows that.'

'But her uncle doesn't?'

'Sonia won't do anything until he has his birthday. Which reminds me of something I was going to put to you as a suggestion.'

'Put it to me then. I'm a good listener.'

'Uncle Shill is going to be eighty on the first of May. The big Eight-O. Think he'll make it?'

'Nothing more certain.'

'One way and another it's going to be a big day and I thought we ought to celebrate it in style. A party would be nice. What do you think?'

'I think it's a great idea.'

'You're only eighty once and I'm quite fond of the daft old sod. Not exactly your typical eighty year old pensioner, is he?'

Ralf raised his glass. 'To Uncle Shillabeer's trigger finger.'

The butcher laughed. 'I take it you're in favour. Could you

mention it to the ladies? We should have to hold it at High Beckles and they will be doing most of the work. Tell them I'll provide all the booze.'

'I'll tell Dad about it, too. He'll be home by then. Something for him to look forward to.'

'That's settled. Good. I like a party. Let's make it one to remember.'

Having eaten they should have been sensible and gone home. Instead they stayed until closing time and had far too much to drink. Needing to visit the Gents before leaving they went together. On entering Ralf had a surprise.

The Bear Hotel had well-appointed cloakrooms, including a large wall mirror over the wash basins. Woozy with alcohol Ralf's brain refused to accept what his eyes were seeing. Of the two men in the mirror he could identify the one on the left, recognising his old College chum Oliver Biggs, the & Son of Biggs & Son Family Butchers. There could be no mistaking his big red face but who was the man on the right?

His father's house possessed little more than a shaving mirror in the bathroom and a dappled wood-framed looking glass in the hall, neither of which had prepared him for what he was seeing now. It was a sobering experience because he had expected to see his old self and was startled to see someone else staring back at him. He leaned down and dashed some cold water into his face before trying again, but with the same result.

He found that he was looking at a younger version of his father. Hair short, eyes steady, jaw firm, a real man at last, muscular and weather-beaten. Could this really be the same Ralf Lassiter puffing and blistered when he tried to saw a log in a summer long gone? The pale academic with the long hair, the faraway expression and the diffident smile? It was, it was, and in a moment of insight he realised that there had been other changes besides those he could see in the mirror.

'Are you all right, mate?' the butcher enquired, also splashing his face with cold water in an attempt to sober up. He was aware that Ralf stood as if transfixed, leaning forward and staring at his reflection in the mirror.

This was because he was experiencing some uncomfortable moments of truth, among them that his cherished PhD did not count for much in High Beckles, a place where he had little to be conceited about. Most humbling of all had been his bittersweet romance with Sonia Shillabeer, failing to treat her with the consideration and respect due to a proud woman.

On the credit side by caring for his father he had behaved honourably and learned to feel compassion at the same time, not an emotion he had experienced before. He reckoned that by learning these painful lessons he had gone some way to redeeming himself, in his own eyes if not the eyes of others. More importantly he knew who to thank. Whatever their other shortcomings the eccentric inhabitants of High Beckles had lost no time in making a man of him.

24

Next morning Ralf was woken by a loud bang.

Or more accurately by a gunshot beneath his bedroom window but at half-past seven in the morning after a night out and far too much to drink it sounded like a mortar shell landing. Holding on to his throbbing head he staggered to the window, opened it and looked out.

There was sufficient light to see Sonia Shillabeer with a gun held up in her right hand, her finger still on the trigger. Standing guard beside her the Witch looked on with interest as he groaned and said, 'Did you fire that gun under my window to wake me up?'

'What are you waiting for, Ralf? We want you to carry for us. Quickly, it's getting light fast.'

'I've only just gone to sleep.'

'What sort of excuse is that? Are you always like this in the morning?'

'Sorry, Sonia,' he muttered, still holding on to his head. 'You wouldn't believe how terrible I feel right at this moment. I couldn't possibly.'

'Hurry up and get dressed. My turn with the gun doesn't come round very often. I don't want to miss it.'

Squinting at her through puffed-up eyes he said, 'You don't mean that thing, do you?' Pointing to the gun she was holding. He recognised it from the collection in Shillabeer's gunroom, a beautifully made twelve-bore shotgun with a sidelock action, one of a pair, a best gun worth as much as a new car.

'What's wrong with it?' she asked, a trifle edgily.

'It makes a loud noise. That's what's wrong with it.'

'How much longer are you going to talk to me through a window? Get a move on, Ralf. You look as if a walk in the fresh air would do you good.'

As his eyes grew used to the early morning light he saw that Sonia was wearing a cartridge belt round her waist, and on her head what appeared to be one of her uncle's cloth caps. Something about the confident manner in which she wore it reminded him of the boastful robber chief swaggering about with his thumbs hooked jauntily in his waistcoat pockets. He expected to get his own way, and usually did, and it looked as though Sonia intended to carry on where he left off.

She had fancied a couple of hours out and about with a shotgun under her arm, looked round for some free labour, and had not hesitated to rouse him from his slumbers with a barrel under his bedroom window. Having claimed his attention she was now ordering him to dress immediately and fall in behind her, and to be quick about it. He knew that he should have refused on principle, making it plain that he had no intention of being bossed about by her or anyone else.

But he didn't. To a man wearing only his underpants, and who had been celibate for many months, the presence of the woman he loved beneath his bedroom window was as much as he could bear. His bed was still warm, he was alcohol aroused and in the mood. How hard would she resist if he ran downstairs and carried her back over his shoulder? Would she give way gracefully? Or would she shoot him?

He swore with frustration and called out that he was dressing as fast as he could and shortly afterwards joined her outside, shivering slightly in the chill wind of a winter morning.

He said, 'Are you sure this is a good idea, Sonia? It's almost light, people are going to hear the bangs and come after us.'

'It's Sunday morning. People get up late.'

'Gamekeepers?'

'They will think they imagined it and go back to sleep.'

'Forgive me, but I don't find that answer very reassuring.'

'You can stop worrying, I'm not going to shoot on the estate. I fancied a try at those tall trees on Galley Hill. It won't take us long if we cut across the top of the park.'

Ralf did not argue but it was still a test of nerve he could not afford to fail. Cutting through the park meant passing close to the house where Captain Ives lived. He could only hope that no early risers were pulling back their bedroom curtains at that very moment. Forcing himself not to appear nervous Ralf plodded dutifully in the boss lady's footsteps as she strode past the backs of a row of estate cottages. He could see lights, which meant that people were already up and about.

He had come to trust the head poacher but was not so sure about his tooled-up niece, however much he loved her. He was wearing his belt with the loops, his pockets were full of short pieces of farm string cut to length, plus a knife and spare cartridges. 'Going equipped', as the clerk of the court says when reading out the charges. Having survived for so long he was fearful to be caught just as the shooting season was coming to an end, and it couldn't come too soon for him. He heaved a sigh of thanks when they finally made it out of the park and off estate property.

Galley Hill was a noted beauty spot, the road zig-zagging to reduce the gradient. It was a dangerous place, often closed after a gale when a tree was certain to fall and block the road. The soil was only inches thin, held together by tree roots, with a steep overhang at the top.

'Up there,' Sonia said, pointing to some towering beech trees with her gun. 'A lot of fat old birds think they have been very clever sitting out the winter in those trees. What do you think, Ralf?'

'I think it was a decision they will soon regret.'

'They will if I can move up a bit higher. They're going to roll all the way down into the road. Can you get down there with the Witch and pick them up for me?'

Ralf wisely made no promises. The hillside was even steeper than it looked through the windows of a car, more like a cliff in some places, and the soil was loosened by recent rain. Sonia was already half way up, but having difficulty. She dislodged showers of stones which in turn forced the local wildlife to wake up and flee in alarm.

Rabbits bolted, squirrels leaped from tree to tree, foxes slunk away and magpies screeched angrily. Pigeons zoomed out of every overhanging thorn tree making a tremendous clatter, helped on their way by a blast from the gun. This made the pheasants fly too, she called out to Ralf that one had been hit. It had come speeding from a tall tree when it was hit, a spectacular shot. With the result that it fell about two hundred feet, landing in some bushes on the other side of the road.

'Fetch it for me,' she called down to him. 'Over there.'

Obediently Ralf darted across the road and retrieved, although not before an indignant motorist had trumpeted angrily. Even on a Sunday morning there was a steady flow of traffic and he feared for his life. Sonia shot two more in quick succession but they landed softly and rolled downhill, the Witch fetching one while he scrambled after the other.

Dislodged stones trickled down past him and two fat roe deer skipped one behind the other across the road, forcing a lorry to swerve. It was hard to see how one young woman with a gun could wreak so much havoc on the local environment in so short a time.

'That's enough, Sonia,' he called out in alarm as a loose rock headed in his direction. 'Come on down.'

'No, you come up!' she shouted back, pointing behind him.

A police car with a flashing blue light was approaching rapidly uphill, most probably responding to an incident rather than pursuing them. Ralf did not wait to find out. Fear gave him wings and with the Witch by his side he shot up the steep slippery slope on his hands and knees as though pursued by a mad bull.

'Are you quite crazy?' he yelled, as she started shooting again before the police car was out of sight.

A boundary hedge had formed at the top and the pheasants who lived there were obligingly committing suicide by planing downhill. This was not the smart option with Sonia

222

Shillabeer lying on her back blasting them out of the sky. She only stopped firing when he arrived alongside, accompanied by the Witch.

Looking cross she said, 'I suppose you want to go home already? I've hardly started.'

'Police cars make me nervous.'

'I don't fancy going down. Can we get out over the top?'

'It's almost vertical just above us. We shall need to move sideways a bit.'

By now the sun had risen and it was a bright frosty morning with crystal-clear visibility. Sonia stood up and slithered between the trees until she was near the top and began looking at the overhang to find an escape route. As she did so she lost her footing and slipped.

Ralf saw her come sliding towards him and flung out an arm. He managed to grab her cartridge belt, which slowed her fall. They began to slide together and might have gone all the way down but instead lodged up against a small tree trunk which brought them to a stop. They were safe, and could fall no farther.

It took a few moments to sort themselves out, freezing where they had landed in case they fell again. Sonia was holding the gun aloft in her left hand, while Ralf's right arm was anchored across her body clutching at a tree root. He found it a very agreeable position, her body half pinned under his, their faces almost touching. Perfectly placed for a kiss.

Ralf stared into her upraised face and wild eyes, and at her body panting after exertion. When she realised what he was going to do she tried to twist herself free, struggling up against his restraining arm. Ralf was only human, and therefore unable to resist temptation. He thought it was high time he asserted himself. He had had enough of being bossed around by Sonia Shillabeer, so he held her down, lowered his head, and kissed her.

It was no ordinary kiss.

Slowly, slowly, she let go of the gun so that she could put her arms round him. It became one of those long yielding orgasmic kisses that leaves both partners weak and shaken. Everything seemed to go quiet afterwards, all the clamour and commotion suddenly stilled.

He removed his arm and helped Sonia to sit up, then brushed away some of the dead leaves and twigs and loose earth from her back. Neither of them spoke. There was really not much more that needed to be said.

Slowly she picked up her gun, Ralf gathered up the pheasants, and the Witch offered to show them the way home. Sonia said, 'She's worked it out. Let's go.'

They followed the dog who led them lower down the hill where they were able to pick up a sunken green lane between tall hedges. It was a longer route but it was safer, and they began the slow trek back to High Beckles.

They were still subdued after the kiss. Ralf did not want to say the wrong thing but could not think of the right thing to say either, and wisely kept quiet. When they were able to walk side by side he placed his hand on Sonia's waist. She let it stay.

All journeys however long or short come to an end. Soon they were back where they started, at Orchard House. He had been carrying the gun for her and handed it over as they prepared to part. For the first time since he told her that he loved her he sensed that she was in a receptive mood. She had always avoided any serious discussion of how the future might work out for them. After the kiss on the hill she was ready to listen.

He said, 'One day we could be going home together. That would be nice.'

'It needs a lot of thinking about, Ralf. We're two very different people.'

'Sonia, what's yours is yours. I shall always want to earn my own living. I'm well qualified and there are a lot of different things I can do. You needn't worry that I might want to be part of the farm. We could live together and still lead separate lives.'

'That's what needs thinking about. I'm not as sure as you

are that it would work.'

'We could make it work. If we really loved one another.'

'So long as you're prepared to wait.'

'Does that mean we have an understanding?'

'An understanding? That sounds very solemn.'

'It's a solemn matter we're discussing. I don't want to lose you, Sonia.'

After a long hesitation she said, 'All right then. We'll start going out together after Uncle's birthday. That isn't long to wait.'

'And until then?'

'It would be better if we didn't keep seeing one another. To avoid complications.'

'I'll agree to that. If that's how you want it.'

Whether she believed him or not it was to be a day of surprises. He felt a warm and wet sensation and on looking down found that the Witch had licked his hand. A sign of affection he had never expected. She had been reading their body language, and seen the kiss for herself. Yet another on the matchmaking team, and one indicating approval. He gave her a pat and she moved closer.

Sonia said, 'There's just one thing I want to say.'

'Yes?'

'I won't hold you to your promise. Not if you need to change your mind later.'

'You mean if my father dies?'

'You might feel differently when the time comes. I know how much working in London meant to you. I wouldn't want you to stay here and be miserable just because you had promised.'

'Oh, I'm the faithful sort, Sonia. I won't change my mind.'

'Whatever happens I shall always remember all the nice things you said to me.'

'I meant them. I haven't said them to anyone else.'

They were still standing close together, with the dog companionably by their side. The time had come to say goodbye and go their separate ways but because he could sense that Sonia was still in a receptive mood Ralf pointed to the top of Beckles Hill. He said, 'One day in the summer when we get a few warm days I'm going to build a fire up there. I've got a sheltered place looked out, a little hollow between the yew trees and the burial mounds.'

She was curious in spite of herself. Understandably so, since the hill belonged to her. 'Why would you need to make a fire?'

'Because I should like to make love to you on the hill. At night, under the stars.' Adding by way of explanation. 'The fire would be to sit by afterwards.'

He thought she was not going to comment but after a long pause she said, 'I'm sure it's very romantic. But not very comfortable if you don't mind me saying so.'

'We won't know how uncomfortable it is until we try. Well? What do you think of it for an idea?'

'You have a wonderful imagination.'

'Don't smile, I'm serious. Love under the stars, a fire to keep us warm. What could be nicer?'

Instead of answering his question she put a hand on his shoulder and gave him a quick kiss on the lips. She said, 'That's for being so good to your father. Even if it doesn't work out for us I shall always remember that you came home to look after him. That's worth something, isn't it?'

Then turned and walked quickly away, the Witch trotting faithfully at her heels.

25

Just when Ralf thought that things were starting to come right for him he had a nasty surprise. Delivered along with the morning mail by their local postman.

He was a man cordially detested for miles around, a nosy-parker and troublemaker by the name of Sid Pike. He may have been disliked but people were scared of upsetting him for fear that their mail would go astray. No one wanted to take the risk, Ralf among them. Sid Pike was a self-appointed ombudsman, marriage counsellor, righter of wrongs and mediator in family disputes.

Having handed over Ralf's letters the postman sat himself down at the kitchen table where he accepted a mug of tea and a slice of marmalade toast. While munching the piece of toast he put on his glasses and had a methodical look through his bundle of mail. He scrutinised handwriting, held letters up to the light, inspected them back and front, weighed and assessed, read all the post cards and circulars, examined stamps and mused on the contents. A man from whom few secrets were hid. Bland and sly-eyed, his cheeks badged with ginger fur, he had found exactly the job that matched his big interest in life – other people's business. He was straight out of children's fiction, Postman Weasel, the enemy of all. He had the ingratiating politeness of the blackmailer. If you had a secret you could be sure that Sid Pike knew it too.

By way of parting conversation he said, 'Your Dad's old chum Captain Ives isn't very happy with life just at the moment.'

'Why is that, Sid?'

'He had a bollocking from the big house. Didn't like it much.'

'Had he done something wrong?'

'The boss man and his rich pals haven't had very good sport this year. Ives got his arse kicked, and serve him right.'

Ralf suddenly felt a lot less pleased with life. Trying not to sound or look worried he said, 'Explain a bit more.'

'Hasn't been half the pheasants in front of them there should have been. Hardly any on some drives. Mind you, if they could shoot a bit straighter that might have helped.'

'Foxes, perhaps?'

'The gamekeepers had already shot most of the foxes round here so he couldn't keep blaming it all on them. Big losses, Ralf. Ives was told to do something about it. Or else.'

'I'll ask my father. He might know.'

'Poachers, Ralf. A gang. That's where the pheasants have gone. And like I said, the Captain has been forced to do something about it.'

Ralf could feel his headache coming on again. He felt sick, too, but did his best to sound unconcerned. 'What makes them think it's a gang, Sid?'

'It's too well organised to be anyone local. They've always lost pheasants, but not on this scale. It's got to be a gang.'

'What sort of a gang?'

'I'll tell you this much, I shouldn't like to get in their way. With all these motorways and fast cars they could come from any of the big cities. Villains, Ralf. Ruthless. Anyone tackling them is likely to get the chop. If you ask me that's why our wankers of gamekeepers never catch up with them. Too scared.'

Ralf was scared too, and with good reason. Shillabeer was already pursuing his hobby into February, well past the end of the shooting season, and showed no signs of wanting to stop. Not only illegal but unsporting as well. Sonia had told him to pack it in, but he refused. Ralf was equally annoyed and threatened to withdraw his labour, only for Sonia to implore him yet again not to let her uncle out of his sight.

Which meant that if Shillabeer went he would have to go too. A chill sense of foreboding suddenly spoiled his breakfast. Something of his father's fatalism had been preparing him for the catastrophe that had been programmed in from the start. Trying hard not to betray himself he enquired, 'What did you say the Captain is doing about it?'

'There's always been deer poaching round here, and sheep rustling. They can live with that but the pheasant losses have been enormous this year. Pheasants are hard to get at in any numbers, and these are better guarded than most. How this gang managed it is a mystery. Hundreds and hundreds of birds they must have shot this winter and carried away.'

'It's serious then?'

'Ives has organised a round-the-clock surveillance team to try and catch them. Crookwatch. That's his code name for it. Says he intends to catch the poachers once and for all and put them behind bars.'

'Sounds a bit drastic.'

'I agree with you there, Ralf. Putting everyone else to a lot of trouble to cover up for his own incompetence. Typical. He should have done something three months ago. A bit late now.'

'Who told you all this?'

'They think it's a big laugh down in the village. Check points, passwords, just about the Captain's level, that is. A real Dad's Army with him in charge. Walks around with a pair of binoculars on his chest. He'll be wearing his medals next.'

'When are they starting?'

'They made a dummy run last night, by way a trial. I'm surprised you haven't heard about it. Combined Ops. They've roped in the Young Farmers Club, the darts team from the pub, the allotment holders, the bell-ringers, you never saw such a pantomime in all your life. Tonight the Women's Institute are going to run a soup kitchen in the village hall, so it's a bit of fun for them too. Tell your Dad about it, Ralf. It might cheer him up.'

'Thank you for letting me know,' Ralf replied, and he spoke the words with complete and utter sincerity. He thought it had been a providential discovery, and the moment he could get rid of the postman he intended to cross at once to the farm and inform Shillabeer that his evening expedition would have to be called off.

Sid Pike snapped the elastic band over his bundle of letters, folded away his glasses, brushed the toast crumbs from his chest and pushed back his chair. Before leaving he unburdened himself still further.

'The Captain and his guvnor in the big house have got friends where it matters, and favours to call in. The last I heard the police were offering to put their helicopter on standby. The boys in blue take poaching more seriously than you might think. It's theft, it's nightwork, and it's guns. Oh yes, you can depend on it. They'll catch them now the toffs have had their sport interfered with. They'll catch the buggers even if it takes half the county police force and a couple of million quid to do it. But if someone breaks into your garden shed and steals all your tools they tell you they don't have the resources to combat rural crime, and hard luck. Am I right? Or am I right?'

'Oh, you're right, Sid,' Ralf assured him. 'You're always right. Thank you for telling me. Thank you very much indeed.'

As soon as he had driven off in his red post van Ralf hurried in search of Sonia's problem-child of an uncle. She had taken the day off to attend a farm sale and so would not be there to hear from him the postman's alarming news. The sale was many miles away, she had left early, and was unlikely to return until late in the evening, and if delayed not until the next day. She suspected that her uncle was up to something and had asked Ralf not to let him out of his sight until her return.

Jed was tucking into a big fried breakfast and Shillabeer was spreading marmalade on triangles of toast when Ralf clanked open the latch and entered the kitchen. Still in an agitated state of mind he began telling them about the Captain's plans for catching the villains who had been poaching game from the Beckles Court estate.

Shillabeer had been reading through his post while he ate and peered at Ralf over his tiny spectacles. He made calming gestures with his hand. 'Not so fast, Ralf. I'm having my breakfast. What Captain Ives gets up to in his spare time is nothing to do with us. Sit down and have something to eat.'

Ralf ignored this and repeated his warning. 'They think it's an armed gang at work. Half the village is turning out to catch us. Doesn't that worry you?'

Predictably Shillabeer was less impressed. 'You've been listening to the postman again. No need to take any of that seriously.'

'Too damn right I'm going to take it seriously. So should you.'

'You're not telling us anything new. They always say it's an armed gang. Do I look like an ex-SAS man? Do you?'

'The time has come for you to choose a new hobby. The sooner the better. Tonight would be a convenient time to start.'

Shillabeer treated him to a patient smile. 'If they think it's a paramilitary gang then they won't be looking for us, will they? Who is going to believe that you and me shifted all those birds? No one. Not in a month of Sundays. So take it easy, Partner. No need to get all worked up and excited.'

'Sounds a bit of a laugh to me,' Jed added as his contribution. 'Bronchitis is all they'll catch. If it starts to rain they'll go home. Not many people can stick a whole night out of doors.'

Ralf had been exasperated and spoken forcefully but was soon reduced to pleading with Shillabeer instead. 'You promised Sonia you wouldn't go out while she is away from the farm. There's even more reason not to go now that I've told you about the vigilantes ganging up on us. No point in taking unnecessary risks.'

Shillabeer looked puzzled. 'What risks are we talking about now, Ralf?'

'I'll tell you what risks. It's Captain Ives, his two gamekeepers and the estate workers and the tenant farmers and the shooters from the clay-pigeon club. All men who can handle guns and would love to use them on us, given a chance.'

'No need for you to concern yourself, Ralf. The Witch and me can handle it on our own for once. Take the night off.'

Ralf gave up. He knew Shillabeer well enough not to go on arguing a lost cause and returned to the Orchard House even more agitated than when he left. Something seemed to tell him that this was the night when it would go horribly wrong, a dead weight of apprehension that stayed with him throughout the day.

So when night fell it was with a heavy heart that he once more clanked open the iron latch at High Beckles. Only to find that Shillabeer had changed his tune. Artful as ever he was at his most soothing and reasonable. 'Just an hour out with the gun, Ralf,' he wheedled him. 'We'll be back long before Sonia gets here. I don't want to upset her any more than you do.'

'Pike wasn't kidding about the vigilantes. They really are out in force tonight. I've checked.'

'It needn't interfere with us, just a bit of fun for the villagers. They're polishing up their badges because they think they're going to catch a gang. They always blame it on a gang. Everyone does. They write articles about poaching in the posh Sunday newspapers and it's always a gang. They never learn.'

'You speak as though it has nothing to do with us. But it's us they're talking about. Us they want to catch. I'm not sure you understand that.'

'Don't spoil it for me, Partner. Next winter I'll find myself a different hobby, and that's a promise. Christ knows what but I'll think of something if it will make you and Sonia happy.'

'How many times have you promised that, I wonder?'

'Be a pal, Ralf. One last time.'

'It's too risky.

'I shall be eighty years old on the first of May, you know that, don't you? The Witch has finally had it, too. God damn it, do you suppose we want our fun to come to an end?' Shillabeer put his hand on Ralf's arm. 'We always knew there had to be a last time but we've been putting it off. Just once more and then we'll pack it in for good.'

On hearing her name the Witch's ugly snout appeared from under the table, her opaque malignant eyes reminding Ralf that a little token dissent was fine so long as he backed down quickly and did the master's bidding. Shillabeer was determined to go and short of sedating him or locking him up Ralf had no choice except to go with him and try to keep him out of trouble.

So he gave way and soon they were making their usual procession out of the farmyard and following his favoured route through the yew trees and juniper bushes on the steep slope of Beckles Hill. Ralf's ears were finely attuned now. He could recognise the short sharp bark of a vixen, and most of the other animal sounds, often borne so quickly on the wind that they passed by as swiftly as the darting hares and silent night rooks flapping through the darkness.

Their route took them close to the ancient burial mounds on Beckles Hill and as always he pondered on why the Shillabeers loved the hill so much. Just owning it was not enough, there had to be a better reason, and the obvious one was that they belonged there as of right, through ancestry and continuous occupation. Sonia's wayward uncle obviously thought so, perhaps his father did too. Old hilltop settlements exert a spell on those with respect for the past and Ralf felt its bewitchment more strongly than ever. The dark mysterious remains of the ancient yew grove, the long dead ancestors in their burial mounds, the running of the deer and its fleet-footed huntress made it a magical place where the hours and the centuries passed as one.

To prove it Shillabeer swaggered in front more jauntily than ever with his thumbs hooked in the pockets of his green quilted shooting waistcoat. Sonia had told him 'no', Ralf had told him 'no' but once again he had got his own way and hummed a triumphant little tune to celebrate his victory.

Behind him his pathfinder dog also trotted proudly, another delinquent pensioner who loved the hill, her tail curled back between her back legs in a flourish of italic script.

Ralf toiled behind with the gun. When Shillabeer waited for him to catch up he said, 'No need to tell me. You feel lucky tonight.'

Shillabeer felt lucky every night so it was a true statement and they walked on again, allowing Ralf to resume his train of thought. He was thinking about Sonia, and the kiss on Galley Hill. He could recall at will the smell of the loose earth, the slither of stones, the rough grasp of the tree root, the sound of the gunshots still ringing in his ears, and Sonia's warm body panting with exertion pinned under him. Bright morning sunshine and her eyes wide open in alarm as his intention to kiss her became clear. But what a kiss! It had been a long passionate heart-and-soul kiss that had haunted him ever since. Because it was a betrothal kiss that bound them more closely than a hundred legal documents. A kiss from which there could be no going back.

He had promised her a wedding fire on the hill, a promise he had every intention of keeping. It was an idea that pleased him, even if a touch pagan. Incantations to the moon, well they would have to be optional, but making love to a wild and beautiful huntress under the stars, with a fire to sit by afterwards, should be more than enough to keep the ancestors happy.

Romantic, too, and not just a one-off. No, it was something they could do for many years to come. And in the fullness of time, when they grew too old to make love outdoors, they could still light a fire and watch the moon and feel close to the ancient people buried there. He had told Sonia of his plans and whether she believed him or not at least she knew what was in his mind.

So he smiled to himself as he trooped along behind the robber chief. There is a time for dreaming, and a time for reality. But which is which? Occasionally but not very often the two overlap and merge, making it difficult to be sure.

26

'Cats,' Shillabeer mused aloud as they walked along a field-edge path side by side. 'No friend of the pheasant. A cat with a taste for pheasant chicks can do a lot of harm on a big shoot. Did you know that, Ralf?'

'No. I did not know that. Along with most other people, I suspect.'

'Some of those big rats are almost as bad. A determined rat will clear a nest of chicks one after the other until they're all gone. Stoats, weasels, badgers, they all have their share, and foxes have more than their share. Hedgehogs, too. They eat the eggs, shells and all.'

'They do?'

'Then there are the hunting birds, they like a share too. Sparrow-hawks spot the chicks as soon as they start to move, a real menace they are. So are owls and crows but gulls are the worst. They eat anything dead or alive and they just love pheasant chicks. A gamekeeper has many enemies, Ralf. Many enemies and few friends.'

'Which category do we come in?'

Shillabeer ignored this and continued with his lecture. 'Pheasants that live in the wild don't suffer from much but idiots like Captain Ives have spoiled things by using so many antibiotics and other medicines. Wild birds are hardy and can fend for themselves but there's too many of the other sort around now.'

'I've heard my father say the same.'

'Penned birds get the roup, that's an infection of the lungs. Coccidiosis is nasty too, you can always tell it because their eyes close up. Erisypelas, that's inflammation of the skin. Fowl cholera is worst though. Always fatal that is.'

'Doesn't sound much fun, being a pheasant. Why am I not

surprised?'

'Blackhead used to be a problem but they don't seem to suffer with it so much these days. Partridges can get trike,[1] not that you see many grey partridges these days. Trike is serious, they go on eating as if nothing was wrong but lose all their flesh. A lot of young birds have the gapes, it's caused by worms. You need the vet to deal with those two particular problems.'

'Thank you for explaining it to me.'

'I promised you that I would tell you about some of the things pheasants have wrong with them, but I kept forgetting. Old age, Ralf. It's a bugger.'

'The alternative is worse, believe me. '

'Perhaps you ought to make a study of the pheasant and its ways. Vicious little sods they are, pecking one another's eyes out the second they leave the shell. Nature's way, isn't it? Survival of the fittest.'

'Not many pheasants survive when you're on the warpath.'

'I haven't finished telling you about the things they can have wrong with them, such as white diarrhoea. Nasty, that is. They suffer with parasites, too. Lice for one, red mites for another. Real pests they are because there isn't much you can do about them. It's a constant battle. Bad weather. Disease. Predators. So you see, Ralf, game birds don't have it easy all the time.'

'Or any of the time if what you're telling me is true. I expect the local pheasants wish you had chosen a different hobby for your old age.'

'You talk too much,' Shillabeer said sourly. 'What's the matter now?'

Ralf had come to a stop at the end of the field and drew something to his attention. 'The moonlight,' he said, pointing upwards. 'Take a good look.'

'You're right, Ralf. It's a long time since I've seen it this bright. That weather forecast fellow on the telly needs an ounce of lead shot up his bum, and I'd like to give it to him,

---

[1] Trichomoniasis

the number of times he's got it wrong lately.'

'Where were you heading?'

'Shearcroft. There's an old willow tree down by the river that is always full of birds at this time of year. Know where I mean? There's Swanmead on one side of the river and Shearcroft on the other.'

'Too far. You promised a short walk.'

He paused to consider. 'We've been making good time because of the moonlight. It's not a very big willow tree but if I'm in luck there will be all you can carry. Step it out, Partner. I've got an itchy trigger finger tonight. I think we're in for a good haul.'

Ralf did not like what he was hearing, and feared the worst. Shearcroft was on the wrong side of the river. It was easy enough to cross over as they descended the hill but once down into the valley their escape route back to High Beckles would be cut off.

A thick white mist was drifting over the river when they arrived. With the mist had come frost, a stinging white rime, achingly cold on the ears. They stumbled along the uneven river bank but soon Shillabeer had to admit that he did not know where they were. The dazzling moonlight shining on the swirling mist made an impenetrable barrier and closed them in. Ralf could see nothing on either side. He was not happy, and said so, forcefully.

'You never hear me swear,' Shillabeer reproached him. 'Pass me the gun, I think this is the tree I was looking for. If not it's one very much like it.'

'It's almost ten o'clock. We were late starting out and it's time to go back already.'

'Oliver can still sell them. It's easy money.'

'You wouldn't like it if Sonia got back first and found you out with the gun.'

'You worry too much, Ralf. This won't take us long.'

He had already boasted that he intended to shoot cock birds only to give the hen birds a chance to recover their breeding numbers. Whether it was the right tree or not it served his purpose equally well. The wretched creatures craned their necks to lean over curiously and peer down the spout of his gun. Because it was so light other birds began to fly, a pigeon rocketed out with a tremendous clatter, making him curse. The Witch lost control and began to plunge about in the reeds where the low willow branches trailed into the water. Ralf hissed at both of them to calm down.

At the same instant a church clock struck the hour.

It was Long Beckles church and Ralf had heard its metallic clanking chime too often in his bedroom at home to be mistaken. The moment it started striking Shillabeer seized his arm in a panic. With good reason. Because of the thick white mist they could not see the church, or indeed any other buildings or lights, but the chimes were so loud and so close that they both knew instantly they could not possibly be anywhere near either Shearcroft or Swanmead. Two places much farther up the river where the clock would have sounded faintly in the distance.

'Bloody hell,' Shillabeer swore. 'Where are we, for God's sake?'

'I don't know either,' Ralf admitted, taking the gun away from him. There could be no doubt that they had strayed deep into enemy territory and ended up in the park close to the big house itself. Worse still they knew they were on the wrong side of the river. They stared at one another in horror, knowing they were in imminent danger of being caught, but not sure which way to run.

They dithered until the sound of the last stroke died away. Even then it seemed to go on ringing in Ralf's ears. It was not a particularly melodious chime for the clock of a medieval village church but it had plenty of muscle and continued winding its way down the frost-chilled river valley in a prolonged and slowly fading echo.

In a surge of adrenalin-charged panic they turned their backs on the river and fled uphill. Soon they came to a long narrow clearing between two pheasant coverts that gave them a fix. It was a feature known as the Long Ride but instead of ambling horses it saw three scared poachers running for their lives.

The moonlight was so bright that the trees cast a shadow. They were almost at the top when the Witch snarled a warning. They froze in their tracks and saw the black outline of approaching men, their guns and sticks clearly visible against the skyline.

All three responded in the same instant. Shillabeer, Ralf and the Witch turned and ran back downhill the way they had come. They had almost reached the bottom when they saw a second line of men advancing from the opposite direction. Trapped. They heard shouts that told them they had been spotted and heard the roar of engines starting up. Powerful headlights shafted in their direction and Ralf suddenly discovered that he was very, very frightened.

'Well?' Shillabeer asked him as soon as he could draw breath. 'What do we do now, Partner?'

'If it's all the same to you, Mr Shillabeer, I don't think I want to be a partner any longer. Would you accept my resignation, please.'

He was too out of breath to reply, panting heavily with his head between his knees. They had hurried a mile uphill as fast as their legs would carry them and then run all the way down again. The Witch whimpered in agitation and Ralf's nerves suffered a cataclysmic meltdown. The moment of capture had finally arrived, just as he knew it always would.

'What the hell are they doing now?' Shillabeer asked him, still short of breath.

They could hear vehicles shunting about and the plummy patrician tones of Captain Ives giving orders. Ralf said, 'I think the Captain is lining the cars and tractors up so that their headlamps all point in the same direction. The beaters are going to circle round behind and walk us in against the lights.'

'Sorry about this, Ralf.'

'I bet you're not half as sorry as I am.'

'We're on the wrong side of the river. That was my fault. You can blame me.'

'It's your fault for coming in the first place. After I'd warned you not to.'

'Too late now. Can we get out of this? Where's the nearest bridge?'

'They will have the bridges guarded, won't they? Not a chance.'

'The mist will hide us if we can get closer to the river. What do you think? We might be able to give them the slip down there.'

'Better than standing here waiting to be caught. You go first.'

Cautiously they began moving sideways through the trees until they came to the edge of the water meadows. Ralf whispered, 'I don't suppose you know where there is a boat?'

Shillabeer whispered back, 'No. But I know where there is a ford.'

'You do?'

'It's just round the next bend in the river. Not far from Beckles Mill.'

'We've had a lot of rain this winter. Won't it be too deep?'

'Have you got a better idea?'

'No, but I think I know where you mean. Will you be able to find it in the dark?'

'There's a white post on the bank. On the other side from us.'

'It's worth a try. We've got to get past the mill first.'

The mud along the river bank had a brittle crust, sometimes frozen hard enough to bear them up but mostly they sank down with a squelch and had to extricate each boot in turn. The coarse rushy grass was stiff with frost, the moonlight reflecting off the water with startling brightness.

Fortunately for them the young men guarding the bridge had a couple of girls keeping them company. They could hear laughter and see the glow of cigarettes. As well as being distracted by the girls the young men were facing in the opposite direction so by going as wide as possible, and with the aid of the mist, they were able to edge past.

Now all they had to do was find the ford.

Which wasn't easy. They were looking for the white post and also for the depressions in the bank where people had crossed in the summer months. It was almost like studying a photographic negative where the black and white areas are reversed, but they found it in the end. The white paint had flaked off, and it was half obscured by a swag of thick grass, but having found it they knelt on the bank and looked across.

'Bugle Boy Ford,' Shillabeer said. 'That's what my Aunt Edith always called it. Never thought to ask her why. Do you know, Ralf?'

He didn't, but made a mental note to ask his father next time he saw him. He would know, just as he would have known the answers to a lot of other questions Ralf had never thought to ask him.

'Bastards,' Shillabeer wept in annoyance, as some voices came closer. 'How many men does it take to catch a poacher these days? They ought to have something better to do with their spare time.'

'When we're drowning in the river we shall wish they had caught us.'

It was only an insignificant river, scarcely more than a trickle in a dry summer. For several months of the year the stepping stones of the ford were visible above the surface of the water and no one using them needed to get their shoes wet. Now it was winter, and after plenty of early February rain the river looked as wide and impressive as the Mississippi.

Crouched side by side on the bank they saw how deep and icy cold the water was, how swiftly it turned the corner and creamed along the distant bank. Pleasant gurgling sounds emphasised the weight of water flowing past. The stepping stones were visible beneath the surface but a long way down. Anyone trying to wade across risked losing balance and being swept away.

'Too deep for me,' Shillabeer apologised. 'Sorry, Ralf. I wouldn't have a hope.'

His opinion was shared by the Witch. She could read the game as well as they could, and didn't fancy their chances. She whined and grizzled with apprehension until Shillabeer put a comforting arm round her shoulders. Ralf saw them both look up. High Beckles was not very far away in distance but it was on the other side of the river. How to get across, that was the problem.

'You first then,' Ralf said.

'Don't make jokes at a time like this. Try it,' Shillabeer urged as the voices of the search party came ever nearer. 'Jump in and see how deep it is in the middle.'

Ralf looked into the water. The reflection of his face was black and wavering, as though seen in the glass of an antique mirror. Although he could see the first of the blanched stones it was obscured by long tendrils of waterweed, played out like the hair of a drowning woman.

He slipped in, shuddering with cold, his feet clawed for the feel of the stones on the raised pathway under the fast running water. They were worn smooth and surprisingly slippery. He fixed his eyes on the white post and began to wade across with the gun held above his head. He kept going until he reached the other side, throwing the gun up on to the bank.

'The Witch next,' Shillabeer said, after he had waded carefully back again.

'You mean you never taught her to swim?'

'The water's too cold, she would never make it. Carry her for me, Ralf.'

Without arguing he picked up the Witch in his arms. She was surprisingly heavy, and because of her long legs, awkward to carry. She trembled and whimpered but also licked his face, her way of thanking him for the ride. He dumped her safely on the bank and then waded back for Shillabeer.

He jumped on Ralf's back, a small but solid weight densely packed with knotted muscle. 'Good man, good man,' he whispered. 'Almost there. Keep going.'

He shouldn't have said it because when they were only one

step away from the other side Ralf's right foot slipped off the last stone and he trod into deep water. On his own he might have recovered his balance but with the extra weight on his shoulders he slowly began to tip sideways, and finally plunged them both headlong into the river.

He went under, almost paralysed with fear and shock as he was immersed in the icy water. He surfaced almost immediately and after floundering wildly for a few seconds soon reached the bank and held on for dear life, gasping and choking.

Then looked round for Shillabeer, and couldn't see him. He must have gone under, and stayed under. Ralf's first thought was that he had failed Sonia. Never mind that it was an accident waiting to happen, one he should have prevented, and hadn't. He knew Sonia would never be able to forgive him. All the worst consequences that could follow flashed through his brain and past his eyes, too full of river water to see properly.

With her uncle dead before time Sonia would be unable to pay off the inheritance tax and be forced to sell the farm to raise the money. The beautiful romance he hoped for would have ended before it had properly started. There would be no lovemaking on Beckles Hill, no fire to sit by afterwards. Their children would never be conceived and so would never be born to grow up in the old family farmhouse. His father Tom Lassiter would die, he would go back to London and be miserable for the rest of his life.

Up to his waist in icy cold water he sobbed loudly with despair. At which point Shillabeer rose to the surface, a long way downstream. He must have been swept there by an underwater current but half wading and half swimming Ralf caught up with him and pulled him out, just as he was going under again. In one mighty effort he heaved him up on to the bank, knowing it was likely to be his only chance.

He fully expected that immersion in the icy river would have killed him with shock. But it hadn't, or not quite. To Ralf's amazement he soon came round, after much spitting and coughing. Then sat up and began cursing viciously.

'The sods,' he wept. 'I could have drowned.'

'At least we're on the right side of the river now. Are you able to walk?'

'If it kills me. Get going, Ralf. The bastards are coming after us again.'

They could now hear voices on both sides of the river and only the swirling white mist saved them. 'The gun,' he whispered. 'Don't leave my gun behind.'

'I've just fetched it. Come on, I'll help you up.'

They had not noticed the faint night wind but now it knifed them to the bone. Their teeth chattered and their clothes hung wetly to the skin but with the Witch encouraging him on one side, and Ralf's hand under his armpit on the other, Shillabeer managed to cover half the uphill distance back to High Beckles.

Just when they thought they were safe the Witch snarled another warning. It was bad luck. The bright moonlight had been fading fast and the moon was now obscured by dark clouds. The night would soon have swallowed them up but their route had taken them straight towards a posse of vigilantes parked in a gateway within half a mile of the farm.

This had been their escape route and the effort of a detour was beyond them. There is a limit to human endurance and for the last hundred yards Shillabeer had only been staggering. On seeing the faint lights from the parked vehicles, and hearing the voices of the watchers, he sank to the ground and refused to move. The Witch immediately did the same, collapsing in exhaustion as though dead.

'Run for it,' Shillabeer whispered, as Ralf knelt beside him. 'Get going. You can do it easily from here.'

Instead Ralf tried to raise him from the ground, alarmed at how cold he felt. He said, 'I'm going to call out for help. They can take you to the farm. Or to hospital, if necessary.'

He grabbed Ralf's arm in a fierce grip. 'It's too late. We're done for, the Witch and me. Don't worry about us. Save yourself.'

'You're going to die of hypothermia if you don't get your wet clothes off pretty soon. Come on. I'll carry you if necessary.'

'Ralf, believe me I would sooner die than see you get caught. Leave me the gun and get going. You know the drill. Circle right round and go in the back way.'

'No. I'm going to call out. You need help.'

'Don't do it. Run, Ralf. Run.'

Instead of running Ralf stood up to surrender, and would have done so, except that at the same moment there came the sound of a gunshot.

A loud shot. It was almost like a young cannon going off, and was followed soon after by another and even louder shot. In the frosty silence the sound seemed to go on for ever. Then came a third shot, the echo racing down the length of the river valley before dying away.

Immediately there were excited shouts from the men in the gateway. Ralf could hear them saying they had seen a light moving around in the trees. Another shot was fired and this time they did not hesitate. Doors were slammed, engines started up, headlights were switched on, and one by one in a convoy they disappeared into the distance.

'Sonia,' Shillabeer whispered, struggling up on one arm. 'That's my Dad's old twelve-bore she's shooting off. What a gun! I'd know it anywhere. She must have got back home and come after us.'

'Can you walk?'

'Just needed a bit of a rest. Fine, now. Lead the way, Partner.'

They still had half a mile to walk, most of it uphill, and by the time they reached the farm they had slowed to a crawl. Ralf was not only carrying the gun and Shillabeer but half carrying the Witch as well. It was the weary trudge of a defeated army.

They were met by an anxious search party. First came Jed with a lamp, then Queenie muffled up in coat and boots. And finally Sonia, carrying the gun and looking cross. The three poachers awaited her wrath.

'Nice work, Sonia,' Shillabeer whispered, greeting her with a kiss. 'The sods had us cornered. You did well there, my girl.'

'I saw all the people in the village. What went wrong this time, Ralf?'

'We fell in the river.'

She drew breath to scold but changed her mind when her uncle pitched at her feet. And then rolled over as though dead.

27

Shillabeer was immortal, and so did not die. Jed picked him up in his arms and carried him into the house and up the narrow back stairs. Sonia ran him a hot bath and between them they managed to get him undressed.

'I'm all right now,' he protested feebly. He had good reason to be apprehensive, flinching at the sight of Queenie in her apron with her sleeves rolled up, and scalding steam rising in clouds from the bath.

There was nothing soft about Shillabeer when they succeeded in removing his clothes. Cigarettes and gin had pickled him into the texture of saddle leather. His bristly tough little body was held together with lumps of knotty muscle and bunched sinew as hard to the touch as steel and plastic. Not quite immortal perhaps, but with a tenacious grip on life.

Ralf wisely left them to it and went downstairs to the kitchen and made himself a hot drink. He removed his coat and jumper and hung them to dry on the Aga rail. In contrast to the uproar above the only sound he could hear in the cloistered calm of the kitchen was the snuffling of the Witch in her malodorous basket by the stove.

After a slow start they had gradually warmed to one another. The Witch would never have won any prizes at a dog show but in Ralf's eyes she was redeemed by her high intelligence, and by her devotion to Shillabeer. This had prolonged her life by giving it meaning and purpose. Her deerhound ancestry lifted her level with his waistcoat pockets, if he gave her ugly head a scratch she closed her eyes and sighed with pleasure. She had trotted proudly beside him for the whole of her life, as devoted to him as a child to a favourite teacher.

Ralf had become increasingly intrigued by the way in which Shillabeer and the Witch appeared to be able to convey information to one another. Was it a faculty which had become lost with the evolutionary process? Every so often a party of university students would ask permission to excavate one of the burial mounds on Beckles Hill. They never found more than a few broken pots or some fragments of bone, or a shaped flint or two, but this did not deter them from writing up their findings into learned papers and doctoral theses. They would have found out more from studying Dick Shillabeer and his dog instead, living descendants of the ancient people whose pathetic remains they picked over with such minute attention to detail. Shillabeer and the Witch had survived down countless centuries because they could hunt, and were at one with the wild creatures who shared the hill with them.

He heard a sound and turned to see that Sonia had come downstairs into the kitchen. She seemed surprised to see him but he moved forward quickly and took her hand, asking her what she would like to drink.

'Whatever you're having,' she said, and watched as he busied himself with the kettle. She had driven a long way to her sale and back again before dashing to their rescue. She spoke slowly, clearly exhausted. 'I left them to it. Jed and Queenie are trying to get Uncle dried off and put to bed.'

'I can picture the scene.'

'Do you think he will suffer any ill effects?'

'I doubt it, knowing him. But considering what is at stake perhaps he ought to see a doctor tomorrow. Just in case.'

'He hates having anything done for him. Tell me what happened.'

'He insisted on going out. I couldn't stop him. I tried, but he was determined to go. Sorry, Sonia. I don't suppose you were very pleased when you got back and found us gone.'

'I think this will have been the last time. He's getting too old, and he knows it.'

'It was touch and go until you fired the gun.'

'How did you come to fall in the river?'

'We tried to wade across the ford. With him on my back.'

'It's far too deep in the winter. You could both have drowned.'

'It seemed a good idea at the time. I wouldn't have wanted him to miss his birthday party.'

'It's time he acted his age. Thank you for rescuing him. He said you dived under and pulled him out.'

'So long as he survives. That's the main thing.'

She put out a hand. 'Your clothes are wet through. You need a hot bath too, Ralf.'

They had been speaking in whispers, staring at one another like sleepwalkers. After spending so long in the open air they were overcome by the warmth of the kitchen, practically out on their feet with fatigue. While they spoke they had also been slowly moving towards one another.

He said, 'Just now I was remembering the first day I came up to the farm. You were waiting for me with a gun under your arm.'

This made her smile. 'It wasn't personal, Ralf.'

'And you were being guarded by the Witch. She was doing her duty and protecting you from strange men.'

'We had been ratting.'

Ralf refused to be put off by this unromantic revelation. He could sense that she was receptive, her eyes watching him sleepily. 'It was a hot day. You were wearing a white dress. And a straw hat. That's when I fell in love with you, Sonia. On the spot. Love at first sight. Nothing can ever take that memory away from me.'

'You've told me before. In the doorway. Nice. Thank you.'

'I promised you that we would make love on the hill. With a fire. And we will, as soon as it is warm enough. Then sit and watch the sun rise.'

'With or without my clothes? You don't want me to dance around naked to watch the sun come up, do you?'

'Something tells me you don't think I'm serious.'

'I'm never entirely sure with you, Ralf. You're not making fun of me, are you?'

'Would I joke about things like that?'

'Tell me about the fire.'

'It's to sit by after making love. We can take the Witch if you would feel safer.'

'I must say it all sounds rather uncomfortable. Do I have to?'

'Yes. You do.'

By now they had come close enough to kiss, their faces almost touching. For the first time he could feel Sonia's body softening. Normally taut and disciplined from hard work and an unflinching purpose, she had suddenly relaxed. She began to lean, he could feel her weight, her warmth, her breath. They raised their arms for an embrace and he knew that she had finally yielded herself up, something he had not expected, or hoped for, but which miraculously seemed about to happen.

It didn't, because at the very moment their lips met they heard a noise from beside the stove. Followed by an ominous and unaccustomed silence. The familiar background accompaniment of snuffling and grunting from the huge wickerwork basket beside the stove had suddenly, and finally, stopped. They both turned and saw at once that the Witch had just that moment died. The old bitch was still curled up in the basket but her head lolled over the side in the unmistakeable stillness of death.

Ralf knelt and put his hand on her chest but her heart had stopped beating. He was emotionally distressed by this sudden death, seeing it as an ill omen. 'She ran a few miles tonight,' he said in a voice that trembled. He gave her a farewell pat. 'I guess it was one night out too many. It had to happen.'

Sonia also knelt beside the dead dog, her eyes filling with tears. 'I know death has to come but it's sad when it does.'

'She was your dog, too.'

'She was. Yes.'

'You never did tell me how she directed you over to Huckle. That night we got lost. You said it was a family secret.'

'There are a lot of things I haven't told you, Ralf. But I

will one day.'

'That's what you always say.'

'Poor Uncle Dick,' Sonia whispered tearfully, as they both continued kneeling beside the Witch. 'How am I going to tell him?'

It is a matter of some contention as to whether or not a dog has a soul, immortal or otherwise, but assuming that Shillabeer had one Ralf thought he would willingly have shared it with the Witch. She was the child he never had, the companion of every waking hour, the most trusted of friends.

He replied, 'You needn't worry. I think he'll know already.'

28

It was time to honour the promise Ralf had made to his father. Two days after the Witch died the weather turned sunny and mild. Although February was only halfway through it was enough to justify a return to Orchard House. And more importantly, to the garden.

First he had to square it with the authorities and made an appointment to see his father's doctor. 'Fine by me,' the doctor said, making no objection when they met in the Matron's office. 'There seems little point in keeping Tom here if you are willing to look after him at home.'

'It's what he wants.'

'Quite a test of character for you, Ralf. Looking after a seriously ill relative is never easy.'

'I'm sure he will try hard to be no trouble.'

The man he was speaking to had been his own doctor until he left home at eighteen, and had also treated his mother during her short illness. Now elderly, but with great distinction of manner, he was Edinburgh trained and still spoke with the accent. Ralf had good memories of this courteous medical man and knew that he was sympathetic to his father's determination to battle it out to the end.

'Doesn't like taking medication,' he acknowledged with a smile. 'And doesn't care much for doctors, either. I know, I know, and who can blame him? But don't be afraid to call on us if you need help. We usually have a card or two up our sleeve.'

'I will.'

'Continuous thoracic pain is hard to bear, not to mention a lot of other disagreeable symptoms as time goes on. Unless he suffers a heart attack and dies quickly. That is a common outcome in this sort of situation.'

'I shall make him as comfortable as possible. And remember what you say.'

Being an old hand the doctor knew the question Ralf was inhibited from asking, and answered it for him. 'How long? The pick-up time was rather late, which didn't help. Early diagnosis is essential and in your father's case we did not have it.'

'Would it have made any difference?'

'Probably not but there are several shots in the locker these days. Even surgery might have been considered earlier on.' He winced feelingly. 'Tom wasn't keen. Can't say I blamed him.'

'Not long then?'

'He is a strong-minded man, which helps. And physically strong too, of course. But it's not a nice thing to have wrong with you, there is no point in pretending otherwise.'

'Thank you for telling me.'

'I shall be retiring myself later in the year. Old age, Ralf. It comes to us all in the end. Along with a lot of aches and pains and unpleasant surprises. Try and postpone it as long as possible.'

'I shall certainly try. Thanks for the tip.'

'I'm sure you will, a sensible chap like you. Pleased to see you looking in such fine fettle. You're in your prime, laddie.' As they parted at the door he added, 'Ralf, be thankful that you're not a doctor of the medically qualified kind. How many nights have you been called from your bed?'

'Very few.'

They both smiled, which relieved a sombre conversation, and they parted on good terms. Ralf had thought a lot about the nature of illness since his return home. He had come to realise that the malfunctioning body, the hurt mind and the broken spirit are one and the same, part and parcel of any breakdown in health and equally needful of cure. Though not a religious man he considered that his father's great skill as a farmer, and his closeness with the natural world, surely entitled him to a more easeful death than the one booked in for him.

A return to the old architect's scented garden would at least restore his independence and give him a sense of achievement, so to that purpose Ralf now turned his mind. With the Witch dead his poaching activities had come to an end. He had begun cleaning up the house in readiness for his father's return, and laying in stocks of food and drink, especially drink, starting with a big bottle of his favourite brandy.

'Tomorrow,' he said, going straight in to tell his father the good news. 'It's fixed. Ten o'clock in the morning. That suit you?'

'I only wish it could be today. But thank you for arranging it.'

'Do you have a special diet I should know about?'

'Ralf, a cheese sandwich sitting at my own table would be a feast.'

'I expect I can do better than that. Queenie has started making you some pies. And a cake. You won't go hungry, I can promise you that much.'

'Good old Queenie. Thank her for me next time you see her.'

'I've brought in the logs from that old apple tree you made me saw up. They should burn a treat. And smell nice, too.'

'It can't come too soon for me. Not that they haven't done their best for me in here. I'm grateful, of course I am. But it's not the same as being in your own place, is it?'

'No, Dad. Not at all the same.'

'What's the weather like today?'

'Warming up nicely.'

'I hope so, not just for my sake, but for the farmers. Did you know that Sonia came to see me yesterday evening?'

'That was kind of her. What did you talk about?'

'The farm, mostly. Looking after livestock at the end of a long winter isn't the easiest job in the world. These are difficult times to be in agriculture, Ralf. And they aren't likely to improve for a long time yet.'

'So I believe.'

'Even a well-run farm comes to the end of the food supply and needs some warm weather for the grass to grow. If I could order some sunshine for her, I would. The estate could do with some as well.'

'It's not your worry now. You would have coped, whatever the weather.'

'That's true, I would.' He held up his hand to detain Ralf who was already pushing back his chair and edging towards the door, anxious to continue the Orchard House spring clean. 'Don't go, just for a minute.'

'Is there something on your mind?'

'Sonia told me about Dick's old dog going on. That was sad.'

'I was going to tell you later.' Ralf shrugged an apology and spread his hands. 'Didn't think it was something that would cheer you up.'

'A death in the family deserves a mention. That was one clever dog, Ralf.'

'She was Sonia's dog too.'

'Yes, the Witch really was one of the family, no doubt about that. Dick would have felt the loss.' He lowered his voice. 'Sonia was pleased that you helped to bury her on the hill. That was good of you, Ralf.'

'How much did Sonia tell you?'

'She said that you drove Dick's Land Rover halfway up the hill. Then you and Jed carried the dog in a blanket nearer to the top.'

'That's how we did it, yes. Jed had gone up earlier to dig the grave. Next to where the Witch's mother was buried.'

'I remember the mother dog well. Not quite so much daylight under her as the Witch but that didn't stop her being the fastest thing you ever saw on four legs. She was Saul's old dog. Saul Shillabeer, Sonia's father. He planted a yew tree to mark the grave.'

'I saw it. Growing nicely.'

'Sonia said she cried when the Witch was lowered in. How did Dick take it?'

'He was a bit subdued. Never spoke a word. I helped Jed to fill in the grave.'

'Thank you for doing all that. I'm sure they appreciated it.'

'I was upset too, Dad. Sorry for not mentioning it. Bringing you news of a death didn't seem quite the right thing to do, just when you were hoping to leave.'

'Death is something you get used to, working on a farm. Nothing and nobody lives for ever. Well, I've heard all your news and you've heard all my news so I guess it's time for you to be about your business.'

Ralf stood up again. 'Yes. Got to go, Dad. The big clean-up. Lots to do.'

'Don't bother on my account. Some dirt and muddle will seem a bit more homelike after this place. I can't wait to get the smell of disinfectant out of my nostrils.'

'There's plenty of fresh air waiting for you at High Beckles.'

This made his father smile. As Ralf stood up and headed for the door he added, 'I don't suppose you … ?'

'You suppose wrong,' Ralf said, removing a small bottle of brandy from his inside jacket pocket. 'Exchange is no robbery so I'll take the empty one back with me. They never found your hiding place, and it's a bit late now.'

'God bless you, my boy. Till tomorrow morning then. I'll be ready and waiting.'

When Ralf was back once more in the Orchard House he stood scratching his head as he tried to work out the best order to do all the jobs that needed to be done for his father's homecoming. Even one non-smoking clean-living bachelor created a surprising amount of domestic junk, particularly in the bathroom and the kitchen. So where should he start? On the oven, the bath, the refrigerator, or the back porch? Which was a disgrace to the nation it contained so many filthy boots and items of clothing torn on barbed wire.

Inspiration came in the bedroom when he contemplated the basket of dirty washing needing to be done. A start! He bundled up all the sheets and pillow cases and towels as well as his vests and underpants and socks and took them down to Long Beckles as a special treat for Cousin Daisy. Also to inform her and her husband George that contrary to their expectations his father was leaving the hospice and returning to High Beckles. They were suitably surprised but sent their best wishes and repeated their offer to be the refuge of last resort.

'And that includes you, Ralf,' Daisy informed him. 'Our spare room will always be available if needed.' Eyeing him more suspiciously she said, 'You look a bit different somehow. What have you been getting up to at High Beckles? You're twice the man you were when you came home last summer.'

Making a mental note never to tell anyone for the rest of his life how he had spent the winter at High Beckles, or to let anything about his poaching activities slip out through carelessness, he returned to the Orchard House and spent the rest of the day cleaning and tidying it room by room. Next morning he drove out again, this time to Northbeck where his father was packed up, dressed and waiting on the doorstep. No one had really believed that Tom Lassiter would come out of the hospice alive. He not only came out, he walked out unaided and upright. The senior nursing sister accompanied him to the car, where Ralf helped him in. She seemed astonished at the idea of anyone wanting to leave and kept asking if he was doing the right thing. They thanked her for her concern but knew she would never understand why he wanted to leave however long they explained it to her, and wisely never tried.

'You made it, Dad,' Ralf said in admiration, opening the front door of the Orchard House and ushering him in with arm extended.

'I did,' his father agreed. 'You're right there, son. I bloody well did.'

Ralf thought it would take several days if not weeks for him to readjust but he was wrong about that, just as he had been wrong about a lot of other things where his father was concerned. The months in the hospice were erased from his memory the moment he lay back in his own armchair and stretched out his boots to the fire. Ralf poured him a tumbler of brandy with hot water and sugar, he tuned in to the sports channel on television and it was as though he had never been away.

The next morning he was up early and out into the garden. 'Work to do,' he explained when Ralf expressed concern. 'Don't worry, my son. I shan't overdo it. Little and often, that's how I shall go about it.' He waved a proud hand at the emerging flowers. 'Daffodils. Pansies. Primulas. The first tulip almost there. It's all happening! The Spring, my favourite season. Leave me to it, Ralf.'

A week of spectacular early morning frosts with bright sunshine came next. Although Ralf continued to urge caution his father revelled in the cold clean air and went out early so that he could breathe it in and admire the view.

'Marvellous,' he enthused. 'You have no idea how sweet fresh air is until you've been crated up in one of those hospital places.'

'Always plenty of fresh air up here, Dad. If we could bottle it and sell it we would make a fortune.'

'I don't want to sell it, I want to keep it for myself.' It was a heady morning of dazzling frost and brilliant sunshine. He clasped his hands to his chest the better to breathe it in. 'It's great to be alive, my boy. Would you want to leave all this a moment before you had to?'

'No,' Ralf agreed, standing beside him to share the view. 'I wouldn't. I should hold on as long as I possibly could.'

'That's how I feel. I haven't handed my notice in yet, and I don't intend to.' He pointed to the wide border that ran the length of the garden. 'Flowers coming everywhere. Another few weeks and it will look a picture. I can hardly wait.'

It was as near a state of grace as an unbeliever was likely to get and Ralf sensibly left him alone to enjoy it in his own way. Birds began building nests, the bees came out of their hive and started work on the flowers, the weather turned pleasantly warm and his father finally had what he longed for all the winter, another chance to wander about in the garden and help ease it back into life.

Ralf remembered his father telling him soon after they arrived at High Beckles that just to sit in the garden felt like being on holiday. The magic still worked, even more so, although in the nature of all holidays it would one day come to an end. Ralf could only hope on his father's behalf that it did not come to an end too soon.

Meanwhile life went on. After the death of his dog Shillabeer no longer wanted a drive every day. He missed her terribly and found it difficult to settle. They still managed a tour round once a week, usually on Mondays by taking a delivery to Oliver Biggs in the deserted farm buildings at nearby Claypits Farm. Along with everyone else Oliver suspected that there was something going on between Ralf and Sonia but neither he, nor Sid Pike the postman, had been able to find out exactly what.

'You're both keeping very quiet about it, that's all I can say,' his father grumbled. 'When are you going to let us in on the secret?'

'There isn't anything going on,' Ralf replied truthfully. 'Not at the moment, anyway. When it does, if it does, I shall tell you first. That's a promise.'

'I don't want to intrude. It's just that asking a man in my condition to be patient is asking a bit much. You know how I feel about Sonia.'

'I do. Yes.'

'A daughter-in-law would be very special to me, Ralf. You can't blame me for wanting it more than anything. If you and Sonia made it as a couple I should die a happy man. Even happier if you got married and settled down here.' He sighed. 'She's as bad as you. She won't tell me anything either.'

'Don't keep talking about dying, Dad. It upsets me.'

'Sorry, son. I won't do it again. Or embarrass you by asking about Sonia. I should have more sense. Everyone likes to keep their love life private, of course they do. Especially when there might be a marriage on the end of it. I shall say no more.'

Ralf was sorry not to be able to tell him what he most wanted to hear. There was a simple explanation, namely that his own moment of truth with Sonia Shillabeer had not yet arrived. They had kept to their agreement to stay out of one another's way until her uncle's birthday, much to the puzzlement of the matchmakers. By doing so they had outwitted family and friends, even the postman, by keeping their love affair and their plans a private matter. A conspiracy that bound them together by staying apart. They did not want to tell anyone else because they did not know themselves how it was going to work out when their moment of truth finally arrived.

They soon would though, because the long waiting period was almost over. March seemed to pass in a flash and as soon as they were into April it became a simple matter of counting off the days. With the warmer weather came easier times on the farm. The grass grew and the animals grazed, no longer needing to be fed every day, and the pace of life began to slow down after the efforts of the winter.

Preparations for Dick Shillabeer's eightieth birthday celebrations on the first day of May were well under way, and taken seriously, everyone involved aware that it was a significant event in the family history. Everyone seemed to be waiting. There was a feeling of suspense. An expectation of change, and something exciting about to happen.

Ralf felt it most of all. His return to his birthplace had been a strange episode in his life, one he had never expected to go through, and which had changed him more than he would have believed possible. There was now a dreamlike quality about his exile in High Beckles, a retreat and sanctuary from the real world. What would happen when the time came for him to return to his former life? He was in no hurry to find out and took refuge in his father's fatalism. Whatever would be, would be.

His father was miserable because there came a spell of cold

wet weather in the middle of April which restricted the time he could spend in the garden. Until one morning, at the end of the month, when they drew back the curtains and found that it had suddenly changed for the better. In an unpredictable climate the forecasters were confident that a mini-heatwave was heading their way. It was true. Next day the sun shone out hot and strong, the temperature soared, and Tom Lassiter was happy again.

'Lovely,' he said, touring round the garden in a straw hat and shirtsleeves. 'Just what the doctor ordered. Anyone would wait a long time before they heard me complain about the weather being too hot.'

'I arranged it for you personally,' Ralf told him. 'You won't do any digging in this heat, will you?'

'No fear of that. The seat under the plum tree will do me nicely for the rest of the week.'

He folded his arms contentedly. Although he continued to lose weight and was stooped and moved slowly he did not seem to be in any pain or unbearable discomfort. He still liked to talk in his slow gravelly voice, and still spoke a lot of sense in Ralf's opinion. Although it had happened in a roundabout way he had inadvertently found the place above all others where he wished to end his days. For the first time in a busy life he was free of responsibility and care.

One day when they were sitting together on the seat under the plum tree, now coming into blossom, he said to Ralf 'I often think about the old architect fellow who used to live here. Loved his bees and used to fuss over them and talk to them. It always puzzled me that he seemed so happy and contented in such an isolated place. Now I know why.'

'He certainly made himself a nice garden.'

'I wish that I had taken the trouble to get to know him a bit better. He must have been an interesting man to talk to. Too late now. Always the way, isn't it?'

'I'm afraid it is, Dad. Always the way.'

'He did well in life, and that's what Mother hoped for you. I've never enquired how your career is going. I know that

Mother secretly hoped you would become a professor. What are your chances of that now, Ralf? Not quite so hot, I suspect.'

'I haven't quite given up hope.'

'There is always a price to pay. That's true, isn't it?'

'Most things in life are a trade-off, I find. Yes, to gain a little you usually have to give a little first. No telling how it will work out.'

'You're right there, son. Never mind, that's all in the future. Right now I'm starting to think about the party. Looking forward to it.'

He was not alone because everyone loves a party and the feeling of pleasurable expectation began to escalate as the first of May approached. An event that had once seemed far off in the future was now only a day away. Queenie had several women from the cottages she could call upon for help and there was a frenzy of cleaning and cooking as the final countdown began. The blissfully warm weather continued without a break and did not disappoint when May Day finally arrived.

This was Dick Shillabeer's long awaited eightieth birthday, and a big day in the calendar at High Beckles. Ralf did not even go into his study or open his laptop, he joined his father on the seat under the plum tree instead.

He said, 'Well, he made it, Dad. Always thought he would.'

'I've known Dick all my life and he's been a good friend to me. You know that.'

'He's been a good friend to me, too.'

'Even these days eighty is a fair age. And I'm just as pleased for Sonia's sake.'

'I am too, Dad. Very glad.'

'I can remember the day seven years ago when he signed the farm over to her. She seemed very young to me at the time. It must have seemed a lifetime away to her.'

'I don't know what the first six years were like. The last one was a bit nerve-racking.'

'Farming is a rough trade, even for men. Sonia hasn't put a foot wrong in all that time, and probably never will now. Quite an achievement when you think about it.'

'You can share the credit. She told me more than once how much she appreciated the help you gave her.'

'Well, from now on when she looks out of her bedroom window practically everything she sees in front of it will belong to her. Eight hundred acres is a lot of ground to own. Must be a nice feeling.'

'A very nice feeling. Couldn't be otherwise.'

'Got an appetite for tonight? We're going to need one, I reckon, the amount of food they've been cooking. Not that I shall be able to eat very much but I don't intend to go hungry either.'

'We've waited long enough.'

'So let's enjoy the party.' He stood up and began to make his way indoors. 'I hate to leave all this lovely sunshine but I think I shall be sensible and have a rest first. Something tells me we're in for a late night.'

Ralf began his preparations in good time with a bath and a shave, after which he dressed in his party best. He could not help feeling excited. It was the date he had looked forward to for many months, and Sonia for several years, so they both had something to celebrate. Because it also marked the end of their agreed waiting period.

Tomorrow, if all went well, they would make the match-makers happy by stepping out together.

29

Looking more than ever like a retired country parson Shillabeer was at his most silvery and respectable, taking an innocent pleasure at being the centre of attention. With his faded blue eyes he blinked round shyly to see his friends dressed up for the small dinner party arranged to mark his eightieth birthday.

The meal was held in the rarely used family dining room and when the time came they filed in and took their places. Shillabeer presided at the head of the table and indicated that Queenie should sit on his left and Ralf's father on his right. Jed moved in beside his mother and Oliver Biggs sat next to him. This left Ralf and Sonia, with Sonia in the middle between him and his father.

Parties always begin with everyone on their best behaviour. Queenie wore a new print frock and some make-up. She had been to town to have her hair done and was transformed. Her son likewise. For the first time ever Ralf saw Jed cleaned up and looking extremely smart, his hair washed and tied back in a ponytail. He was already into party mode, having polished off a bottle of wine with Oliver Biggs before the meal had even started.

Ralf wore a bow tie as his contribution to making the occasion special. Shillabeer was giving him seigneurial beams of approval from the head of the table and he was reminded of the day he arrived and could hardly take his eyes off Sonia. And still couldn't. Which seemed to please the others and he was aware of the general goodwill towards them. It was a party that got off to a splendid start and got better as it went along.

'Went to that farm sale at Mardle today, Tom,' Oliver Biggs said between mouthfuls. 'A lot of good stuff on offer and most of it went cheap.'

'How did the machinery sell?'

'Plenty of bargains to be had. Most people kept their cheque books in their pockets. I didn't stay long.'

'Always a shame when farms have to sell up.'

'You're right, Tom, it is. But Sonia won't have to and that's why we're having a party. We've got something to celebrate so I'll give you a toast. Ready everyone?' He pounded the table and raised his glass. 'Here's to the happiest days of my life. Spent in the arms of another man's wife.'

'He means his mother,' Ralf explained to Sonia.

'Jokes aren't very good if you have to explain them, Ralf.'

'I heard that,' Biggs said, pouring out more wine. 'Nothing a man enjoys more than to feel his fingers curling round something smooth and firm. And you should know, Ralf!'

'He means a glass,' Ralf explained.

'I was thinking of a bottle actually,' the & Son said, opening yet another. 'You're not keeping up with me. Tom? Jed? Big ones all round. I bought a crate of the best wine they had in the shop. Every grape individually trodden by the peasant girls of …' He picked up a bottle and squinted at the label. 'Hungary, it says here. Not quite sure where it is exactly but I know how they feel. What comes next, Queenie?'

No one else could have got away with such terrible jokes but Biggsy's crate of wine and his good nature soon had them laughing and talking. Parties take on a life of their own and this one had a theme, a central point of interest which brought it alive. In this case it was an eating and drinking contest between Jed and the butcher. Even before the meal began Jed's mother was scolding him not to eat too much, or too fast, and once started kept nudging him to slow down. A fierce air of competition developed and both men were unstoppable. Neither could be restrained and shovelled it in at a tremendous rate.

The food was piled high on the polished mahogany table, most of it roast meat needing carvery skills. A rib of beef, a leg of ham, a generous selection of poultry and game, sausages, stuffing, bowls of sauce and mustard, dishes of potatoes and peas, all washed down with oceans of rich gravy. After which there were some elaborate fruit dishes which must have tested Queenie's cooking skills to the limit, jugs of thick cream and other equally unhealthy delicious goodies. However much they ate there always seemed just as much left. It was a feast, and they recognised it as such.

Nor were Jed and Oliver Biggs the only ones over-eating. They all ate their share, Ralf included. He watched with interest as Sonia tucked in also, a girl with a healthy appetite. He liked to see her just a little uninhibited for once. It made him very thoughtful. It was an eating and drinking orgy and she did not hold back. He thought the omens were good and the outlook bright for an overdue pair of celibate lovers.

Sonia had been the last to arrive for the party.

His heart had started to beat faster as he heard her coming down the wide wooden staircase and approach along the stone-floored passageway. He could tell from her footsteps that she was wearing high heeled shoes and the moment she appeared in the doorway looked down to see if he was right.

He was, and worked his way upwards from shapely black silk ankles, which made his heart beat faster still, to a dark green velvety dress with long sleeves. Out on the farm she tied her hair back, for the party it was loose. It was long dark lustrous hair, curly at the ends, it reminded him of the day he came up to the farm and found her waiting for him with a gun in her hand and the Witch at her side. An image that was branded into his memory and could be recalled at will, just as he knew it would be until the day he died.

They had not yet taken their places at the table and were standing with drinks in their hands when he heard her approaching. It suddenly seemed terribly important to him which of them she would look for first when she entered the room. If it was not him then their courtship and tender romance was sideswiped before it had left the starting gate. It had to be him, he almost willed it to happen, and was filled with relief and happiness when it did.

She hesitated in the doorway until she had picked him out and made eye contact. Immediately afterwards she greeted her uncle with a birthday kiss and an embrace. Next she kissed Tom Lassiter on the cheek, exchanged a cousinly cuddle with Oliver Biggs, and then stopped in front of Ralf. The room suddenly hushed. Everyone held their breath for a moment, waiting to see what happened next. They were not disappointed. Sonia put an arm round Ralf's neck and kissed him on the lips.

It was done shyly but in public and told the matchmakers all they needed to know. That Sonia had not only secured her inheritance but was announcing her marriage as well. After the kiss they stood side by side with their arms round one another's waists and the birthday party was elevated into a family celebration. Short of bursting into spontaneous applause the reaction was one of warm approval. Ralf's father and Sonia's uncle clinked glasses and beamed and shook hands as though sealing a wedding contract.

As the meal progressed Ralf and Sonia moved their chairs closer together so that their arms and legs were touching. They began to act like lovers, leaning towards one another and whispering. If all women in love are beautiful then Sonia Shillabeer was certainly so. Ralf could hardly believe that she was at last sitting beside him and indicating consent. It was a warm evening and at that moment the grim winter he had endured was erased from his memory.

When it was time to cut the birthday cake Oliver Biggs hammered on the table again. 'Eighty has got to be special. So pay attention everyone. Ralf is going to make a speech.'

Speech making is always an unnerving experience, even among a small gathering of friends, but Ralf had been asked in advance and had it rehearsed. He said all the right things and paid all the necessary compliments. Then they stood and drank Shillabeer's health while he sat and smiled modestly. Finally they gave him a clap and sang 'Happy Birthday.' As parties go it had to be rated as a big success.

After which, one by one, they stopped eating and the

birthday revels came to an end. And who had won? By general consent it was a draw. Jed stared round the table glassy-eyed, his face shiny with grease. He had eaten and drunk himself almost into a state of unconsciousness. And if Ralf had been Mrs Oliver Biggs with six children to educate he would have been alarmed to see the family provider purple of face and ready to burst.

'By God but you did us proud, Queenie my beauty,' Biggsy said, puffing his cheeks and shaking his head to try and clear his thoughts. 'What a blow-out! Have some more wine.'

Tom Lassiter was also in party mood. He had begun by talking to Shillabeer but finished by keeping hold of Sonia's hand and telling her what a lovely girl she was. Older men can get away with such things but he meant what he said and could not hide his delight at the prospect that she would soon become his daughter-in-law.

There now came an unexpected development. Unexpected, and from Ralf's point of view, unwelcome. Without consulting anyone Shillabeer banged on the table with his gin bottle and gave his housekeeper an order. 'Queenie, fetch the cards. Tom and me want to have a game of Nap.'

Unwelcome because Ralf was hoping to spend some time alone with Sonia, was longing to feel his hands smoothing over the dark green velvety dress. He began thinking back to all those nine o'clock kisses in the cold stone doorway, both huddled into winter clothes. Now it was a blissfully warm evening in early summer and she was there, ready and waiting. He thought they had both waited long enough. Their moment had come. Except that it hadn't. He had to sit down and play cards instead.

Napoleon, or Nap for short, was a game much played in the public house where they had gone after the shoot. Ralf knew it as a simple whist type game with an elementary form of bidding. Five cards are dealt and the first card led by the highest bidder indicates the trump suit.

'A pound a trick,' Shillabeer said next, putting some

268

money on the table. 'Any objections? Tom? Ralf? Oliver?' No one had so he handed the cards to Jed. 'You can deal first. No need to shuffle the spots off. Let's get on with it.'

Whether the ladies minded or not they were excluded from the card school, leaving the men to battle it out on their own. Ralf and Sonia exchanged rueful glances, once more reduced to communing without words to make their feelings plain. Ralf shrugged and turned his eyes upwards as though to say, 'We've waited this long, a little longer won't hurt us.'

Even so it was not a development that augured well, and they both knew it. The smile vanished from Sonia's face. She had been languorous and relaxed but now sat on a chair by the door with her hands clasped, looking tense and anxious. The same thought occurred to her, as it did to Ralf, that his father should have been allowed to go home to bed as soon as the party was over.

There is nothing like the chink of coins and the sight of money to focus the mind. At a pound a trick a run of losing hands with the other players to pay out every time was enough to hurt, and they sobered up quickly. It was almost midnight when they sat down to play, and they did so with grim determination, shirts unbuttoned, silent and concentrating.

The bidding was tight but after two hours a clear winner emerged. Shillabeer was not easily parted from money but his age was against him and he lost steadily. Jed depended on luck and cunning but these are unreliable friends and after holding his own for a long time he too started to lose. Biggs could not keep a poker face and groaned every time he was dealt a poor hand, with the result that he also was a net loser. Ralf broke even but did not get the hands and settled for keeping his losses to a minimum. Which meant that only his father was winning. He was on a roll, the cards fell his way and the stack of coins and bank notes in front of him began to mount up.

Sonia and Queenie brought in coffee at regular intervals. The room became unbearably hot, Shillabeer smoked cigarettes and the butcher lit a cigar, which made it worse, and they played hand after hand without a pause. The sums of money and the piles of banknotes grew still larger, the butcher's curses more vicious, but no one volunteered to leave the table. Only Shillabeer grew increasingly irritable as he worked his way down a bottle of gin and continued to lose.

Sonia sat with her arm along the back of her chair while she watched the cards being played. This had the effect of pulling the velvety green dress tightly against her body, a sight that caused Ralf considerable anguish and disappointment when he thought how much better his time could have been spent. A sight that caused him even more concern was to see his father's eyes. They were dark with exhaustion, while at the same time burning with excitement and a desperate will to win.

'Deal them round again, boys,' he urged. 'One more hand. One more hand.'

Not only Ralf but the others were beginning to watch him with increasing unease. He was enjoying himself so much that he did not care about the consequences. After all those melancholy months in the hospice wondering if he would ever see the outside world again this was like going to heaven. A drink in his hand and a game of cards with his friends was all he would have asked for, granted a last wish, and he did not want it to come to an end.

'Don't stop,' he pleaded. 'It's your deal, Dick. See what you can find for me this time.'

His face was lit up with a kind of feverish strength to maintain this final despairing grip on life. He snatched up the cards the moment they were dealt, then leaned forward eagerly to put in his bid.

Queenie came to sit beside Sonia, who had never once taken her eyes off the card players. They could both tell that something bad was going to happen. They sat away from the table and watched intently as the cards fell. It was now three o'clock in the morning and Ralf was more asleep than awake, playing by instinct. This went for Jed and the butcher as well. They had also had enough and wanted to stop.

Shillabeer was a night-hawk and not in the least sleepy. He still contested every point keenly and after a long run of losing hands he started to win back some of the money he had lost. This cheered him up. 'Mine, I think,' he said smugly as he took the last trick. 'Time we showed these youngsters how to play this game, Tom.'

'Deal them round again,' he pleaded. 'One more hand, Dick. One more hand.'

Ralf awaited the outlook with fatalistic calm, knowing that the inexorable sequence of events that had begun the moment he answered Cousin Daisy's telephone call was about to be concluded. Only the two older men at the table were able to muster the will to bid, both holding their cards secretively under their noses as though it was a matter of life and death. Which for Tom Lassiter is exactly what it was. Another hour passed. Through the window the first glimmer of dawn began to lighten the sky. In the dimly lit room the circling faces were white with fatigue as the danse macabre came to an end.

'Deal them out, boys,' Tom pleaded. He saw that the others had come to a stop and could play no more. 'Deal them round again. Another hand.' When there was no response he managed to gasp for the last time, 'One more deal, boys.' But the side of his face had begun to twitch, his sightless eyes had become the windows of an empty house, and the cards slipped from his fingers one by one.

Jed carried him to an armchair and within a few minutes he had died peacefully. They all stood round the chair, not knowing what to do or say. Queenie and Sonia cried, and Jed looked scared. Oliver Biggs poured a glass of whisky and put it in Ralf's hand, while Shillabeer came and put an arm round his waist by way of condolence.

Thus Ralf Lassiter witnessed his father's death, faithfully discharging his duty as a son to see him out of this world as decently as possible.

'That was a good party,' he said, raising his glass. 'A bloody good party. No one could have had a better send off. I shall always be grateful.'

30

Tom Lassiter's funeral took place in warm sunshine. It was not a sad occasion as funerals go. The well-attended service in Long Beckles church was more in the nature of giving thanks for a life usefully led. Even so death is very final and no one enjoys seeing a coffin lowered and a life ended.

The local farming community turned out in force, as did the estate workers led by Captain Ives. Cousin Daisy and her husband George considered themselves the chief mourners and were first to the graveside for the committal. There was nothing those two enjoyed more than a good funeral and a chance to dress in black from head to foot. Also to shake their heads sorrowfully over a man who swore, smoked, drank spirits and bet on horse races, and who consequently died young. Or young by their standards of piety.

The bereavement was most keenly felt by the small community of High Beckles, and Ralf included himself among them. A brief episode in their lives had come to a sudden end and they were unsure about the future. None of them could predict what would happen next, or how it would work out for them individually.

Shillabeer had hardly said a word after the shock of seeing his friend die in front of him. With the Witch also gone his age finally caught up with him and instead of swaggering about on the farm he spent the days until the funeral just sitting at the long kitchen table doing nothing and saying less. Jed and his mother were also quiet and serious, knowing that things would never be quite the same for them again.

This applied to Ralf most of all. His father's sudden death had drawn his absence from London to an abrupt end. As if he had taken a plunge into a bath of cold water he found himself catapulted straight back into real time. The spell had been lifted. His reason for coming to High Beckles in the first place, and the pressures on him to stay, no longer had any relevance. He was free to go. They all knew it and they all expected that he would soon vanish from their lives again, this time for ever.

Ralf was unprepared for the emotional effect that his father's death would have on him. Right up until the last moment he could never quite convince himself that the illness was terminal. Somehow he imagined that his father's strength and courage would prolong his life by many months, if not indefinitely. A year had not been long enough to befriend him properly. Now that it was too late he regretted bitterly the wasted opportunities to visit, the failure to take any interest in his affairs, or to help him through his own bereavement. He was choked by remorse as well as a sense of loss. Even in illness his father had been a formidable presence in the house and Ralf found his empty chair a poignant reminder that he could have been a better son.

Sonia had wept at the funeral. This moved Ralf to tears himself, it was a tragic occasion all round. Hopes and dreams go down with a coffin, particularly those involving other people. He recalled the feeling of apprehension and foreboding he had experienced that first morning when he drove uphill to High Beckles in his father's car. He was supposed to be in Los Angeles with a new job and a bright future in sunny California, and knew himself to be in the wrong place at the wrong time. So it had proved.

He could not help wondering what would have happened if he had ignored Cousin Daisy's appeal to return home. Would the outcome have been much different if he had kept to his plans and headed for America instead of High Beckles? Probably not. His father's illness would have run its course and both their lives would have been free from complications. With hindsight he conceded that he might have made the wrong decision.

True, he would not have met Sonia Shillabeer, but this would have spared them both much unhappiness. Mindful of all their various promises he and Sonia were acutely aware that their moment of truth had finally arrived. Vows of undying love pledged under duress in the winter seemed a little more open-ended and up for review as the May sunshine beamed down. With Shillabeer's birthday safely passed, and his father's funeral just taken place, they had no further claims on one another.

Ralf had invited the mourners to join him in the local public house afterwards for the traditional drinks, eats and farewells. There is always a feeling of relief after a funeral, a sense of duty done and customs respected. Ralf was grateful for the condolences and words of sympathy that took the edge off a bleak occasion in any man's life.

When everyone had gone he made a return visit to the grave, now filled in and covered with flowers. The headstone had been taken away to have his father's details added to those of his mother but even so it was an affecting experience and he would not be sorry when the day was finally over. While deep in thought at the grave he became aware that Sonia had come to stand beside him.

She was wearing black, and looked pale. She had sat with him at the funeral and helped him to sort out some of his father's clothes and belongings in the days after his death. Ralf had been glad of her support but realised that this had now come to an end. Nothing had been said about their future but her body language spelled out a sad message, that it was not a future they would share together. Their romance, such as it was, had come to its natural end.

Common sense had prevailed. The shock of the death coinciding with her uncle's birthday had put Sonia back into real time as well as him. The magic had gone. Stern reality had put love to flight. The differences between them were too great and would have made for an increasingly unhappy situation. A marriage would never have worked out for them, and they both knew it and accepted it.

When she appeared beside him in the churchyard he knew what she had come to tell him. He was sad about it but knew it had to be. It was a time for being practical and sensible, so there was no point in prolonging the unhappiness. They stood for a moment without speaking, both looking at the grave with its mound of flowers. When it was time to speak he said, 'Thank you for being so nice to my father all those years while I was away. It meant a lot to him.'

'He was special to me.'

'Poor old Dad. I shall miss him.'

'We all will.'

He steered her away from the grave towards the lych gate that led out of the churchyard. The funeral had been held in the morning and it was now a warm and sunny afternoon. From some of the taller trees on the far side of the church they could hear the gentle background cawing of a rookery. The nests were built high, sure sign of a fine summer to come, if his father's folklore was to be believed. It was a peaceful sound, one his father would have heard every day of his working life, the farm being just out of sight behind the trees. Ralf could see the old family home not far away, and also the main street of the village. He was sad at the prospect of leaving it behind for a second time. It was like being eighteen again, and once more on his way to London.

He said, 'Well, here we are, Sonia. Came round quickly for us, didn't it? Too quickly. We never had a chance to find out whether it would have worked or not.'

She touched his hand. 'I'm sorry, Ralf.'

'You're giving me an easy escape route. You don't have to.'

'I said I wouldn't hold you to your promise. It was always going to end like this, wasn't it?'

'Life can be a bit of a sod sometimes. Dad thought it was all worked out for us in advance.'

'He told me the same. He could have been right. He was right about most things.'

'At least he saw us together at the party. It was what he wanted more than anything, so he died happy.'

This made Sonia cry. She dried her tears quickly and said,

'It would be silly to go through with it just to please other people. Uncle knows. I didn't tell him, he worked it out for himself that you would soon be going. He'll miss you.'

'It might have ended up differently if we hadn't had that game of cards.'

'Too late now.' She shrugged and forced a smile. 'I've got the farm to run. And you've got your career. They don't go together.'

'It's true. They don't.'

She touched his hand again. 'I shall never forget you, Ralf. Or the nice things you said to me.'

'But we have to behave like two sensible adults? You're right, we do.'

'When will you go back to London?'

'At the end of the week. The solicitor seeing to the will says I needn't stay any longer. Dad's affairs are straightforward, they can send me any documents that have to be signed. George and Daisy are coming tomorrow to have their pick of the furniture and anything else they want. A house clearance firm is coming for the rest.'

'I know it's a sad day for you. I'm sorry to make it worse.'

'Much better to get it all over with in one go. Good luck with the farm, Sonia.'

He offered his cheek but she kissed him on the lips instead before hurrying away, visibly distressed. Ralf had to concede that she had handled a difficult situation well, or as well as any parting of lovers could be said to go well. She had wanted to avoid being hurt but in a love affair you always get hurt, as she had just found out. He was hurt too, but secretly relieved to have had the decision made for him. Now all he wanted to do was leave as soon as possible.

Doubly so when he heard the red post van slither to a halt outside Orchard House next morning. In every situation however dire there must be a redeeming chink of light, and this was his. Realising that he would soon be free of Sid Pike for ever made him feel better, if not much better, but his father had always cautioned against upsetting the postman so he forced himself to remain polite one more time.

'This one in the white envelope is from London,' Pike announced, walking in without being invited. 'Thick and fast now, Ralf. It's from your college. Open it up quick, it looks like good news to me. I can always tell. A job offer, that's what I reckon it is. A biggie. What a bit of luck for you.'

'No, I've won a prize, a holiday in Tromso. Any idea where it is? I could do with a holiday.'

'Norway, I've delivered about twenty so far. That's not the letter I meant.' He pointed. 'That's the one from your college, don't keep it to yourself, Ralf. Looks as if you've landed a plum job in London, lucky bugger. You were due for some promotion and I reckon this is it. Am I right?'

'Not everything that comes from London is a job offer, Sid. Mostly they're after money.'

'Just kidding me, aren't you? Well done, mate. I was sure you would make it back again. Tom would have been proud of you.'

'You seem in an awful hurry to get rid of me.'

'Glad we had a nice day for the funeral, Ralf. Made all the difference, didn't it? Went off very well, I thought. Wonderful turnout we had.'

'You sound as cheerful as George and Daisy.'

'I shall be seeing them later. Any messages?'

'Yes. You can tell Cousin Daisy that I'll phone her next time.'

'She will appreciate that, I'm sure. Ah well, can't stay chattering, much as I should like to.'

'Not going are you?' Ralf enquired, as the postman backed off. 'Don't you want a cup of coffee? My last chocolate biscuit? A look through the rest of your letters? To use the lavatory?'

'In a hurry this morning,' Pike said. 'Sorry, Ralf. Can't stop. A big round today and lots to do.'

Ralf knew very well what he wanted to do which was hotfoot it to the farm and tell them the latest. Their friendly neighbourhood postie was skilled at reading the expression on people's faces, they told him all he needed to know. Never mind that he had got it wrong, horrible Pike would pile it on, saying how Ralf couldn't wait to pack his suitcases and take it on his toes with a glad shout, leaving High Beckles far behind and everyone in it, including Sonia Shillabeer.

Well, for once the meddlesome mailman was behind the times, just as he had never really been able to read the game during the doomed romance with Sonia, if their fraught and edgy courtship could truthfully be described in such a way. Hardly surprising that he was still getting it wrong, a friend they could all do without. It was difficult to salvage much satisfaction from a lost cause but Ralf felt that he and Sonia had taken Pike on at his own game and got the better of him. Outwitting the nosy postman had been a pleasure they enjoyed equally. The only pleasure they had enjoyed together, as things worked out.

31

Ralf was soon safely back in London, and breathed a huge sigh of relief. He was back where he belonged and felt most at home. The comforting noise, the exciting pace of life, the familiar surroundings, the constant hustle and bustle, were all much to his liking. Having been breathing clean country air for so long he was also conscious of the city smell, and he liked that too.

The friend who had put him up while he waited to catch the plane to Los Angeles a year ago obliged him once more on his return. Now that he had a base in London again Ralf began seeking out job opportunities to resurrect his career with least delay. He had lots to do, many people to see, and many explanations to give in response to questions about his missing year and sudden change of plan.

Without appearing to be unduly evasive he dodged the questions as best he could, surprised that so many people wanted to know. His former colleagues were intrigued by the change in his appearance, and assumed it had occurred during a year spent by the pool. If not in sunny California where had he got his weather-beaten tan? His muscles? What had become of his long hair, his pale face and his diffident manner? Ralf wisely wasn't saying.

For the first time in many months he was able to join in conversation that did not revolve around guns, dogs, lamps, deer, pheasants and gamekeepers. There had been times when he wondered if it would ever happen and he knew it had been a close run thing. He was able to evade most of the questions that came his way but his friend with the house knew about his father's illness and was more persistent. He wanted to know how things had worked out between them, and how he had spent the time between leaving and returning.

Ralf was reluctant to divulge any information at all, least of all about his misadventures with Shillabeer and the Witch, something he intended to keep quiet about for the rest of his life. Still less was he inclined to talk about his mishandled love affair. Having explained why his job in America had fallen through he was obliged to answer reasonable questions about his father's illness and eventual death. He still found this distressing and the constant probing had the unhappy effect of stirring it all up inside his head again.

From the moment of his return to London he had made a conscious effort to forget the events of the past year, and to bury the memories as deeply and permanently as possible. He succeeded during the day but at night it was a different matter. He went to sleep easily enough but then woke in the early hours of the morning, the dreaded time for all insomniacs. He was unable to prevent himself reliving the experiences of his lost year, often in acutely vivid detail, beginning with his first morning at home. He had been impressed by the number of trees, even more than he remembered from when he lived there. Through his bedroom window he had looked out over a landscape painted entirely in green.

Helping his father to pack and then move out of the family home had generated a feeling of insecurity that had taken a long time to subside. A combination of anxiety and panic had prevented him from thinking straight. What he could not have believed when he drew back the curtains on that first morning was that he would come to know all those woods and open spaces individually by name in his capacity as Shillabeer's birdman. Among them Swanmead and Shearcroft, two places lodged firmly in his memory. As were Doggrell's Copse, The Holt, Bellwether Hollow, The Chantry, Packhorse Meadow, Edney's Piece, Dauncey's Bottom, Stunch Thicket, Twenty-acres, The Spinney and Foxley Paddock. A recital of English place names.

It had been a bizarre experience for someone of his occupation, one he could hardly believe had happened, but which he had survived and which was now thankfully over.

And already fading into a dreamlike anthology of sights, sounds and smells. Especially the smells. The kitchen at High Beckles, for example, redolent of dog basket, tobacco smoke, muddy boots and roasting meat. Less pleasant to remember was the sickly odour of disinfectant that permeated the hospice at Northbeck. In contrast again to the Orchard House garden, sonorous with bumble-bees and potent with the scent of flowers. Not difficult to work out why his father had been so anxious to exchange one for the other.

As for sounds, the iron latch on the kitchen door would clank in his memory for ever. As would the blood-freezing snarl of the Witch, and the echo of Sonia's shotgun racketing down the frost-chilled valley on the night when he toppled Shillabeer into the river. The sight most securely programmed into his memory was of his first meeting with Sonia. It was imprinted deeply into his subconscious mind and could be recalled at will. He still remembered hearing the gentle click of her gun, whirling round to find it pointing in the general direction of his kneecaps.

She had been wearing a white slim-fitting linen dress, her face half in shadow beneath a straw hat. It was a hot day and her arms were bare to the shoulder. Combined with the gun and the watchful manner she had made a lasting impression on his memory, the heiress of High Beckles guarding what was hers. Standing protectively beside her the Witch was doing likewise, both observing him dispassionately but giving nothing away about how they assessed his chances of survival in their tough frontier outpost. Not great, he imagined.

He had proved them wrong by staying the course, by doing everything that had been required of him, and then some. Which included risking life and liberty by acting as haulier for the lunatic Shillabeer while he pursued his dangerous hobby. How had he ever been persuaded to do such a thing? It seemed almost impossible, in retrospect. He had done it to honour the solemn promise he made to his father, namely that he could return to the house and the garden he loved so much. And because Sonia Shillabeer had promised him a kiss. Two very compelling reasons at the time of making them.

From thinking about Sonia, which he found painful, he went on to thinking about the farmhouse at High Beckles. A rambling old house with a big front hall and upwards of twenty rooms, plus lots of passageways, staircases and landings to make it seem even more spacious. A house for which the past still existed. This was because nothing was ever thrown away. The belongings of all the long-dead Shillabeers and their children still remained in wardrobes, chests of drawers and cupboards, upstairs and down, almost as if they still lived there. The attic above and the cellar below had never been cleared out and were still crammed with old family possessions. It was a miracle that the house and its contents had survived intact and unchanged into modern times.

It would have been an enchanting house for young children to grow up in, and an exciting farm to explore as they grew older. But suppose there were no children to play dressing-up games with the old clothes in the attic, no girls to saddle a pony, no boys to fish by the river? Suppose Sonia followed the example of the previous Miss Shillabeer and ended up bent over a stick tending the geese on Beckles Green? That was less pleasant to think about in his bachelor bed at five o'clock in the morning.

Why had he been so easily seduced by the dark hill with its yew trees, its running deer and ancient burial sites? And by the secretive inhabitants who guarded it so jealously? It occurred to him as a possible explanation that perhaps his father, like the Shillabeers, had also been descended from the prehistoric people who had lived and died there. In which case as his father's son he too had a claim on the hill, one that could explain why it had cast a spell over him while he lived in its shadow. A spell that should have been broken at the moment of his father's death and set him free but which instead rose to the surface of his consciousness in the early hours of every morning.

32

A year has passed.

Life at High Beckles had gone on much as before but was still subdued. Dick Shillabeer was finally coming to terms with what it meant to be retired. With no shooting best friend, no dog, no hobby and no one to drive him around in his old Land Rover and provide him with a captive audience he mooched miserably about the farm all day until it was time for meals. Jed and his mother carried on with their work, Queenie inside the house and Jed outside on the farm.

Only Sonia displayed a positive attitude. She had a farm to run and applied her mind. If she had any regrets or second thoughts about what might have been she never allowed it to show. She made it plain that she could manage perfectly well on her own, thank you. Just as she always had, and just as she always expected to be, alone, coping and single for the rest of her life.

No one expected to hear from Ralf Lassiter again. Except that one day towards the end of June the iron latch clanked and Jed swaggered into the kitchen. It was noon, it was sunny, it was hot, and it was time for his cooked lunch.

Before forking in his first mouthful he said he had some news to tell them. Jed had his own plate on which all his meals were served. It was an oval willow-pattern carving plate, big enough for a mayoral banquet. He did not recognise the existence of salads. Summer or winter he expected to be provided with proper food and tucked into an emperor-sized steak and kidney pudding.

'Well?' his mother prompted him.

'Well what?'

'You said you had some news to tell us, Jed. What is it?'

Using his sleeve to mop the sweat from his forehead and

the gravy from his chin he replied, 'I saw Ralf this morning. Thought you might like to know.'

He certainly had their attention. 'Where?' Shillabeer asked him.

'In the town. Sonia sent me in to get some disinfectant for the sheep.'

'What was Ralf doing in the town?' his mother asked him. 'Did he say?'

'Looking for somewhere to live. That's what he told me. Wants to buy a flat. I met him as he was coming out of one of the estate agents.'

'But why? Is he coming back here to live?'

Not one to be diverted from the serious business of eating Jed gave them the rest of the news in instalments, between mouthfuls. 'Got himself a teaching job at the College. Starts there in September.'

'Does that mean he's moving back here to live?'

'That's what he told me, yes. Anyway that's not all.'

'There's more?'

'I asked him if he was going to pay us a visit.'

'Don't keep stopping, Jed. What did he say?'

'You're never going to believe this. He said he would give us a look-up when he was ready. There was something he wanted to do first.'

'Stop eating for a moment. Tell us what he said.'

'He said he was going to have himself a fire. A fire on the hill.'

'A bonfire, do you mean?' Shillabeer asked him. 'On our hill?'

'Yes. Near the top. Among all those humps and bumps.'

'Why would he want to do that?'

'How should I know?' Jed answered back, while continuing to eat. 'I didn't ask him to explain himself. Christ, but it's hot today. Why would anyone want to light a fire? Has he gone soft in the head, or what?'

It was his mother's turn to speak. Not to him, but to Sonia who had been sitting on the other side of the table listening to their conversation. 'Are you all right?' Queenie enquired in alarm. 'Not crying are you, Sonia? Whatever is going on here today?'

Jed sat back and put down his knife and fork. 'How about that? Did I say something wrong? Ralf can build himself a bonfire if he wants to, can't he? Provided he doesn't ask me to carry any wood up there for him.'

It did not take Dick Shillabeer and his housekeeper Queenie many seconds to realise the implication of Jed's news and exchange looks of surprise, hope and expectation. They turned their gaze on Sonia who dried her eyes quickly and stood up from the table. It was an emotional moment and Sonia's voice faltered as she reacted to the news. 'I shall be upstairs if anyone comes for me.' She paused, hesitated, then rephrased her words more precisely. 'If Ralf comes for me. That's what I meant to say.'

So that was how it ended up.

There is a time for dreaming, and there is a time for reality. But which is which? Sometimes it is difficult to be sure. Sometimes, with luck, they overlap and come together.

End

www.ingramcontent.com/pod-product-compliance
Lightning Source LLC
Chambersburg PA
CBHW060526260626
47161CB00003B/776